Violent Peace

Paul R. Evancoe

WingSpan Press

Printed in the United States of America

Published by WingSpan Press, Livermore, CA
www.wingspanpress.com

The WingSpan name, logo and colophon are the trademarks of WingSpan
Publishing.

ISBN 978-1-59594-336-1

First edition 2009

Library of Congress Control Number 2009925408

This book has been officially security-reviewed by U.S. government authority. Security review does not imply U.S. government approval or endorsement of this story or the written content.

Cover designed by Michelle Cronin Shroyer, Reboog Design and Travis Getz, Getzsolutions. Cover picture courtesy of the U.S. Department of Energy.

For more information about the author, questions and answers, previous and future books, scheduled book signings, etc., please visit the author's web site at: www.paulevancoe.com

Also by Paul Evancoe

Own the Night

For Beaner, Elwood, Rocky,
P.S., Robb and Poopsie

Acknowledgments

To my friend and best selling author, Vince Flynn, you remain da man! To my friend and best selling author, Steven Pressfield. I am grateful for your friendship and coaching. Here's looking at you kid. To my friend and acclaimed author, Ben Small, thank you for the critique, suggestions and the bottom line. I owe you. To my former classmate and longtime friend, Bruce Duncil, I humbly accept your criticism because you're always spot on. I anxiously await your book so I can return the favor. To LCOL Jay Cook, USAF (ret) and COL Jack Niemyer, USMC (ret), thanks for all the rotor-head flyboy help and for keeping me real. To my cheerleaders, Dr. Daryl Witt, Jeremy Ward and Jon Roark, thank you for keeping me on task. To Dr. Irwin Binder and Vince Vecera, since I can't say why, I'll just say thanks – I appreciate your professionalism and patriotism. To my story editor, Geri McCarthy, thanks for the spice - "Hooyah!" To my line editor, David Collins, you done good. To Michelle Cronin Shroyer and Travis Getz, thanks for the great book cover. To Marlene Smith, the best executive assistant on the planet. Thanks for keeping me out of trouble.

And most importantly, thank you to those who serve. You know who you are.

Book One

Chapter 1

The Caspian Sea, February

The forty-two-foot Sea Ark heaved violently as it plowed through the heavy seas. The Caspian Sea was no place for such a small boat in February, much less on a stormy night. Outside the Sea Ark's cramped pilothouse the temperature was well below freezing with an added wind chill that drove the relative temperature down another twenty degrees. Although the boat was equipped with state-of-the-art radar and GPS navigation system, it was nearly impossible for Third Captain Hernako Kulzsolph, the officer at the helm, to hold the boat on a coherent heading. Kulzsolph was a native born Kazakh who had eighteen years of service as an officer in the former Soviet Navy onboard Komar-class patrol boats home based in the Black Sea. He was a skilled helmsman with hundreds of hours of experience operating at night in stormy winter seas. Even so, the ride was very rough.

Boucher was staring intently at the color digital radar display monitor mounted low on the console in front of him. After serving twenty-five years as an officer in the U.S. Navy's elite SEAL Team, he'd had his fill of small boats and rough seas, especially in the dark, but he was answering his country's call. He had been specifically asked to lead this mission and he knew he was the right man to get it done. His mind momentarily drifted to the steamy jungles in Cambodia where, a year ago, he and some of his men from his old SEAL Team platoon had recovered a large quantity of gold from a cargo

1

plane's crash site. As a result he was now a very wealthy man. He certainly didn't need to work ever again, but here he was. *Damn rough seas*, he cursed in his thoughts.

He braced his six foot three inch, two-hundred and fifteen pound body between the instrument console and the navigator's chair to keep from being thrown into Captain Kulzsolph who was standing at the helm to his right. The low drone of the boat's powerful twin diesel engines was barely audible above the near-deafening roar of the green water as the waves slammed over the boat's bow and rushed backward over the deck, frothing against the aluminum pilothouse. It seemed that for every wave the Sea Ark crested, it submarined through the next two.

"The contact is at zero three zero degrees at a range of twenty six hundred meters. He's doing about ten knots. Try to ease up his stern. We need a positive ID on him," Boucher shouted to the interpreter who instantaneously relayed the order to Kulzsolph at the helm.

Kulzsolph nodded in acknowledgment while keeping his eyes fixed on the gyrocompass. He carefully inched the twin throttles forward, increasing the boat's speed a few knots to better negotiate the quartering seas and maintain his heading.

Except for the dim red lights illuminating the control panel and the radar display, the Sea Ark was completely darkened, operating without interior cabin lights or exterior navigation lights. A six-man Kazakh Special Squad waited in the heated cabin below the boat's pilot house. The squad's Officer in Charge was Second Captain Rajakovics, a native born Kazakh, who had served eleven years in the former Soviet Navy as a Spetsnaz officer. At the end of the Cold War he left the Soviet Navy and returned to his native Kazakhstan where he had since served as an officer in the Kazakh Navy. He was a well-experienced naval commando with plenty of combat experience with the Russian Spetsnaz in Afghanistan.

In an effort to gain first-hand knowledge of the rogue ship they were preparing to board, Rajakovics had worked undercover as a crewman onboard the Iranian owned "Rakish" for the previous six months. This yielded some very necessary intelligence on the ship's movements, cargo handling procedures and crew routines. In fact, it was his intelligence "tippers" that confirmed that the Rakish would be transporting a very special cargo this night for an Iranian buyer far to the south. Rajakovics knew that while some faces of the ship's crew changed from cruise to cruise, the crew's routine remained relatively the same. Because of his primary knowledge, Rajakovics would lead the commandos on this mission.

The naval commandos of the Kazakh Special Squad had been secretly

2

trained and equipped years earlier for underway ship boarding by a team of former U.S. Navy SEALs as part of a highly-classified "black" CIA counterproliferation program. Now retired SEAL Commander Jake Boucher had led this team of former SEALs whom he personally picked for the mission. In fact, the new Director of National Clandestine Service at the CIA, Navy SEAL Vice Admiral James Thornberg, personally requested Boucher based upon his previous Nuclear Emergency Support Team experience and his knowledge of certain highly classified operational plans that pointed toward Iran's quest to both develop and procure nuclear weapons on the black market. Thornberg had been brought out of retirement to assume the DNCS job at the express request of the President himself.

And now, Boucher was back with the men of the Special Squad he had trained years earlier as their operational advisor and Nuclear Emergency Support Team (NEST) qualified technical expert. The commandos sat in silence, waiting for the Sea Ark to maneuver into position along the Rakish's port side aft quarter. Boarding underway in rough seas was always dangerous and doing it at night in freezing weather increased the danger by several magnitudes.

Boucher squinted through his night vision goggles as they approached the ship from its stern. Its silhouette, barely discernable between the sea and sky, suddenly loomed ominously through the darkness.

"I see it dead ahead, about three hundred meters. I see its name."

Boucher strained to make out the faded white letters painted across the ship's rusting stern.

"R - A - K… it's the Rakish!" he said. Pulling his NVGs up to his forehead, he looked directly into the steel eyes of First Captain Chercinko, the Kazakh officer in command. He and Chercinko had worked together several times previously when Boucher and his SEALs were training the Kazak Special Squad in ship boarding procedures. Even though Chercinko spoke almost no English and Boucher spoke almost no Russian, they had become friends both professionally and socially.

"It's show time!" he said pointing out into the darkness.

As the interpreter translated Boucher's words into Russian, Captain Chercinko was already shouting orders to Rajakovics in the dim red-lighted cabin below to ready his men. The Special Squad, dressed completely in black, pulled their fleece-lined parkas over their wool sweaters and carefully adjusted the tabs on the sleeves and waist. Donning their soft body armor overtop of their parkas, they systematically adjusted the chest straps to allow free arm movement. After pulling their black balaclavas down over their faces they put on their gloves. All of the squad members were armed with FN Five-Seven silenced pistols worn in gunslinger-style ballistic nylon leg holsters. They also carried FN P-90 silenced sub-machine guns slung muzzle down behind their shoulders within easy reach. Both guns fired deadly armor piercing 5.7 millimeter high velocity ammunition capable of easily penetrating an opponent's body armor out to one-hundred meters and kill the wearer. These commandoes looked fierce and they were indeed every bit of what they looked.

From the Sea Ark's darkened pilothouse, Boucher watched through his night vision goggles as two crewmen moved out on deck systematically removing the weatherproof vinyl covers from the boat's three pedestal-mounted thirty caliber machine guns. Completing the removal of the bow gun's cover, the two crewmen carefully moved to the starboard and then the portside guns. Dressed in heavy foul weather clothing, the crewman looked like over stuffed teddy bears as they carefully loaded and charged the guns on the boat's darkened deck readying them for immediate use if needed.

Chercinko glanced over at Boucher with a faint smile and gave him a thumbs-up. In a heavy Russian accent the captain reported, "Good to go."

"Let's do it!" Boucher replied with an affirming nod. The Kazakh interpreter immediately translated Boucher's words to all the others.

Chercinko calmly ordered Kulzsolph to make the boarding approach while the interpreter translated the order in English back to Boucher. Boucher could feel the knot in his stomach growing. It seemed he always felt that way just prior to executing this type of operation.

There're just some things you never get used to, he thought to himself.

The Special Squad filed quietly through the pilothouse out to the boat's slippery pitching weather deck. Kneeling along the outside bulkhead of the Sea Ark's pilothouse they braced themselves from being thrown overboard by the boat's sudden course changes imposed by the heavy seas. Two crewmen now manned the bow and starboard machine guns aiming them up at the silhouetted ship's deck dead ahead. Skillfully maneuvering the Sea Ark through the heavy seas, Kulzsolph quickly advanced the small boat to a trailing position about twenty meters directly behind the ship. Boucher could feel the boat's transition from the heavy seas to the relative calm of the ship's frothing wake as the ship pressed the waves flat in its path.

Without speaking, Boucher placed his right hand on Chercinko's shoulder and pointed ahead at the ship. Chercinko in turn nodded over at Kulzsolph who immediately throttled the Sea Ark's powerful turbo charged Detroit diesel engines to twenty-three hundred RPM's as he simultaneously spun the boat's wheel hard to the left. The Sea Ark lurched forward, diving into the rough seas bow on. Chercinko quickly maneuvered the small boat along the ship's port side. He then spun the helm wheel to the right and skillfully swung the Sea Ark against the ship's side, holding the boat in place by matching the boat's course and speed with the ship's. For a moment, Boucher tried to imagine a theme park ride that could rival this action and of course, he knew there were none. He also knew the reality of a real-world operation like this one and that a mistake here would be fatal.

As the Sea Ark and the ship kissed opposing sides, two members of the Special Squad quickly raised a long aluminum painter's pole similar to the type used for painting high ceilings. This particular pole however, was uniquely modified for ship boarding. In place of the paint roller, it had a small specially made titanium grappling hook fastened to its tip. A mountain climber's caving ladder was attached to the eyelet on the grapple's shank and trailed down along the length of the pole. The caving ladder had narrow aluminum/magnesium alloy rungs about the diameter of a pencil strung between two high strength aircraft-type lightweight wire cables spaced about six inches apart.

The squad member holding the painter's pole expertly hooked the top end grapple over the Rakish's lifeline that ran along the edge of the main deck fourteen feet above. The lifeline was made from one-quarter inch diameter wire cable strung between metal stanchions that were welded to the deck to provide a sturdy safety railing. Two squad members tested its strength by momentarily hanging on the caving ladder. As they maintained tension on the ladder, Rajakovics mounted the ladder and began the treacherous climb up the ship's side. He knew that a fall would likely result in him being crushed between the Sea Ark and the ship's side. Should he survive the initial fall, he certainly would risk being sucked into the ship's propeller as he washed back towards the ship's stern. On top of all that, he would undoubtedly suffer hypothermia if he wasn't immediately rescued, which meant the mission would have to be aborted. But, he was the Squad Leader and lead is what he intended to do.

Years earlier, Boucher and his SEALs had trained the Special Squad to understand that there was only one option when boarding underway, and that was to make the climb up the narrow caving ladder successfully. As Rajakovics reached the top of the caving ladder he quickly clipped a snap link with a nylon cord fastening the ladder's top around the lifeline support stanchion. This served to firmly secure it so that neither the grapple nor the lifeline needed to be relied upon as the caving ladder's primary anchoring point. Following this task he drew the pistol from his holster and vaulted over the lifeline onto the ship's main deck. Like a chimp effortlessly springing to the ground from a low branch above, he landed lightly in a crouched position on both feet. On deck, he disappeared in the darkness.

Within seconds the other five commandoes of the Special Squad successfully made the three meter climb up the ship's side and had boarded. On the Sea Ark below, Chercinko ordered Kulzsolph to maneuver the Sea Ark away from the ship's side. Slowly easing the throttles backward, he allowed the boat to slide rearward along the ship's side to the stern. Maintaining a discreet distance from the ship's stern, he brought the Sea Ark into a trailing position about one hundred meters directly behind the ship. Except for the rolling swells remaining behind in the ship's wake, the ride in this location was good.

Boucher mentally pictured the Special Squad conducting their mission onboard the darkened ship. He had conducted similar missions with his SEALs many times during his twenty-five-year military career and somehow the tactics were almost always identical. *By now they were moving forward along the main weather deck heading for the amidships watertight door that led below to the ship's hold. They were cautiously confident but not overly aggressive. Their rules of engagement were clear. They would not shoot unless they had to and Boucher hoped they would not have to. Mission compromise was simply not an option.*

CIA Headquarters, Langley, VA

"We just got the report. They're onboard."

"Thanks, Marcus. I'll inform the Director. By the way, are you tracking the Israeli military exercise?"

"Yeah, it looks like they're refining their tactics for a preemptive attack on Iran's nuclear weapon development facilities."

"Yes, that's exactly what they're doing. We figure they'll launch their attack sometime soon. The Navy is forward deploying several carrier battle groups to the Indian Ocean region and the Eastern Mediterranean to put Iran and Syria back in their box in the event they counterattack. You realize how serious this is, right?"

"Believe me, Ian, I get it. I just hope we're not too late. We need that nuke."

<u>Chapter 2</u>

New York City, the same time

"And now ladies and gentlemen, on behalf of the Atomic Scientists of America, it is my great honor and privilege to introduce a renowned scientist and today's guest lecturer, Doctor Simon Barnhart."

The ASA president stepped away from the podium and extended his hand to the old gentleman seated to the left of the podium. The applause sounded like a thousand Fourth of July firecrackers crackling simultaneously through the auditorium. The old man slowly stood from his chair. A faint smile penetrated through the weathered lines on his distinguished face. He sucked in a long breath through his teeth and stepped to the podium. Barnhart bowed humbly to his audience as he raised a hand to calm the applause. The standing ovation gradually subsided and the onlookers took their seats. Except for a few coughs, the auditorium went deathly silent. Barnhart opened the notebook on the podium before him and adjusted the microphone. He peered at the audience across the top of his reading glasses and into the faces of those who anxiously awaited his words.

"Thank you for the warm welcome. I want to thank Doctor Steinberg for the privilege to address you today."

Barnhart smiled, pausing momentarily to take a sip of water from the glass in front of him. He carefully returned the glass onto the podium with a faint clunk and continued.

"Historically, few nations have had the technical expertise, material resources and money to develop a nuclear weapon capability. The nations that do possess a nuclear capability compose the elite 'Nuclear Club' leaving the rest to rely upon conventional weapons for deterrent defense or, in some cases, offense. That, I believe it's fair to say, has changed during this decade. Proliferation of nuclear weapons technology and the special nuclear material required to build a nuclear weapon has remained a top national security concern for the United States and the international community as a whole. The potential that a stockpile weapon could be acquired on the black market has been escalated by today's politically correct agendas of openness, technology transfer, and declassification. These sources, fueled by the U.S. government's feverous support of the global information highway, not to mention its recent nation building failures in the Middle East, may give rise to previously unthinkable weapons of mass destruction becoming available to terrorists and rogue nations."

He looked up from his notes recognizing several reporters in the audience. Even though he had addressed similar audiences before, he was always suspicious of the media misinterpreting and misquoting him.

"Ever since the Manhattan Project, the prevention of illegal acquisition of highly enriched uranium, plutonium, and associated nuclear weapon technology has topped the list of U.S. National Security issues. The demise of the Soviet Union, and the breakup of its former empire into independent states that are now more or less aligned with the world community, has caused concern over their ability, and in some cases desire, to maintain tight control over former Soviet nuclear stockpile weapons and the special nuclear material required to build nuclear weapons.

"Iran's steadfast refusal to allow international inspectors access to their reactor operation records and samples of spent fuel is a signal that Iran is breeding weapon grade plutonium through dedicated reactor operations. Reactor cycles dedicated to breeding weapon grade plutonium leave distinctive radiological signatures that can be detected through proper diagnostic comparison of reactor operations and the isotope content of the fuel rods. The fuel burn rate records should be consistent with the isotope content in the fuel at any period of inspection."

Barnhart hesitated again quickly glancing around the auditorium. It seemed that everyone was paying attention. It wasn't easy for him to dumb-down topics like this so even the non-technical non-scientific types could understand the subject matter. After all, Barnhart wasn't a university professor who made his claim to fame as a paper tiger in a classroom. He was a man who had spent his entire adult life designing and building nuclear

8

weapons. Emphasizing his coming words, he held up a curved finger as if to caution his listeners.

"There are of course, several variables involved that can make verification extremely difficult if not nearly impossible. The type of reactor is important. For example, United States designs require reactor shutdown to refuel or replace fuel rods. This provides both a great margin of safety and an unmistakable power signature fluctuation that is easily detectable. On the other hand, Russian, and perhaps Iranian reactors do not generally require shutdown to change out fuel rods. Thus, these reactors do not provide the same telltale power signature, making verification difficult without their full cooperation. This may be the driving reason that the U.S. offered Iran U.S. reactor design technology in exchange for Iran allowing International Atomic Energy Agency inspection of several selected facilities."

Barnhart took another sip of water, peering at the audience over his reading glasses as he swallowed. This time he wiped his lips with the back of his hand before continuing.

"No matter what country, friend or foe, special nuclear material, as well as the required processing and weapon manufacturing facilities have historically received the highest national level security attention. In view of the relative few nations that exclusively possess a nuclear capability compared to those who desire to acquire such a capability, it has always been a case of the 'have' verses the 'have nots'. The truth is simply that the safeguards and security that have been rigorously applied to the nuclear program, across the worldwide spectrum of nuclear weapon research, development, stockpile maintenance and support, worked. Proliferation of nuclear weapons had, until the post cold war era, remained in check. However, there are new concerns resulting from the still evolving new world order and the unknown intentions of some Middle Eastern nations. The new potential threat may not focus on weapon development as it has in the past. Today's threat may include a wide range of non-traditional elements so abstract that intelligence analysts may simply not recognize the indicators."

Barnhart cleared his throat and then pushed his reading glasses further up onto the bridge of his nose. He momentarily stared at one man sitting in the second row directly in front of the podium. Barnhart was now on a roll. He was deep into his area of expertise and it showed. He barely glanced down at his notes as he spoke. He straightened his posture and removed his reading glasses.

"Additional proliferation stemming from nuclear weapon development by Iran, China, Pakistan, and North Korea heightens concerns that such weapons, lacking the rational controls brought on by an understanding of world community deterrence, could be sold or ransomed for purposes other than those pertaining to their national security as sovereign nations. Although there can be little argument over the technical sophistication required to build nuclear weapons, or that the nuclear threat has correctly been the World's dominant focus over the past four decades, it may now have several rivals that require equal attention. Iraq demonstrated that a nation with the willingness and resources to send students abroad for scientific and engineering training in dual-use technologies could develop extremely sophisticated, indigenous capabilities for high technology weapons and their delivery systems. The possibility that a rogue nation like Iran has acquired new and more sophisticated technology in this manner leading to weapons of mass destruction is real. The issue is how those dual-use technologies will be applied and if so, to what kind of weapon."

The Caspian Sea, the same time

The Rakish's Iranian crew numbered less than ten and only four of them were awake and on watch. Two of them were in the ship's pilothouse steering and navigating the ship through the angry sea that lay in their path. The mate navigating at the ship's wheel occasionally checked the radarscope for contacts of other vessels but the small Sea Ark was completely invisible to him amongst the sea clutter resulting from the heavy seas. The third person on watch was an engineer who was in the engine room rebuilding a leaking fuel-water separator. The fourth man, an armed roving patrol who made routine hourly security rounds, was drinking coffee in the ship's galley trying to warm up after his last bone chilling excursion outside on the main weather deck. None of them had any idea that their ship had been boarded or that a search of their cargo hold was underway. In fact, they didn't even know what their cargo was. As far as they were concerned this was just another shipment of boxes and bulk cargo. A routine shipment that began at Astrakhan, Russia along the Volga River on the north shore of the Caspian that would end with a delivery to Randar-e Anzali on the Caspian's south shore piedmont at the foot of Iran's Elburz Mountains.

Except for some occasional static, the Sea Ark's radio was silent. Even though the chances of compromise were slim, both Chercinko and Boucher waited impatiently for the Special Squad to report. In the tossing pilothouse Boucher's thoughts drifted to the issues that got him here. Thoughts going back to the time following the demise of the Soviet Union, when he was in NEST training under Doctor Simon Barnhart, the key architect of the newly formed United States/Russia Bilateral Non-proliferation Regime. Memories about the thousands of nuclear warheads and the missiles to deliver them that were to be dismantled over the next number of years by both sides to reduce the nuclear threat. It was no secret that because of Russia's economic decline, living conditions were austere in both Russia and the now fledgling republics that once comprised the former Soviet Union. The Russian black market, controlled by the Russian Mafia, continued to flourish. Anything could be bought if the money was right. Anything, as Boucher well knew, even a nuclear weapon.

Most frightening to Boucher was the possibility that a former Soviet stockpile weapon would simply vanish from inventory records. The Russians had actually kept their nuclear stockpile inventory records in logbooks using handwritten ledgers, not secure computer spreadsheets like the U.S. used. He knew how easy it would be to fudge an inventory to cover the loss or theft of a stockpile weapon. His mind raced through the scenario... *in any event the stockpile weapon would be classified as a loose nuke - providing that the intelligence community would be lucky enough to detect the weapon's disappearance.* He knew better than most – *the only thing required to make a loose nuke operable is a replacement fire set.* As the former Director of the Nuclear Emergency Support Team, Boucher knew that building a replacement fire set could easily be done without detection because the parts required were not unique and therefore not tracked by the intelligence community.

Then his thoughts shifted to the treasure hunt that he and the men of his old SEAL platoon had undertaken last year, their launch point in Thailand, finding the C-130 crash site in Cambodia, the canal intersection and its bamboo foot bridge, their escape from the Chinese Spratly fortress and the Plans that revealed a Chinese plot to provide nukes to Iran so terrorists could attack the U.S., and of course, the Luminous - the secretive underground faction that issued power and took it from those they deemed disloyal or uncooperative. He shuddered again at the thought.

"Vostorg," a single word in Russian crackled loudly from the Sea Ark's radio startling Boucher's thoughts back to the reality of his present location. The interpreter immediately translated it to Boucher.

"He said, 'Joy'."

Boucher looked over at Chercinko who barked a command into the mic of his squad radio. Two static-filled clicks immediately followed, acknowledging receipt of the order by the Special Squad onboard the ship.

The Sea Ark surged forward beginning its second approach toward the ship's side. Kulzsolph headed the boat to the ship's port side boarding position where the caving ladder still hung, stretching down to the water.

Boucher winced, knowing this time he would be the one having to make the treacherous climb to the ship's deck.

He zipped his waterproof fleece-lined jacket all the way to the top and put on a dark brown multi-pocketed bass fisherman's inflatable life jacket over top. He pulled his navy knit wool cap down over his ears and put on his gloves. Chercinko held a small black nylon backpack up and helped Boucher get his arms through the shoulder straps. Boucher snapped the waist strap in place and looked back over his shoulder.

"Ready," Boucher calmly reported.

Chercinko followed Boucher through the pilothouse door, helping to steady him as they moved forward along the boat's pitching deck toward the caving ladder. Boucher was admittedly no spring chicken, but he was amazingly fit. What he lacked in youth he made up for in determination.

Kulzsolph once again accurately positioned the Sea Ark alongside the ship next to the caving ladder. Chercinko grabbed the ladder, pulling it onto the Sea Ark's deck. Boucher always contended that getting safely onto a caving ladder from a pitching boat alongside an underway ship was kind of like getting a foot into the stirrup of a running horse from the bed of a moving pickup truck with the expectation of climbing into the saddle. With a boost from Chercinko he carefully stepped off the tossing boat and slowly pulled himself up the ladder pausing briefly at the top before climbing over the ship's lifeline into the waiting hands of two members of the Special Squad. On deck, he glanced back down at the shadowy boat below and gave an assuring wave to Chercinko who waved back in acknowledgment. The Sea Ark once again trailed quietly rearward until it was swallowed by the darkness behind the ship's wake.

Onboard, Boucher was led forward along the ship's dark weather deck to an amidship's port side watertight door that accessed the ship's interior. The two Special Squad members cautiously opened the door and motioned Boucher to follow them inside. The three men moved quickly through the dimly lighted passageway cautiously crossing an intersecting passageway. A short distance further they entered a narrow steel stairway leading below. As they guardedly descended several flights of steep stairs, they were met by another squad member posted in a defensive position beneath the bottom-most flight of stairs. They entered an open hatch and climbed down a steel ladder encased inside a narrow escape trunk cylinder arriving in the ship's cargo hold two decks below.

A red flash caught Boucher's eye coming from the opposite side of the cluttered cargo hold and he instinctively crouched. The commando behind him returned the signal using his red lens flashlight and the three men made their way around the variously sized cargo boxes to the other side of the cramped hold where they met Rajakovics. He was standing by a locked metal container about the size of an average office desk. In the dim red light Boucher could see that Rajakovics had placed an open backpack next to the container.

Boucher knelt down on one knee next to the open backpack. Using his red lens flashlight he peered inside to examine the radiation detector it contained.

"Gamma, neutron, Pu-239," he whispered. "Damn!"

He carefully slipped off his backpack and opened it, exposing an electronic device that resembled a military-style radio with complicated knobs, switches and LED flat screen digital readouts covering its top face. The device was a portable radioisotope spectroscopy unit. He then pulled a small laptop computer from the pack and checked the electrical connections linking the two devices together. As he switched both devices on, several small red, green and yellow colored lights flashed which gradually all turned to green. Switching his digital watch to the stopwatch setting, he sat down leaning back against a cargo crate next to the crate in question.

Pointing at his watch, Boucher pantomimed *ten minutes* to Rajakovics who was standing guard beside him. Rajakovics nodded sternly, silently acknowledging his understanding of Boucher's requirement and patiently returned to an alert security stance. Boucher removed his gloves, unzipped his jacket and rolled his wool cap up above his ears. He drew in a deep breath and held it momentarily before exhaling. The air in this deep hold smelled stale and moldy. He was at home dealing with stress but for some reason he was really feeling it this time. His thoughts momentarily drifted to Laytonsville, Maryland, his home and his son. His eyes filled with tears at the thought of his son, Doug.

Doug, who would have been thirty-two next month, was Boucher's only child. At age five, his son had survived an automobile collision that had ended his wife's life. Boucher was still an active duty SEAL officer at the time of the accident. Unable to raise Doug alone, he placed him in Valley Forge Military Academy so he would get a good education and learn discipline. It had worked. Doug went on to college and graduate school at USC where he earned a Ph.D. in biology. He did a post doctoral study in Saudi Arabia in ichthyology and joined the U.S. State Department's AID program. He was posted in Kuwait where he had been working for several years as an ichthyologist on a fishery project at the time of Iraq's invasion. He disappeared and was not heard from again. Barbara Badger, the Deputy Chief of Mission at the U.S. Embassy in Kuwait, reported that Doug was believed to have been taken prisoner by terrorists. The State Department later investigated his disappearance with negative results. Doug was never found.

Captured al Qaeda officers denied any knowledge of his capture or his demise. The State Department's official line was that he was presumed dead but Boucher never accepted that. Doug spoke Arabic like a native from the many years he had spent studying and working in the Middle East. For that matter, his naturally black wavy hair and dark suntan allowed him to easily pass as an Arab among Arabs. Boucher continued to hold the belief that Doug was alive, perhaps incarcerated, but alive. While he was to some extent capable of getting over the loss of his wife, he could never give up on Doug.

Forcefully redirecting his thoughts to his present location, he checked his watch. Five minutes had expired. Only five more minutes and they could leave. He was nearly certain that the spectroscopy he was gathering would reveal a fissile plutonium source inside the nondescript metal container he was kneeling beside.

Maybe it is just irradiated reactor fuel or maybe it is a nuclear weapon. A weapon purchased on the black market. Either is unacceptable, but a loose nuke is truly diabolical. If it is a nuclear weapon, it would clearly confirm Iran's quest to develop and possess a nuclear weapon arsenal. Perhaps they will use it against Israel or some European nation friendly to the U.S. As a notorious state supporter of terrorism, Iranian agents might even try to smuggle it into the United States and nuke an American city like Washington or New York. Boucher cringed from the thought of a nuclear detonation taking place in a U.S. city. *The death toll would be overwhelming and the destruction catastrophic. The economy would falter and turn the U.S. into a second world economic power within a few days of the attack. Oh shit...*

He knew this better than most people because he had discussed that very scenario many times with his old friend Simon Barnhart, one of the few remaining scientists alive today who helped develop the thermonuclear bomb with some of the original Manhattan Project scientists at Los Alamos.

He stood momentarily and impatiently checked his watch before returning to the kneeling position beside the ID equipment. As his digital watch beeped twice marking ten minutes elapsed time, he switched off the spectroscopy ID unit and dumped the data into the computer's hard drive. Clicking on a program icon he ran a quick analysis program on the data and interpreted the spikes displayed on the computer's color screen in much the same way that a cardiologist reads a heart EKG.

What he saw was not good news. "Damn," he mumbled under his breath.

Chapter 3

New York - the same time

Barnhart took a quick sip of water and cleared his throat. "An event worth noting occurred in Europe this year that attracted little media attention. It involved the theft and sale of special nuclear materials or SNM. I'm going to use the abbreviation, SNM, from now on. This was also the first ever case that involved the attempted sale of a measurable quantity of SNM. This incident involved enriched uranium reactor fuel pellets stolen in Romania and offered for sale on the black market. These pellets were only enriched to five percent and were classified 'fresh' fuel, having never been used in a reactor. The level of enrichment was far below weapon grade requirements and therefore useless unless further enriched. If used as reactor fuel, these pellets could have possibly been made into weapon grade plutonium, but the quantity was insufficient for that purpose. The only possible weapon application for this type of low grade SNM could be for use in a 'low tech' RDD, short for Radiological Dispersal Device. An RDD when exploded causes low level contamination by simply spreading radioactive material over a localized area. RDD construction utilizes a conventional explosive surrounded by radioactive material. When exploded, the radioactive material is pulverized and carried outward by the force of the blast spreading it as radioactive particulate dust upon the surface of the blast radius."

Barnhart emphasized the words blast radius by putting his hands together and quickly flinging them apart. He continued without missing a beat.

"It is important to understand that an RDD does not produce a nuclear yield associated with an atomic bomb. There is no mushroom cloud, searing heat, or release of lethal gamma radiation. Unless this low-level radiation particulate is taken internally, the radioactive material is of little danger to human health or consequence to the environment. The detonation of such a device would no doubt provoke a media feeding frenzy and result in undesirable localized surface contamination, but it would not cause apocalyptic mass destruction of life and property. The RDD, however, should not be discounted as inconsequential. It is indeed a means to discretely contaminate a selected target and requires only a radioactive source material, not necessarily SNM, and rudimentary explosives technology to construct and employ. I am of the opinion," Barnhart cautioned with a slight pause, "that the RDD may likely debut as the terrorist's weapon of choice during this decade."

Extending both his hands in front of himself, Barnhart formed a shape about the size of a grapefruit.

"Hypothetically," he explained, "a mass of six to eight kilograms of weapon grade plutonium, Pu-239, or a larger amount of highly enriched Uranium in the isotope U-235, is sufficient to make a nuclear weapon. It is no easy matter to procure that amount of weapon-grade material without detection. And it is several hundred magnitudes more difficult to handle it, machine it, and fabricate a working nuclear weapon. Nonetheless, if there is indeed a suitable quantity of SNM awaiting a buyer, a considerable threat exists. Without equal, the European continent is most vulnerable to nuclear terrorism and may unknowingly already be at great risk.

"The lesson that can be taken from this is that since 1966 when such cases began being investigated, evaluated, and documented, until today, a total of about nine hundred reported cases proved to be scams involving bogus material. Proliferation controls have largely worked. Only the more recent cases involved actual SNM. The integrity of the former Soviet military and science communities must be recognized as effectively contributing to the disallowance of such an occurrence. But, things clearly changed after the Cold War ended and the Soviet Union went out of business."

Barnhart stopped and peered down at his notes. It was obvious he wasn't studying them. Rather, it was as though he was ordering his thoughts. It was so quiet in the auditorium even the smallest cough or sneeze was amplified. Barnhart finally looked back up and continued.

"Today's proliferation concerns range a broad spectrum of issues that involve radical states with zealot agendas, such as North Korea, to dedicated terrorist organizations like al-Qa'ida or Hamas. Or Iran, for example, who supports Hamas' continued violent terrorist campaign against ethnic and religion-based foes like Israel, with little regard to innocent bystanders or collateral damage. It is these miscreant states and knavish groups that cause many a sleepless night for the national security analysts who monitor them and attempt to assess their activities. Proliferation no longer involves just the haves and the have nots, it's global."

Barnhart cleared his throat and removed his reading glasses. Before proceeding, he quickly glanced around the room and noted he still had everyone's attention.

"As many of you know, last week, the president's Press Secretary unveiled the Administration's non-proliferation and export control policy. This policy is in an attempt to establish a framework to prevent the proliferation of weapons of mass destruction and the missiles that deliver them. In this framework the president outlined three major principles to guide U.S. non-proliferation and export control policy. The first is to make non-proliferation an integral element of U.S. foreign relations. The second is to seek expanded trade and technology exchanges with nations, including former adversaries, that abide by global non-proliferation norms, and the third involves building a new consensus to promote effective non-proliferation efforts while integrating economic goals."

Barnhart replaced his reading glasses and quickly thumbed to the bottom page of his notes. He picked up the page and studied it momentarily, then continued.

"In this policy statement the president reaffirmed U.S. support for a strong, effective non-proliferation regime and provided brief descriptions of the policy's key elements. These policy elements focus on the following. One: control and security of fissile material. Two: application of dual-use technology export controls. Three: strong support for the renewal of the 1968 Non-Proliferation Treaty. Four: strong support for the International Atomic Energy Agency's efforts to detect clandestine nuclear activities. Five: promotion of the Missile Technology Control Regime guidelines as a global combat missile non-proliferation norm, and Six: to make special efforts to address the proliferation threat in regions of tension such as the Middle East, the Korean Peninsula and South Asia."

Barnhart put the page back down on the podium and took another quick sip of water. He again removed his reading glasses and then gripped both sides of the podium as is if to steady himself.

"Simply stated, the current U.S. non-proliferation policy appears to be enigmatically linked to the economic concerns of export controls. Phrases used in the policy such as, 'The United States will harmonize domestic and multilateral controls to the greatest extent possible,' are, in my opinion, misaligned with the real-world realities of the potential threat of a weapon, or weapon development technology, falling into the hands of terrorists."

A few gasps could be heard in the audience and Barnhart nodded in the direction he heard them coming from as if he agreed with their surprise.

"An informal off-line consensus appears to be growing among intelligence analysts and nuclear weapon experts," Barnhart said with a tremble in his voice. "In view of the hundreds of nuclear warheads being moved back into the U.S. and Russia for disassembly and reprocessing, the chance of an accident or loss of inventory seems *imminent*!"

The Caspian Sea, the same time

Boucher could taste the acid forming as his stomach tightened. It was definitely weapon grade Plutonium-239 and, by the look of the preliminary spectroscopy analysis, it was a sufficient quantity of material to produce a fission yielding bomb. Some of the spectral data suggested that it was surrounded with high explosives. It was the reality of his worst nightmare. He quickly saved all the data on the computer's hard drive and saved a back up copy on a flash drive that was plugged into the computer's USB slot. He removed the flash drive and sealed it in a small waterproof case which he tucked into an inside pocket of his parka, closing the pocket's Velcro flap. Next, he carefully replaced the ID unit and computer into his backpack. He zipped his parka, pulled his knit cap down over his ears and pulled on his gloves. Without speaking, Rajakovics lifted Boucher's backpack up and helped him put it on ensuring that the shoulder straps were not twisted. He silently gave Boucher a thumbs-up and pointed to the ladder on the other side of the hold. Rajakovics stepped in front of Boucher grabbing him by his parka sleeve leading him briskly across the dark hold through the maze of cargo boxes toward the ladder.

Two squad members met them with their sub-machine guns at the ready. They all cautiously climbed the ladder to the hatch above with Boucher in the middle of the procession. A fourth squad member met them at the top hatch and they all began the steep climb up the multiple stair flights to the passageway leading outside to the ship's main deck. As he reached the top of the final flight of stairs Boucher held up his hand signaling that he needed to stop.

"Give me a minute, boys. I just need a minute," he whispered between deep breaths.

The Kazakhs didn't understand a word of English but they understood Boucher's request. Two squad members took up a defensive position at the top of the stairs while the others pressed themselves along the steel bulkhead next to the door ready to engage anyone who might enter.

Boucher's face was cherry red. He leaned on the stair rail taking deep breaths and exhaling slowly. His resilience was amazing for a man of his age. In less than a minute he had recovered his strength and was ready to resume the trip out. Rajakovics nodded to his men by the door. They slowly opened the creaking steel door and entered the dimly lighted passageway. Rajakovics followed with Boucher at arms' reach. Except for the rustling sound made by the fabric in their clothing, the five men moved noiselessly down the passageway toward the watertight door leading outside onto the ship's weather deck.

The two Special Squad members in the lead cautiously crossed an intersecting passageway while the others remained behind, standing close to the passageway's steel bulkhead wall. Boucher watched as one of the Kazakh commandos took up a defensive position on the corner of the intersection while the other stepped a few feet further down the passageway toward the door. The squad member in front of Boucher took up a defensive position on the intersection corner opposing the squad member on the other side of the passageway. This allowed the commandos a full range of fire both up and down the intersecting passageways and a means to provide maximum security for Boucher as he crossed this high threat area. Even so, Boucher took no chances and drew his pistol.

Rajakovics took Boucher's arm from behind and ushered him to a position close to the corner of the passageway intersection. This position kept him out of a direct line of sight from anyone who might step into the passageway. As Rajakovics glanced toward his comrade across the hall for the okay to cross, Boucher heard a metal door slam open along the intersecting passageway. From their defensive positions at the intersection, the two Special Squad members immediately opened fire with their silenced P-90 sub-machine guns. With his sub-machine gun at the ready, Rajakovics shoved Boucher against the passageway's steel bulkhead stepping in front of him as a shield.

The puff-puff sound of the silenced sub-machine gun shots were answered by one shotgun blast. The buckshot instantaneously impacted against the steel bulkhead across the passageway from Boucher, tinning a saucer-size gray metal splotch through the wall's tan-colored paint. Then, there was the thud of a body hitting the steel deck. The two Special Squad members on the intersection corners immediately charged forward toward the body and the open door the guard had just come through.

Rajakovics motioned the commando on Boucher's right over to the corner. The commando cautiously peered around the corner and reached back without looking, taking hold of Boucher's parka. Rajakovics grabbed Boucher by the arm and whispered a command to the commando holding his parka. Together they whisked him across the passageway intersection towards the watertight door leading outside onto the weather deck.

Boucher had just enough time to glance down the passageway where the shotgun blast had come from to see one squad member lifting the dead guard's body over his shoulder while the other was picking up the sub-machine gun's expended brass casings from the deck.

Using the barrel of his submachine gun, the commando leading the procession down the passageway, tapped on the metal watertight door that led outside to the main deck. His two quick taps followed by a single tap were answered by a single tap from outside. Relaxing somewhat, the commando slowly pushed the door open and stepped outside motioning the rest of the squad to follow. As the commando stepped outside into the darkness, Boucher could see a shadowy figure with a sub-machine gun at the ready relax his posture as he apparently recognized one of his own. A sudden chill from the rush of freezing cold wind permeated Boucher's parka as he stepped through the open door and out onto the ship's dark slippery weather deck.

Boucher glanced back toward the open door in time to see the two commandos who had engaged the guard emerge from inside. One commando was carrying the dead guard draped head down over his right shoulder with the guard's shotgun in his left hand. The other commando was walking backward providing rear security with his sub-machinegun held at the ready against his body armor's breast plate. The commando carrying the guard effortlessly heaved the shotgun and body over the ship's side in one fluid motion. Except for some blood in the passageway inside, there would be no other evidence of what happened.

The sixth squad member who had been waiting outside hastily led the boarding party to the ship's stern. Rajakovics hurried to the lifeline on the stern of the ship and flashed his red lens flashlight into the darkness toward the Sea Ark that was following astern just out of visual range to the naked eye. The rest of the squad took up defensive positions aiming their submachine guns forward along both the port and starboard decks.

Boucher caught a strained glimpse of the shadowy boat making its approach through the ship's white frothing wake. As it came into view, he saw the boat veer left and head toward the caving ladder that was still swinging from the port side life line stanchion. The Sea Ark effortlessly tucked in alongside the ship next to the caving ladder. Members of the Special Squad hurried Boucher to the ladder helping him over the ship's side. Boucher began his climb down the ladder. Chercinko, was standing on the boat's deck below, pulling the bottom of the ladder into the Sea Ark to keep it from being caught between the boat and the ship. Now poised above the tossing Sea Ark, Boucher waited for the small boat to heave up to his level on a wave crest before releasing his grip and jumping to the boat's deck. He was particularly careful to ensure that he would land on the Sea Ark, not in the water between the ship and the boat. Timing was paramount.

Waiting for the Sea Ark to rise on the crest of a swell, he let go of the ladder pushing himself away from the ship's side with all his strength. His short free fall ended as Chercinko grabbed Boucher's parka and muscled him up to a stand-up landing. Chercinko quickly ushered him to the relative safety of the boat's pilothouse as the six commandos of the Special Squad hustled down the ladder and successfully re-boarded the Sea Ark. Easing away from the Rakish, the Sea Ark disappeared far into the darkness leaving the caving ladder playfully swinging in the wind blown surf along the ship's port side.

Onboard the Rakish two heavily clothed men emerged on deck and headed directly to the starboard side lifeboat. They were carrying a waterproof plastic shipping container about the size of a small two-drawer file cabinet between them. The men carefully lifted the container into the lifeboat and secured it to the cargo tie down eyelets on the boat's deck with some nylon line. A third person emerged from a watertight door on the ship's stern and hurried forward towards the lifeboat. The two men already in the boat seemed to pay little attention as the third person climbed in.

The third person, indistinguishably dressed from the other two, slapped them on their shoulders and simply shouted "okay" in Arabic. The female's voice was nearly drowned out by the noise of the wind and surf. Although the sound of a woman's voice was unusual onboard ship on a stormy winter night in the middle of the Caspian Sea, no one beyond those in the boat heard her. The three of them quickly lowered the boat to the water, started the boat's diesel engine and cast off the bow painter maneuvering the boat to a westerly heading. The rigid hull semi-inflatable lifeboat was easily negotiating the following seas as it sped away through the darkness, undetected by anyone.

The Sea Ark maintained steerage way in trail about a half mile behind the ship. Inside the Sea Ark's warm pilothouse, Boucher eased his backpack to the floor. Looking directly at Chercinko, Boucher spoke slowly and deliberately.

"Captain, I can confirm there is a nuclear weapon in that hold."

The interpreter simultaneously translated his words.

"They are still at least two days away from Iran but you're going to have to stop this delivery. If Iran gets possession of that weapon who knows what they'll do with it. The bastards might even try to take out Tel Aviv."

Chercinko remained stoic. Turning away from Boucher he stared out of the pilothouse window into the darkness for several moments. Suddenly he turned and barked out an order to his men who were now all safely inside the heated cabin below, "Po-to-pit!" Rajakovics, who led the Special Squad, immediately acknowledged the order and rose to his feet producing a small radio transmitter about the size of a cell phone. The interpreter looked at Boucher in total bewilderment as he translated the order. "He said, 'Sink it'!"

Before Boucher could digest the gravity of the order, Rajakovics keyed in a numeric code on the transmitter and pressed the red send button. The ship, now about a thousand yards ahead of the Sea Ark, was instantaneously illuminated in a blinding bright white-hot flash that expanded from its hull below the water line outward almost as far as the Sea Ark. The flash immediately diminished and was followed by the heavy concussion thud of a high explosive detonation moments later. The Rakish heaved up in a plume of water and flames then slowly rolled onto its starboard side, breaking in half. There was little sustained fire as the bow section quickly slid beneath the Caspian. The ship's stern floated on its side for three or four minutes intermittently spouting orange flames and then slowly disappeared beneath the sea.

Boucher was caught completely off guard and his anger flashed.

"What the hell did you just do?" he shouted at Chercinko. "That's a blatant damn act of war! Are you fucking crazy?"

Chercinko grabbed Boucher by the shoulders like a man trying to console his best friend. Chercinko spoke in English with a heavy Russian accent.

"Jake, it-dis-de only way."

Boucher realized that while the Special Squad was aboard the ship, they had planted explosive charges deep below the ship's waterline in apparent anticipation of what he might later confirm. The Kazakh intelligence network was significantly better than the Central Intelligence Agency's capability to ascertain accurate information in this region. Boucher was dumbfounded not only from Chercinko's actions in sinking the ship but also from his sudden apparent understanding of the English language.

"You rat bastard, Chercinko! You've understood exactly what I've been telling you before it was translated! Why Captain? All I want to know is why?"

A faint smile appeared over Chercinko's face.

"To give to you and your country – how you say - plausible denial." He then continued in Russian with the interpreter who was translating his words into English. "If I would involve you and fail, you and the U.S. would take the blame. If I take the action and fail, then only I fail. I am sorry my friend, but it was necessary to accomplish our mission. Iran will not get that weapon and this entire operation has never happened. It is winter and ships sink in the Caspian Sea all the time. This one is little different."

Although Boucher was upset, he couldn't find any serious flaw in the Captain's logic.

"Okay, Captain," he responded, "but you must realize that I'm going to have to provide an honest report of tonight's events to my government. I don't know what will come of this. There is no discounting the fact that there was a nuke on that ship and that the ship was heading to Iran's north shore. Perhaps you did the world a favor tonight." Boucher paused and lowered his voice. "Maybe this is the way to enforce counter proliferation policy. Maybe we shouldn't play by the rule of law when the terrorists and proliferators don't give a damn who they kill!"

As the Sea Ark made its way back toward Fort Shevchenko, the Special Squadron's homeport, Boucher went below to the warm cabin. Most of the commandos were already asleep. He removed his outer garments and settled back against the foam-padded bulkhead. It had been a long night for them all. He studied the faces of the men around him, wondering why he had been asked to accompany the Kazaks on this mission if the plan had been to sink the ship all along. He was troubled because it didn't seem that the means justified the end. Boucher yawned as his tired eyes fluttered. Even in the tossing boat he had no trouble falling asleep.

New York City, the same time

Most everyone in the audience was nodding in agreement which encouraged Barnhart to continue at his current level of detail.

"In the event that control of a stockpile weapon is lost - you know, a loose nuke - it is then defined as an improvised nuclear device, or IND. An IND significantly differs from a dirty bomb because an IND, when detonated, has the potential to provide the yield of an atomic bomb. An IND has a working physics package surrounded by the explosives to detonate a nuclear explosion. All that may be required to render an IND operable is a replacement fire set. Developing a fire set would certainly require technical competence, but not disciplined scientific research and development. The type of technical competence required could be found in thousands of former Soviet weapon technicians who are out of work. A high tech laboratory would not be required either. A modern machine shop and electronics repair capability would probably suffice. A source of detonators and high explosives would be necessary, but acquisition of high explosives is perhaps the easiest part of the problem as well as the least traceable because of global availability. As we have already experienced this is the most likely way that a rogue nation or terrorist group will acquire a nuclear weapon or other weapons of mass destruction. The odds of such an event occurring again are probably low but the consequences, as we know, are unarguably high."

Barnhart paused to again look around the room.

"I am here today to restate my belief that there can be no margin for error in our policy or response. It is widely known there are numerous illicit sources for the necessary precursor materials and components required to build an atomic bomb. We must stand firm and insist that the governments composing the nuclear club take every precaution necessary to prevent terrorists from gaining nuclear weapons. The scientific community and government must join together on this because there is simply too much at stake to do otherwise. Thank you for your attention."

Barnhart stepped back from the podium as the president of the ASA stepped forward to shake his hand. The thunderous applause drowned the ASA president's words as he thanked Barnhart for the appearance.

Chapter 4

Los Alamos, New Mexico, several months later

The weather in June at Los Alamos seemed to always be a dichotomy of seasons. Large snowy patches remained frozen in the north hillside shadows draping down from the mountaintop several hundred feet along the ski paths. The ski lodge, located a few thousand feet below, was built by the Government in the early nineteen forties for the private use of the lab employees who had little social life during the development of the atom bomb. Even with the snow on the hill above, the temperature on the lodge's sunny patio was a comfortable sixty-eight degrees.

Longtime friends Simon Barnhart and Jake Boucher were sitting across from one another at a weathered blue wooden picnic table on the flagstone patio. Both men were loosely clad in open collar summer attire.

Barnhart was a Ph.D. nuclear physicist who had completed his post-doctoral study in the fall of 1957 at Berkeley on a program associated with theoretical spontaneous fission and quantum mechanics. As a young graduate of renowned brilliance, Barnhart was recruited by Doctor Oppenheimer as a project scientist working in the fast-neutron group beside such famed scientists as Doctors Teller, McMillin, Manley and Serber. He went to work at Los Alamos in early 1958 to design and build atomic bombs in an arms race with the Soviet Union During the 1960s he spent months on end at the Nevada Test Site conducting experimental nuclear blasts, both above and below ground, to test various warheads he had designed. He was credited as the primary architect of, and driving force behind, the formalization of Los Alamos National Laboratory's Applied Computational and Theoretical Physics Division or "X division" as it later came to be known. Barnhart retired from Los Alamos National Laboratory in 1991 and since, had acted as a consultant to Los Alamos National Laboratory and other various government agencies. Clearly, Barnhart was a man of science. If he had an ego, it was well disguised in his intellectual prowess. Few nuclear physicists in the world were more experienced than Barnhart and even for his age, none were more competent.

Barnhart adjusted his well-worn pocket protector that was overflowing with pens of various sizes. "You see, Jake," he droned in a monotone, "like Oppenheimer began the Manhattan Project, Iran began with the development of a uranium 235 weapon."

"Why uranium?" Boucher asked jokingly. "Because it's relatively available in its enriched form and because that is where the sum total of their theoretical experience and experimental research focused. Right?"

Barnhart smiled, knowing years earlier Boucher had been one of his brightest students. "Yes, it's because they simply don't have the theoretical data available on plutonium weapons - at least not yet. However, there is strong evidence that they have experimented with explosive implosion, a science still fledgling to them, and hydrodynamic explosive shots to learn the physics required to send a neutron into an atom's nucleus and cause a fissile chain reaction."

"That's the reaction that releases the tremendous energy associated with atomic weapons, better known as the 'yield'," Boucher playfully responded to his former teacher.

"You always were my favorite student, Jake. It's so good to see you."

Boucher noticed that several people sitting at other tables on the patio were watching Barnhart. Most of them, no matter what age, had pocket protectors similar to Barnhart's. Boucher concluded years earlier that the pocket protector was a ready means to identify scientists. Their behavior was interesting to him because it seemed that they were waiting for Barnhart to look their way. When he did, they would greet his gaze with a smile and a subtle wave. It was obvious that Barnhart held legendary status at Los Alamos. "Please continue, Si."

Barnhart lowered his eyebrows and nodded consent.

"Intel revealed that Iranian President Mahmoud Ahmadinejad promised his generals that he would have a uranium bomb ready for delivery to the Army by the beginning of 2006. Based on Iran's weapon development program the CIA didn't feel that was achievable until perhaps 2012, but went forward to our president with an expedited 2006 timetable for derailing that delivery anyway. Even when it became obvious that these expectations would not be realized by Iran during 2006, the CIA and the Defense Department urged the destruction of Iran's nuclear development facilities anyway."

Boucher sighed impatiently. "Has Iran developed a gun-type weapon?"

"Yes, Jake. They apparently decided their developmental focus for the first bomb would be on the gun-type uranium weapon rather than pursuing a more scientifically demanding implosion-type weapon even though it would ultimately have greater destructive power.

"So they built their first bomb for use against Israel, correct?"

"Well, I suppose that's safe to assume. But you must understand, the weapon they developed is still untested and therefore unproven. Their primary concern has been for the corresponding acquisition of, or where necessary, the development and manufacture of, dependable very specialized bomb components and that is a profound challenge. It is important to remember there is a great difference between a theoretical laboratory device and a deployable weapon. But, North Korea stepped up to the plate and provided Iran not only much of the necessary technology required to build a bomb but the vast majority of the materials. While the interoperability of weapon components is always a top reliability concern in a working weapon, North Korea still served to accelerate Iran's realization of a successful nuclear weapon program."

Barnhart paused to clear his throat.

"You see, Jake, we need to bring our troops home from Iraq before Iran has a deployable weapon or I fear they might test it on our forces in Iraq."

Barnhart pointed a crooked finger to the mountain ridge on his right. Boucher had heard this story many times before from Barnhart and knew what he was going to be told, but out of respect he acted interested.

"When I first came to Los Alamos the Army had armed patrols on foot and horseback combing those hills. Fortified observation posts with long telescopes were strategically placed on the mountainsides surrounding the lab to provide the earliest warning of intruders. In fact, if you look over there," Barnhart said, pointing to a distant mountain, "you can see the remains of a concrete observation bunker on that exposed rock face. Can you see it?"

Pretending to strain, Boucher focused on the distant hillside about two miles away. "Yes, I think I see it. Did they ever shoot anyone?" he asked jokingly.

* * *

What Barnhart and Boucher didn't see were the two men, wearing sniper-style camouflaged Ghilli suits, hidden beneath the low branches of some small spruce trees located about one hundred and fifty yards up the hill from the ski lodge's patio deck. The men were each wearing small earplug headphones attached to parabolic disk-shaped listening devices aimed at Barnhart. The feed from the small amplifiers at the base of the hand-held devices led to a hard disk recorder and a secure radio. The two men were so well camouflaged that a person would almost have to step right on them to find them.

Barnhart took a massive bite of his corned beef and tomato sandwich and continued talking with his mouth full, chewing between words.

"For that matter it's a nasty drive up the mesa to Los Alamos. Did you see where the old road used to run off to your left when you drove up here? That little winding one lane dirt road was all we had until 1958 when the government built the road you used today."

Barnhart paused for what seemed to be an unexplainably long time to swallow. His eyes fluttered as he subsequently drew in a long breath through his teeth.

"Yes, Jake, I was told there was occasional machine gun fire from those hills. There were rumors that intruders were shot but no one ever saw any bodies."

The North Atlantic Ocean, the same time

The nondescript coastal freighter made its way through the Atlantic's slow rolling swells several hundred miles west of Mauritania. Otherwise, the seas were unusually calm. A gentle breeze warmed the bearded face of Abdul Adja Rahman, the freighter's master, as he stood on the ship's open bridge. He squinted into the blue sky above. *God is great!* he thought smiling to himself before returning inside the pilot house.

Soon he would arrive at the point in the ocean only marked on his navigation chart by GPS coordinates. Rahman smiled to himself. *It is indeed a great day. It is the beginning of the end for the Great Satan and the infidels. Islam will finally dominate the world and be the one true religion just as the prophesy predicts.*

He imagined how his home country of Algeria, along with Libya, Tunisia and Morocco, the once feared Islamic 'Barbary' states, would regain their past glory.

We will again raid the coastal villages and kill as many of the 'non-Muslim' men and women as possible. We will collect the booty of young non-

Muslim women and sell them as concubines in Islamic slave markets. Allah prescribed Islamic law to provide for the sexual interests of Muslim men by allowing us to take four wives and to have as many concubines as our fortunes allow. Allah will reward Islam's true believers and my fortune will be great. It will be glorious!

Rahman smiled again knowing that all he had to do was to complete this assignment and he would be rich and prophesy would become reality. His attention returned to the GPS navigation screen above the ship's helm. It would not be much further on this heading, perhaps an hour more of sailing, and when they arrived it would be dark.

No one will be watching. It is time to get God's hand ready to swim.

Rahman had waited a lifetime for this singular piece of undersea oil exploration technology for it provided the difference he and his fellow devout believers needed.

It will dive to depths previously unreachable and easily recover the divine weapons that have been lying on the ocean floor out of reach for over thirty years. The nuclear warheads are there and we will use them against the very infidels who built them.

All Rahman needed to do was retrieve some of them - two or three would be enough.

We will install a new fire set in each of them and make them operable again. Islam will become an instant nuclear power and be feared. Israel will be wiped off the face of the earth forever. The United States will be powerless to respond and its demise will be next. This attack will bring The Great Satan to its knees and Islam will reign for a thousand years. Praise be to God!

The thought of it made him almost giddy with joy.

Los Alamos National Laboratory, the same time

"Tell me about Iran's clandestine nuclear weapon program."

Barnhart stood, gazing down into the valley below as though he was searching for a cue card to read from. Barnhart's focused silence seemed to exaggerate the sound of the wind blowing through the tall Aspen trees next to the lodge. Peering back at Boucher over his thick-lens glasses, the tall, slim, white haired sage scientist began to explain.

"The story actually begins in Iraq."

"How so?"

"In June of 1981, Israeli war planes unilaterally attacked Iraq's nuclear reactor facility located at Tuwaitha, completely destroying it. Many thought that the operation was conducted by Israeli commandos who had covertly placed explosive charges on the inside because the strike was so surgically effective with so amazingly little collateral damage. In a United Nations Security Council forum, the United Sates, along with other member nations, publicly protested the Israeli attack."

"Yes, I remember the incident and that it was little more than a small blip on the news media's radar scope."

"But not disclosed to the world was the chain of events that led to the Israeli strike against the facility and how their targeting and bombing precision was achieved. Also not disclosed was the fact that Iraq had a clandestine nuclear weapon development program. And, Jake, it was Iraq's program that ten years later turned out to act as a catalyst for the first Gulf War and ultimately provided Iran's start in its own nuclear weapon development program."

"What?" Boucher mumbled.

Barnhart took a disinterested sip of cold coffee from his foam cup and sat back down. He propped his upper body on his elbows while loosely holding the cup in both hands up close to his mouth.

"As early as spring of 1980, Israeli intelligence provided the U.S. government indicators and warnings about Iraq's true intentions to secretly divert nuclear source materials from superficially peaceful reactor operations for weapon purposes. Even today a trail of espionage, deception and international intrigue is still surfacing, leaving many people who analyze such events to doubt that Iraq ever departed from its quest to develop nuclear weapons after the first Gulf War."

Boucher interrupted in astonishment. "1980? How do you know that?"

"Because in 1980 I was a member of an IAEA safeguards inspection team scrutinizing Iraq's Tuwaitha nuclear reactor facility which was nearing completion. The Osirak reactor plant at the facility was bought from and built by the French because the French sold Iraq one of their French-designed Framatome reactors. The reactor was nearly finished and in the process of being readied for fuel loading."

"You never cease to amaze me. I've known you for the last twenty years of my professional adult life and you still amaze me with the stuff you've done."

Barnhart smiled and went on.

"Following our detailed review of Iraqi reactor fueling progress reports and other nuclear-related scientific records, I grew suspicious of Iraq's true intentions and purpose for the reactor. Although they claimed it was for peaceful purposes there were just too many inconsistencies in their reports and in what their scientists and engineers had to say. Besides, why would a nation like Iraq, that is so rich in fossil fuel, pursue nuclear power to generate electricity?"

Boucher lurched forward, "Did you raise the red flag?"

Barnhart didn't even flinch. "Not at the time because I wanted to confirm my assumptions, and I knew I would be returning for additional progress inspections. Jake, you must consider that when an IAEA inspector makes such an accusation the data better be irrefutably accurate."

"Of course. Sorry."

Barnhart took a final gulp of cold coffee placing the cup down flat on its bottom with a loud pop. He again aimlessly stared out into the valley below as he spoke.

"I returned to Iraq about five months later. I prepared a personal inspection agenda in addition to the IAEA inspections in an attempt to confirm my suspicions. After spending about four weeks conducting a close review of previous IAEA data, and then comparing it to the new data, my analysis led me to believe that Iraq was indeed diverting nuclear source materials in the form of enriched uranium reactor fuel pellets to a clandestine nuclear weapon development program."

"Did the Iraqis suspect that you were up to something?"

A faint smile appeared on Barnhart's distinguished face. "Jake, you know I'm just a simple scientist." Barnhart continued before Boucher had a chance to reply. "In view of the potential threat, I was very concerned and felt it prudent to warn the American consulate in Baghdad."

Barnhart blew his nose several times in a napkin.

"You're killing me, Si. What happened in Baghdad?"

"Sorry," he replied as he balled up the napkin and wedged it down into his empty cup. "At the U.S. consulate in Baghdad, I revealed my findings and concerns to two embassy officials by the name of Mark Hann and Jon Patrick. Hann was the Political Officer, and I had to go through him first to get to the Ambassador. I had met Hann several months earlier during some briefings back at the State Department in Washington, DC. I'm not sure exactly what Patrick's status was there because he didn't talk very much and I never saw him again. Well, actually I did months later, but that's when I realized he worked for the DNCS at Langley. Who knows, he might have been the CIA's Chief of Station."

"The COS?" Boucher questioned thoughtfully.

"You see, Jake, Hann seemed to think the information I provided was inconclusive and therefore he discounted it as insignificant. According to a State Department friend of mine who had worked closely with Hann on an interagency counter-terrorism program, Hann was politically connected and definitely not to be trusted. Well, you're not here to talk about that, now are you?"

"Yes, I absolutely want to hear it. You never shared this level of detail with me before. Please continue, Si."

Barnhart scratched the side of his head.

"Hann had little stomach for controversy and apparently didn't want to be seen as an alarmist. I don't believe Hann ever did formally report my findings to the White House through State Department channels. Or, if he did, my findings were so bureaucratically watered down that they were not taken seriously. More likely, if Hann did report it, the information would have been included as part of a CIA intelligence report and would have been classified to the point that its' author probably wouldn't even have been appropriately cleared to read it. I suppose I'll never know for sure."

Boucher could see that Barnhart was clearly irritated with the memory of that time.

"In fact, I was blackballed by Hann because I was insistent and would not accept his assertion that my findings were lacking coherent fact and thus incomplete."

"Blackballed? How so?"

"Yes! Blackballed, Jake! Hann said that he would brief the Ambassador. What he really did was leak a lie to the IAEA that I was attempting to indict Iraq, and that most certainly did not help my credibility within the IAEA. I didn't find out the purpose of his agenda until years later."

"What was it? What was Hann's agenda?""

"To shut me up and discredit my assertion that Iraq had a clandestine nuclear weapon development program, and their so called plans to build commercial nuclear power plants were a cover! I'll tell you why later!" Barnhart exclaimed.

"What happened then, Si?"

"I returned to Washington in the fall of 1980. With the help of a well-placed friend, I gained the attention of some congressional staffers who arranged for me to present my findings before several members of the Senate Select Committee on Intelligence. The revelation that Iraq was deeply embroiled in a clandestine nuclear weapon development program, with direct links to their so-called peaceful reactor program, seemed to go unheeded again. What I didn't know then was that they knew exactly what Iraq was up to but didn't want the beans spilled for political reasons. Here's where it gets sort of convoluted."

"Damn, Si, you lost me back at the Embassy in Baghdad."

Barnhart stood up and looked down at Boucher. "Come on, Jake," he coaxed, "let's go to my house and drink some beer. I want to tell you more about my findings."

The two men slowly walked off the patio and clanked down the grated metal stairs leading to the gravel parking area below. As they got into Boucher's rental car Barnhart pointed back up toward the mountain behind them.

"You know, up there, you're eleven thousand feet above sea level. You can see into Colorado from the top. You ever been up there?"

Boucher smiled and nodded, "A bunch of times."

"I mean, when was the last time?"

"Spring, five years ago, remember?"

A nondescript white Ford cargo van was parked on the opposite side of the gravel parking lot. A red fiberglass extension ladder was clamped to the right side of the van's roof rack. A white PVC pipe with caps enclosing each end was strapped to the driver's side. Two small antennas mounted in the center of the van's roof were barely visible. There were two men sitting in the front seats wearing painter's overalls and eating sandwiches. Neither Boucher nor Barnhart noticed the weathered van's presence.

Boucher started the engine and headed out of the gravel parking lot toward the asphalt road leading down the mountain. Shortly thereafter, the van slowly pulled out of the parking lot following well behind. Boucher carefully navigated the car down the steep narrow road that twisted toward the sprawling Los Alamos National Laboratory complex below. Barnhart began to reveal more facts about the Israeli attack.

"In January of 1981, Israel requested U.S. government assistance in determining what weak points might exist from missile hazards in the U.S. Westinghouse-designed nuclear reactor. A request of this nature was not alarming because the U.S. was in the process of marketing nuclear reactors to Israel. And, a well-designed and constructed reactor, like the U.S. Westinghouse reactor, had ample systems protection from missile hazards caused by things like steam explosions. So, the U.S. responded to this seemingly innocent request from a stellar friend and ally by having the Department of Energy provide a four-man, hand picked team of reactor experts to answer the Israeli request. Although I was not a formal member of this team I was invited to sit along the wall as a note taker during the meetings."

Barnhart paused to draw a deep breath, yawning as he slowly exhaled.

"Excuse me, I didn't sleep very well last night."

"You feeling okay, Si?"

"Yeah, I just have a lot on my mind. Where was I?"

"You were sitting along the wall taking notes."

"Right. Right. Anyway, Ron Cruse, a senior Energy official and personal friend of mine, was the team leader for the U.S. side. The Israelis were particularly interested in the reactor's containment structure design and the missile hazard shielding around the reactor itself along with its supporting auxiliary and backup systems. Keep in mind that the missile hazards I'm referring to primarily focus on things like steam explosions and high pressure lines bursting. The Israeli delegation was also very interested in the reactor system's layout and the detailed positioning of individual equipments within the containment structure. You see, the Israeli team took great interest in questioning me at every opportunity, both during coffee breaks and over dinner after hours. Based upon the types of questions they asked, I privately suspected that their interest in me was more than religious brotherhood."

"What do you mean?"

"It was as if they were trying to recruit me to work for them. I subtly made it clear that although I'm Jewish, I am an American first. I've always felt that anything beyond that is superficial to what I am."

Boucher simply nodded and smiled over at Barnhart.

"Anyway, I soon realized that many of their questions focused on the similarities and subtle design differences between the Westinghouse design and French Framatome design. I raised this as an issue of concern to Cruse, but Cruse accused me of being insensitive to the obvious politics involved in important bilateral exchanges and flatly told me to back off. It was his impression that these types of technical questions must be asked to evaluate the overall safety of the reactor's design. While unstated, he clung to the premise that the overarching purpose of the Israeli query was innocent."

Barnhart put his right hand outside the open window waving it up and down playfully in the buffeting airflow as he went on with his story.

"The Israeli delegation departed the U.S. a few weeks later with all the reactor plant blue-prints and design details they asked for. The U.S. team was satisfied that they had done their job and had given the Israelis confidence in the safety and safeguards protection inherent in the Westinghouse design. I remained troubled over the disclosure because in my opinion, it went beyond good technical marketing. I instinctively felt that there was some abstract relationship to their line of questioning and the Framatome reactor design, but at the time, I couldn't find the link. Only months later did I see what the information we provided the Israelis was truly used for."

Barnhart sat up and pointed ahead.

"Ahhh, turn right at the light and take the second left toward White Rock."

"Roger," Boucher replied, having visited Barnhart's home countless times before. Even so, Barnhart always provided driving directions as though it was Boucher's first time.

"During the early nineteen eighties the proliferation of nuclear technology and materials seemed to be unchecked. The Cold War between the superpowers was in full swing. Nations already possessing a nuclear weapon capability were elite and became known as the 'Nuclear Club.' Israel, a member of the Club, expressed public concern that Iraq, close to having the reactor capability to produce weapon grade, special nuclear material, might have a corresponding weapon development program. Alright, Jake, we're almost here. Turn right into the driveway of the fourth house on the right."

Boucher turned the car into the driveway and stopped it a few feet away from the walk leading to the house's front door. Barnhart's low ranch-style home was uniquely situated on the edge of the mesa overlooking a long deep canyon leading down to the Rio Grande River about five miles distant.

"You know, Jake, I've been fixing up this house for the past twelve years and I'm still not finished."

"I know, Si."

Chapter 5

The Pentagon, Arlington, VA.,
the same time

Mr. Ian Lester, the newly appointed Assistant Secretary of Defense for Special Operations and Low Intensity Conflict, was in heated conversation behind closed doors on his secure telephone equipment or STE as everyone called it.

"Yes Ambassador, he's disclosing some very sensitive information and it must be handled before it creates irreparable damage to our national security. There is no other way. It is now in your hands." Pausing to listen for a moment he replied, "Look, I don't give a shit how you do it! Just get him out of the equation...yeah, you too!" Lester bristled as he hung up.

Lester was a typical white, middle-aged political appointee who achieved his lofty position by helping run the President's election campaign. His appointment as ASD/SO-LIC was a political payback. Like so many political appointees in the Washington, DC metro area, he was eminently unqualified to hold such an office. He fancied himself an elitist and loved to boss people around, especially those he considered at a lesser station than himself. He was politically connected and party loyal with his fellow appointees throughout the government who all stuck together to keep the network cemented which in turn kept their circle of power mutually strong.

Dialing his secretary's two-digit office intercom number Lester commanded, "Kim, put a call in to Jon Patrick at the National Security Council. I need to talk to him secure. Do it ASAP. Tell'm it's important!"

"Yes, Sir. Right away, Sir," the woman quickly replied.

A short while later the STE located on the credenza next to Lester's desktop computer monitor chirped out a ring. Lester answered the call, picking the telephone hand set up on the second ring.

"Lester," he snapped in his best deep baritone voice. "Oh, hi, Jon. Thanks for taking my call. We may have a problem with our old friend Doctor Barnhart. I received word about a half hour ago that he's in the process of disclosing some sensitive material to some ski lodge friend of his." Listening for a few seconds to the response on the other end of the phone, Lester continued. "Well, I think we should take preemptive action and so does Fuller over at the Agency." Listening for a few more moments, he again replied. "Good, Jon. Get some folks on it immediately. You know what to do and how to make it happen. I owe you one."

Lester slowly hung up the phone and rested back into his brown leather executive office chair. Congratulating himself he whispered, "Damn, I'm good!"

And, perhaps he was good because he left no audit trail behind in the event things went sour. This sort of business was always conducted by telephone call, using a secure telephone. There was no way to monitor the conversation unless you could sit next to the parties involved and listen to their conversation. More importantly, there was no paper trail that could come back to haunt those involved should an investigation occur. This was commonly known in the Washington DC beltway political circles as being "Teflon-coated," because nothing could be stuck to you.

Picking the secure phone back up, Lester direct dialed a local number. "Yes, this is Secretary Lester, please connect me – four, five, six, one-four, one-four. Thank you."

Routing outgoing calls through the White House switchboard was commonplace to prevent a caller ID audit trail. Before saying anything Lester pushed the secure button on the phone to encrypt the conversation.

"Hey, it's me. Do it," Lester ordered.

He then paused, listening intently to the voice on the other end before responding.

"No rules....do it any way you can, but get it done!"

He listened again, briefly and slowly began to anger.

"Look, it doesn't matter one way or the other. If you can use him to our advantage, great! Just don't screw it up!"

Listening again he interrupted.

"What do you mean you don't like it? Of course he knows you. So fucking what! It has to be done and you're going to do it! I want a briefing on the concept of operations in two hours."

Lester listened again, briefly, before speaking. His face was slowly turning red as his anger grew.

"I know we didn't plan for this eventuality but we can turn this into something that will work to our advantage. You have two hours."

Lester hung up the phone slamming it back on the hook.

"Damn, you're a knuckle-dragging shit-for-brains!" he angrily grumbled as he stared at the telephone.

Lester had strong political ties at the CIA from a Middle East posting he had in a previous administration. He was a master of manipulation and was mercenary in his modus operandi. Over the years he had been directly involved on-scene or facilitated several unofficial "black" operations like the selling of arms to Afghanistan and the laundering of foreign donations from China for the President's election campaign in exchange for political favors that included precious metal and scrap iron sales in support of the Favored Nation Trade Agreement with China. He had a well-established network of strategically placed senior government officials whom he could call upon for almost anything. His foreign contacts, in other so called "governments friendly to the United States", were equally impressive. Lester was known throughout the administration as the man to call when a dirty job with sensitive political implications had to be done right the first time. They also knew him as a man whom you should never turn your back on.

A briefer arrived at Lester's Pentagon office about two hours later and was ushered directly into Lester's office by his secretary.

"Mr. Mason is here, Mr. Lester," she announced.

Lester remained seated.

"Please show him in, Kim."

As she left the office she closed the door behind her ensuring that it was latched. The man sat down in a chair in front of Lester's desk and pulled a flash drive from his shirt pocket, throwing it on the desk in front of Lester. Lester took the small flash drive in his hand, studying it momentarily before looking up at the man.

"Alright, Bill," Lester said, "let's cut the chase and see what we have here."

Lester inserted the drive into the USB port on his computer and clicked the mouse several times, opening the file on the computer's display screen. Lester carefully read the document for a few minutes before commenting.

"Okay...Phase one and two look alright but I don't like phase three. I take it you think our friends will cooperate?"

Mason was now leaning over the corner of Lester's desk in an attempt to see the computer screen.

"Yes," he replied, "they will help us. They'll have to. Hann is on scene and has personally taken charge. He'll make it work one way or another."

Lester glared at Mason as he spoke. "You damn well better hope they'll play ball with us because if they don't we'll all go down over this and shit flows downhill. Do we understand each other?"

Mason looked away, hesitating a moment before answering. "Let me remind you that without the rest of us your shit is real thin. Don't ever forget that! And don't think for a second that you're where you are because of your resume. You're here because we put you here. We can finger you on the Fort Detrick anthrax job you and that scientist friend of yours bungled any day of the week we want. You might even overdose just like your scientist friend did. So fuck you, Lester!"

Lester sat back in his chair without comment. He removed the flash drive from his computer and tossed it onto his desk close to Mason.

"He didn't overdose and you and I both know it," he calmly replied. "He didn't bungle the job either. He sent the anthrax to all the threats you identified. He did what was asked of him and served his purpose. Then you had him killed so there was only one story – the government's. Even if he had gone to the media no one would have believed him. You planted e-mails in his computer and had your shrink accomplice confirm notes from therapy sessions with him that never occurred. There's no question about how capable you are so don't worry about me, I get it."

Mason snatched the drive and returned it to his shirt pocket.

"See-ya round, Mr. Lester," Mason sarcastically sneered.

Lester returned the sneer. "Yeah, around, Mr. Mason."

Mason left the office without looking back and intentionally left the door open behind him.

Lester sat with his elbows on the desk, cradling his head in his hands and massaging his forehead in deep thought. He had worked closely with Mason on several other "black" operations and while he really didn't like Mason, Lester knew that he would get the job done and personally see it through to successful completion - he would *Deliver the Message to Garcia*. Lester had total confidence in Mason's ability to both manage the operation and cover his ass. Mason once told him that a successful operation had only a few basic rules: Never rely on anyone who has less to lose than you do. Take no prisoners. And, never ever look back as you leave the scene. Lester knew firsthand just how much Mason and all his operatives lived by those rules.

After taking a few deep cleansing breaths, he picked up the secure telephone and keyed in a new number on the keypad. Only after pressing the secure button when the person on the other end answered, did he speak.

"Yeah, it's me. All I want to know is how soon."

Pausing while his question was being answered, he doodled with his pen on the yellow legal pad before him on the desk.

"Okay, I understand. I want you to contact Hann and step the schedule up by five days." Pausing again, he listened to the voice on the other end. "Yeah, I understand that. Pay them whatever it takes. This is not the time to argue over a few dollars. The money is immediately available."

The voice on the other end was apparently arguing with Lester. Lester was beginning to show his frustration.

"Look, we'll pull it off! Just let me worry about our friends over there. This has got to be done. We need Barnhart in this with us."

The voice on the other end interrupted, but Lester fired back.

"Yeah, they'll play! Mason has Hann in his hip pocket and he will take care of the details."

Listening momentarily, Lester snapped, "If you think the good doctor is going to be a problem then assign one of your people to him to keep him out of trouble. Look, I have to go."

Lester carefully placed the phone back on its hook.

The picture he had doodled on the yellow notepad in front of him was a mushroom cloud with several arrows crossing beneath it. Below the arrows he had drawn several small boxes with an X in each box. Lester tore the page from the pad and folded it in half. He stood up from his desk and carried the folded page over to the shredder beside the FAX machine, located next to the window. Lester paused and gazed out the window unemotionally. Without looking down at the shredder he inserted the page into the cutter slot and pressed the green button. As the machine buzzed to life the yellow page was instantly transformed into confetti with pieces too small to reassemble. He remained standing there, blankly staring out the window at the many rows of white grave markers lining the hillside in Arlington National Cemetery directly across the street from his Pentagon office.

Chapter 6

White Rock, New Mexico, the same time

Both men entered Barnhart's home through the heavy solid oak front door. To the right, a large family room opened away from the kitchen with a massive red stone fireplace filling one entire corner of the room. The room's outside walls were all glass from ceiling to floor which provided a spectacular view down the canyon that was only partially obscured by some native Juniper trees and Ponderosa pines. Boucher could easily see why Barnhart had remained there following his retirement from the Lab. The town of White Rock was even smaller than its neighbor city, Los Alamos. It certainly didn't have much to offer in the way of social activities found in Santa Fe, but it sure had natural beauty and above all, serenity.

Making himself at home with remote controls in hand, Boucher switched on both the stereo and the television to talk shows. He then turned on a pedestal-mounted oscillating floor fan, separating the kitchen from the family room, and carefully aimed the airflow into the kitchen.

Barnhart began to speak, his voice barely discernable over the noise created by the radio, TV and fan. "Israel sternly cautioned both its friends and potential enemies that Iraq would not be allowed to bring its Tuwaitha reactor on line because of the direct threat Israel felt Iraq posed to regional security if allowed to possess the resources to develop nuclear weapons. In nothing less than a tactically brilliant surprise attack, Israel unilaterally bombed the Iraqi nuclear reactor facility at Tuwaitha, completely destroying it. Only then did the relationship between the U.S. Westinghouse reactor design, Iraq's French-built Framatome reactor and the Israeli raid come to light," he said flaring his left hand above his head to emphasize the word light.

"I remember the Israeli attack but I'm not sure I'm following you."

Barnhart walked over to the refrigerator in the adjoining kitchen and pulled open the door while looking back at Boucher.

"Beer?"

"Yes, thanks."

Barnhart retrieved two beer bottles from the back of the top shelf and opened them. He returned to his chair, handing a beer to Boucher. Barnhart took a long swallow then wiped his sleeve across his mouth.

"You see, Jake, from the late 1960s through the 1970s the U.S. and Europe thrust forward in an attempt to develop energy independence from fossil fuel. Back then, the use of clean nuclear power generation as an alternative to environmentally polluting fossil fuel power generation methods was very promising and seemed to provide an acceptable solution to the looming future power requirement demands. At the time, selling and building reactors for nations was big business, not to mention the national prestige it provided."

Barnhart paused to take a small swallow of beer before continuing.

"Even between friendly nations, international espionage that targeted each other's reactor designs and their related technology was running rampant. The French Framatome reactor was nearly an identical clone of the U.S. Westinghouse reactor and that was more than just coincidence. You see, the French designed their Framatome reactor in about a third of the time that it took Westinghouse. Comparatively, the French had amazingly little research and development cost and as a result they were able to undercut the U.S. cost proposals on the international reactor sales market. The Framatome reactor was, for that period, a good, very safe system because it was for all practical purposes identical to our Westinghouse design."

"Are you suggesting that the French stole our design secrets?"

"No! I'm not suggesting anything!" Barnhart decreed. "I'm telling you they stole the Westinghouse design right under our noses and copied it almost to the millimeter!"

"So is that the Israeli tie?"

Barnhart held up his index finger and quickly took two gulps of beer before replying.

"The Israeli intelligence community knew that the French had cloned the Westinghouse reactor design. They exploited this knowledge to reverse engineer the Westinghouse reactor's design weaknesses and strengths in planning their attack against Iraq's Framatome reactor. That's why they wanted our Westinghouse reactor data. The arrogant bastards never had any intention of buying our Westinghouse design. This overt process of detailed technical collection against the U.S. by Israel, in addition to their other covert tactical collection in and around Iraq's reactor, provided all the information required to plan and flawlessly execute a surgical strike against Iraq's reactor."

"Jezzzz! Did anyone even have a clue what the Israelis were up to?"

Barnhart forcefully set his beer bottle on the glass-topped end table and leaned forward toward Boucher.

"There are some who believe the U.S. was a witting accomplice to the Israeli attack. There are unconfirmed reports that the Israelis used U.S.-supplied laser guided bombs in the strike. That would have certainly required specially equipped aircraft and U.S. sponsored training for the Israeli pilots. It would also account for the impressive accuracy attained in the strike. But the fighter-bomber aircraft sold to Israel by the U.S. at the time were not laser equipped by Congressional decree. It would have been against U.S. law and outside any authority of the Executive Branch to provide them such advanced weapons."

"Shit!" Boucher gasped. "This is some incredible stuff, Si."

Barnhart smiled as he reached to reclaim his beer.

"Some credibly speculate that the various bomb targets were laser illuminated by Israeli Special Forces ground elements, operating clandestinely within laser aiming range of the Iraqi reactor facility. This could account for the extreme accuracy of the bomb hits and at the same time reduce the requirement for airborne laser target illumination."

"That's correct; I used them numerous times when I was still on active duty in the SEALs. Portable laser target designators provide pin point accuracy and, once they're in place they can be remotely operated, which greatly reduces the risk of compromise." Boucher gulped down the last of his beer. "But do you think we gave them the portable laser units too?"

"I doubt it because such laser target designator devices were available worldwide and the Israelis still would have had to have laser guided bombs and compatibly equipped laser target designation-capable aircraft."

Barnhart took a quick swallow of beer and turned toward Boucher.

"There is some evidence that suggests the U.S. provided Israel access to raw, un-assessed strategic overhead intelligence so that Israeli planners could assess the imagery for themselves. Keeping in mind that Iraq was not an enemy of the U.S. during that time, a second benefit of such an unprecedented intelligence disclosure of unanalyzed super secret spy satellite imagery by the U.S. to Israel could have been to keep the number of witting personnel on the

U.S. side to a bare minimum. This would have acted to further insulate the U.S. from complicity in the ensuing Israeli attack."

Boucher shrugged as if to beg a question, "And the truth?"

"The truth?" Barnhart repeated to himself. "Well, I suppose the truth no doubt lies somewhere within classified Pentagon and CIA files. Nonetheless, it is an example of the sort of international intrigue that leads to public distrust of Washington's policies and fuels belief in government secret deals that are made behind the public's eye and without their consent."

"Why do you suppose the Israelis just didn't go to the French and ask them for the Framatome reactor design just like they asked us for the Westinghouse design? I mean, wouldn't that have been much easier?"

Barnhart choked at Boucher's question as he drained the last swallow of beer from the bottle.

"The French?" Barnhart coughed. "Those assholes wouldn't give the Israelis the time of day, or anyone else for that matter!"

"Wait a second, Si. My last name is French," he joked, "pronounced, Buu-shure and I'm not an asshole – am I?"

Barnhart chuckled, "Just slightly, but you're only part French and besides, your French blood has been diluted by numerous American generations of Bouchers."

Boucher laughed. Barnhart became serious again and immediately returned to his point.

"If you look at the politics of the time, the U.S. was completely in bed with Israel, and Israel couldn't afford association with France's eccentric de Gaullean policies or France's previous Suez Canal franchise with the Arab world. Also remember that Iran was holding Americans hostage. And, Iran was at war with Iraq. We were in dire need of oil and Iraq was supplying much of it. Hell, Iraq was our ally. At the same time we didn't want Iraq to join the nuclear club. It's probably safe to assume that Israel was going to bomb Iraq's reactor with or without our help and what the U.S. government apparently decided to do was to manipulate the circumstances so we could have our cake and eat it too. Hey Jake, are you still thirsty?"

Barnhart returned to the family room and handed Boucher a fresh beer, then walked over to the largest window that offered a clear view of the Rio Grande River snaking through the valley below.

"You know, a black bear visits my backyard almost every night. The furry bastard loves to raid my garden."

Boucher acknowledged with a smile.

"Whatever happened to the Iraqi reactor fuel after the Israeli strike, Si?"

"That's a darn good question." Barnhart continued peering mystically through the window as he answered. "Following the Israeli strike against Iraq's reactor in 1981, an IAEA safeguards inspection team was dispatched to assess the extent of damage to the reactor and, I was again a team member."

Boucher studied his old friend carefully. It was as if Barnhart was mentally reliving the experience as he spoke about it.

"Destruction of the reactor facility was total and remarkably, their enriched uranium fuel stockpile was all accounted for. Well, at least on paper and by volume it was."

"But it really wasn't accounted for?"

"Well, close analysis of actual fuel samples recovered by the IAEA after the attack revealed that the level of enrichment was not the same as the stuff we had checked months earlier."

"So was it the same stuff or not?"

"Although subtle, my analysis showed the percentage of enrichment of the fuel was different than that assessed prior to the Israeli raid. I had the data to prove it wasn't the same stuff. Like before, I went to the American embassy in Baghdad to report my finding. I was told that Hann had been reassigned but his replacement, Jon Patrick, met with me. Although I was deeply suspicious of his agenda I gave him a copy of my notes containing my findings. It was clear to me that he had little familiarity with nuclear stuff. Although he didn't actually say it, he suggested that I was again being an alarmist. I was frustrated because at the time I had no idea why the embassy would refuse to even consider my findings."

"Why didn't you go through the IAEA? Wouldn't they have been concerned and elevated it to the proper international level for action?"

"I'm sure they would have, Jake, but you have to remember that we were allies with Iraq and if I would have raised the red flag on them it could have significantly damaged our relationship. Don't forget, we needed their oil."

"What then, Si?" Boucher impatiently asked, again shifting his position on the couch.

Barnhart maintained his fixed stare out the window. In a low, almost inaudible voice he answered.

"I returned to Los Alamos several weeks later and was directed to immediately go back east to Washington to the DOE headquarters for a debriefing of my Iraq trip. That wasn't an uncommon event in itself, but that isn't quite what happened."

Boucher sat at attention. "What do you mean?"

"I reported to the DOE Assistant Secretary for Military Application and Stockpile Support as ordered, expecting the normal niceties and an informal debriefing around a table of my colleagues. But, I was ushered into the SCIF down in the basement instead and debriefed by some CIA intelligence analysts from Langley and guess who else - Hann and Patrick!"

Boucher was now on the edge of the sofa. "What did they want to know?"

Barnhart turned back to the window and continued at a slower pace.

"Their line of questioning was antagonistic and skillfully designed to see if I had any inside information from which a correlation might be made, scoping Iraq's nuclear weapon development program. Of course, they promised me that no matter what I said the 'non-attribution policy' would be in effect."

"Oh yeah," Boucher interrupted, "I remember the Intelligence Community's good old non-attribution policy promise from the last job I did for them in the Caspian. They're a bunch of introverted, egocentric bastards, those freaking intelligence-types! They're a damn solution looking for a problem!" Boucher, obviously irritated by the memory of the non-attribution policy, gulped a quick mouthful of beer. "The American people don't have a clue what these people are really about or what they're really up to!"

Barnhart smiled and took several swallows of his beer before continuing.

"You see, Jake, there were two weeks of follow-on debriefs after that first meeting. All the rest were held at the CIA's Langley headquarters. I never saw Hann again, if that was even his real name, but Patrick attended every single meeting. There were usually four to five other people involved each day. They always used first names and their behavior towards each other led me to believe that they were a mix of CIA Case Officers and other inter-agency players who didn't normally work together. Their individual political agendas occasionally emerged from behind the facade. Nevertheless, I attempted to provide them the very best information I could and although they videotaped every meeting I truly didn't think that they were interested in the technical details I was offering. They weren't from the scientific community, of that I'm sure!"

"Can you give me an example of the kind of stuff they focused on, Si?"

"Of course I can. They wanted to know the level of destruction at the plant. In fact, they referred to it as battle damage assessment."

"Yeah, BDA. That's a military term. But surely, they had satellite imagery and other firsthand on-ground reports of the destruction resulting from the Israeli strike."

"One would certainly think so. But I was more puzzled by some of their questions, especially those that dealt with the Iraqi scientific community and my ties to them. The entire debriefing process was unnerving for me. I felt as though I was being interrogated, not debriefed. Actually, looking back on it now, it was an interrogation. I remember leaving for Los Alamos after the debriefings feeling as if I had been violated. It wasn't fun and I didn't like being treated like a foreign agent by our own people."

"Si, what else did you tell them?"

Barnhart turned away from the window and walked up to Boucher's chair. He seemed to be contemplating the question.

"I'm going to reveal things to you that I have never discussed with anyone else. I may not trust the intelligence community's non-attribution policy, but I trust you."

Barnhart again peered through the window and began talking as though he was reporting on an activity that was happening before him.

"Many analysts believe that following the strike, Iraq continued to clandestinely purchase and stockpile enriched uranium from sources like North Korea, China and at the time, maybe even South Africa. I believed that Iraq might even have obtained a small quantity of SNM, perhaps obtained on the black market and smuggled there, from one of the Soviet states. Iraq unquestionably proceeded with the procurement and development of the specialized equipment and facilities for their nuclear weapon program. Looking back, I think it is unlikely that our intelligence community was initially aware of this Iraqi effort because of the dual use aspects of much of the type of equipment required to develop nuclear weapons and the fact that most intelligence analysts simply don't have the scientific or technical background to recognize and identify the purpose of such components. It is exactly what Iran is doing today and ironically we face the same intelligence issues."

"Iran is buying SNM from anyone they can and they're crazy enough to risk sanctions and maybe even attack if they are caught at it?" Boucher scoffed. "So why don't I find that hard to believe?"

Barnhart began pacing in front of the windows and speaking as though he was lecturing in a university classroom.

"Well, let's take a look at history, Jake. In the mid-1980s Iraq's border war with Iran was going badly and was becoming a costly drain on Iraq's resources. Iraq had already demonstrated its willingness to use chemical weapons, both on the battlefield against its Iranian foe, as well as within its own borders against its own people. The Soviet Union was in the process of going out of business and a new world order was beginning to take form. The West was more interested in keeping the oil flowing from the Persian Gulf and courting oil rich states like Iraq, Kuwait and Saudi Arabia than in controlling potential proliferators. Patrick's entire line of questioning was focused on how to keep the oil flowing, not on stemming Iraq's nuclear proliferation."

Boucher barely said the words, "Yes, but," when Barnhart cut him off.

"If Saddam had nuclear weapons, he too could gain membership into the elite nuclear club. With nuclear weapons he would also have an intimidation factor not possessed by Iran or, for that matter, any other Gulf state. Nuclear weapons would turn the tide of the war against Iran and undoubtedly shift the Middle East's balance of power in Saddam's favor. With nuclear weapons, Iraq would possess both a threat to Iran and a strategic deterrence to Israel's anti-Arab policies. Or, for that matter, he could launch a devastating surprise attack – a first strike against Israel and wipe it from the face of the planet making him a superhero to the Arab world. A well funded nuclear weapon program was clearly in Iraq's best interest and I believe that Saddam had every intention of making it so."

"That's not surprising to me, Si, but it still requires a huge undertaking and a strategy like that isn't easy."

"Easy? Who said it was easy? Here's how they did it. Over the next several years Iraq sent its brightest students to the very best schools in the United States and abroad for scientific and engineering training in dual-use technologies. This state supported effort was a well-organized campaign to acquire new and more sophisticated technology to develop indigenous capabilities for high tech weapons and their delivery systems. If the U.S. intelligence community detected this and correlated its true purpose, they did little to curb its potential threat. In my opinion, it is far more likely that they completely overlooked it. And, that allowed Saddam to exploit these available intellectual resources and establish his weapon program."

Barnhart paused and sucked in a long breath while clenching his teeth.

"This might be a good example of what I'm talking about. At the beginning of the first Gulf War in 1991 an FBI source whom I trust, told me that the FBI investigated the locations of Iraqis in the U.S. He said that he was astounded to find that the majority of foreign students going to several major U.S. universities specializing in nuclear engineering, nuclear physics, health physics, and related nuclear sciences, were Iraqi. This was seen as an indicator to some analysts within the intelligence community, leading them to believe that Saddam already had a well organized state supported nuclear weapon program."

Barnhart turned to face Boucher.

"Ironically, even those analysts on the conservative side believed if Saddam didn't yet have a weapon he was dangerously close. Of greatest concern to us all was the belief that if Saddam did succeed in getting his hands on a nuclear weapon he would undoubtedly use it if he felt the benefits were worth the risks of potential retaliation."

"Are you telling me that we suspected Iraq was developing the bomb for the past twenty years and did nothing about it?"

"It was more than suspicion," Barnhart insisted. "I think it's fair to assume that we knew at the highest levels of government and allowed it to happen. Jake, we must factor politics into this as well. The Palestinian homeland issue was just as hot a media topic then as it is today, maybe even hotter. Israel was displaying more and more distrust of Washington and we're back to that today, especially with our current administration. We had an entire embassy staff being held as hostage in Iran and we had a very weak president who felt compromise was the primary tool on which to base his foreign policy and military strategy. Our peanut farming president thought he could use his Kum-Ba-Yah diplomacy to control the oil flow in the Middle East, gain the release of our hostages held by Iran, a nation that opposed us with it's every fiber, and win the Cold War arms race against the Russians by playing croquet and drinking mint juleps with Leonid Brezhnev. Carter drove our military's readiness down to the point where it was little more than a hollow shell. He gutted our intelligence community and stood by naively smiling as the U.S. economy nose-dived and inflation ran rampant. If there ever was an opportune time to take advantage of a weakened and unfocused United States that was surely it. And, the world's bad actors knew it and did just that."

The television seemed to capture both Barnhart's and Boucher's attention simultaneously as a picture of an above ground nuclear detonation flashed on the screen behind large blue letters that read, "Fox News Alert." The picture faded into a full frontal of Jamie Lessiak standing along Pennsylvania Avenue in front of the White House. Barnhart grabbed the TV remote and increased the volume. She began the report.

"Examples of terrorists employing weapons of mass destruction are few and far between. This has led many analysts to erroneously conclude that the threat posed by weapons of mass destruction in the hands of terrorists is on the decline. Ironically, just as momentous changes point toward the peaceful resolution of the historic Palestinian-Israeli territorial claims over the boundaries of the Palestinian State and Hebron, another outbreak of deadly violence has occurred along the Israeli-Lebanon border. Recent terrorist outrages linked to al-Qa'ida, Hamas, Hezbollah and eight other lesser known but related radical-Islamic terrorist groups, are raising special concerns about Islamic extremism."

Lessiak glanced down at her script again as though she had her message memorized instead of reading it from the television display prompter located next to the camera in front of her.

"It is incongruous that, just as the extraordinary movement toward peace among Israelis and Palestinians was being celebrated, the process was assaulted by a contrary dynamic in the region. Islamic extremism and terrorism, of which al-Qa'ida and Hamas share as two of the most dangerous manifestations, has once again jeopardized a fragile peace and regional stability. Most of these groups are implacably opposed not just to Israel, but to secular Palestine. They are committed not only to wrecking the peace process, but to a broader agenda of imposing a radical version of Islam throughout the region, and to confrontation with the West. How should this threat be assessed and, what can be done to limit it?"

Again pausing momentarily, Lessiak turned toward the White House in the background before continuing her dialog.

"Iran, as President Banner has pointed out, is the world's leading state sponsor of terrorism. Iran is responsible for murdering many Iranian dissidents abroad. It has broadcast a fatwa calling for the murder of those it opposes. It directs, finances, and supplies its terrorist surrogates like al-Qa'ida and Hamas, and it has vowed to eradicate Israel. Iran can only restore relations with the civilized world by abandoning terrorism. That notwithstanding, Iran continues to ignore warnings from the international community that its behavior is intolerable. Iraq, Iran's neighbor to the west, continues to move toward democracy and opposition to terrorism. The president's warning issued here at the White House only moments ago was loud and clear."

Lessiak turned back to squarely face the camera.

"Should any terrorist act be directed at the United States, its allies or interests, that employs the use of a weapon of mass destruction, the United States will retaliate swiftly and decisively in kind. This is Jamie Lessiak, Fox News at the White House."

Barnhart immediately lowered the volume.

"Interesting report but sadly she doesn't have a clue."

Boucher smiled, "Si, are you implying our government's position isn't as serious in its support of Israel as it should be?"

"The issue is this," Barnhart responded, seeming not to catch Boucher's sarcasm. "Countering weapons of mass destruction and countering terrorism are directly related because they both commonly involve the same state supporters. Although much of our national strategy emphasizes stemming the proliferation of weapons of mass destruction and their means of delivery, today's programs are either marginally successful or dysfunctional failures."

Barnhart glanced out the window then turned to again face Boucher.

"You see, Jake, these exceedingly expensive non-proliferation programs may be in concert with the letter of the strategy, but not with the spirit. In truth, they are little more than disjointed and competing. They provide the illusion of progress, but in actuality they contribute little to the substantial enhancement of U.S. security."

"So you're saying our rear ends aren't as secure as we think they are. What's the solution, Doc?"

Barnhart thoughtfully grunted, took a swallow of beer, and then drew in a characteristically deep breath.

"Well, it seems the solution could be to first recognize that there is a difference in program composition and purpose between non-proliferation and counter-proliferation. Non-proliferation programs are primarily intelligence-oriented proactive programs that focus on prevention. On the other hand, counter-proliferation programs are operationally-oriented and focus on the operational response to a clear threat of an incident about to take place or already underway. As a solution, the U.S. government places all these programs under the non-proliferation umbrella and I am here to tell you that this has never worked and probably won't ever work. I think it's safe to assume that for all the non-proliferation successes involving the detection and intercept of nuclear materials on the black market, there are probably a number of unsuccessful detections. To be sure, detection is not a perfect science. I think we must assume that nuclear materials, and maybe even the weapons themselves, have already slipped through and may be in the hands of rogue nations or terrorist groups who would use them against anyone they consider enemies."

"Okay, I follow you. There are real problems in the world and we need to prioritize them. I've been saying for years we need better, more reliable means to detect rogue weapons and keep the terrorists from using them against us?"

Barnhart leaned forward toward Boucher.

"The need to detect and prevent the use of weapons of mass destruction by terrorists is addressed in the U.S. National Strategy as a priority. You see, Jake, most analysts believe the greatest threat involves the use of an improvised chemical or biological weapon or, a low tech radiological dispersal device. But as you well know, compared to a nuke, none of these are true weapons of mass destruction. In my opinion the use of such weapons will wreak havoc and will likely catch those targeted completely unprepared within a small local area, but such an attack will not be otherwise devastating. In comparison, the use of an atomic bomb is unacceptable by all international understanding. The strategy makes clear that an attack of this nature will be perceived by the U.S. as an unacceptable escalation to the level of violence that could drive significant military retaliation if state complicity is associated. That's what Miss Lessiak is talking about. She just doesn't explain it very well."

"No argument, Si, I got it and I concur."

"Good, Jake. Now here's how the detection issue factors into the puzzle. As you know, solid intelligence is the key ingredient for successful counter proliferation and counter terrorism. Our strategy addresses intelligence but falls short of recognizing the necessary role that it plays in both policy and operations. As you well know, the U.S. intelligence community is composed of several agencies and departments, not just the CIA as the public commonly believes. The intelligence community is itself competing and compartmented, and as a result it is largely ineffective."

"You got that right, Si. There's certainly no big picture as the Hollywood movie scripts would have us believe."

"Correct, Jake. Moreover, the inter-agency members involved in countering the wide variety of threats posed have the appropriate level of clearance and a need to know, but most often they are excluded or do not have access to the information they need. Intelligence needs to be disseminated, not harbored. Significant improvement of this one area would result in measurable success not only in countering proliferation, terrorism and drug trafficking but in deciding when and how to employ U.S. forces."

"I thought that was fixed following 9-11 when President Bush created an intelligence czar to coordinate the entire intelligence community and force them to play nice together?"

"Fixed?" Barnhart smirked. "You got to be shit'n me, son! All the Director of National Intelligence does is pile an additional layer of bureaucracy onto an already top heavy bureaucracy. Help isn't help unless it's asked for, and the intelligence community didn't need any or ask for any. All they need is for Congress to remove the restrictions they imposed over the past thirty years and the intelligence community will become effective again. Just let'm take the gloves off!"

Boucher stood and walked over to the window, again peering over the mesa below. "Safe and arming systems exist in virtually all nuclear weapons. Don't you think the intelligence community knows how easy it would be to make a black market weapon functional?"

Barnhart joined him at the window.

"Perhaps, but most of them don't understand or remember the difference between an IND and an RDD."

Barnhart held up a crooked index finger to emphasize his point, continuing as though he was in a university classroom.

"Granted, an IND's replacement fire set may not provide as efficient a detonation as the original design fire set, but the destructive difference between, say a twenty kiloton design yield and a ten kiloton rogue yield, is really only measurable by the destruction it wreaks on the target where the bomb is detonated. If it is detonated in a highly populated city environment the difference can easily be measured by the breadth of death and destruction. If it's detonated in a rural environment it might be measured by its indirect effects from its expanse of radiological fallout contamination down wind."

Turning to face Boucher, Barnhart hinted a faint smile.

"Both are terrorizing and neither is particularly pleasant to experience."

Boucher winced. "Yes, I understand your point."

At that moment the window behind Barnhart shattered followed by a splintering bullet impact on the door jam across the room. Barnhart and Boucher both instinctively hit the floor.

"Holy shit! What was that?" Barnhart exclaimed.

"Stay down and follow me!" Boucher yelled. "Don't give'm a target. Stay low!"

Boucher and Barnhart crawled on their hands and knees from the living room through the kitchen to the hall leading into the garage. Boucher reached up and carefully cracked opened the hall door leading into the garage. He quickly peered through into the garage.

"You got the keys to that SUV?" he asked pointing at a black Ford Expedition backed into the right side of the two-car garage with its front end facing the door.

Barnhart pulled some keys from his pocket and fumbled through them as he passed them to Boucher. "It's the black key."

Boucher motioned for Barnhart to follow him. The two men low crawled across the garage floor to the Expedition. "Get in and stay low!" Boucher shouted.

Boucher reached up and opened the driver's side door and slid into the seat, quietly easing the truck's door closed behind him. Barnhart did the same on the passenger's side.

"Okay Si, I'm going to give it a second after I start it up and then I'm ramming through the door. There are probably more of them out there waiting to take another shot so we need the element of surprise. Ready?"

Boucher paused momentarily as he glanced over at Barnhart. Barnhart's face was drained of color as he nodded agreement.

"Don't worry, we'll make it okay."

With that he started the Expedition's powerful engine, slammed it into drive and switched on the four wheel drive option.

"Hold on, Si!"

He floored the gas pedal commanding the heavy truck to leap forward, exploding through the closed garage door without the slightest hesitation.

Large panels of the door were launched across the street. Boucher skillfully threw the powerful Expedition into a controlled skid at the foot of the driveway. Lurching sideways onto the black asphalt street, he eased off the gas pedal and perfectly aligned the weighty truck's direction with the center of the street. He floored the gas pedal again and the Expedition sped down the narrow street.

"We're heading down the mountain!" Boucher yelled toward Barnhart who was pressed back in his bucket seat in an attempt to stabilize himself.

"How about the police? Call the police!" Barnhart shouted back.

"The Los Alamos police?" Boucher winced. "They can't protect us."

"Protect us from what? I thought the bullet that broke the window was a careless hunter or something."

Several miles down the road Boucher took a hard right turn and swung the Expedition onto a gravel road that led into a deep canyon. Slowing to a maneuvering speed on the bumpy road seemed like a snail's pace compared to the wild ride they had moments earlier.

Boucher slapped Barnhart's knee. "Si, that bullet was no accident. It was a warning! If that sniper would have wanted to kill you he could have done it several times over the past hour. Barnhart shook his head in doubt. "Jake, what is going on here?"

Without answering, Boucher continued along the gravel road about another half mile, keeping the truck hidden from the main road by the dense underbrush that lined the side of the ravine. Neither he nor Barnhart spoke. He finally turned the Expedition onto a gravel ramp leading back up onto the main road.

Boucher's mind raced...what he had heard over the past several hours was not recorded anywhere. It was a raw, historical account given by a man who had been personally involved. Boucher mentally recounted some of the day's experiences. They were followed. They were spied on. They were shot at and now they were trying to get away. Boucher looked over at Barnhart and studied the old man's weathered face. My God, Boucher thought to himself, this is the kind of close-hold information that's never made public. He noticed a coyote standing next to a brush thicket about fifty yards ahead. The coyote seemed quite at home and was not alarmed at their presence. Boucher smiled as he felt a weird exhilaration. It was a feeling he hadn't had since he and his guys went on their treasure hunt a year ago.

Chapter 7

The road to Santa Fe

It was now dusk as the Expedition sped along the road to Santa Fe. Barnhart seemed quietly oblivious to his surroundings and hadn't spoken to Boucher for some time. Boucher found his old friend to be very complex, a dichotomy of several professional cultures, yet, he could find no conflict of purpose. Boucher smiled to himself thinking Barnhart was about as solid a citizen as he could imagine one could be.

"When we left the ski lodge this morning, I noticed two men in a white work van followed behind us," Boucher said breaking the silence. "They remained well behind us most of the way to your house. I didn't think they were a threat."

"I didn't notice them. Who do you think they are?"

"They're definitely pros. They're about a half mile behind us right now. Look back to your right on the hill as we round this next curve and you'll see a white van."

Barnhart looked back and caught a glint of white van moving along the road well behind them contrasted against the dark rock masse.

"Si, I'm not sure I'm buying this simple scientist routine you've been playing. What's this all about?"

"I suppose you're right, Jake. You need to know the complete story."

Boucher checked the rear view mirror again and mumbled to himself, "Simple scientist my ass!"

Boucher sped up, steering the Expedition deliberately through the turns of the winding road with almost perfect turn geometry and the skill of a seasoned Le Mans race driver. He checked the rear view mirror over the course of a minute with several quick glances.

"We're out of their reception range by now. I don't think they'll try to catch up."

"What reception range are you talking about, Jake?"

Boucher accelerated as they exited the turn. He looked over at the old scientist and reassuringly patted him on the shoulder.

"Si, we're dealing with two issues here. First, I think it's fair to assume that we have been under surveillance for some time. Number two. Since visual surveillance has significant limitations we can assume that they bugged your house and maybe even this truck. I assumed that the white van has monitoring receivers onboard and that is why they attempted to stay within transmission range of the bug's small radio transmitters. These miniature transmitters work on FM radio frequencies and can only be received in a straight line of sight. That means in mountainous terrain like we have here, the receiver must remain close enough to visually acquire the target. You know, line of sight, in order to maintain continuous reception."

Barnhart smiled. "It's personal, Jake. They want me, not you."

A baffled Boucher was trying desperately to understand.

"But who are they?"

"Maybe the intelligence community or some other government agency?"

"I did the Caspian Sea ship boarding operation for the CIA. Why would the CIA be interested in what we are talking about? Shit, why don't they just ask me?"

"Did you ever stop and think that they may not be the ones who are doing the spying?"

Boucher had a look of confusion on his face. "Si, this is getting pretty bizarre."

Barnhart gave Boucher a fatherly glance. "Sometimes I'm not sure who I am anymore but I know I'm not the enemy."

Boucher shook his head. "Me either. So who are those guys?"

"I'd bet they're privateers. The administration can't risk another public relations catastrophe, especially one that involves their conducting covert operations against U.S. citizens here in the United States. They've already lost enough credibility with the American people over the last few years. Congress would kill their budget."

"But Si, who would be interested in you to the point that they would go to this extreme to intimidate you into silence?"

"At this point Jake, I'm not sure but I do know it's done all the time."

"But why you?"

"It seems there are some who see me as a threat to their agenda. We're at a point in the state of our government where the tail is wagging the dog. That's why I'm trying to impart some of this information to you, Jake. I'm telling you information that needs to be brought out into the light and exposed to the American public and to our elected officials. This country," he added with a pause, "is in deep shit and we need to fix it before it's too late!"

"Not the Luminous again," Boucher muttered. "I thought I put them out of business!"

Onboard the aircraft carrier USS John Stennis, in the Indian Ocean

Iran was again holding the world energy hostage. For the second time in slightly more than a year Iran was stockpiling their crude oil onboard leased supertankers which shorted the demand and artificially drove the price per barrel to nearly $185 dollars. The move additionally tied up over fifty percent of the international tanker fleet. This not only put a huge delivery strain on the remaining available international tanker fleet but reduced the amount of crude available to the U.S. and the industrial European nations. Russia and China, the main consumers of Iran's oil, were now buying from the Saudis and Venezuela in direct competition with the U.S. over the limited supply available. While the situation with Iran was continuing to deteriorate from an artificially contrived fossil fuel availability perspective, Iran also blatantly refused to stop its commercial nuclear power initiatives and its related but secretive, nuclear weapon development program. Its open threats to wipe Israel off the face of the earth fueled further Western concern that if given the opportunity, Iran would indeed carry out their threat. The world expected Israel to take unilateral action against Iran's nuclear weapon development facilities but nothing had happened yet. The newly elected U.S. President knew that when it did, Iran, maybe Syria too, would retaliate and the only way to prevent that would require a swift and overwhelming U.S. bombing campaign against Iran.

The petty officer of the watch startled Cherrington as he reported, "Admiral, the COD is inbound."

COD, or carrier onboard delivery, is a two engine turbo-prop plane with sufficient range to ferry cargo and personnel to and from the deck of aircraft carriers. It is equipped with a tail hook so it can land on a carrier underway and takeoff with the assistance of the catapult.

"Very well. Advise me when he's twenty minutes out."

"Aye, Sir."

Rear Admiral Cherrington eased back in his captain's chair on the carrier's flag bridge and took a sip of lukewarm coffee. Cherrington was in overall command of a massive battle group composed of three aircraft carriers and their many escort ships totaling twenty-six surface combatants and three fast attack submarines. It was the largest single U.S. Navy task force assembled since the Gulf War and it was there, ready if needed, off the coast of Iran.

Admiral Cherrington, a Naval aviator himself, had been chosen to command this unique task force because he was combat experienced and had a reputation of being a no nonsense commander. His ships were spread out over two hundred miles of ocean making them harder targets for an air or missile attack coming from Iran. He had positioned one carrier and its escorts inside the Persian Gulf which made him nervous because of the restricted maneuverability in those waters, especially when running combat operations. He took some comfort knowing that his carriers and the Navy and Marine attack squadrons that inhabited them were ready to launch a massive Alpha strike the moment the President gave the order. He hoped it wouldn't go nuclear but he was ready to do what had to be done if it did. He had six B-61 nuclear bombs available onboard each of his carriers and two nuclear tipped cruise missiles ready to launch from each of his submarines. With that firepower he could turn every major city in Iran into a glass covered parking lot and still have some nukes to spare in case Syria raised its ugly head.

He glanced up at a small brass plaque in front of him located above the bridge window. It was a quote from famed World War Two Admiral, Arleigh Burke, on the three principles of leadership that Cherrington had adopted as his own.

Know your stuff.
Take care of your men.
Be a man.

He looked upon these words of wisdom when the pressure was extreme. He often wished that he could have known Burke but that was a different time in history. He fully appreciated that now was his time and silently reaffirmed his vow to follow Burke's three principles.

"Admiral, the COD is twenty out."

"Very well. Please advise everyone that I will greet Admiral Thornberg on the flight deck after he is piped aboard."

"Aye Sir."

The road to Santa Fe, the same time

The two men sped along in silence for the next several miles. Boucher kept mulling over everything that Barnhart had told him and the events that had transpired over what he thought was going to be a quiet lunch with an old mentor and friend. Barnhart suddenly spoke.

"You see, Jake, international concern with Iraq prior to the Gulf War focused on Saddam Hussein's secretive and extremely well financed nuclear weapon development program. Compelling evidence pointed to Iraq's internal ability to produce nuclear feed materials and special nuclear material, either in the form of highly enriched uranium, or plutonium."

Quickly glancing over at Boucher to ensure he was paying attention, Barnhart continued.

"The intelligence estimates during the late eighties attempted to scope Iraq's weapon program. These estimates generally concluded that in terms of people, equipment, facilities, and available fissile material, Saddam probably already had developed a nuclear weapon, or was dangerously close to doing so. This posed a threat of immeasurable height and one that the non-proliferation regime could not allow to continue."

A faint scowl appeared over Barnhart's face, "Aha."

"Saddam's invasion into Kuwait may have provided the catalyst for an inevitably necessary purpose."

"So we bombed them back into the stone age, right?"

Barnhart smiled. "That purpose was the total destruction of Iraq's nuclear weapon program. In comparison, the liberation of Kuwait was little more than an aside to the far more important objective of keeping nuclear weapons from Saddam and ultimately out of the hands of terrorists who would not hesitate to use them against the United States or Israel. This single, yet never publicly reported upon objective was perhaps the only way to genuinely assure the long term security of the region."

Boucher interrupted. "So you're telling me Saddam's invasion into Kuwait was allowed to give us an excuse to invade Iraq and put a stop to Iraq's weapon program?"

Barnhart nodded in affirmation. "There was little doubt that a government like Saddam's, who would not hesitate to use chemical weapons against its own citizens would likely use nuclear weapons against its adversaries. Remember that time in history, Jake. The Government of Iraq was becoming recklessly belligerent and increasingly dangerous. Saddam had to be stopped. Our Ambassador to Kuwait at the time, April Gillespie, essentially gave Saddam the green light to invade. You don't think that was coincidence do you? Hell, at the time we were allies with Iraq. Her message to Saddam was well scripted by Washington. She was later criticized by the media and she became the scapegoat for the public record, but her charade was necessary so Saddam would invade Kuwait. Saddam became the invading bully and that provided us the international and neighboring Arab-nation support we required to put his weapon development program out of business and get him back into his box."

Boucher seemed dumbfounded. "But, Si, why wasn't this made public?"

"The answer lies within the intelligence community, Jake. It's probably safe to assume that because of the level of classification and compartmentalization surrounding the issue, few people were able to put it all together. Secondly, and as I suggested previously, the intelligence community has historically masked its incompetence in secrecy. This preserves its singularity and integrity as the 'know-all authority' even when they're dead wrong or down right clueless."

Boucher scratched his head as he began to ask, "But..."

Barnhart interrupted him. "Factor this into your analysis, Jake. Throughout the Gulf War, Iraq's nuclear weapon facilities were relentlessly attacked in an attempt to destroy both existing and future nuclear weapon development capability. The intelligence community was divided over assessing how advanced Iraq's nuclear weapon program was. Some believed that Iraq already possessed nuclear weapons while others concluded that none had yet been developed. But," Barnhart said with a slight hesitation, "virtually everyone agreed that Iraq had a weapon development program. Regardless, the stakes were too high to take any chances. Keeping in-mind that the intelligence community was mum during the decade prior to the Gulf War, it seems a bit illogical to me that once the war began, the intelligence community could suddenly make such an astounding revelation."

Boucher wasn't sure where this was all going to take him, but he felt privileged to be the one that Barnhart had chosen to reveal the information to. He felt that the perceptive old gentleman sitting next to him somehow knew that too.

"Si, we need to get off this highway and lay low for a few hours so the dust can settle before we go on to Albuquerque. I'm going to stop at Gabriel's Restaurant and make some calls on his land line. I have friends who will help us."

* * *

Because of its small size and altitude, the drone from the unmanned aerial vehicle above them was nearly undetectable from the ground. It was little more than a model plane with a wingspan not much larger than a seagull but it was equipped with a very sophisticated low light video camera and transmitter that provided a real-time picture of what it saw back to its operator on the ground.

Chapter 8

The Road to Santa Fe

A few miles further down the road Boucher abruptly turned left off the highway onto a narrow dirt road running behind the parking lot of Gabriel's Restaurant. The road dead-ended at the base of a small rocky hill several hundred yards away. It was dark now and the scrub desert foliage separating the dirt road and the parking lot provided the Expedition excellent concealment from the highway. With Boucher in the lead, he and Barnhart quickly crossed the unlighted gravel parking lot behind the restaurant and quietly entered through the back door. This was not so much a precaution for Boucher as it was his preferred modus operandi. He always parked there and entered the restaurant from the rear employees' door.

As they walked down a narrow hall toward the dining area a large burley man rapidly approached Barnhart.

"Doctor Simon, my old friend," the man declared with a strong Latino accent. "How are you today?"

The man broke into a toothy grin and hugged Barnhart, nearly squeezing the breath out of him. Pushing Barnhart backwards, the man grabbed the old scientist's hand, shaking it as though it was barely attached.

"Hey Si, I bet you five bucks you never guess who's been asking about you?"

That got Barnhart's full attention.

"Who?"

"Nobody!" the man replied slapping Barnhart on the back with his meaty paw while laughing heartily.

Barnhart was clearly delighted to see the man. "Manuel, you old bag of mule shit, how the hell are you?" he replied with a chuckle.

Manuel slapped Barnhart's shoulder again.

"S.O.S.D.D. You know.... same old shit, different day."

Manuel laughed again, slapping Barnhart on the back. He then turned his attention toward Boucher who was next to suffer Manuel's affectionate greeting.

"Hey, Jake, this is just like old times having you and Simon here again."

"Manuel, Si and I have had a most interesting day and I thought you might be able to help us find a quiet place to talk."

Boucher was six feet three inches tall and built like a brick shithouse but even so he felt his hand disappear as Manuel shook it. It was like shaking hands with someone who was wearing a baseball catcher's mitt.

"Welcome, my old friends, welcome! Please follow me."

Barnhart nodded to Boucher and the three men proceeded down the hallway a short distance to a small private room off to the side of the main restaurant. Manuel stepped inside and held the door open.

"Here's your old table my friends. We have spent many evenings sitting here drinking red wine trying to understand women." Manuel chuckled at his own words. "But, we always forget to write down the solutions and then we can't remember what we said in the morning. Oh well, I guess you can lead a horse to water but you can't take it with you!" Manuel, clearly proud of his feeble attempt at humor, fought back another hearty laugh.

Barnhart placed his hand on Manuel's huge arm.

"Thanks, Manuel. We might have been followed. Would you mind keeping an eye open? Jake and I will need some time together. Manuel, we will need to use your phone."

"You will be okay in here. I will bring you the phone," Manuel said smiling as he carefully closed the door on the way out.

Barnhart and Boucher seated themselves across from each other at the small four-person table. Boucher spoke first.

"Okay, Si, you were telling me about Saddam's clandestine weapon development program and that the U.S. knew about it since 1980 and intentionally did nothing about it. You said that the Gulf War brought the problem to a head. What then?"

"Sounds like you're paying attention, Jake, that's good. That's very good. But before I go on with the Gulf War let me back up for a minute because there are some other issues involved in this that influentially matrix into the outcome." Barnhart sat back in his chair. "When President Reagan took office he properly deduced that the way to win the Cold War against the USSR was to drive them into economic downfall."

"Bankrupt the bastards. Right?"

"Yes. Reagan knew that if he presented a credible enough challenge, the Soviets would take the bait. He saw that the Soviet's Achilles heel was their lack of available hard currency and he reckoned that oil was the key to the Soviet's source of hard currency. So he tripled the U.S. foreign aid to about three billion dollars each for Egypt, Saudi Arabia and Israel. The Saudis increased oil production, as did the Kuwaitis. OPEC took a nosedive as oil prices dropped below twenty dollars a barrel. Egypt aligned itself with the U.S. and bought our military hardware instead of the Soviet's while at the same time they made peace with Israel. This nearly eliminated the only source of hard currency the Soviet's had to fund their war machine. In 1988 Bush forty-one, grabs the reins from Reagan. He can now deal from a position of strength thanks to his predecessor. He knows that the remaining wild card standing in the way of an unlimited oil flow to the United States is Saddam Hussein. He knows that without oil the U.S. economy will not flourish. He knows that Iraq has a nuclear weapon development program that, if allowed to mature, will jeopardize the Middle East peace process and change the balance of power."

Barnhart stopped talking to take a sip of water.

"Good info, Si, please continue."

Barnhart nodded his consent.

"So Bush forty-one knew he had to nip it in the bud but he needed a reason to bomb Iraq with the full support of Iraq's Arab neighbors. He allowed Iraq to invade Kuwait, then, sufficiently demonized Saddam for doing so even after Ambassador Gillespie gave Saddam the green light. Bush formed a coalition of nations the likes of which had not been seen since World War II and the first Gulf War was history." Barnhart paused for a second to collect his thoughts before continuing. "At the conclusion of the first Gulf War, the International Atomic Energy Agency was charged by the United Nations Security Council with investigating, ascertaining the status of capability, and ensuring the neutralization of Iraq's nuclear weapon program. All the evidence suggested that prior to the War, Iraq possessed a technically competent and well-financed approach to redundant and multiple paths of production of special nuclear material. Since special nuclear material is the key component of a nuclear weapon..."

Boucher interrupted, "Do you realize what you're implying, Si?"

Barnhart held up his crooked index finger stopping Boucher's further inquiry.

"In fact, it was this belief that drove priority targeting in the initial bombing raids against Iraq at the start of the first Gulf War. Virtually all known and suspected nuclear weapon developmental and component production facilities were attacked with varying degrees of destructive success. Many of these targets were bombed again and again because battle damage could not be accurately assessed or initially confirmed."

Boucher nodded silently at Barnhart who nodded back approvingly.

"An additional concern that still plagues the U.S. today is the real possibility that Iraq concealed some of their critical nuclear weapon development research and development programs in deep underground facilities dispersed in remote parts of the country." Leaning towards Boucher he softly questioned, "Scary, isn't it? And, guess what? It gets worse!"

Boucher peered back at him, meeting his stare. "Shit!" he whispered. "I'm not sure I want to hear this."

Barnhart flashed a reassuring smile at his friend and went on.

"As a result, a requirement demanded of Iraq upon its surrender was complete and unconditional disclosure of their nuclear weapon program as well as their full cooperation with the systematic inspection and subsequent dismantlement of any capability that could directly or indirectly lead to current or future nuclear weapon development. This task was levied upon the United Nations under the International Atomic Energy Agency. Under its charter as the multi-national watchdog for proliferants, the IAEA began almost immediately. The first thing they did was to send their multi-national inspection teams throughout Iraq in an attempt to prevent Iraq from hiding critical records and equipment that could mislead the IAEA's scoping of Iraq's true intentions and capabilities. And yes," Barnhart said anticipating Boucher's question, "I was one of the senior members of the team. I was there, finally with the full attention of not only the IAEA, but the CIA. The findings of the inspection teams confirmed the claim I made twelve years earlier that Iraq was indeed deeply involved in a clandestine weapon development program. The IAEA formally reported that Iraq was involved in the kind of research associated with nuclear weapons development, which Iraq adamantly denied until Saddam's son-in-law, Lieutenant General Hussein Kamel Hassan and his brother Saddam Kamel Hassan defected to Jordan in 1995 and confirmed the IAEA's report."

"What else?" Boucher questioned.

"For example," Barnhart stated, "there were significant quantities of highly enriched uranium in the form of unirradiated reactor fuel in Iraq's possession. Pre-war intelligence estimates claiming that Iraq could produce a nuclear explosive within a few months explicitly assumed that this material would be diverted from peaceful purposes and used in nuclear weapons. Iraq consistently claimed that no HEU had been diverted for weapon purposes." Now, frowning, he said, "The IAEA inspection teams painstakingly accounted for all this material later, confirming Iraq's claims to be true. Even so, this was not good enough."

"Jezzz, Si. This is some incredible shit. Why didn't you share this with me when you were mentoring me at Los Alamos?"

Barnhart's wrinkled face reflected a faint smile.

"The IAEA had underlying concern that there was the possible existence of a clandestine stockpile of illicitly obtained Special Nuclear Material well hidden somewhere inside Iraq. Apparently, this was the major factor in the U.S.'s decision to destroy Iraq's reactors, nuclear explosive development facilities and equipment fabrication capability. I believe," he said as he thoughtfully scratched his head, "that it was this destruction that set the Iraq nuclear weapon development program back by at least ten years and bought the world time to better control the proliferation of weapon-related nuclear materials and fabrication equipment."

Manuel entered the small room with a liter carafe of red wine and a tray of appetizers.

"So nice to see you are both enjoying yourselves," he commented as he filled the wine glasses and placed the appetizers on the table. "It looks quiet out there," he motioned with sweeping left arm across the room as though the walls were transparent. "Here's my phone."

"Thanks, Manuel," Boucher replied. "Please be sure to let us know if any who are unworthy arrive."

Manuel grunted and left the room once again carefully closing the door behind. Barnhart turned his full attention back to Boucher.

"The destruction of the Iraqi nuclear weapon capabilities was no small task. It took not only painstaking inspection and detailed data collection, but intense data correlation and evaluation so that key facilities and equipment could be properly eliminated thereby most impacting a stop to Saddam's program."

Boucher interrupted. "But what kind of indicators did the inspection teams look for and how did they determine Iraq's nuclear weapon development status with any degree of confidence?"

Barnhart took a sip of red wine and sloshed it around his mouth for a moment before responding to Boucher's question. "That's a good question, Jake, a very good question."

Boucher took a quick gulp of wine spilling some on the white cotton tablecloth. Without comment, Barnhart passed Boucher his napkin. He took pride in his old student and friend even if he didn't know how to sip wine.

"You must surely remember there are specific technical areas common to all such programs that can be evaluated to ascertain a program's status. These program areas are very difficult to conceal from inspection. Thus, when these specific areas are detected and analyzed they reveal program progress. It's really not all that difficult but one must be completely familiar with weapon design because of the physics limitations surrounding the critical mass requirements and particular design characteristics common to all nuclear weapons. Jake, you and I both know there are only so many ways to build a weapon that will work. It makes no difference which nation's weapon development program you're looking at because everyone is similarly limited by the physics involved. It is the physics limitations inherent in all designs which is a universal constraining factor."

Barnhart sipped his wine and popped a salsa covered tortilla chip into his mouth, munching it loudly.

"Si, you taught me all that years ago when I was going through NEST training. I'm asking *how you* evaluate a weapons program."

Barnhart washed down the chip with a swallow of wine.

"It's not all that hard," came his monotone reply. "The IAEA based its evaluation of Iraq's nuclear weaponization program on eleven primary technical areas common to all nuclear weapon development programs. Remember, it doesn't matter who is doing the development."

Pointing toward Boucher he slowed his delivery. "Those areas are: Initiator Development, Lens Development, Main Charge High Explosives Development, Dedicated Facilities for Testing, Fissile Metallurgy, Other Material Science, Dedicated Fabrication Facilities, Firing and Fusing Systems, Codes and Computations, Lithium and Tritium, and finally something we call, Weapon Design Options."

"Got it!" Boucher replied. "Please continue."

"Sure Jake, but let's eat. I'm hungry enough to eat a horse."

Boucher's laugh was quickly ended by a series of excited knocks on the door. Manuel burst into the room, closing the door sharply behind.

"Simon, Jake, we have three visitors! They're checking the lounge area. I don't think you should go to your car. They might have somebody out there. Give the keys to me. Stay here, I'll be right back!"

Boucher threw the Expedition's keys to Manuel and nodded concurrence. Manuel dimmed the lights in the small room and eased through the door, carefully closing it behind.

Barnhart peered across the table at Boucher. "They're the same guys from this morning aren't they?"

"They got'a be. What do you think they want?"

"They want to prevent me from going public. They can't afford to have the truth known."

"I can't believe, if the FBI knew about this, they would allow a foreign government to get away with..."

Boucher stopped in mid sentence as Manuel hastily reentered the room.

"Follow me! Quickly!" Manuel ordered with uncharacteristic strain in his gravelly voice.

Onboard the USS John Stennis in the Indian Ocean

Admiral Cherrington led Admiral Thornberg to the Flag Staff Conference Room located directly behind the Flag Bridge. The two admirals had met previously while Thornberg was still on active duty but they were from two dissimilar cultures within the Navy. Jim Thornberg was a retired SEAL and Dennis Cherrington was fighter pilot. Thornberg now held the powerful and prestigious position as the CIA's Director of National Clandestine Service. While still given all the Navy protocol a retired admiral deserves, his current DNCS position far eclipsed his previous Navy career accomplishments. It was most unusual to have the DNCS himself visit a front line battle group. Cherrington knew it had to be important. He had prepared an executive-level briefing for Thornberg and had members of his key staff along with the CAGs from all three carriers present. Thornberg was seated at the head of the table beside Cherrington, facing three flat screen monitors on the opposing bulkhead.

"Sir, once again, I want to welcome you to the Stennis and my battle group. My staff has prepared a briefing for you that we would now like to present. Please feel free to interrupt at any point should you have a question or comment."

"Thank you, Dennis. It is a pleasure to be here with you and back at sea in the company of warriors. Before we begin I want to make it clear to everyone why I'm here. The President asked me to come here and personally brief you. In short, based on indicators and warnings, the President believes within the next two weeks there is a better than an eighty percent chance that we will be running offensive, perhaps pre-emptive, combat operations against Iran. He wants you to understand what the tripwires are and the national security implications of these actions should he direct engagement. As you may already know, the President signed a secret finding four weeks ago authorizing a covert offensive against the Iranian regime. The finding covers a geographical area of operations ranging from Afghanistan to Lebanon. This directive authorizes sweeping covert and overt actions ranging from military support of Iranian opposition groups, to assassination of key officials, to direct military attack against both military and industrial targets deep in Iran."

Cherrington glanced around the table at his senior officers. The concern on their faces spoke volumes. Cherrington pointed to the flat screen monitor and nodded to his staff briefer. The monitor immediately flickered to life.

"Admiral Thornberg, I'm Captain Ward, Admiral Cherrington's N-3. Here's our readiness picture."

Ward pointed to the flat screen in the middle as it flickered to life showing a listing of all the ships in the battle group. The screen on the left showed a map of the Eastern Mediterranean and Middle East region and the location of all the battle group ships. The screen on the right showed a map of Iran with all the primary and secondary targets marked in red.

"The battle group is fully operational. Here're our carriers' locations. The USS Abe Lincoln is operating about one-hundred miles north of our current position here in the Indian Ocean. The USS George Washington is in the lower Persian Gulf. The USS Ronald Reagan is deployed to Japan and is available to surge forward and reinforce us when needed. The USS Theodore Roosevelt is on its way here from the Atlantic Fleet and should be in strike range within the next seventy-two hours. She and her escorts will take up position here, close to the Iranian–Pakistani border. The USS Dwight Eisenhower and the USS Saipan left Norfolk three days ago and are on their way to the Mediterranean where they will take station off the Israeli-Lebanese coast in case Syria get's involved. The Marines on the Saipan and on the ships in the Amphibious Ready Group accompanying her will be ready to reinforce Israel if a ground campaign results from Syria, or even Egypt for that matter. The Ike battle group will be there in six days."

"Who's commanding the Ike Battle Group?"

"Rear Admiral Todd Buster. He's a surface warfare black shoe and a perfect fit if things run amuck ashore, especially if we need to reinforce Israel. The ARG is commanded by Commodore Tom Laverne. He and his battle staff are onboard the Saipan."

"I was just curious. I never met either one of them and I'm headed there after I leave you. Please proceed with your briefing."

Ward pointed to the flat screen on the right which now showed a map of the Pacific theater of operations.

"The Kitty Hawk and the Truman are on their way home after a ten month deployment here in the Gulf and Indian Ocean. They're currently astride of the Marianas. If we need more firepower we can turn them around and resupply them underway. The USS Iwo Jima and the USS Peleliu will rendezvous in our A.O. within the next forty-eight hours."

Ward put his pointer on the right flat screen, moving it along the Strait of Hormuz locations he identified as he spoke.

"They will be available to secure the Iranian strongholds of Sirri, Abu Musa Island, and the Greater and Lesser Tunbs, located in the deepwater channel here in the Straight of Hormuz. It is paramount that the Marines secure these islands at all cost if we are to close and hold the Straight. Any questions, Admiral?"

Thornberg sipped his coffee and nodded approvingly.

"Sounds like we're ready. Thank you, Captain."

Thornberg hesitated a moment and patted his hand gently on the table top.

"Gentlemen, I have some very close hold information that I want you all to be aware of. About three months ago we intercepted a rogue FSU artillery nuke onboard an Iranian ship in the Caspian. Indicators and warnings point to an Iranian-backed Hamas-run operation to acquire nukes on the Russian black market for use against U.S. interests in the Middle East or, God forbid, against the U.S. homeland. Even now we are still unsure what the target or targets are. We are certain, however, that Iran is aggressively attempting to acquire nuclear weapons on the black market or from other sources. I have a team of operatives on their way to a Middle Eastern location to ferret this out and locate these nukes before they can be used. Clearly, if these nukes are used against U.S. interests abroad, or the U.S. homeland, the President will order immediate retaliation against Iran and that will fall squarely into your capable hands."

Cherington cleared his throat. "If we strike Iran it's probably going to get ugly. Obviously, we'll have losses. Our plan is to take out their coastal missile batteries and radar warning sites. At the same time we'll run a massive first and second wave Alpha strike against Tehran. Our plan is to fly our inbound attack line along the east side of the Zagros Mountains following them all the way north to Tehran. If we lose any aircraft along the way in or out, the SEALs and Marine Force Recon will conduct the combat search and rescue of our downed pilots and recover them. If any of our planes are hit in or around Tehran they'll try to make it over the mountains and ditch in the Gulf where we'll have some of our guided missile frigates waiting. If that isn't possible they'll try to punch out over the Great Salt Desert to the south. The Air Force will employ strategic bombers from their bases in Europe and the U.S. They have also forward deployed a number of their bomber and tanker assets to Turkey, Saudi Arabia, Guam and Diego Garcia."

Cherington watched as Thornberg studied the map on the flat screen.

"There's one more thing you need to be aware of," Thornberg cautioned. "Three nights ago Russian commandoes raided two Georgian military airfields located in South Ossetia. With our help, Israel had a secret agreement with Tbilisi to use these two airfields to launch their air strike against Iran's nuclear development facilities. These airfields were critical to the Israelis because launching their fighter-bombers from South Georgia sharply cut the flying time by three and a half hours to Northern Iran and Tehran, where most of the nuclear facilities are located. It also kept them over the Caspian Sea so they wouldn't need to get U.S. clearance to over fly Iraq air space thereby keeping us non-complicit."

"Jezzz. It doesn't get much worse than that," Cherington offhandedly remarked.

"I'm afraid it does. We got the Israelis the use of those airfields by providing the Georgians arms supplies and technical training. That also provided a cover for U.S. and Israeli technical advisors under the guise of Georgia's desire to join NATO. When the Russians took those airfields they captured some very sensitive spy equipment to include several extremely sophisticated stealth spy drones."

"UAVs?"

"Yes. We provided them to Israel. They were flying collection missions over Iran and Syria and sharing the raw intelligence with us."

"What triggered the Russians?"

"For the last two months, the Israelis have been collecting imagery and electronic intercepts over Southern Russia as well. We're not yet sure how we were compromised. All we know is that Russian military engineers have dismantled the equipment and sent it home. It's safe to assume they will pass their analysis on to Tehran and Damascus."

"So I guess we're on our own," Cherington blurted.

"I sincerely hope it doesn't come to that, Dennis. Out of self interest, the Saudis are working very hard to reduce the threat of war in the region. They know that war will close Hormuz and stop the flow of oil. They also know they will be vulnerable to Iranian attack. Their primary interest is to protect their mushrooming wealth and their inflated oil profits. Their driving reason to keep the peace is so capitalist in motivation it's laughable. Nonetheless, they are trying their best to pacify Iran and keep the status quo. Let's pray we intercept those rogue nukes before they can be used or otherwise end up in Iranian hands."

Gabriel's Restaurant, the same time

Barnhart and Boucher followed Manuel down a short hallway toward the kitchen. Manuel stopped short of the closed kitchen door and pointed to a low half door located on the outer wall on the opposite side of the hall.

"It will be a little cramped but it leads outside. It used to be the wood box for the oven in the kitchen. This way!"

They entered the small dark room. Manuel took Barnhart's hand and quickly gave him instructions in a low whisper.

"Go to Indian Jack's house on the reservation. I'll meet you there as soon as I can. Do you remember how to find it?"

"Yes," Barnhart whispered.

Manuel carefully unbarred and opened the small outside door. Boucher could see the moon shining through the foliage that lined the rear exterior wall of the restaurant. Manuel cautiously crawled outside and extended a hand to assist Barnhart through the small opening. Boucher followed.

"Be careful, my brothers," Manuel whispered before returning inside through the small opening.

"Manuel, I need to take your cell phone with me. Okay?"

Manuel gave Boucher a thumbs-up gesture and quietly pulled the small outer door closed. Boucher gently tugged on Barnhart's shirt signaling him to follow. Staying in the shadows, the two men quickly moved across the narrow gravel driveway behind the restaurant to a low broken down picket fence surrounding the perimeter of the unpaved parking area. Using a broken tree limb as a step they sprang over the fence, disappearing in the shadows of the low desert scrub brush. Boucher slowly led Barnhart about one hundred yards from the restaurant grounds where Barnhart collapsed on some shale rocks in the bottom of a shallow wash.

"We will wait here," he said in a loud panting whisper.

"Si, we may have a bunch of unknowns chasing us. You say the FBI knows about this and doesn't give a damn? And you claim this is all happening because they just don't want you to go public? Doc, what could be so damn sensitive that would drive a conspiracy like this against one man?"

"It's what I came across during my time with IAEA when I was destroying Iraq's nuclear weapon development facilities." Barnhart swallowed hard. "It's working nukes, Jake! The bad guys have'm and our government is sitting on the information! The conspiracy involves both the good and the bad guys.

Our highest government officials know and they're keeping it a secret from our citizens!"

Boucher stood up just far enough so he could look through the tops of the scrub weeds back toward the restaurant. As he did, the Expedition sped from the parking lot towards Santa Fe with its tires squealing as it hit the asphalt road. A single car pulled out of the parking lot and followed a few hundred yards behind.

"That ought to keep'm busy for a while." Boucher smiled confidently at Barnhart. "Manuel is trying to decoy them away from us. He'll lead them onto the reservation a few miles down the road and lose them. That should buy us some time."

As Boucher and Barnhart watched, a fireball erupted about a mile down the road in the direction the two vehicles had sped. Orange gasoline-fueled flames rose several hundred feet above the road, illuminating the night sky, followed by the sharp crack of a high explosive detonation.

"Those murdering sons-of-bitches!" Barnhart gasped. "Manuel was one of my oldest friends."

"I'm sorry," Boucher whispered.

The two men sat silently in the darkness. Barnhart was still staring in the direction of the explosion. The dim starlight glistened on the shiny tears streaking down Barnhart's weathered cheeks.

"Si, we need to get away from here!" Boucher whispered.

Barnhart nodded and slowly stood up in a low crouch surveying the area for signs of movement. Boucher cautiously led Barnhart deeper into the low scrub-covered hills. After a brisk paced mile, Barnhart stopped in the shadows of a large rock outcropping where he sat down on a rock to catch his breath. He motioned Boucher to join him.

"Indian Jack lives on the reservation about a mile from here. I think he'll let us borrow his truck."

Barnhart slowly slid off the rock and sprawled out on the clay earth using the weathered rock as a pillow.

"Give me a few minutes to catch my breath. These bones aren't as young as they used to be."

"Si, I need to make quick cell call to get some of my guys moving."

Barnhart nodded his okay without speaking. Boucher dialed and waited. He got Leon Patterson's answering machine.

"Pat, I need your help. I have Simon Barnhart with me. We're in trouble. We're being chased and whoever it is just murdered my friend Manuel just down the road from Gabriel's restaurant. We're on foot, heading to Indian Jack's house on the reservation. We'll hole up there as long as possible. Please let Billy Reilly know what's going down. Do what you can. I trust your judgment, my friend. You have this cell number on caller ID. Unfortunately, the battery is almost gone. Out here."

* * *

Thirty minutes had passed. Barnhart looked like he had fallen asleep.

"Hey Si, how you doing?" Boucher questioned in a low whisper.

"Not bad for a Monday," Barnhart replied without opening his eyes. "I suppose this kind of situation is not all that new for you?"

"Actually, it is. I'm usually being shot at. We need to keep moving."

Boucher cautiously stood and scanned the surrounding area. Barnhart slowly sat up and painfully got to his feet. The two men moved silently away under the moonlight, intermingling indistinguishably with the shadows cast by the scrub growth and rocks.

Two hours later after crossing several rocky ridges and a shallow wash, they cautiously approached Indian Jack's small adobe house. They moved, deliberately remaining in the shadows of a junked car that was permanently parked about seventy five feet from the back of the house. Using it as concealment, they kept it between them and the direct line of sight from the house. The house stood alone except for a small doghouse that was located on the far end in what seemed to be the vast New Mexico desert. The house was completely dark inside. Even the dog hadn't awakened. Boucher and Barnhart carefully surveyed the area for signs of movement before exposing themselves to change their location. Both men crouched slightly as they cautiously moved from their covered position behind the car out into the moonlight toward the back door of the house. Boucher could feel the hair on his neck standing on end as he led Barnhart towards the house. He instinctively felt that something wasn't right but they had no alternative but to proceed.

Pressing himself against the outside wall of the house next to the back door, Boucher peered through the door's small window. He cautiously stepped to the side of the door and knocked several times and nodded to Barnhart.

"Jack, Jack, please come to the door, it's Simon Barnhart."

Boucher leaned forward to peer through the door's dirty window again. A small dim flashlight glinted inside and appeared to float through the darkness toward the door.

Barnhart spoke again. "Jack, it's Simon. Please open the door. I need your help."

As the door opened, Boucher quickly slipped inside pulling Barnhart with him.

"Jack, where are you?"

74

Boucher noticed the pungent smell of cigar smoke. As the door closed behind, a powerful white-hot flashlight beam scorched directly into their eyes completely ruining their night vision.

"Welcome gentleman. We've been expecting you," a slightly accented voice boomed from the darkness in front of them.

"Who's that? Where's Jack?" Barnhart demanded. "Jack, are you in here?"

Boucher knew all too well what was happening. He could taste the copper flavor in his mouth brought on by the rush of adrenalin. He knew they had walked right into a trap and it was now too late to do anything about it. He grabbed Barnhart's forearm and squeezed it in an attempt to prevent him from doing anything that would cause a violent reaction from the darkness. Although it repulsed Boucher, he realized that in order to survive they would have to follow orders and cooperate.

A second powerful flashlight coming from a different part of the room switched on. The narrow beam danced across the floor and lifted directly into Barnhart's face.

"Both of you lay face down on the floor. Do it now!" the voice behind the flashlight commanded.

Boucher nodded to Barnhart and they both lay face down with their arms and legs spread. A third man came from behind and loosely bound their hands behind their backs with a plastic tie-tie.

"Doctor Barnhart, I thought you retired and gave up these silly games?" a new voice said coming from the direction of the flashlight. "You really just never quit, do you, Doctor?" the voice asserted with a familiar sarcasm.

Barnhart couldn't identify the name behind the voice but he knew he had heard that voice before.

"What do you want?"

"Why Doctor, after all these years, you of all people should realize what we want. We just want you to do the right thing," the voice playfully replied.

Barnhart kept trying to place the voice coming from the darkness. He heard it before but where?

"He doesn't know anything. Let him go and I'll cooperate," Barnhart said referring to Boucher.

"Sorry Doctor, you have already revealed far too much to Mr. Boucher. You should have considered the consequences before you talked, but then you never did think things through before talking, now did you. We have a problem and you are both a part of it!"

At that instant Barnhart recognized the voice. It was Hann from the U.S. Embassy in Baghdad years before. Barnhart was more angry than afraid.

"What have you assholes done with Jack?" he demanded.

"Ohhhh...it's Jack is it? Well, Jack apparently had an accident," Hann sarcastically reported.

Contrasted by the flashlight's beam, Boucher couldn't help but notice the grimace on Barnhart's face. It was not a look of fear, but rather one of total hate and disgust. It was the kind of look that a kindly old gentleman like Barnhart should have been incapable of. There was no doubt in Boucher's mind that Barnhart would not allow this to go unanswered.

Radio static crackled in the adjoining room. Boucher could hear some garbled words but he couldn't make them out. In a matter of minutes the drone of an approaching helicopter could be heard.

With a motioning flashlight, the voice in the darkness ordered, "Outside, gentleman. If you do anything other than what you are told, it will not go well for either of you. Is that quite clear, Doctor?"

Barnhart grunted acknowledgment. With Boucher close by his side they proceeded outside through the open door into the moonlight. As they passed by Jack's rusty pickup truck they saw a man's body laying face down in a pool of black-looking clotted blood. The man had been shot in the back several times. Lying to his right was a dead dog, also shot several times. Barnhart hesitated for a second at Jack's body.

"Ahh Jack, I'm sorry," he whispered.

Barnhart and Boucher were taken to a clearing in a dry wash located a short distance from Jack's house and ordered to sit down along its perimeter. One of the guards administered a jabbing needle to the back of Barnhart's arm and then did the same to Boucher. Boucher saw Barnhart briefly look over at him and nod reassuringly before the old scientist slouched forward. Boucher felt his head pound. His ears began to ring so loudly he could barely make out the whining jet engine noise from the helicopter approaching overhead. He briefly saw the helicopter circle against the moonlit sky as it began its landing descent. He glanced back toward the house and saw two men each dragging a lifeless body towards the landing zone clearing. As Boucher's vision began to blur from the effects of the drugs, he wondered if he would ever wake. Boucher's eyes fluttered in surrender to the drugs and he slumped over against Barnhart, unconscious.

The North Atlantic Ocean, the same time

The sea was unusually calm and Rahman took it as an epiphany from God; a sign that *His Will shall be done*. He had expertly positioned his small ship precisely on the point the GPS identified as the salvage area. His all-Arab crew had hoisted the Deep Submergence Remotely Operated Vehicle over the side and launched it on its dive toward the sea floor a mile and a half below. Rahman himself would take the controls of the DSROV when it neared the target. He would have the honor of securing the retrieving lines to the nuclear-tipped missiles that were strewn around the sunken Soviet submarine's final resting place.

The DSROV had been descending for the past several hours and it was getting close. Rahman studied the instrument cluster on the control panel in front of him. The DSROV's rendezvous and docking sonar was painting a clear picture of the wreckage that was strewn across the ocean bottom. Rahman, now at the controls, turned on the lights and video camera and skillfully brought the DSROV into a hover about fifty feet above several cylindrically shaped objects. He adjusted the DSROV's down angle to better aim the camera at the objects.

Rahman found this whole operation to be very easy. The German-built DSROV was purchased by a Muslim-owned oil exploration company located in Abu Dhabi. Its advanced deep submergence capability wasn't restricted by export controls and no one in the West paid any attention to the sale or purchase of such technology, especially if earmarked for oil exploration. Rahman had trained on its use for the past four months using a computer simulation provided by its manufacturer and had become very good at precision positioning the DSROV and using its manipulator arms with nearly human dexterity. And now, he was actually operating the real DSROV a mile and a half below the surface of the sea.

How easy this is, he thought.

Then he saw the first missile illuminated by the DSROV's bright flood lights. The long cylindrical shape had a coating of silt on its top surfaces resulting from years of submersion. The Soviet's red star, painted on the cylindrical body, stood out clearly as it rested proudly upon the gray sea floor. He marveled how perfectly intact the warhead appeared to be. He leaned back from the video monitor and momentarily studied the picture. It was indeed a fantastic sight to behold.

Rahman smiled as he silently reasoned. *Recovering it will be a simple matter. Praise be to God.*

He carefully maneuvered the DSROV to within easy reach of the manipulator arm. The arm's gripper-hand held a stud gun. He slowly extended the arm until the stud gun was in precise contact with the missile's body just behind the seam that attached the warhead's rounded nose cone. He adjusted the angle so that the stud gun was precisely perpendicular to the missile's cylindrical body. Then he pressed a button on the control panel and fired the stud gun, sending a small tungsten carbide harpoon-shaped stud into the missile's aluminum sheathed body. The back end of the stud was tethered to a high strength lightweight cable reel and several inflatable buoys. He carefully backed the DSROV away from the cable reel and remotely inflated the buoys. The buoys began to ascend as the wire they were tethered to unreeled from its spool. Rahman smiled, knowing that when the buoys reached the surface, his crew would retrieve them and then winch the attached missile up to the surface for recovery.

Rahman kept the DSROV's lights on the missile and watched to ensure that everything was going as planned. He was pleased to see that it was. *Allah is great!*

After a few minutes he turned the DSRV back toward the debris field and sought out another missile. The second was just as easy to recover as the first. Following that, he found a third missile and completed the same recovery procedure. He then carefully maneuvered the DSROV away from the ascending buoys and their tethers and turned the controls over to one of his crewmen.

While he knew it would be daylight by the time they would be hoisting the missiles onto the ship's deck, it didn't matter. There were over sixty nuclear warheads lying on the sea floor around the world and even though their location was publicly available no one monitored those sites – no one! He was confident that they would not be bothered and once the torpedoes were onboard they would remove the nuclear warheads as they sailed to Algiers. There, the warheads would be off loaded and taken to a laboratory where they would be reconditioned and refitted with new explosives, detonators and fire sets. Rahman didn't know the exact location where that would be accomplished or who would take part, but he did know that he would be called upon again to carry the three warheads to their final destination. He would be told when and where to deliver them when the time was right and he would ensure that God's will was fulfilled. He believed in the importance of his contribution to the next thousand years of Islamic dominance. He was honored to have been selected for a mission so important and surely he would sit beside Allah for all eternity because of it. *Praise be to God.*

Chapter 9

Nevada Test Site

The sleek Lear 35 was westbound, descending through twenty-three thousand feet. Boucher awoke with a splitting headache. A bright light was shining in his eyes. For a moment he thought he was still inside the little adobe house with that blinding flashlight beamed on his face. Turning away from the reading light that was shining in his face, he squinted into fuzzy focus only to see Barnhart, unconscious, in a seat directly across from him. His perception was as blurred as his vision. The steady whine of the plane's jet engines and outside wind noise blunted his thoughts.

Boucher attempted to sit up but could not. His body felt as though it wasn't connected to his brain. After several groggy tries he realized that his ankle was shackled to the bottom support strut of the seat. As he looked around the small jet's cabin trying to get his bearings, he saw Hann coming his way.

"How are you feeling this wondrously fine morning?" Hann asked loudly.

Boucher glared without replying.

"Okay, I bet you wonder where we're going? Well, you're getting an all expense paid vacation for a debriefing. We'll be there in another twenty minutes or so. If I or any other members of the flight crew can be of assistance in making your flight more enjoyable please don't hesitate to ask."

Boucher winced. Although he felt total contempt towards Hann he sat quietly scowling back at him. His immediate concern was Barnhart's condition. Barnhart, still unconscious, was in the middle of a choking cough. Boucher reached over to Barnhart and gently shook his shoulder.

"Si, wake up. Si..., wake up."

Barnhart came to a dizzy consciousness not realizing what Boucher was trying to say. Although completely disoriented, Barnhart managed a weak smile as he slowly worked his body up from his slump into an upright sitting position. Barnhart stared at Boucher and attempted to speak. His voice was trembling and weak.

"Jake, what are? I mean...where are we going?"

"I think we're heading west. Judging by the moon's position, I think we're headed west."

Barnhart had a puzzled look on his face.

"West? What's out west that could possibly involve...?"

Boucher peered through the small window and studied the ground. "I can't imagine, but I'm judging that we're at an altitude of about twenty thousand feet and descending."

Barnhart slowly turned to the window and intently studied the ground below. It was just before dawn and he instantly recognized what he saw below. He could make out several expansive dry lakebeds pock marked with dozens of craters. He could see two huge drilling towers, now stationary relics, still erect above the holes they were drilling when the underground test ban treaty went into effect. Over his long affiliation with the nuclear weapon development program he had helped make many of those craters that created the moon-like topography below. Barnhart had no doubt that they were above the Department of Energy's Nevada Test Site.

He could now clearly make out the Sedan Crater. Measuring over a quarter mile in diameter, it is the largest crater on the test range; in fact so large, that it can be seen with the naked eye by astronauts in earth orbit. He remembered the day he helped Doctor Teller ready the thermonuclear warhead and then in 1962, lower it down a hole six hundred thirty feet deep where it was detonated. The resulting one hundred kiloton yield nuclear detonation threw a twelve million ton plume of earth several hundred feet toward the sky, scattering car-size rocks a half mile from ground zero. Half the earthen plume fell back into the hole refilling it to today's depth of three hundred and twenty feet. The blast also registered four point four on the Richter scale and the artificially caused earthquake was felt over seventy-five miles from ground zero. It was a grand experiment to see if a nuclear bomb could be used for peaceful purposes such as blasting out canals, or for mining. Because of the persistent radioactivity that covered many of the eastern states following the blast, the experimental project, named Operation Plowshare, was deemed dangerous to health. Thus, Congress concluded that additional experiments were undesirable and pulled further funding from the project. Even in his predicament, Barnhart nearly smiled from the memory of those glory days.

The Yucca Mountains bordering the test range cast a long snaking shadow along the desert floor from the bright moon. The small jet continued its descent as it followed along the mountain tops occasionally dipping a wing to make small course corrections. Barnhart was jolted from his memories of happier days by the sound of Boucher's voice.

"Si, my head feels like I took a round right between my eyes! Can you tell where we are?"

"It's not where we are, it's where are we being taken."

Boucher, rubbed his head and squinted across the aisle at Barnhart. Barnhart hesitated for a moment and then inhaled deeply, releasing his breath hissing through his teeth.

"If my guess is correct, we'll be landing at 'Groom Lake' just over the mountains from the Nevada Test Site." Boucher looked like he was going to ask a question but Barnhart shook his head *no*.

"Don't ask...it's the same place the tabloids say the Roswell space aliens were taken. It's Area 51. It's been in the movies and in the folklore since 1947. Groom Lake is a super secret Air Force base located a hundred miles from nowhere. They do all the 'black' programs there under some of the tightest security in the government. I visited it once while working on a non-nuclear electro-magnetic pulse project back in the mid-80s before the stealth bomber was revealed to the public. And," Barnhart whispered, "I caught a glimpse of not only the stealth bomber but the replacement for the SR-71 Blackbird. They had to build a completely new runway to accommodate it. They still haven't admitted the existence of the hyper-sonic SR-75 Aurora, but I saw it and it's incredible."

Barnhart looked back out the window at the terrain below.

"But, I really can't imagine why they are taking us there."

The Learjet made a perfect lights-off landing touching down on the base's darkened runway. Even though the plane had slowed sufficiently to turn off the runway by mid-point, it continued to taxi to the last ramp before turning onto the taxi way. Barnhart peered out the small window beside him but could see no lights. He had heard the rumors many times about Area 51. Planes would land between Russian satellite passes so as not to be observed. At night, the base was always kept completely darkened except when safety overshadowed operations compromise and that was rare.

Area 51...Space aliens. Give me a break! Boucher thought to himself.

Barnhart looked at Boucher in surprise, "What did you just say?"
"Err, nothing. I was just thinking."

The plane taxied at high speed for several more seconds before finally slowing to a sharp halt inside an unlit hanger where the plane's engines wound down to a quiet stop. Boucher recognized the metallic creaking sounds of the heavy steel hanger doors and the buzzing drone of the powerful electric motors winching them closed. As the doors met, slamming to a close with a loud boom that echoed through the huge hanger, the plane's door was opened. Two armed security guards entered the plane carrying red lens flashlights and made their way to Barnhart. One of them held Barnhart in his seat by the shoulder while the other guard unlocked the leg shackle from Barnhart's ankle.

"Sit still until we tell you to move!"

They unshackled Boucher using the same procedure. A guard flashed his light across both Boucher's and Barnhart's face.

"Okay, gentleman, follow my red flashlight and don't anyone attempt to be a hero."

Boucher stood, straightening his legs in a crouching stretch before following the guards. The hanger was pitch dark. The only sound was that of an idling car engine. Stepping down from the airplane's small stair to the hanger floor the guards turned and helped Boucher and Barnhart off the stairs. Once on the hanger floor, they were led a short distance through the black to a waiting cargo van. No one spoke. They were placed inside the van and the side door was closed with a slam. As it drove outside into the early morning darkness, Boucher realized there was a metal privacy partition between the front driver's seat and their seat that prevented them from seeing out the front window. There were no windows where they were seated and except for a few pinholes of dim light entering through the opaque rear window screens, the van was completely dark inside.

"Listen up, Si," Boucher whispered. "We're in deep shit and I'm not certain how this is going to play out. I think we entered a tunnel facility a short distance back because we've been running down the same artificially smooth gradient for a while. These bastards are serious players. But, they want something one of us has or they would have capped us back in the Santa Fe desert. They need us alive and we need to use that knowledge to manipulate the circumstances. Whatever happens we need to try to stay together."

Barnhart slumped backward into his seat. He was tired, hungry and frustrated. His thoughts shifted to the Steak House located inside the cafeteria at the government-owned village called Mercury. It was about seventy miles away on the opposite end of the expansive test range that contained more square miles than the entire state of Rhode Island. Mercury was where all the scientists and technicians stayed during the experimental nuclear blasts on the Nevada Test Site. He remembered the numerous times he sat in the Steak House tired, hungry and frustrated but somehow a T-bone steak with broiled shrimp wrapped in bacon, accompanied by some 90 point Merlot always helped ease his anxiety. Those were good days when everyone had a clear mission - defeat the Soviet Union - and his memory of them was consoling.

The van came to a jolting stop. They could hear the creaking rumble of a heavy door rolling closed behind them. Blinding bright light flooded the van's interior as the van's sliding side door was pulled open. Three guards dressed in tan desert camouflage, wearing brown balaclavas and dark red lens goggles appeared at the van's door and ordered the two men to disembark. Boucher and Barnhart climbed out and stood stiffly side by side, with their backs against the van. The guards took Boucher and Barnhart by the arm and led them through a heavy steel door that was latched to the wall in the open position. Boucher noted that this door was a blast door similar to those he'd seen many times before throughout government underground complexes.

The guards led them along a brightly lit concrete tunnel that took a sharp turn to the left, then along its length another hundred yards to a passageway leading off to the right. Boucher had toured an underground complex like this many years before, located close to Camp David in Maryland. That was the underground site where the Pentagon would move its operations headquarters in the event of nuclear attack. Now, inside what otherwise looked like a regular above ground office, the guards stopped in front of a heavy gray vault-like metal door which had a digital keypad combination lock mounted above the stainless steel door handle. The lead guard swiped his ID badge across the card reader next to the door and entered a numeric code. The card reader's red light flashed several times, then turned yellow for several seconds before turning green. As it turned green, Boucher heard metallic clicks as the locking bolts were electronically withdrawn around the vault door. The guard pulled the heavy door open and led the way inside a large, well lighted conference room.

An adjoining room equipped with one-way glass appeared to be behind the wall at the far end of the room. A horseshoe-shaped mahogany conference table was located in the center of the room. A dozen or so overstuffed leather-covered executive type swivel armchairs lined the table's outer edge. Secure telephone units and small flat desktop microphones were positioned on the table in front of each chair. There were several large flat screen video monitors grouped on the wall opposite the projection room. Closed circuit, remotely controlled video cameras were hanging from the ceiling in each corner of the room and all were aimed down at the conference table. Four computer work stations lined the wall opposing the door, each with a red label on its front designating the station *SCI / Classified Use*. Both Boucher and Barnhart had been in many rooms that resembled this one over their careers and to them it looked like a conference room of any of the emergency operations centers that could be found beneath most of the federal government agencies' headquarters in Washington, DC.

The guards ordered Boucher and Barnhart to sit down at the head of the table facing the wall screens. Several minutes passed. Hann and one other man abruptly entered the room. Boucher observed that Hann was carrying an orange-colored file folder that had the word *ACTION* printed on the front cover beneath "Top Secret" in large block letters. They sat down along the side of the table with the computer workstations to their backs. The guards waited for a nod from Hann before leaving the room. On the way out the guards slowly closed the heavy door behind them. Hann opened the folder and paged through some of the documents inside.

"Well now, gentlemen, I suppose you are just dying to know why we brought you here?" he asked without looking up.

"That might be a start," Barnhart replied in a low voice.

Hann shook his head ruefully before looking up at Barnhart.

"You want to know why? I'll tell you why! It's because you are out of control! You have been a constant pain in my ass since I first met you in Baghdad and that pain has only grown worse. But don't you worry, you're going to get another chance to contribute your expertise." he sneered, emphasizing the word expertise.

Barnhart erupted in anger.

"You sons-of-bitches are a bunch of murdering bastards and I wouldn't help you if the whole country depended on it!"

"Well guess what, Doctor…it does! You and your friend, Boucher, here, are going to save the country from the greatest threat posed since the Third Reich. Not from a Russian nuclear attack and not from a weapon launch as you know one. You're going to save us from a nuclear terrorist attack," Hann blurted back sarcastically. "Interested now?"

Barnhart had by now regained his self control and fixated a steely-eyed stare at Hann.

"Go to hell, Hann! It's you and your asshole friends that this country needs to be saved from!"

Hann smiled back at Barnhart.

"Don't be too sure of that, Doctor. We have a mutual enemy that must be neutralized."

Hann stared intently at Barnhart with his characteristic sneer. He lowered his voice making an appeal directly to him.

"Your country needs your help – both of you. We need your help to do it without compromising the President. If the other side thinks the U.S. government is officially involved, then we are all truly screwed."

Boucher rolled his eyes at Barnhart. Hann began his briefing focusing on Barnhart.

"We had to bring you both here because we weren't sure what information, or to what extent, you have revealed information to Mr. Boucher or anyone else for that matter. When we lost you at the restaurant we couldn't be sure what Mr. Boucher might do with his information. The only prudent caution was to bring you here for your own protection."

"Protection my ass!" Boucher shouted. "I suppose you're going to tell us that you were providing protection when you blew up the car Manuel was driving and shot Indian Jack! You assholes don't protect people, you murder them."

Hann sat up straight and glared at Boucher.

"Well let me tell you how it really was. We didn't blow up that car or murder your friends. We were tipped that you were going to be targeted and we were trying to save both your and your friends' ass. We just couldn't get there in time."

"If you didn't do the killing, then who did?" Boucher demanded.

The older distinguished gentleman sitting beside Hann slowly stood and placed his hand on Hann's shoulder as if to assure him. Hann nodded and left the room.

"First," he said with a faint smile appearing on his face, "I want to apologize for the hardship that you have had to endure. My name is Fuller, Marcus Fuller. I am representing the Director of Central Intelligence. Please make yourselves comfortable. Doctor Barnhart, I assume that you know where you are?"

Hann returned to the room pushing a cart containing deli-style breakfast sandwiches, water, coffee and assorted fruit juice drinks.

Fuller continued. "Gentleman, you must be very hungry. Please help yourselves. If you need a bathroom call, Mr. Hann will escort you. Mr. Boucher," he said pausing momentarily, "we don't have an answer, at least not yet. We have still not confirmed exactly who the killers are but we think we know. The FBI has the case and is investigating as we speak. And, by the way, the FBI knows you're both with us. You are here because we once again need your help. Admiral Thornberg personally directed us to request your help. You may call him if you wish using the secure telephone in front of you. If you want to hear it directly from him, go ahead and call, please feel free."

Boucher moved the phone in front of him. "Yeah, I want to hear it from the Admiral."

Fuller nodded toward the one way window. Moments later the red light flashed on top of the phone. Fuller nodded at Boucher. Boucher picked up the handset.

"Jim, this is Jake, are you there?" Boucher visibly began to relax as he listened. "Okay, I'll consider it. Out here."

Walking toward a large flat screen video monitor on the wall, Fuller pulled a laser pen pointer from his shirt pocket and tested it by flashing a red dot on the wall as the monitor flickered to life.

"Are you up for it?" he asked looking back at both Boucher and Barnhart.

"Proceed," Boucher curtly replied.

Inviting Boucher's attention by pointing to the pictures of three men displayed on the wall-mounted video flat screen, Fuller continued.

"We believe these men are responsible for the attack on you and for killing your friends. They are Saudi-born expatriates now living in the U.S. They are members of an Iranian-based militant Islamic fundamentalist splinter group. They're funded and led by the Saudi multi-millionaire Sheik Abdule bin Omessi who is opposed to any Arab peace settlement with Israel and who sees the United States as a tool of Satan. We believe Omessi is targeting you because you have been instrumental, unwittingly I might add, in preventing his organization from obtaining what they really want."

"And just what do they really want?" Boucher whispered.

"To permanently stop the peace process between Israel and the Palestinians. Yes, Mr. Boucher, the artillery-fired atomic projectile on the ship you and your Kazaks intercepted in the Caspian was really bound for them. How they may have tied its loss to you is still a mystery to us."

Barnhart hadn't looked up from the gaze he had fixed on the tabletop in front of him until that statement. He studied the pictures of the three bearded men for a few moments and then looked over at Boucher who was clearly captivated by the man standing before him. Barnhart's mind was racing as he tried to piece together the events of the past thirty-six hours.

"Jake," he said in a low voice, "if we agree, we will become an inseparable part of this and it will become a monkey on our backs. We will never be able to reveal any of this. How do you feel about that?"

"Well Si, we've come this far together but now we're probably going to need some help. So, as long as we can pick our team, I say W-T-F, let's do it!"

Fuller nodded, "You may pick your team."

Barnhart sucked in a deep breath and glared at Fuller. "I know where this is going," he said. "You involve Boucher's men and you now have cause to legally gag them for national security reasons. It's typical Agency bullshit and you know it! But since we all know how this game is played I suppose we have little choice."

Fuller's smile faded.

"Actually, you both do have a choice. You can turn your backs and refuse to answer this call to help your country, or you can help prevent one of the greatest threats to world peace since the Gulf War. And yes, we're all in this together. And, together is the only way we will succeed."

Boucher put his elbows on the table and cradled his head in his hands slowly rubbing his temples. "I want Leon Patterson, Frank Moss, Bill Reilly, Jack Doyle, Johnny Yellowhorse and Mojo Lavender in on this. I may bring in some others later if I need more manpower."

"Consider it done. Patterson called us after you left him your voice mail. That's how we knew where to look for you. He's already offered to support your operation. I will trust you to bring the others in. Anything else?"

"I may need to call on a few additional operators who are one-hundred percent loyal to me. Is that going to be an issue?"

"No, I understand your relationship with your extended team. I trust you and your men understand the security sensitivity surrounding this mission." Fuller paused and smiled. "I realize you are all independently wealthy but we will cover all the costs that you incur. Now, may I please have your attention?"

Boucher nodded his agreement as did Barnhart.

"Our latest electronic intelligence intercepts leads us to believe that Iran is close to obtaining a nuclear weapon capability. This is also based on human intelligence collected on two counter-smuggling operations that we ran in conjunction with our friends in Russia, the Ukraine and Kazakhstan over the past several months. The first operation is the one that you, Mr. Boucher, participated in that took place in the Caspian. We later confirmed that the nuke you discovered in the cargo hold of that ship was an AFAP - a former Soviet Union 152mm artillery-fired atomic projectile that was bought on the black market and was on its way to a Saudi buyer. That buyer was Sheik Omessi. We believe Omessi intended to provide it to the Iranian Talibans for use by the radical Islamic fundamentalists he supports. As part of the deal, we think it is very likely that the Government of Iran may also be a player because of their links to terrorist surrogates like Hezbollah and their open threats to annihilate Israel."

Fuller paused, sipping from his water glass.

"The second operation occurred last week and it also involved an act of smuggling. We believe that a full-up former Soviet Union stockpile weapon was acquired by an unconfirmed party on the Russian black market. Omessi may or may not be our man here. We simply can't confirm his hand in the play so far. This weapon is believed to be a SS-19 single reentry vehicle containing a single fully operational warhead. We now believe it was smuggled out of Eastern Europe through the Suez to the Red Sea and offloaded in Aqaba, Jordan. We are uncertain how it will be transported through Jordan."

"Jordan?" Boucher questioned.

"Yes, everything we have points to Israel as the destination. As you know, a likely means of transport would be to submerse it in the liquid of a tanker truck to shield the radiation signature from detection. At any rate, all we have at this point are some inconclusive intelligence leads."

Boucher interrupted Fuller. "What about Jordan?"

"Jordan is a friend and is fully cooperating thanks to King Abdulla."

"What about Iran?"

Fuller took another sip of water.

"We haven't been able to determine any direct complicity involving the Government of Iran, but we believe that the weapon will ultimately be delivered to a radical Iranian-supported splinter group of Hamas. We think the weapon will probably remain hidden in Jordan for the next several weeks while the transportation route is rehearsed and the mode of transportation is decided. If Iran gains safe and arming control of this weapon the potential threat is beyond calculation as you certainly can well appreciate. As I'm sure you already know, Iran is currently being assisted by China and North Korea in the development of a ballistic missile that has the range to deliver a nuclear warhead to Israel and maybe even as far as Central Europe."

Barnhart was doodling on a notepad in front of him. Boucher noted that Barnhart had drawn intersecting arrows which resembled a flower bouquet.

Pausing briefly, Fuller again sipped his water before continuing.

"Our operatives inside Jordan are tracking this as closely as they can but we can't put them in a position to sniff this thing out in time to prevent it from falling into Iranian hands. We can't actively search for it in Jordan without the risk of alerting both Iranian and Saudi agents. There is an additional wild card involved here as well. Electronic intelligence has revealed that Hamas is up to something more sinister than their attack on the World Trade Center. Indicators lead us to believe they intend to explode something big within the next several months, perhaps in a terrorist attack against Israel."

Fuller paused to readjust his glasses.

"Since this is not a nuke of U.S. origin and we're not sure where it is, and it doesn't appear to directly involve an attack on the U.S., the President has decided not to use our military to intervene inside Jordan. However, if we can nail this down he would not rule out conducting preemptive operations against Iran. Quite obviously, a preemptive strike would be seen by the world as an act of war. And, the President doesn't want to alert Israel because that could seriously jeopardize the fragile peace process between Israel and the Palestinians or for that matter, between Israel and Jordon if that pot is stirred."

Barnhart raised his hand to interrupt Fuller.

"Have you informed any of your most trusted Israeli or Jordanian contacts from the intelligence side?"

"Not yet. We feel it's premature to notify them at this point because we haven't confirmed the location of the weapon or that they are, in fact, a potential target. When we narrow down the location and confirm the presence of a weapon, we'll bring them in accordingly. Again, the President doesn't want to risk stifling the peace process which is so vital to regional stability."

"But don't you think Israeli intelligence knows what's going on?"

"It's likely they know about it in general terms but it is unlikely they have the specifics we have."

"How about the Russians?"

The glint of a faint smile came over Fuller's wrinkled face.

"We felt out the Russians, informally of course, regarding their potential interest in assisting us - since both nukes are former Soviet Union weapons. They declined to acknowledge the loss of inventory control, much less agree to cooperate in any disablement and recovery operations. They're obviously saving face. That said, they know the deal and have informally agreed to share intelligence on the matter. This is where you fit into the equation."

Fuller turned and nodded toward the one way glass behind him and then continued.

"Doctor, you are an internationally respected scientist. The Iranians are familiar with your work and respect you from your IAEA inspection days prior to and following the Gulf War. We want you to go to Iran as part of a special IAEA verification team. Your stated purpose will be to confirm Iran's nuclear reactor fuel enrichment compliance. As you know, Iran is still believed to be very close to developing its nuclear weapon capability and their acquisition of a Soviet stockpile weapon could significantly accelerate them to near instantaneous success."

Barnhart interrupted Fuller.

"But Iran hasn't allowed the IAEA inspectors into the country. What's changed?"

"A lot has changed. With the help of the Russians we have secretly negotiated a deal to lift sanctions on Iran in exchange for them to allow the IAEA back in. Ahmadinejad went for it like a bee to honey because it will keep him in money, in power and restore Iran's pre-Gulf War influence in the region. In turn, we get an opportunity to take his pulse on the nuclear weapons development progress and you certainly know the rest of that story as well as, or better than, I do."

"The Russians are already selling Iran enriched uranium reactor fuel so the Iranians don't have to make their own. Oh yeah," Barnhart mumbled, "what about the French? Are they still interested in trying to find the reactor hidden under that housing complex in Tehran or have they given up?"

Fuller sat quietly smiling at Barnhart's rant.

"And how about the feed material plant in Qom? Or, how about the enrichment facility Iran has concealed in Yazd?"

Fuller remained impassive as he stared across the table at the two men, finally focusing on Barnhart.

"I see your memory remains quite keen, Doctor Barnhart."

Fuller shifted towards Boucher.

"Mr. Boucher, you and your team will travel to Jordan under non-official cover. You will be an investigative journalist researching background on the ancient city of Petra. You will of course be adequately backstopped. You will be traveling with your assistant, Sandra Morrison, who will also act as your interpreter and..."

Boucher loudly interrupted Fuller in mid-sentence.

"Whoa! Whoa! Wo...! I don't have an assistant!"

"Of course you do, Mr. Boucher," Fuller said smiling. "In fact, perhaps it might be appropriate to have her join us and let her finish this briefing."

As Fuller took a seat across the table from Barnhart the door opened and Sandra Morrison strode to the front of the room next to the television monitors. Boucher was curiously attracted to this stunning woman of obvious middle-eastern descent. It appeared to Boucher that she practically floated across the room above an unobservable stride. Her slender grace and sculpted features were accented by her tight fitting cotton khaki slacks and white sleeveless blouse, which served to contrast her penetrating dark brown eyes. Boucher was beginning to like this partner-assistant idea more and more by the second.

Sandra Morrison was a career CIA Case Officer who joined the Agency right out of graduate school. Holding an undergraduate degree in Health Physics with a double masters' degree in International Intelligence Affairs and Middle Eastern Affairs, she was natively fluent in Farsi, Hebrew and Arabic and spoke enough Russian to get by. She was a late 40s-something beauty with a mind that rivaled her looks.

"Good morning Dr. Barnhart and Mr. Boucher." Her English was flawless. "My name is Sandra Morrison. I go by Sandra and I would appreciate it if you would call me by my first name. I will now begin the briefing." She smiled warmly at Boucher, making direct eye contact. "We will set things in motion overseas and with the media so as to put a very positive international spin on both the inspection that you will lead, Dr. Barnhart, and the media coverage that you will head, Mr. Boucher. This should encourage the Iranians to cooperate and hopefully give you the access you may require. Dr. Barnhart, you will need to locate and work with one of our deep cover operatives already in place inside Iran. That officer's agent network is currently postured for chemical and biological weapon proliferation and he will need your expert assistance in diagnostics and disablement when the nuke is located."

Barnhart nodded in agreement.

"We are now concerned that this operation could compromise him and for that reason we will need him to come out with you if possible. He is one of our best." Continuing with an admiring smile she said, "I suppose it's fair to say that you are as well."

Boucher gave his old friend Barnhart a knowing look.

"Simple scientist my ass," he mumbled under his breath.

"Excuse me?" Morrison asked Boucher.

"Nothing. Sorry."

"Dr. Barnhart, some of Mr. Boucher's handpicked team will backstop him and me throughout the operation. You and Mr. Boucher have worked together for many years so I don't need to go into more detail about that here and now.

Morrison now turned her attention to Boucher.

"Mr. Boucher, we..."

Boucher interrupted Morrison. "Ahh, I go by Jake. I mean, please use my first name."

"Certainly, Jake," Morrison replied, her eyes twinkling above a flirtatious smile.

"Jake," she emphasized, while bowing slightly in his direction, "for the next two days, you, your team, and I will attend intensive area familiarization briefings at the CIA's Langley, Virginia headquarters to get you all prepared for this operation as quickly as possible. Using special radiation detection devices, we will act as searchers. The camera equipment that you and I will carry will have covert radiation detectors built into them so that we can search for the weapon based upon Doctor Barnhart's leads. We will also have miniaturized GPS transponders with us so that in the event we locate the weapon we can tag it for tracking and military intervention should that become a viable option. We will all deploy to Jordan the day following our training. I apologize for how brief the training is, but we are dealing with a mission of the highest urgency and we cannot afford the luxury of time."

"Why wait until the next day?" Boucher casually asked. "We can deploy the evening we finish training on my private Gulfstream 450."

"That works for me if your team can drop us off in Amman. They can continue on to Aqaba and get started. We'll catch up with them the following day if need be. Dr. Barnhart will fly there separately with his IAEA team."

Pausing, she momentarily engaged both the gaze of Boucher and of Barnhart, respectively, before continuing. Boucher nodded his approval.

"Last, it is my belief that our analysts are wrong on this one."

Fuller straightened up in his chair. At that moment, Boucher sensed that Sandra could be trusted because she was not regurgitating the party line. She appeared not to notice Fuller's concern at her statement as she continued.

"I know that statement could be considered heresy by some, but the weapon has still not been confirmed to have been moved from Aqaba, so that is where we should begin our search. I believe that this weapon may not be bound for Iran. I also believe there is a target already designated for this weapon by those who currently possess it and a handoff is unlikely. Additionally, I believe the target is somewhere other than Israel. It may be bound for the United States. And finally, I believe this mission has a significantly greater chance to fail than it has to succeed. Gentleman, I will now address any questions that you have."

Boucher was too mesmerized to ask, even though he had many questions. He had never met a woman who was so obviously competent, in control, confidently independent and lavishly beautiful, all wrapped up in a single sexy package.

Wow! he thought, while trying to resist the temptation to look her up and down, *I wonder what my chances are?*

Book Two

Chapter 10

Amman, Jordan, three days later

Located on a hilltop with a commanding view of the surrounding city, the Amman Marriott is nothing less than elegant. Boucher and Sandra had just finished checking in. They were seated on a third floor balcony enclave overlooking the mammoth marble-clad lobby below having morning coffee. Boucher found it curious to watch the oil-wealthy Sheiks, dressed in traditional Arab headdress garb, busily come and go below. Most of them were accompanied by exceptionally attractive young women concubines, dressed in high fashion European business clothes. Boucher had been to Jordan while he was still an active duty Navy SEAL officer. In fact, he met Prince Abdulla while he was still a colonel in the Jordanian Special Forces during a joint U.S.-Jordanian counter-terrorism exercise and found him to be a superbly intelligent and exceedingly delightful man. Boucher loved Jordan's rich history and held great respect for King Abdulla. Sandra's soft voice jolted him back to the moment.

"We'll remain here overnight. I have a lunch meeting today with the COS at the U.S. Embassy. I need to get on top of any last minute leads. You can enjoy the pool while I'm gone," Sandra playfully suggested. "It should only take me a few hours."

It wasn't hard for Boucher to pick out the foreign intelligence agents in the lobby below. Several appeared to be reading the paper while others sat alone, chain smoking cigarettes, trying to provide the appearance of being uninterested. The CIA counter-intelligence briefer had cautioned Boucher about the high population of Iranian, Iraqi and Israeli agents throughout Jordan and warned him to observe operational security (OPSEC) continuously. That meant he had to pay especially close attention to what he said and how he acted so he wouldn't blow his cover and compromise the mission.

Of the many CIA briefings that he attended over the past several days, he found those involving counter-intelligence and counter-surveillance the most interesting. Because he was an old hand at both, he viewed them as a science. He was also sensitized to the political-military strategic aspects of the Middle East and to the dynamic influence of the Islamic Fundamentalist's movement, both traditional and militant. He understood the basics of the long held dislike that the Arabs had for the Jews and why they will likely remain enemies for many more years to come.

In a way, he was very grateful to have been drawn into this. There was no doubt in his mind that Sandra, his new partner, was not only the most highly capable woman that he had ever met, but also one of the easiest to look at.

"Jake," she uttered softly, startling him out of his daydream, "I'll see you back here in a few hours. Stay out of trouble."

With that, she flashed a disarming smile at him as she stood. Carelessly slinging her handbag over her left shoulder, she strode away. He watched the curves of her sexy figure sway through her form-fitting, silky dress as she seemed to glide down the three flights of marble stairs leading to the lobby door below. At the foyer, the dark-haired beauty turned and glanced back up at him with the hint of amusement in her penetrating eyes. She then turned away abruptly and disappeared through the hotel's front revolving door. Boucher could hear his heart beating.

Sandra returned from the embassy to the hotel about mid-afternoon to find a message from Boucher in her mailbox at the main lobby desk. The message read, *Please join me by the pool. Jake.* She walked to the pool and found a sleeping, sunburned Boucher lying facedown on a fully-reclined lounge chair. Sitting down on the edge of the chair next to his, she bent down close to him.

"Jake, wake up," she softly coaxed. "Come on sleeping beauty, wake up."

Boucher slowly opened one eye, then the other, and found himself inches away from the open front of her silken dress, staring right at her braless breasts.

"I've died and gone to heaven," he whispered without looking up at her.

Realizing that she had unwittingly offered Boucher an almost full view of her bare bosom, she consciously decided to remain in the same revealing position a few seconds longer, enjoying the attention from this attractive man. However, as she was beginning to feel the hot sun on her back, she abruptly sat up, shifting sideways far enough to allow the sunshine a direct path to Boucher's face.

"Damn," Boucher exclaimed as the sun's brightness temporarily blinded him. "Did you have to do that?"

"Sorry," she answered in a soft purr. "You're alive, this is not heaven, and we have work to do. Come on."

Grunting in displeasure, Boucher raised himself up on his elbows before speaking.

"I thought this was supposed to be an all-expense-paid vacation for two. What'd you find out?" he asked as he squinted into her dark brown eyes.

Taking a quick look around to make sure that they were not in earshot of anyone else, she cautiously whispered.

"Based on satellite imagery and ELINT intercepts, Langley believes that the item of concern is in fact here in Jordan. It appears a ship arrived at Aqaba two days ago and the item may have been moved north by truck to Petra. If that is where it's hidden we have our job cut out for us. We need to drive there now and begin our search the first thing in the morning."

Boucher sat up. "Petra?" he questioned. "Why Petra?"

Sandra smiled patiently.

"Come on," she said softly. "Let's get our gear and hit the road. We have a three and one half hour drive ahead of us. I'll tell you all about it on the way there."

As they left the pool, neither Sandra nor Boucher noticed the two men who were sitting in the outdoor dining area on the other side of the pool deck. One of the men dialed a number on his cell phone and spoke in Yiddish. Both men slowly stood and cautiously followed behind.

The drive south from Amman to Petra wasn't all that bad, or so Boucher initially thought. With Sandra at the wheel, Boucher had time to enjoy the rugged beauty of the Jordanian desert. Highway 15, comparable in construction to any modern interstate in the U.S., was virtually absent of cars. However, it did have an abundance of fast moving eighteen-wheelers hauling everything from petroleum to gravel between Aqaba, Jordan's only seaport at the far south end of the country, and Amman, its capital city and main population center to the north. Boucher tried to visualize his location as they headed south. Iraq bordered Jordan's desert to his left – due east.

Aqaba and the Red Sea were straight ahead to the South. The Dead Sea and Israel, bordering the Dead Sea, were on his right – straight west. The rugged Edam Mountains bordering the Dead Sea on Jordon's west side were distantly visible from the highway. It was hard for Boucher to imagine how a lifeless, barren, desert like this one, could once have been in the heart of the lushly foliated Fertile Crescent.

Speeding along at one hundred and forty kilometers an hour in their rental car, Sandra continued her Petra briefing.

"The COS said that NSA intercepts revealed that the item of concern has been transported from Aqaba to Petra. We're the only assets available so we're going in as journalists doing a feature story on the ancient city. We need to confirm the presence of, or the lack of, special nuclear material."

Boucher smiled to himself when Sandra referred to people as *assets*. Boucher forced his attention back to Sandra's comment about Petra.

"Why do you suppose the bad guys would pick Petra as a place to hide a nuclear weapon?" Boucher asked. "Why not just transport it across the Arabian Peninsula to the Persian Gulf and boat it over to Iran?"

Sandra contemplated Boucher's statement for a moment before answering.

"Petra is unlike any other place on the planet. It consists of hundreds of man-made caves that were literally carved into solid rock. It was built by free people during the Nabatean Empire. Because it was hidden in the mountains and there were only two ways to enter the city through a narrow gorge, it provided natural protection and made the city easily defendable. It was also on the path of the major trade route that ran from Aqaba, on the Red Sea, through the mountain passes leading to the Dead Sea. Later in the century the Romans also inhabited the city but never enforced their rule upon it. Did you see the Indiana Jones movie where Sean Connery starred as Indiana Jones' father? Remember the search for Christ's chalice led them to a hidden building carved into the rock face at the base of a deep gorge? Well, that building, along with dozens of others just as impressive, actually exists in Petra."

Boucher blinked back at Sandra. "But why Petra? Why hide a nuke in the middle of a damn tourist attraction?"

Sandra frowned, quickly glancing over at him before returning her eyes to the road ahead.

"I've given that some thought and I must credit the opposition with providing us an extremely difficult challenge. As you well know, a nuke weapon made from plutonium has a unique gamma-neutron radiation signature. Searching for such a weapon in a modern city environment is difficult even if we know approximately where it is. So if you use the natural shielding of solid rock, hide the weapon in a cave in an area where there are thousands of caves to choose from, it would require that those persons searching for it either get real lucky or bring enough people and equipment to systematically search every cave. There is one other complicating factor as well. Virtually all rock contains natural uranium which emits a higher than normal background radiation signature. The rock in the Petra area is rich in natural uranium. I understand that we must try to focus our search on plutonium's unique gamma-neutron radiation signature but that will be like looking for a needle in a haystack. Additionally, because of the size of the miniaturized sodium iodide detectors built into our cameras we are physically limited in our detection range and ability to accurately segregate the spectra. That means we will need to investigate every suspect detection hit we get above background."

Boucher laughed. "That will take us the rest of this year. I'm more concerned about what we do if we actually find the damn thing!"

Boucher was privately wondering why Barnhart wasn't here with them instead of playing IAEA inspector in Iran because he was the disablement expert. Sandra, sensing his discomfort with the plan, attempted to further explain.

"What we are searching for is a former Soviet SS-19 reentry vehicle warhead, Jake. It's big, heavy and nasty to move around. This isn't a suitcase weapon out of some Hollywood movie. We're dealing with the physical limitations of reality. The opposition might be clever in their choice of hiding spots, but without some serious help they're not going to lift a quarter ton RV up the face of the gorge to hide it in a cave two hundred feet above street level and radically risk a chance of compromise. You can bet your next paycheck if we know about this, the Israelis probably do too, and the Mossad will be watching every potential avenue that weapon can come from and go to, as well as watching the Russians and us."

"The Mossad?" Boucher shouted. "I worked with those dicks back in the 80s."

Sandra looked over at him and chuckled. Boucher had not seen her like this before. He studied the dimples in her cheeks and the lovely creases that formed beside her mouth and eyes. Her laugh seemed to generate from deep inside her. It made him desire her even more.

Sandra recovered her serious expression and continued. "The COS shared some other late-breaking intelligence with me on Israel. Israel is apparently in the process of running another major military exercise like the one they did last year based on a pre-emptive strike against Iran's nuclear weapon development facilities. They've also gone into the Gaza and amassed a bunch of armor along the Syrian border. Syria is at war-ready status and is countering the Israelis by amassing armor and troops on their side."

"I think the Israelis are nuts."

"Maybe, but I think they're posturing for a thrust deep into Syria. That will give them the option to pivot back to the west as they withdraw from Syria and invade Lebanon. A pincer move like that will trap the terrorists operating there and give the Israelis the opportunity to destroy them. That strategy will effectively nip any potential counteroffensive against Israel in the bud."

Boucher contemplated Sandra's words without comment as he studied her. The whole package was compelling. Brains and beauty - perhaps the most classically beautiful woman Boucher had ever known. He knew he was being irresistibly drawn in. He silently vowed he would be there whenever she needed him.

About an hour later Sandra turned right off the Highway 15 onto Highway 88 that transitioned to a winding secondary road. At the speed Sandra was driving, the bumpy asphalt surface occasionally caused the car's rear wheels to break traction. The result was a skid-like lurch and a momentary loss of control that she skillfully countered, but she didn't slow down. Boucher noted that she was negotiating the turns perfectly using the same driving techniques he himself had learned many years before. Curiosity got the best of him.

"So Sandra, where does one learn to drive like this?"

"Driving school, where else? I've actually attended several different driving courses. Did you ever hear of BSR? Bill Scott Raceway is the name. It's a Le Mans race track in Summit Point, West Virginia, not far from Charles Town. It's where the Agency conducts crash-bang training. It's a great course. I've also been to the ITI counter-terrorism driving course in West Point, Virginia. That's a good course too. They drive on an old airport runway. That one's not quite as fast or exciting as a Le Mans track, but its still great training. I also had the opportunity to train with the SAS in the UK a number of years ago. They have a combat town with houses, shops and so forth, where they trained the SAS for operations in Northern Ireland against the IRA. That was a unique driving experience learning how to negotiate cramped city streets. Of course, I do my driving requals every chance I get when I'm driving a rental car. Sometime when we're not working I'll teach you how to do J-turns and bootlegs. It's some serious fun."

Boucher smiled. He had been to those same driving schools along with several others throughout his previous SEAL career but he wasn't about to spoil the moment by telling her.

"Yeah, J-turns and bootlegs...I like that stuff."

Sandra smiled and nodded assuredly without taking her eyes off the road. Slowing the car slightly, she turned left onto Highway 49. As she sped up Boucher realized they were now gradually gaining altitude. The road was rising up to meet the mountaintops ahead. Boucher saw some trees for the first time since leaving Amman. As they ascended along the winding road he saw some farm crops growing in fertile fields alongside the road.

What a switch, he marveled to him self, *a half hour ago we were driving through a barren desert and now we're about twenty-five hundred feet up in the mountains bordering the Dead Sea and there is topsoil and green vegetation.* Even the air was pleasantly cool and moist.

After following the narrow winding road across the mountain ridges for about a half hour they began to descend. Several miles later Sandra stopped the car along the narrow shoulder of the road. She slid across the seat next to Boucher and leaned over him to his open window.

"Look down there," she said pointing out the window. "See that village?"

He looked where Sandra was pointing to the valley a thousand or so feet below.

"That's the modern village of Petra," she said. "Old Petra is hidden in a deep canyon behind that mountain over to the right of New Petra."

Boucher squinted into the distance. Far below he could make out the modern village of Petra, nestled deep in the valley, completely surrounded by rugged mountains. From the number of small adobe-type dwellings, Boucher estimated the population to be about two thousand, maybe less. The adobe-like houses were all very small, mostly constructed from rock and mud, the same building materials that have been used in the region for thousands of years. The architecture was equally as antiquated. To Boucher, these buildings looked more like ancient ruins than an inhabited village.

"Sandra," he asked, hoping to savor the nearness of her body a little longer, "where again is the part of Petra located that we're interested in?"

Sandra, still leaning over Boucher's lap, pointed down towards the right side of the small village below.

"It's on the other side of that mountain. New Petra is actually located just outside the deep gorge entrance to ancient Petra. We'll enter old Petra with the tourists the first thing in the morning. We have reservations at the Petra Hotel tonight. It's not exactly a four star hotel but it's the best one in town, or perhaps I should say, the only one in town."

Sandra realized that she was nearly on top of him when she felt her breast fully pressing against Boucher's chest. Boucher acknowledged her directions with a smile and a nod, but couldn't help the flicker of desire that shone in his eyes as they met hers. Sandra quickly returned to the driver's side of the seat, put the car in gear, and headed it down the mountain road to Petra.

"Have you ever been married?" she asked awkwardly.

Boucher winced. "Yeah, she was killed in an automobile accident many years ago."

"Any kids?"

"Yeah, one son. We weren't close. He was working on a fishery project in Kuwait when Saddam invaded and was never heard from again. How about you?"

"Never married. No kids. Guess I just never found the right man."

Boucher grunted without comment. Inwardly, he hoped she just had.

The two checked into the hotel and Sandra's description of it was validated to Boucher. The rooms were small, the tap water had a pungent odor and the beds were hard and lumpy. The view, looking out of the hotel window on downtown new Petra, was even more underwhelming. The small village was littered, congested and austere. He and Sandra met for supper. She had changed clothes and was now dressed in a very loose-fitting, nondescript, off-white, cotton dress. If not for her intense natural beauty it would have made her look very plain. Boucher truly had to remind himself not to stare at her.

Because of the crowded restaurant and close quarters, Sandra and Boucher couldn't carry on any meaningful discussions. They did have the opportunity to discuss their childhoods, families and future goals but it was not a revealing conversation. Boucher was intrigued by her and couldn't help but wonder what she thought of him.

Following supper, he would have loved to get better acquainted with her but they returned to their rooms and turned in early to get a good night's rest for the next day, a day that they both knew would be physically demanding.

The morning came much too soon for Boucher. Jet lag had caught up with him. He met Sandra for breakfast in the hotel's small dining area. She was wearing khaki hiking shorts with tan leather, ankle-high hiking boots and a faded, gray cotton T-shirt. She looked sensuous no matter what attire she wore and that wasn't lost on Boucher. He studied her movements and her curves.

"Take plenty of bottled water along in your backpack," she warned. "It's going to be a scorcher out there today."

For the most part, they looked like any other tourists. Not many Americans visited Petra and there was no hiding the fact that he was an American. Boucher remembered Barnhart telling him that most Middle Easterners could pick an

American out of a crowd in a heartbeat, so trying to hide it almost never worked. Sandra, on the other hand, looked Middle Eastern and had comparable native language skills. All she needed to do was dress appropriately and, except for her ravishing natural beauty, no one would ever give her a second look.

Sandra and Boucher began their entrance into Petra as any other tourists would, at the tourist center ticket counter. The tourist center was located next to the narrow gravel wash that led into the ancient city of Petra. As they proceeded past the Arab vendors trying to sell souvenirs and horseback rides, Boucher stopped, facing Sandra.

"This is a gravel wash, right? And it runs a half a mile or so down that direction into Ancient Petra, right? It's clearly too narrow to drive a car or truck through. So, riddle me this, Miss Morrison?" he asked in fun. "How did the opposition get a quarter ton RV warhead into Petra?"

Almost at that moment a horse drawn cart went by, carrying eight tourists. The cart had automobile tires on it and was having no problem riding on top of the loose gravel.

"Okay, never mind. It was a dumb question. I shoulda known. I'll pay closer attention to detail in the future. I'm a dumb ass."

Sandra flashed Boucher a warm smile.

"They might have used a cart like that one but they also use small, four wheel, all terrain vehicles like you see hunters use in the States. These folks only appear to be undeveloped. Believe me, they have access to the same stuff we do. They just choose to not demonstrate it publicly."

Boucher smiled back at Sandra. They strolled along the wash toward the cave dwellings of Petra without talking. After a short distance, Boucher offered her his hand. She took it without hesitation. Though they continued on in silence, the warmth of this simple contact had a profound effect on each of them.

They came upon the first caves prior to reaching the narrow passage leading into the ancient city and began the radiation search. Using their camera-detectors, the two systematically worked their way down the wash, searching for plutonium's characteristic gamma-neutron radiation signature. At the bottom end of the wash they entered the narrow passage leading into the ancient city's main avenue hidden deep in the mountains ahead.

Boucher marveled at the engineering genius of the ancients who built Petra. It was easy to see how they took advantage of the streambed that cut through the solid rock forming this hidden entrance. The remnants of a paved street that had gutters cut into the rock for drainage during the seasonal rains could still be seen at places. At some spots the gorge narrowed to about eight feet wide. Boucher soon saw why Petra was so naturally defensible.

"So Sandra," he inquired, "just how did the Tangos get the RV in here?"

Boucher used the word Tangos as slang for terrorists to see if he could get a reaction from Sandra. Many of the CIA briefers used that term.

Sandra stepped to the side of the wash along the vertical rock face of the deep gorge. She turned to face Boucher, warmly placing her right hand on his forearm. He could see the morning sun brightly illuminating the brownish-red canyon walls above her and the twinkle in her dark brown eyes that seemed to reflect the same colors.

"Providing that the item of concern is here at all and, if I was a gambler, I'd bet the Tangos—you did refer to them as Tangos didn't you—brought it in here using a horse-drawn cart. You know, the cart with car tires probably like those we saw up by the visitor center. Those carts are used by most of the vendors, or should I call them vengos, to haul in their goods."

Boucher chuckled aloud. "Vengos - imagine that."

She liked when he laughed and that was seldom, but she didn't want to reveal too much of her attraction, so she pretended she hadn't heard his comment.

"A cart like that would attract no attention because they travel this wash frequently after hours while the area is closed to tourists. Come on, Indiana Jones," she said, motioning to Boucher, "it's not much further to the Temple of Doom."

"Okay, but only if I get to drink from the Chalice and gain everlasting life with you."

Boucher realized the moment he said it that it was a slip. He hadn't meant to say "with you," but he had.

"I mean, ahhh..., we can drink from the Chalice together."

Realizing he blundered again, he uncharacteristically dropped his arms limply by his side as if surrendering all defenses.

"Actually, you can drink from it and I'll watch," he said embarrassed by his own bumbling.

Sandra caught every word he said. She liked this old warrior's naive honesty. In fact, she found him to have a captivatingly gentle personality with an entirely appealing intellect. She knew she had to attempt to remain completely professional. Personal feelings would only serve to complicate matters and could indeed risk mission failure. She decided to act as if she had disregarded his comments.

"No one will drink from the Chalice if we don't find the item of concern. Come on," she urged briskly stepping away. "We have work to do."

As they rounded a sharp bend in the gorge, the temple came into full view. Boucher was awed. The temple's massive facade, about three stories high, was ornately sculpted into the gorge's solid rock face. It was indeed a work of art.

"Let's get some pictures," Sandra enthusiastically chanted. Taking Boucher's hand, she led him to the temple's dark entrance.

Sandra remained standing in the temple's cave-like entranceway while Boucher went inside the dark, cavernous, main room. The rising sun was now shining brightly through the doorway behind Sandra like a spotlight behind a stage silhouetting her form as she methodically scanned the entry area. Boucher could see shafts of bright sunlight occasionally beaming between her legs and, for a moment, it looked like the spot was white hot. Boucher jolted, realizing that he had been fixated on her crotch. Embarrassed at himself, he quickly turned away, raising his camera back to his eye so she would not catch him staring at her. He could only think one thought, *Damn, you're beautiful!*

Over the next several hours Sandra and Boucher systematically searched every cave that was accessible on foot along the main street of Petra. Most of the caves required them to climb up the small eroded rambling pathways cut into the vertical sides of the gorge's rock face to gain entry. During a steep climb up to one cave, Boucher was in the lead with Sandra close behind. As Boucher bent forward to reach for a handhold, he glanced back over his shoulder to check on Sandra. She was so fixated on his ass that she didn't realize he caught her watching him. He glanced down several more times during the steep climb to find that she was still checking him out. Boucher sensed the chemistry between them from the moment they met back in that underground room at Groom Lake. Well, at least as far as he was concerned there was chemistry. Now, the mere thought of her was a completely distracting turn-on.

By late afternoon they had searched their way to the point where the canyon began to noticeably widen and the architectural facade, as well as the man-made caves themselves, became more massive. Sandra and Boucher inadvertently met face to face as they both squeezed through a narrow opening leading to the outer room of a three room cave they were searching. The cave, located about seventy-five feet above the gravel street below, even had windows carved into the outer wall which provided a cooling air flow. Neither Boucher nor Sandra said a word. The intense eye contact between them made words unnecessary. It was at that moment that Boucher became overwhelmed with his need for her.

Sandra sat down in the shade on a flat bench carved into solid rock next to the cave's entrance and leaned back on her backpack. She took a swallow of water from a nearly empty plastic bottle and poured the remainder over her face. The water trickled down over her face onto her shirt, making the thin cotton fabric nearly transparent. At that moment a gust of cool breeze wafted through the cave.

"Wow! Does that ever feel good," she said smiling in Boucher's direction.

She lay back with her eyes closed, taking deep breaths trying to relax for a few moments. Boucher could see the water glistening on her soft cheeks as it ran down her slender neck to her cleavage. Arching her neck over the makeshift backpack pillow, her cotton T-shirt was tightly stretched over her breasts. Her nipples looked like they would pierce the thin fabric as her chest heaved slowly upward with each breath.

Boucher slipped off his backpack and sat down next to her, quietly gazing down at her. Without a word he bent and softly kissed her lips. Sandra eagerly returned his kiss, instantly slipping her fingers through his hair and then moving her hands down to grasp his broad shoulders. Several minutes passed as they became embroiled in the passion of their kisses. Boucher forced himself to push back slightly, looking intently into her desire-glazed eyes.

"Sandra," he whispered, "you know what this is going to lead to?"

She lowered her lids and nodded.

"I know. I've been fighting this all day...I surrender," she whispered seductively. Caressing his neck and back, she coaxed Boucher on top of her.

As he pulled her into his strong embrace, he heard himself almost involuntarily rasp out the word.

"Hooyah!"

Her soft whimpers echoed through the cave.

Chapter 11

Iran, the same day

Barnhart arrived in Tehran. As a member of the IAEA inspection team, he was there to review some facility destruction progress records and conduct several routine site inspections of Iran's weapon development facilities to ensure United Nations compliance. He had been fully briefed at Langley during the previous three days. His briefings were held separately from Sandra's and Boucher's to keep the detailed plans for both compartmented from the other, thereby reducing the risk of mission compromise. Barnhart had been down this road many times before and fully understood the operational security requirements, or OPSEC for covert operations like these.

Following the first Gulf War, Barnhart had spent numerous months in Iraq with the IAEA during an intense two year effort aimed at systematically dismantling Iraq's technical capability to develop nuclear weapons. During that period, as reported by the IAEA, Iraq's laboratory equipment was either rendered useless or removed. Design, testing and fabrication facilities were destroyed under the close supervision of the IAEA. The IAEA after-action report, following this effort, officially concluded that Iraq's nuclear weapon development program had been effectively halted. It also concluded that as a result, Iraq's nuclear weapon development program was set back eight to ten years. Unfortunately, as Barnhart well understood, no one, except Saddam, really knew if the IAEA was truly successful.

On the other hand, Iran was a different animal and Barnhart knew it. Iran openly threatened the use of nuclear weapons against its neighboring states within the region, especially Israel. Iran supported Islamic fundamentalism and encouraged terrorist actions against the West, funding its miscreant programs with its colossal oil profits derived from sales to mostly Russia and China. It might have already succeeded in its quest to acquire a nuke on the black market from some other source like North Korea or the former Soviet Union, if not clandestinely developed one on its own.

Now, more than ever, Barnhart believed Iran could easily conceal its real nuclear weapon development program and its supporting facilities underground, somewhere in Iran's vast mountain expanse. He privately believed that was where the plutonium weapon development was taking place. He also believed Iran already had constructed at least one nuclear weapon which was likely a low tech, easy to build gun-type uranium weapon with about the same yield capability as the atomic bomb dropped on Hiroshima in World War II.

But this trip to Iran was very different from all his previous IAEA inspection visits to Iraq years earlier because he was looking for a stockpile warhead; a warhead of Russian origin, possibly smuggled into Iran by terrorists - terrorists who had been paid very well. His objective was to make covert contact with a CIA operative, locate the weapon, provide a scientific and technical evaluation of the weapon's condition based upon available HUMINT. And if possible, providing he could gain access to the weapon if he found its location, he was at the least going to attempt to disable it. If he didn't have the time to disable it then he was going to destroy it. Either way he knew that he had to stop it from being used.

After eating dinner, Barnhart went for a brisk walk. He knew that his every move was being watched by Iranian intelligence agents but he was not able to identify them. He returned to his hotel room about thirty minutes later. Moments after his arrival his Blackberry chirped a notification that he had received a text message. The message was not good news.

///CONFIRM ITEM OF CONCERN NOT, REPEAT NOT, IN IRAN// DESTINATION AND TARGET UNKNOWN//ROUTE UNKNOWN// TARGET UNKNOWN//HAMAS COMPLICITY CERTAIN//NO DIRECT IRAN STATE COMPLICITY DETECTED//BELIEVE IC IS ONE FIVE TWO MILLIMETER ARTILLERY FIRED ATOMIC PROJECTILE// LOCATION UNDETERMINED BUT DESTINATION MAY BE ISRAEL// ETA NEXT FORTY-EIGHT HOURS//SATCOM ALT//YOU SEVENTEEN HUNDRED POINT BRAVO//ME TWENTY-TWO HUNDRED POINT ECHO ALT//END///

Barnhart's greatest concern was that the 152 mm nuke artillery round the agent referenced in the message was inherently dirty, radioactively speaking, especially if exploded at ground level. The detonation and resulting mushroom cloud would carry radioactive particulate into the lower atmosphere. As the plume collapsed it would contaminate an expansive footprint spreading lethal radiation miles over the downwind area. If such a weapon was detonated close to the Kuwait border under the right weather conditions, the radiation could easily affect thousands in Kuwait City. If detonated near the Dead Sea in Jordan, radiation could blanket much of Amman and portions of Israel, with a potential casualty toll numbering in the thousands. *But where did the artillery nuke come from and what is the target? What happened to the SS-19 warhead he was sent to find?*

He noted the instructions in the text message's last line. If he had any information to pass back to the operative prior to their meeting, he was to pass it via a text-message, using the Blackberry with a dead drop alternative, no later than seventeen hundred hours local time. If a dead drop was used, he was to make the drop at point bravo which was a predetermined location that only he and the operative knew. In this way the operative could abort the meeting and still get Barnhart's reply. If the operative had to abort the meeting he would reply via a twenty-two hundred hours dead drop back to Barnhart at point echo, the alternate location.

His first concern was to get this new information to Sandra and Boucher. They would need to know that the SS-19 reentry vehicle warhead they were looking for might instead be a 152 mm Russian-made tactical artillery nuke. More than before, he now suspected it was probably still located in Jordan. Barnhart could send that message to Sandra over the IAEA-supplied portable International Maritime Satellite M-terminal transmitter. Using his laptop to both encode the message and burst transmit it to one of the four INMARSAT satellites in geosynchronous orbit high above the earth's equator was easy. The INMARSAT would efficiently retransmit his message to any electronic address on the face of the earth. Reaching Sandra's Blackberry was a sure thing as was the CIA's Langley address. Both needed to know of this new development.

Barnhart typed the message into his laptop, addressing it to Sandra and the CIA's Langley Headquarters.

///AGENT REPORTS ITEM OF CONCERN NOT, REPEAT NOT IN IRAN//DESTINATIONANDTARGETUNKNOWN//ROUTEUNKNOWN// HAMAS COMPLICITY STRONGLY SUSPECTED//NO IRAN STATE COMPLICITY DETECTED//BELIEVE IC MAY BE FSU ONE FIVE TWO

MILLIMETER AFAP//INFO NOT VALIDATED//BELIEVE SS-NINETEEN RV STILL POSSIBLE//SEARCH FOR ALL//GOOD HUNTING//END///

Barnhart moved the computer's cursor on top of the "encrypt/save message" icon and double clicked on it. This one key stroke served to encrypt and compress the message into a burst file and save the file as outgoing mail. He followed that with a separate message for the operative working with him in Baghdad.

///MEET NOT TOMORROW//REPEAT: MEET NOT TOMORROW// REQUIRE ITEM OF CONCERN GPS LOC ASAP//WILL ARRANGE IAEA INSPECTION//INTERROGATIVE YOUR ASSIST IN FOLLOW-ON//REPLY DROP MSG POINT X-RAY//END///

Barnhart then set up the M-terminal INMARSAT and opened its small computer laptop-like lid whose flat outside surface doubled as the antenna. Aiming it through the window using a small compass, he peered along its side, then up at the sky as though he could see an imaginary spot. Using the small compass he quickly adjusted the antenna's angle and direction towards the satellite orbiting a hundred miles above. With a few small antenna adjustments, the INMARSAT was purring with a strong signal tone denoting that it had a solid signal lock on the distant satellite. Working methodically, Barnhart connected the computer's modem to the data port on the INMARSAT and pressed the return key on the computer. The computer automatically dialed the INMARSAT number and in a fraction of a second the messages were sent. As the computer screen reported that the messages had been successfully sent, Barnhart quickly collapsed the INMARSAT's lid antenna and returned it to its nylon carrying case configuration.

At this point Barnhart could do nothing more than wait for a reply that would hopefully contain some answers to his questions. Without those answers, he would continue the IAEA inspection agenda in the blind. He realized the puzzle had just become significantly more complicated. With the location of the artillery nuke unknown, he continued to wonder what had happened to the SS-19 warhead. *Could the CIA have gotten that wrong? Or was there indeed, a second nuke somewhere in Jordan?* He hoped that he wasn't too late.

The next morning Barnhart listened to the BBC news broadcast on a small battery-powered clock radio that he had brought along. The top story was about a Hamas rocket attack against the Israeli settlement of Kiryat Shmona in North Galilee. The attack, using Chinese-built Katyusha rockets, came during mid-morning. One of the rockets scored a kill of eight children and a woman when it exploded indiscriminately inside a day care center. Another killed two Israeli soldiers standing on a street corner. A third blew up beside a crowded bus stop killing six commuters. Scores of others were left wounded and bleeding in the attack. The Israeli people demanded retaliation against the Hamas terrorists operating from bases located well inside Lebanon. The Israeli Prime Minister vowed to the world, "Retaliation against the cowards who killed innocent women and children would be swift and devastating."

Barnhart knew what that meant as did the rest of the world. Within the next several days Israel would likely launch a massive air strike against Hamas strongholds in Lebanon. Israeli armed forces would also probably use long range artillery and tanks to sustain the strike. They would extract a death toll from where they believed the source of the attack against them stemmed. If state complicity could be proven they might even attack Iran. Barnhart shuddered at the thought. The balance of power was already extremely tenuous in the Middle East. While Egypt and Jordan had made peace with Israel setting the lead for other Arab countries to follow, Israel was still hated by the Palestinians and the Arabs as a whole. A clear escalation of the level of violence by Israel against a country like Iran could unite the Arab nations against Israel.

Ever since the Gulf War the United States had provided the only stabilizing force in the Middle East. True, the U.S. had taken its licks during June of 1996 with the terrorist bombing of the Air Force barracks in Dhahran, the two U.S. Embassies in Africa in August of 1998, and the Yemen pier side bombing of the USS Cole in October of 2000, but American resolve had prevailed. Barnhart anguished over his knowledge that a nuke could be on its way into terrorists' hands. Would the terrorists target Israel? He knew all too well that Israel was a member of the nuclear club and possessed its own nukes. He also knew that Israel would not hesitate to retaliate in kind if attacked with a nuke. To complicate matters, Iran now had ballistic missiles capable of delivering a nuclear warhead as far ranging as central Europe. *Israel had unilaterally attacked Iraq's Tuwaitha nuclear reactor to prevent them from building a bomb. Might they also attack Iran's missile and weapon development facilities now, especially if they believed that Iran has, or is close to having a nuclear weapon?* Still fully clothed, Barnhart lay back in his bed falling into a restless sleep.

Later that night Barnhart's laptop chirped like a beeper startling him awake. Sitting up on the edge of the bed he typed in a code on the computer keyboard and the LCD color screen instantly displayed a text message transmitted from Langley via satellite. The concealed receiver in Barnhart's laptop had recorded the decoded message.

///MULTIPLE SOURCES CONFIRM IOC LOCATION SOUTHERN JORDAN POSSIBLE SEARCH UNDERWAY//RVDZ WITH TEHRAN POC NOT ADVISED//COORD ALL WITH COS AMMAN//WILL ADVISE FURTHER WHEN INFO AVAIL//END///

Barnhart understood. Langley confirmed that the nuke might be in southern Jordan. He knew the only trained and equipped operatives available to conduct a clandestine search were Sandra and Boucher. Clearly, they would have to remain in Jordan while he would continue with the IAEA inspection. He would expand his search to include suspected fire set development facilities with the hope of finding a clue that would both identify and locate the Item of Concern, or IOC, as a loose nuke was referred to. The agent operating in deep cover inside Iran supporting Barnhart's effort was his point of contact, or POC, and he was not to attempt a rendezvous. Barnhart assumed that the Iranians were watching his movements too closely and his POC couldn't risk compromise. And of course, he was to coordinate everything through the CIA's Chief of Station at the American Embassy in Amman.

Barnhart uneventfully recovered his second dead drop the next day as planned. The news this time was even more distressing. The undercover operative reported that the weapon was indeed a small yield 152 mm nuke artillery round and that its modified fire set had been built in Iran's Karaj facility. The agent reported that even though the IAEA had inspected this facility previously and found it to not be part of an active weapon development program, the facility had apparently succeeded in concealing its true purpose.

Even so, this information didn't track for Barnhart. Langley sent him looking for an SS-19 warhead still sheathed in its' cone-shaped reentry vehicle. The artillery nuke was very small in comparison to a reentry vehicle. A ninety-five pound artillery round could be man carried while the SS-19 RV weighed a quarter of a ton. This disparity in the information was perplexing to Barnhart. He was becoming more convinced that there really was a second loose nuke, one that the intelligence community had not detected. *But what was its origin? Could it be a black market nuke from the former Soviet stockpile? Or, maybe the information was incorrect. Perhaps it was nothing.* Barnhart decided to follow his gut feeling and assume the information was valid and that there was a second nuke, but he needed proof. He would have to conduct a surprise inspection and try to find out for himself.

The next morning Barnhart set out for Karaj, well west of Tehran. The drive north to the facility was uneventful. The two Iranian escort vehicles maintained a close vigil on him, but otherwise did not interfere.

During Barnhart's inspection of the Karaj facility's records, he had the opportunity to interview two nuclear engineers who had studied and received their Ph.D.'s in the U.S. Barnhart had difficulty understanding how educated men could consciously support a government like Iran's. These scientists were not like the fundamentalist radicals who drove suicide car bombs into a target and self destructed to gain a place in heaven. They were highly educated men who had lived and studied in the United States for a number of years. Like him, they were men of science.

During the inspection he unexpectedly met with Doctor Jamal Gulzar. Gulzar was the Doctor Teller equivalent of Iran's nuclear weapon program. Barnhart had met him years earlier when Gulzar was doing his post doctoral study in the U.S. In fact, Gulzar had actually spent several weeks working with Barnhart as an intern at Los Alamos. Barnhart took full advantage of his professional relationship and reputation as a Manhattan Project grandfather during the meeting. He knew that Gulzar spoke fluent English so he decided to get right to the point.

"Jamal, have you built a weapon?" Barnhart gently insisted as only an old and trusted scientist could to a peer.

"As we have many times revealed to the IAEA, we have experimented with the physics involved and have investigated the development technologies, but we have never built a weapon," Gulzar replied as if he were reading his response.

"I can't accept that Jamal. I have every reason to believe that you have developed an implosion weapon and that your government intends to use it. We are both loyal men who have followed our government's calling. As you know, I helped build the bombs that led to the Cold War with Russia and China. Today, I'm not particularly proud of what I did and I will share with you that it continues to cause me great anxiety. But your cause cannot be compared to mine. If you explode a nuclear weapon against an unclear enemy you will be labeled a terrorist. The level and extent of retaliation against Iran will be beyond your wildest dreams and your country, as you know it today, will cease to exist. You and I share the power of knowledge, the know-how to design and build a weapon. Can you not understand what I am trying to tell you?" Barnhart pleaded, emphasizing his last few words with an uplifting hand gesture.

"Yes, we have much common ground," Ghoushe replied forcefully, "and my enemies are not unlike your enemies. I fight the Great Satan that threatens my culture as you fought the Communist Satan who threatened yours. I do what I must to protect my country from aggression. It is those outside the Arab world who are the terrorists, not us. We must be strong enough to protect ourselves. We do not need the West to provide guidance to the Arab culture, a culture superior to any other of this world. We see the West, and especially the United States, as arrogant and self serving. We fight to defend what is ours with the tools available to us. That may be accomplished through the martyrs of our day or, through the technical means of our decade. We will not yield to the infidels. We will do whatever it takes to achieve and maintain our unity."

Barnhart winced slightly as he looked the Iraqi weapon expert straight in the eyes.

"I have investigated your program since the Gulf War and there are simply too many inconsistencies to discount the fact that you have been clandestinely developing a plutonium weapon. I ask you again, do you have a weapon?"

"No!" Gulzar insisted, "We do not have a weapon! And, I might add Doctor Barnhart, I am a man of integrity regardless of what you might believe of the politics!"

Barnhart could feel the hair on the back of his neck stand up. Looking away he picked up his notebook and stood without further comment. He simply didn't believe Gulzar. He believed that Iran had at least one weapon, maybe more and he now recognized the region's balance of power was more tenuous than he had previously anticipated.

As Barnhart departed, Gulzar partially blocked his path gesturing in an attempt to shake his hand. Gulzar grabbed Barnhart's hand and pressed a small folded piece of paper into his palm.

"Good day Doctor Barnhart, it is my pleasure to see you again," Gulzar softly said.

Barnhart did not reply. He simply clutched the small note, being careful not to alarm any would be onlookers, and casually placed his hand in his pocket. Turning away from Gulzar without expression, he departed the office.

Returning to his car, Barnhart opened the door and sat inside on the front seat where he read Gulzar's note in privacy. Scrawled in pencil it read: Semnan. Barnhart knew at once that he had just been given some vital information that might lead him closer to locating the SS-19 RV warhead or the 152mm artillery round. Barnhart recalled the IAEA inspections he conducted following the Gulf War. Even then the data analysis revealed that Iraq was developing nuclear weapons and had the materials, equipment and technical know-how to develop the high speed detonators required for a nuclear weapon's fire set. Although the IAEA had only actually detected a preliminary effort to develop such sophisticated technology, they all feared that Iran had the real effort well concealed at a clandestine location, probably underground.

Gulzar's note was like a light bulb going on in Barnhart's mind. It was now becoming clear as the pieces fell into place. Iran never intended to build a weapon of its own but rather buy an intact weapon through the black market and make it workable by replacing the fire set. He had underestimated Gulzar's integrity as a fellow weapon scientist but he couldn't understand why he had waited until now to reveal this information. Perhaps it was a wild goose chase or a diversion to keep Barnhart from the truth. If the note was valid, Barnhart wondered what he might find at Semnan. Nonetheless he had to investigate the Semnan facility and he now knew just what to look for.

Barnhart typed a message on his laptop computer to the COS in Amman with an information copy to Sandra and Boucher.

///GULZAR REVEALED DEVELOPMENT AT SEMNAN//WILL INVESTIGATE TOMORROW//REPLACEMENT FIRE SET FOR ITEM OF CONCERN POSSIBLE//LOCATION OF IOC UNKNOWN//END///

He than typed a second message addressed exclusively to Boucher and Sandra.

///RCMD YOU NOT LIMIT SEARCH TO RV//ARTILLERY NUKE MAY ALSO BE LIKELY //INTERROGATIVE LANGLEY INTEL INFORMATION INTEGRITY//CU SOON//SB///

With the computer modem plugged into the M-terminal INMARSAT, Barnhart clicked on the send icon and the encrypted messages flashed to the orbiting satellite above where they were instantaneously retransmitted to the appropriate addressees.

Barnhart checked his watch and disconnected the computer modem from the INMARSAT zipping it back into its padded case for protection from the bumpy ride back to the hotel. Barnhart knew he would begin a long day in the morning and that he needed sleep. The drive back to the hotel was uneventful. After a lukewarm shower he instantly fell asleep.

Kennedy Irregular Warfare Center, Office of Naval Intelligence, Suitland, MD

"Sir, I invite your attention to this intercept," Lieutenant Bruce said to his boss. "NSA got it from a cell phone call made by Mohammad Vaziri, himself.

We haven't confirmed the validity of its' content but it was copied from the same cell number he's been using for the last two weeks."

Navy Captain Dean Blackford was the most senior SEAL officer assigned to ONI. He was the Commanding Officer of the Kennedy Irregular Warfare Center which provided dedicated operational intelligence support for the entire SEAL community. He also held the honorary title of "Bullfrog," which is the longest serving SEAL still on active duty. Blackford had risen from the enlisted SEAL ranks to the officer ranks and now had over thirty-nine years combined SEAL enlisted and officer active duty service. As far as the SEAL community was concerned, he was a legend. His hard talking, no bullshit "old school" demeanor was contrasted by his willingness to take the shirt off his back for anyone in need.

"Thanks, Lieutenant. Please save me the pain of reading this and just give me the short version briefing."

"Yes, Sir," the lieutenant smiled. "I expected you would ask me for the abbreviated version."

Blackford shrugged unapologetically. As he sat back in his high back leather chair he spat his chewing tobacco into a coffee cup he used for a spittoon. The cup was half full of spit and nasty looking.

"Well, Sir, it seems al Qaeda might be directing a nuke attack on the Canary Islands."

Blackford almost came out of his chair banging his knees on a partially open desk drawer.

"A fucking nuke attack on the Canary Islands? What fucking nuke? I thought there was only one lose nuke in play and that was somewhere in Jordan?"

"Well, Sir, it seems there may be an additional nuke in play that we previously didn't know about."

"But the fucking Canary Islands? Why the hell would al Qaeda attack the Canary Islands? Unless you're trying to make a bunch of fucking dope smoking, earring wear'n, beach bums glow in the dark, there's nothing there to attack."

"I agree, Sir, the Canarys are nothing more than seven islands clustered along the Mid-Atlantic ridge formed by now extinct volcanoes. The only correlation my guys have made so far that validates this intercept is from previous intercepts referencing a plan they called, 'al-Ta'ir al-Zahabi'."

"So what the fuck is that raghead garble supposed to mean?"

"Translated, it means 'golden bird.' As you know, Sir, truth is always stranger than fiction."

"Golden bird? WTF?"

"Golden bird could mean the Canary Islands."

"Yeah, maybe, but don't you think that's a pretty clever analogy for a bunch of terrorist camel jockey cock suckers?"

"Maybe they didn't come up with it, Sir. Maybe someone a little more sophisticated came up with it."

"You know what, Lieutenant? You're too damn smart to be in the Navy. You need to become a fucking lawyer or a politician or something."

"I'll take that as a compliment, Sir, but no thanks. I like this uniform and besides, I could never be a lawyer, I know who my parents are."

"Yeah, I know you do," Blackford chuckled clearly delighted with his young lieutenant. "Dedicate a cell to work it and get me a concrete answer to this conundrum! I want it soonest!"

"They're already on it, Sir."

"Then carry on smartly."

"Aye-aye, Sir."

Chapter 12

Northern Iran the next day

Barnhart set out for Semnan, several hours east of Tehran, just before sunrise in the IAEA Jeep Wagoner. He was accompanied by two Iranian officers and one government official, leading the two vehicle convoy in an aging Toyota Trooper that had almost as much rust on its body as it did the original tan colored paint. The rolling desert landscape was almost devoid of plant life and looked forbidding. Except for some occasional limestone and shale rock outcroppings, the desert's clay-rock composition was little more than barren wasteland. Occasional ravines creased the desert floor as eerie, dark remains of Old Testament deluges. The predawn sun was beginning to brighten the landscape contours, creating ghostly shadows that made the road seem to disappear into deep crevassing wadis in the desert floor. Barnhart had experienced this illusion many times before, during his travels in Iraq, but this morning, for some reason, it was unnervingly vivid. This desert was very different from the Southwest desert of New Mexico which he had come to love.

As he drove, Barnhart kept mulling over the likely existence of the second nuke. It was troubling to him, not just because there might be another nuke somewhere out there for him to find, but because he couldn't understand where it came from or why the intelligence community hadn't detected it. *After all, loose nukes don't just appear out of the ether. The CIA detected and acted*

116

upon the nuke artillery round being smuggled to Iran via the Caspian, several months earlier. The whole intelligence community knew about that. So where did this one come from? He wondered aloud, "Could this nuke be one and the same?" *But Jake Boucher saw the ship explode and sink. Eye witnesses don't come more reliable than Jake Boucher. True, the Caspian wasn't that deep and a dedicated salvage effort could probably retrieve such an object from the sea floor. But a salvage effort of that magnitude would leave a signature that spy satellites would most definitely detect. So how would that nuke have been removed from the ship's watery grave?*

Barnhart fumbled with the Jeep's antiquated car radio and finally found the English speaking BBC channel. The hourly news broadcast was just beginning. The broadcaster opened with a brief update on yesterday's attack on the Israeli city of Kiryat Shmona.

"The death toll has risen to twelve in Israel as a result of the indiscriminately savage rocket attack on the Israeli city of Kiryat Shmona. Overnight, two more children died from wounds sustained during the attack. Israeli outrage and grief, resulting from the attack, is overwhelming. Israel has closed its borders with Jordan and Lebanon to all Palestinians. And, the Israeli military has been observed moving armored columns and heavy artillery toward the Lebanese border. Israeli Prime Minister Ari Bar-Sela denounced the attack as an act of inhuman barbarism against innocent women and children and vowed retaliation against those responsible. Great Britain, France, the United States and Russia have all denounced the attack as a 'barbaric and unacceptable act of terrorism against the innocent' and 'far outside the bounds of civilized understanding.' They have also expressed their sympathy to the Israeli people. The United Nations Security Council is meeting this very hour, in special session, to determine if there is complicity by a known state supporter of terrorism, specifically Iran or Syria, and if further sanctions can be applied to force a stop to this violence. Meanwhile, the Palestinian government has denied any complicity in the attack and has sent a formal protest to the Government of Israel for its persecution by Israel as a result of the border closings. Tension remains extremely high between the Israelis and the Palestinians. Minor clashes between rock throwing Palestinians and Israeli soldiers have resulted in the shooting of one Palestinian youth by an Israeli soldier."

Ahh crap! Barnhart thought. *Here we go again.* Barnhart knew that if history was any indicator of things to come, Israel would be mounting a major counterattack within the next twenty-four hours, probably in the form of a major air strike against the Hamas strongholds in Lebanon.

The BBC broadcast continued. "Just in: a nuclear reactor fuel processing plant located in Honshu, Japan has experienced a criticality accident. This plant processes enriched uranium fuel rods for Japan's nuclear power plants. Initial reports indicate the nuclear reaction caused by the accidental creation of a critical mass is out of control. Japanese officials are evacuating the local area surrounding the processing plant. The extent of injuries to the plant's ninety-one workers is undetermined, but there are unconfirmed reports that at least two workers inside the plant were subjected to lethal radiation doses and have been taken to hospital. We will keep you updated as this story unfolds. In other news today..."

Double ahh crap! Barnhart thought as he turned the radio off. He knew exactly what the Japanese accident meant. Somebody accidentally moved two masses of enriched nuclear material too close together creating a critical mass. It was now a nuclear pile with its fission out of control. The extent of the consequences would depend on the size of the critical mass and degree of enrichment involved. *Perhaps another Chernobyl?* He had visited that exact processing facility years before as part of a U.S. technical assistance team. Barnhart's thoughts focused on his memories of the plant's layout, then on the process itself. *You have to enrich the uranium and process it before you put it back in the reactor and make plutonium.* He could picture it in detail. *Contamination will surely be nasty, but no mushroom cloud.*

At that instant the asphalt road he had been following turned to dirt, jolting him from his thoughts. The dust cloud, created by the escort vehicle ahead, was so dense that he had to drop back several hundred meters just to safely negotiate the bumpy road at the speed they were traveling. A manic Barnhart drove on, still trying to analyze the events leading to the reported appearance of the nuke artillery round. Arriving at Semnan mid morning, the two-vehicle IAEA convoy entered the perimeter of the complex.

To Barnhart's surprise, security was minimal. Instead of a well maintained and guarded perimeter fence there was only some rusted tanglefoot barbed wire stretched haphazardly along the rock strewn ground. The guards at the entry gate stood inside two small makeshift corrugated tin guard houses, flanking each side of the entryway. Barnhart could see no roving patrols walking the perimeter. Security at the facility appeared to be unusually lax. In fact, it was surprisingly almost non-existent.

The two vehicles proceeded up to a small concrete building no larger than an average two car garage and stopped. The two Iranian escort officers left their vehicle and went inside the building. The Iranian government official also left the lead vehicle and casually strode over to Barnhart's Wagoneer door and spoke to him through the open window.

"You are at Semnan. You will follow me now."

Barnhart opened his car door and eased off the seat to his feet. He felt the stiffness setting into his legs and lower back from the morning's bumpy drive.

"I'm getting too old for this shit," he mumbled.

The Iranian officer heard his voice.

"What did you say?" he abruptly questioned.

"I said this place is so dry I can't spit," Barnhart quickly replied.

The officer grunted and proceeded toward the weathered wooden door of the small metal-sided building. Barnhart took a backpack that contained some of his search and ID equipment from the rear of the Jeep Wagoneer and followed him inside.

The inside seemed almost as dusty as the parking area outside. Several heavily gouged wooden desks, littered with stacks of paper files, were positioned perpendicular to the walls. The desks were each bordered by a three-drawer metal file cabinet that had more rust than gray paint on them. Two antiquated mechanical typewriters crowded the same desktop and looked inoperable, highlighting a distinct absence of computers. The Iranian Army officers manning the desks appeared busy talking on their telephones and shuffling documents. The office looked disorganized and incapable of facility management. Barnhart was greeted by an Iranian Army colonel and a scientist wearing a gray lab coat. His escort introduced him in Arabic and then again in heavily accented English.

"Doctor Barnhart, you are to meet Dr. Sulah Abdulaziz and Colonel Adae."

Barnhart offered a handshake to them both, directing his reply to Abdulaziz.

"I am honored to make your acquaintance, Dr. Abdulaziz. I have heard much about your work in nuclear chemistry and quantum mechanics. It is a pleasure to finally meet you."

Abdulaziz smiled faintly, clearly appearing to understand English. The two scientists shook hands.

"The privilege is for me, Doctor Barnhart. What may I do to assist you today?" he said in almost perfect English.

Barnhart already knew from the CIA files that Abdulaziz was the number two man in the Iranian weapons program and that brilliant nuclear chemist had been educated at the University of Michigan at Ann Arbor where, in 1970, he received his Ph.D. He had a reputation for being innovative, as well as enterprising. He was also a committed Islamic fundamentalist who despised the West.

Barnhart also knew that as long as Abdulaziz remained the number two man in the Iranian weapon program that the program would effectively move forward. Abdulaziz was the shaker and mover behind Iran's nuclear weapon development program and he also had the political clout to get what he needed to get the job done from both the military and the government officials. Iran would have its nuclear capability sooner or later and it would be sooner if Abdulaziz had anything to do with it.

"I would like to review your laboratory records and inspect your facility. I am particularly interested in the fire set development that you have been working on over the past year," Barnhart said.

Abdulaziz looked at Barnhart unemotionally for a moment before replying.

"We are not developing anything, I assure you. We are simply investigating the technologies involved. We are perfectly within our right to do so. The IAEA has inspected this facility and our records many times. I do not see the reason for the IAEA to continue this harassment of our research which is for peaceful purposes."

Barnhart knew that Abdulaziz was lying through his teeth. The only peaceful research Abdulaziz ever did was the experiments he conducted while he was working on his doctoral degree at Michigan.

"I am not passing judgment on your work, Doctor Abdulaziz. I am only confirming to the IAEA that your research is peaceful. I invite you to accompany me throughout the inspection. Perhaps we will find that we have more in common than you think."

Abdulaziz nodded his approval to Barnhart as he spoke in Arabic to the Iranian military officer standing by his side, telling him to allow Barnhart access to the facility.

Barnhart had never visited Semnan before but was well experienced on what to expect. The facility had been built almost completely underground, making it nearly bomb-proof. He knew that the U.S. Air Force had this facility listed as a priority target but even the highly accurate laser-guided bombs, dropped by U.S. stealth bombers, would cause little damage of consequence. As Barnhart walked outside the small administrative office building he noted that the sprawling desert complex had several underground entrances clustered in four to five groups, each shielded by individual revetments. Most of the underground entrances appeared to not be in use. All had heavy steel roll-up doors encased in massive steel reinforced concrete entranceways. They were all large enough to easily accommodate a vehicle the size of an eighteen wheeler with a wide reinforced concrete roadway connecting the entrances that provided heavy vehicle mobility into the underground complex below. A partially sand covered roadway led out of the facility compound disappearing nondescriptly into the sprawling desert expanse.

Barnhart also noted that the site had a sizeable number of Iran's elite Revolutionary Guard cadre along with troops from the Iranian Army's 2nd Battalion, 40th Chemical Brigade stationed outside. Barnhart knew their presence indicated that something very important was either occurring there, or was about to.

Abdulaziz directed Barnhart toward Building 6. Building 6 was really not a building at all. It was actually the access point for three tunnels that led underground. One of the tunnels was marked with a number six painted in Arabic on a plywood plaque above the open roll-up door. Barnhart, with Abdulaziz at his side, entered the tunnel. It took a moment for Barnhart's eyes to adjust to the dimly lighted tunnel as he walked in from the bright desert sun. There was no observable activity inside, just pairs of armed soldiers milling about with no apparent objective. The tunnel made a gentle right turn about thirty yards inside which Barnhart judged to be designed to provide additional blast fragmentation protection. There were several canvas covered military trucks parked with their rear ends butted against a well lighted loading dock. Barnhart could see multiple wooden and plastic shipping boxes of all sizes along the dock but there was no activity.

Barnhart raised his camera with the radiation detector concealed inside it and began to take pictures in a three-hundred and sixty degree panorama. He detected no abnormal radiation. As the inspection party moved further inside the tunnel, Barnhart noted several smaller tunnels leading off the main tunnel. The tunnels each ran about ten yards and ended at double steel doors framed in a massive steel bulkhead that was concreted into the floor, ceiling and walls.

"I will need access to each of the inside rooms."

Abdulaziz again grudgingly nodded approval and signaled the guard to open the first room. Barnhart stepped inside the dimly lighted room and began a search using an IAEA-provided radiation detector. He systematically worked his way around the work benches and storage lockers finding no radiation sources above normal background.

From the scientific instrumentation equipment present on the benches, Barnhart assessed that this area was being used for diagnostic research. The diagnostics consisted of pins and time interval meters, conventional high pressure transducers that were calibrated with a hand operated hydraulic pump in a quasi-static mode and a simple photocell triggered time interval meter. Barnhart recognized that this equipment was probably used to support a number of experiments involving the measurement of plate velocity and the performance of warhead initiator components.

The inspection party then returned to the main tunnel, crossing it to enter a similar room on the other side. Upon entering the room Barnhart searched it with his IAEA radiation detector, again, finding nothing. This room contained sophisticated electronic test equipment, two oscilloscopes and an old IBM desktop computer. There were several experiments set up that had exposed breadboard wiring running to various electronic monitoring sets. Along one side of the room Barnhart recognized a high speed camera. He remembered that the Iraqis had declared two very fast electronic streak cameras to the IAEA back in 1991. At the time, the IAEA was evaluating their prohibition as part of the Iraqi weapon program. Such cameras were necessary for measuring bridge wire detonation time variation. These bridge wires were the type used to connect the detonators of an implosion-type nuclear weapon. The camera wasn't set up but it was there nonetheless and he understood what it meant. Barnhart noted the types of equipment present and photographed everything.

Abdulaziz led the way out of the room to the main tunnel crossing it to enter a third room. This room contained some power supplies, electronic switching devices and a pinhole camera for imaging X-ray spot size. Barnhart immediately recognized it to be a developmental effort toward a high energy flash X-ray system, the type of system necessary to conduct weapon penetrator and core tests.

"So, Doctor Abdulaziz, what are you building here?" Barnhart asked as innocently as he could make himself appear.

Abdulaziz grunted and looked away.

"I would hazard a guess that this is a simulation facility."

With a simulation facility the Iranian bomb researchers could get maximum confidence in their detonator timing and neutron output without actually exploding a test weapon. A simulation of this type would not only save valuable and limited special nuclear material but eliminate the tell-tale result of a nuclear test explosion that would undoubtedly be detected.

Barnhart smiled as he considered what he was observing. *Brilliant, simply brilliant!*

"I want to go to the next building."

It was obvious that Abdulaziz was nervous. This surprise IAEA scrutiny was something he didn't approve of and his program didn't need. He hadn't had adequate time to hide some of the critical elements of his weapon development program and he only hoped that the old scientist conducting the inspection would overlook them.

The inspection party emerged from the tunnel of Building 6 and walked left under the hot sun to the entry way of Building 7. The inspection party watched as the heavy metal roll-up door was raised, screeching and grinding to its full-up position. Abdulaziz again led the way, this time accompanied by two well armed military guards. The interior of this building was similar to Building 6. Except for a forklift, the loading dock inside had no vehicles in attendance, but the dock did have three large heavily constructed wooden crates on it that stood about ten feet high. Barnhart recognized the spray painted signage on the boxes which read "LEITZ 3-AXIS COORDINATE MEASURING MACHINE" stenciled in German and English. He also noted the shipping placard that revealed the shipment had come to Iran via Syria.

Upon entering the first room Barnhart noticed it had a higher ceiling than the rooms in Building 6. The brightly lighted room had well grounded receptacles and utilities. Machine foundations were present with anchoring bolts extending from the concrete floor. A large isostatic press was installed near the right wall and appeared to be operational. There were two automated machine lathes near the room's center, the type used to machine explosives. Barnhart searched the room for radiation with negative results, then immediately photographed everything. From the equipment present and the room's layout, Barnhart concluded that this room was dedicated to weapon fabrication. He nodded to Abdulaziz signaling that he had finished. The party moved to the next room without a word.

This room contained relatively crude light machining equipment and was clearly not designed to support nuclear metallurgy. From the equipment in this room Barnhart ascertained that it was dedicated to general support and beyond that its actual function, if it had one, was impossible to determine. Barnhart's inspection efficiency worried Abdulaziz. He had not expected this old scientist to move so thoroughly through the facility.

Barnhart motioned that he was going on to the next room. Abdulaziz followed a few steps behind with the two guards. The next room was completely empty. The smell of fresh paint was nearly overwhelming. Equipment foundations, grounded electrical outlets and utilities were all in place. Barnhart looked back at Abdulaziz, "What is this room for?" he questioned. Abdulaziz looked around as though he had never been inside the room before. "I think the penetrator program," he replied. Barnhart was familiar with the former Iraqi penetrator program from his post Gulf War IAEA inspections of the Al Atheer facility. The Iraqis had declared that they were developing a uranium armor penetrator. This looked very similar.

Barnhart knew that Armor penetrator design involves the use of a heavy metal core encased inside a conventional heavy machine gun bullet or artillery round. Most often, the metal of choice is depleted uranium, but any uranium metal will work. Following the Gulf War the IAEA inspection teams had discovered an inconsistency in the Iraqi claims and their records surrounding their Depleted Uranium Penetrator Program. Iraqi records showed that the scale of their penetrator program would have required about two-hundred and fifty tons of uranium metal a year. However, using the equipment they revealed to the IAEA inspectors, the Iraqis could only have been capable of producing a few hundred kilograms each year. Additionally, an unalloyed uranium metal penetrator is not as effective as one which is alloyed with other metals. This led the IAEA to believe that the penetrator program was a cover for something more sinister but it could never be proven.

So where did the two-hundred and fifty tons of uranium metal a year disappear to when the second Gulf War began, Barnhart wondered. *Iran? Here?*

Barnhart walked over to the freshly painted wall and took several swipes which he carefully placed inside small, individual hermetically sealed plastic bags for later analysis to see if any radioactive contamination residual was present. He doubted that any radioactivity would be found or, for that matter, that this particular room had been used for such a purpose. A quick radiation search around the room had provided negative results but laboratory analysis of the paint swipe would be conclusive.

"Let's go," he said. "I'm finished here."

Again the inspection party made their way back outside.

Hesitating outside the entrance of Building 7, Barnhart looked at the access road leading to the various underground buildings composing the sprawling desert facility. He saw that Buildings 6, 7 and 8 had well worn paths leading to their entrance ways. In contrast, he observed that Buildings 1, 2, 3, 4, and 5 had sand drifted against the roll-up doors and no sign of wheel tracks leading to them. Buildings 9 and 12 also showed no signs of use, but building 10 had fresh vehicle tracks running through the wind blown sand leading up to the closed steel door.

"Dr. Abdulaziz, I want to inspect that building over there," Barnhart said pointing to Building 10.

The look on Abdulaziz's face provided Barnhart with his answer. Barnhart began to walk toward Building 10. Abdulaziz quickly shuffled up to his side and grabbed his arm.

"Perhaps we should see Building 8 next," he quickly suggested to Barnhart.

"No, I want to go inside Building 10," Barnhart firmly replied.

Barnhart paused momentarily as he looked down at the hand clutching his arm, then back at Abdulaziz. Barnhart never liked being handled by anyone, much less a scumbag like Abdulaziz. With a contemptuous snort Barnhart yanked his arm away from Abdulaziz. Abdulaziz realized what he had just done and quickly released Barnhart's coat.

"Very well, I will comply," he said as he set off walking toward the entrance of Building 10.

Abdulaziz signaled the two guards who were sitting in a shadow at the entrance to open the door. As the heavy door clanked upward, retreating above, Barnhart entered the dark tunnel. This tunnel had a distinct downward gradient unlike the previous tunnels but it didn't make the characteristic curve to the right or left. It was dimly lighted by incandescent lights encased in explosive proof caged glass globes. Barnhart estimated that he had walked at least one hundred yards down the tunnel and was about ninety to one-hundred feet below the desert floor when the tunnel opened into a cavernous room. The room smelled like a city back alley with a disgustingly acidic odor of urine that permeated Barnhart's nostrils.

There were two massive loading docks with heavy lift cranes suspended above on ceiling mounted steel I-beam tracks. The tracks of both cranes led though thick steel blast doors into separate rooms. Using the radiation detector Barnhart scanned the large room. He detected no radiation above normal background.

"I want to go in there, please," he said pointing to the blast door on the left.

Abdulaziz nodded to the three soldiers escorting them. Two of the soldiers unlocked the steel dogs securing the heavy steel door to its frame and slowly pulled the creaking door open. Barnhart stepped up a narrow metal stairway onto the loading dock and made his way inside. Located directly behind the heavy blast doors, Barnhart came to a massive airlock. Once inside the airlock Barnhart and Abdulaziz suited up in white paper anti-contamination suits, or Anti-Cs as they were nicknamed, and then entered the room from the airlock. Barnhart immediately noted that the room was expansive and appeared to be reasonably sophisticated. Its compartmented design indicated a complete understanding of the principals of forming and handling radioactive materials.

The area was divided into smaller rooms with independent pressure differentials for contamination control. There were additional airlocks and several other anti-contamination change rooms. The work areas had multiple hood exhausts with redundant filter systems. One of the larger workrooms contained glove boxes for working on extremely radioactive contaminating sources. Barnhart knew he had hit pay dirt.

Using a spectroscopy ID unit concealed in his camera he immediately took a spectrum. Viewing through the camera detector's viewfinder he saw the presence of gamma and neutron emission.

Plutonium, he thought to himself.

Two automated machine lathes were running in one shop area. In an adjoining room a Leitz 3-axis coordinate measuring machine was being used by two technicians taking precise measurements on some freshly machined metals. Characterization instrumentation was being used in the next adjoining room. Barnhart knew that all this was for one thing - fissile metallurgy. He had finally located the heart of the Iranian nuclear weapon development program.

Barnhart returned to the entry airlock and discarded his paper anti-contamination outer garment and bootees. He said nothing to Abdulaziz. He left that room and headed for the room on the right. The steel blast door was opened and Barnhart entered. This area had no airlock but appeared to be divided into smaller work spaces like the first room. There was a small administrative office containing three desks immediately inside on the right, which was unoccupied. Barnhart paused in the doorway and casually glanced into the office. There was a chalkboard on the wall directly behind the center desk with Arabic writing and what he judged to be fire set sketches on it. Both Abdulaziz and the guard escorts were now several steps ahead of Barnhart. Barnhart quickly photographed the chalk board without them noticing.

Barnhart hastily inspected six smaller adjoining rooms inside the main room. It was clear from the type of equipment present that this area was being used for firing system development. On one of the work benches he saw special capacitors and krytrons typically used in nuclear weapon fire sets. While they appeared relatively crude and inefficient by U.S. nuclear weapon standards, Barnhart knew they would work well enough to detonate an implosion-type weapon.

It was in the last room that Barnhart discovered what he was searching for. This room contained three workbenches with sophisticated laboratory electronic test equipment on them. As Barnhart walked along the length of the second bench he noticed a wiring harness hanging on the wall behind the bench. There were dozens of multi-colored wires in the harness that had Russian language words intermittently printed in silver on the vinyl insulation along the wire's length. Although he had never before actually seen a real Russian made fire set up close and in person, the intelligence reports and HUMINT descriptions where sufficient. He was looking at the wiring harness that connected the fire set detonators to a Russian nuclear weapon. Barnhart wasn't entirely sure what particular warhead the wiring harness belonged to, but he was sure that he had just found the smoking gun.

Concealing his excitement, he continued his inspection and returned to the main room entrance. There, while photographing the room, he also took a spectrum.

"I am ready to go outside. This will conclude my inspection."

Abdulaziz, looking relieved, nodded in agreement and led the way back out the main access tunnel to the desert's glaring sun-baked sand.

By now the sun was low in the afternoon sky and the worst heat of the day had passed. The inspection party walked silently back to the small administration building at the entrance of the compound. Barnhart was deep in thought. If the fire set wiring harness he discovered in Building 10 was the one from the SS-19 warhead he was looking for, then he must assume that the Iranians had replaced it with an improvised version of their own. *That would probably make the warhead operable and therefore capable of a nuclear yield.* He needed to get the digital photos he took to Sandra for the Farsi translation and he needed to study the chalkboard drawings himself.

Inside the administration building he returned the security pass that had been issued to him earlier.

"Doctor Abdulaziz," Barnhart said, "I think we can forego the formalities. The IAEA will contact you through official channels within the next several days with specific questions, comments and findings, regarding this inspection. I want to thank you for your cooperation today. I am most pleased with my preliminary findings."

Barnhart almost choked on his words. He wanted to end the sentence by telling Abdulaziz that modifying rogue nukes to make them operable and placing a weapon like that in the hands of a terrorist group like Hamas or al Qaeda was beneath contempt. He desperately wanted to tell Abdulaziz that he wanted to shove that SS-19 up his ass, pointy end first, but he held his temper and smiled instead.

"Do you have any questions, Doctor Abdulaziz?" Barnhart patiently asked.

Abdulaziz stood by nervously without comment.

"Very well then, I have some distance to cover before night falls. Good afternoon."

Barnhart left the office and returned to his Wagoneer. He wasted no time departing the compound. As he drove away, he mentally reviewed his findings and assumptions. *The evidence shows that this weapon development facility is in its early stages and that it is indeed, a well financed effort underway in terms of facilities and equipment. But, where were the people who do the research; the technicians and the scientists? There was no fissile material, only minor traces of some and that had yet to be confirmed in the swipe and spectroscopy results. There was some evidence of initiator development, fissile metallurgy, firing and fusing systems development, and dedicated facilities for fabrication. There was even some evidence of other material science. And, certainly the SS-19 fire set wiring harness was a consistent and compelling piece of evidence.* Barnhart just couldn't put his finger on it but it just didn't feel right to him and that's why it was so unsettling. It all fit too perfectly with his mission to locate the rogue SS-19.

Barnhart returned to his hotel room several hours later and immediately downloaded the digital camera file and the spectroscopy data to his laptop. He set up the portable INMARSAT transceiver aiming the small lid antenna's face out of the window toward the satellite in high orbit above. He typed a brief message to Sandra and Boucher and the CIA's Langley headquarters explaining his findings. He then attached the file containing the digital photographs and the file containing the spectrums he took. He requested a full review and diagnostics with a twelve hour turn around.

Just before sending the message over the satellite, he stopped short of hitting the return key on the laptop. He sat back in his chair at the small wooden desk overlooking the window and frowned.

"No!" he said aloud. "It just doesn't make sense!"

With that he moved the computer cursor arrow back up to the addresses and deleted CIA Langley headquarters address. He hit the return key dispatching the message to Sandra and Boucher.

Barnhart switched the computer's program over to the digital picture files and found the one with the chalkboards he had photographed earlier in Building 10. He enlarged the drawing area and kept cropping and enlarging the picture until he had a view of the main drawing itself. As he carefully studied the drawing he began to understand what he was looking at. It was a carelessly sketched representation of the inner workings of a nuclear artillery round. The squiggly drawing of an electrical circuit with its components depicted a replacement fire set. The detail wasn't great but it accurately showed how the replacement fire set was designed and linked to the nuclear warhead firing components to make it operable.

He moved the cursor left to a smaller drawing and enlarged it. Barnhart studied its meaning as he stroked his chin in deep thought. All at once he straightened up abruptly. He now understood the squiggly drawings. The nuclear artillery round was linked to a radio firing device. The squiggly line that looked somewhat like a lightning bolt led to a depiction of a distant mountain. The nuclear artillery round was configured so that it could be remotely detonated. The only restriction was that the transmitter had to be in a line of sight to the receiver that was attached to the artillery round. That meant it could be detonated from any position and distance as long as there was no obstruction between the transmitter and receiver, a clear line of sight.

As he sat there studying the drawings Barnhart opened an MRE. He rummaged through the various foil food packets inside and tore open the dessert packet and began to eat the fruit cake. Meal ready to eat, or MRE for short, are the standard U.S. military issue field rations. Barnhart always carried four or five MREs in his bag for occasions when he was too busy to find a restaurant, or when a suitable food source simply wasn't available.

Still deep in thought, he was startled by his computer as it chirped, serving notice that a message had been received. Switching the computer back to "message review" he found a reply from Sandra waiting in his electronic mailbox. He opened the file and began to read it, unconsciously mumbling each word aloud:

/// FARSI NOTES ON MAIN DRAWING DISCUSSES ESTIMATED NUCLEAR YIELD OF BETWEEN FOUR TO SIX KILOTONS // WORDS MEANING "LINK" APPEAR BETWEEN THE MAIN DRAWING AND SMALLER DRAWING ON LEFT SIDE // TOWN OF ZAHIE IN THE BEQAA VALLEY IN LEBANON APPEARS ABOVE THE CENTER OF THE TWO DRAWINGS // PARTIALLY ERASED WORDS APPEARING ON RIGHT BOTTOM CONTAIN REFERENCE TO HAMAS MAY ALSO INDICATE IRANIAN GOV INVOLVEMENT // BARELY VISIBLE IS REFERENCE TO HEBRON (ISRAEL) // INTERROGATIVE, THOUGHT YOU FOUND SS-19 WIRING HARNESS // SUBJECT DRAWINGS SEEM TO BE FOCUSED ENTIRELY ON ARTILLERY NUKE // INTERROGATIVE, WHAT'S UP DOC // SANDRA ///

Barnhart immediately typed a reply to Sandra:

/// BELIEVE SS-19 FIRE SET WIRING HARNESS MAY BE DIVERSION FROM REAL PURPOSE OF BUILDING TEN // NOW BELIEVE FIRE SET ON FSU STOCKPILE ARTILLERY NUKE HAS BEEN SUCCESSFULLY REPLACED WITH RFD COMMAND DETONATION CAPABILITY // NEGATIVE INDICATION OF WORK ON SS-19 // SS-19 WIRING HARNESS WAS OUT OF PLACE // BELIEVE THERE MUST BE A SECOND NUKE INVOLVED // SUSPECT THAT SS-19 HAS NOT AND WILL NOT GO TO THIS FACILITY // REMAIN PUZZLED OVER POTENTIAL TARGET FOR ARTILLERY NUKE // UNODIR WILL CATCH FIRST AVAILABLE FLIGHT TO AMMAN // WILL RDVZ WITH YOU TOMORROW AFTERNOON AT PETRA HOTEL // CONTINUE SEARCH // GOOD HUNTING // BARNHART ///

Barnhart punched the return key sending the message secure over the INMARSAT. He finished eating his MRE and returned the communications equipment and computer to their carrying cases. The old man lay back in the small bed still fully clothed and fell instantly asleep surrendering to his fatigue.

Chapter 13

Amman, Jordan the next morning

Barnhart arrived in Amman via Royal Jordanian Airlines and rented a well worn Toyota van at the airport. He casually drove out of the airport and headed to Petra four hours south. Two other vans followed about a mile behind.

After parking his van in a small public parking lot just to the left of the Petra Hotel's lobby, he supervised as a bellhop brought the two suitcases containing his communications and radiation search equipment inside the lobby. Just as he finished checking in, a hand patted his shoulder from behind. He turned without surprise to see Boucher walk past and head toward the elevator.

Barnhart tipped the bellhop and took the wheeled cart containing his equipment in tow, following Boucher onto the elevator. As the doors closed, Barnhart smiled over at Boucher.

"It's good to see you, Jake."

The two shook hands.

"Where's Sandra?"

"She's waiting upstairs in her room. When do you want to meet?"

"I'm in room thirty-one. Give me a few minutes to tap my kidneys."

Boucher pushed the button for floor three, still smiling widely at Barnhart's definition of taking a whiz. He stood with his back against the

131

side of the elevator so that anyone looking directly in the open doors would have difficulty seeing him. This was an old habit he had developed over the years as a means of protecting himself from someone rushing him as the elevator doors opened. It had actually saved his life many years before when two knife wielding robbers rushed an elevator he was riding in a downtown Cairo hotel. By standing along the side wall, instead of the back of the elevator car like most people do, he was out of the line of attack. This provided him just enough time to push past his attackers and exit the elevator. He realized that Barnhart was standing at the back of the elevator car facing the doors directly in the line of attack should one surprise them, so he made a mental note to pass this technique along as soon as he could. The elevator's chime sounded and the doors opened at floor three.

"See you in a few," he mumbled back at Boucher.

As he stepped out of the elevator Barnhart noted a man sitting in a wicker chair along the wall across from the elevator doors. He had a full beard and was dressed in traditional Arab dress. He was reading an Arabic newspaper and didn't seem to care about, or notice, Barnhart leaving the elevator. Barnhart didn't find the man's looks or behavior to be suspicious in nature, but he took a good look at the man's face and committed that picture to memory nonetheless.

After checking up and down the hallway to see if he was followed, he entered his room carefully closing the door behind him. He immediately went about stacking his communications equipment neatly next to the window. He slowly opened the window drapes just a little at first and peered out at the steep stony slope rising up behind the houses across the street. After studying the surrounding area and satisfying himself there was no suspicious activity, he opened the drapes fully. He then used the bathroom and washed his face. The water had a peculiar sulfur-swamp smelling odor but its coolness soothed his aging skin. Standing in front of the bathroom mirror he observed himself for a few seconds. He then put his finger on the mirror and checked to see if there was a reflected gap between his finger and his reflection. He saw that there was which assured him that that the mirror was not instead one-way glass.

"Another fine mess you got me into," he mumbled to his image in the mirror.

As he walked from the bathroom three knocks came from the door and a familiar voice.

"Si, it's Sandra and me. Open up."

Barnhart recognized Boucher's voice and eased the door open.

"Come on in," he said with a smile.

Boucher, Barnhart and Sandra stood at a small wooden table located in the corner next to a small TV in Barnhart's hotel room. Sandra leaned over and turned on the TV, adjusting the volume to about the same level as normal voice conversation.

"Let's sit," Barnhart said motioning toward the table. "Okay, let's review the bidding and try to figure out where we are on this. You two came up with a dry hole here in Petra. The radiation spectra I took at Semnan revealed that the source was non-fissile and was likely placed there as a decoy to divert attention away from the real thing. My investigation at Semnan yielded some hard data but nothing conclusive. I found what I believe to be the fire set wiring harness of an SS-19. It was there in plain view. I couldn't have missed it. It didn't fit. Beyond some minor indicators, there was no evidence of plutonium work in or around the facility. I photographed the drawing of the artillery nuke on a chalk board in Building 10. This is the drawing that showed a radio firing device design for remote firing. It also had references to Syria, Hebron, and Zahie that were partially erased. The swipes I took in the freshly painted room still require analysis to see if there was any SNM present. The agent I was working with in Tehran tipped me about a second nuke. The Agency has thus far only focused on the SS-19. Why? They should have been aware of the second nuke possibility and warned us. Something smells about this whole mission but I just can't put my finger on it."

Barnhart slumped back in his chair. The three sat momentarily in silence.

"I think there are two nukes, maybe three," Sandra commented. "I think one of them we're supposed to find and the others we're not supposed to find. My concern is that our search so far has taken us beyond anything the Agency briefed us on or expected us to do. I think we have provided some surprises to someone. But, I'm not sure to whom."

Barnhart nodded in agreement as he contemplated her statement and then offered his own opinion.

"I believe there are several dynamics involved here. First, Si, you told me of your experience back in the eighties when you had a smoking gun that could have indicated the U.S. was in complicity with Israel involving Israel's attack on Iraq's Tuwaitha reactor facility. Your information, even though credible, was discredited. Our boy Hann was a key player. This operation, in my opinion, has many of the same inconsistencies. Hann found you again - this time to do another dirty job. And, it seems that the intelligence we were provided was incomplete and perhaps, even misleading."

Boucher looked over at Sandra then back at Barnhart.

"Think about it," Boucher whispered. "Our team consists of a CIA Case Officer with a WMD technical background, a former Nuclear Emergency Support Team qualified retired SEAL commander who doesn't need a job and a Los Alamos nuclear weapon designer. We have been attempting to chase down an SS-19 nuclear warhead alleged to be destined for Iran or other nearby location. Our action has been based on information that was provided by the CIA. You have discovered, quite by chance, the high probability of a second nuke destined perhaps for Syria or Lebanon or maybe even Israel, but no one can nail it down. So far the facts show that the nuke we were sent to find is probably nowhere close to Iran. If anything, it's probably here in Jordan. If my analysis of this situation is even partially close, I would hypothesize that we are all being used to further someone else's hidden agenda. Si, I don't think we're supposed to find anything. I think we are supposed to lend credibility to the chase and as such, report the events as they are revealed to us. We are pawns in a bigger game. This whole thing is a charade and we are expected to be unwitting players."

Sandra took a deep breath.

"I think you make a good point, Jake. We need to take control of our situation and react based upon our own experience. We need to assume that there are two or more rogue nukes out there somewhere. We need to find them and stop them. We cannot assume that our communications with Langley are even being monitored by the right people. While I hesitate to suggest a conspiracy's involved here, I must admit that it appears there is a conspiracy of some order influencing these events and subsequently, our actions. I think the source of the SS-19 can ultimately be validated through intelligence channels. The source of the nuke artillery round is a mystery to me and might also be a mystery to the Agency analysts who are attempting to validate its existence. If there are indeed additional nukes involved, I'd like to know where the hell they came from. They're obviously not stockpile nukes provided by the black market. I don't get it and I can't explain it."

Sandra stopped in mid-sentence as a special BBC news report flashed onto the television screen. The picture showed an Israeli jet bombing a Hamas terrorist stronghold at Zahie in Lebanon.

"This is Timothy Levee-Cline live with BBC News for a Breaking News Report. Moments ago the Israeli Defense Force began air strikes against Hamas terrorist strongholds in retaliation for the rocket attacks last week that struck the Israeli West Bank settlement of Kiryat Shmona and took the lives of ten school children, three teachers and wounded scores of other Israeli civilians."

The TV picture showed a distant Israeli F-16 jet rolling in on its target below. Just before reaching the bottom of the attack arc the jet released several bombs. Then with full afterburner visibly flaming from its tail, it pulled up and climbed almost straight up. Several white-hot flares were ejected from the jet as a countermeasure to decoy shoulder-fired heat-seeking anti-aircraft rockets that the Hamas defenders would inevitably fire at the attacking planes.

A second jet rolled in, streaking nose down in a near vertical decent as the pilot lined up on the target below. The bomb release could easily be seen through the BBC television camera's powerful telephoto lens. The bomb looked like a small black speck falling towards the village below. As it disappeared beneath the rooftops, a horrendous explosion bellowed up, enveloping the retreating jet that had just made the attack. The reporter narrating on the scene exclaimed in astonishment.

"My God! They've finally done it! The Israelis have dropped a nuclear bomb! Oh my God! This is war! This is war! Oh my God!"

Barnhart knew exactly what he was seeing. The initial prompt of the nuclear detonation ringed outward, appearing like a blue-white colored flash. The high velocity blast shockwave could be seen ripping buildings in its path to shreds at mach speed as it radiated away from ground zero. The superheated plasma in the center of the detonation had instantaneously vaporized everything within a five hundred meter radius and was now billowing upward to form the characteristic mushroom cloud.

Barnhart estimated that the television camera crew was located about a quarter of a mile from the explosion. From the BBC's camera perspective he guessed that the crew was probably filming from the side of a hill above the blast area. They would be vulnerable to the lethal gamma radiation resulting from the blast and probably, because of their position, suffer the shock wave effects. His assumption was accurate. The blast shock wave could be seen moving toward the reporter who never finished his sentence. He was in the middle of another "My God!" when the transmission abruptly ended and the broadcast went to static.

"Oh shit!" Barnhart gasped. "From those pictures I would put that yield to be about a kiloton, or maybe like something in the sub-kiloton range. And, it detonated at ground level. I can't believe the Israelis went nuclear."

"That had to be the artillery round," Sandra softly commented. "That Israeli jet didn't drop a nuke. The nuke was already there. It was just made to look like the Israeli jet dropped that nuke. The Israelis don't have a weapon that small in their inventory."

Boucher interrupted, "Sandra, how do you know that?"

Kennedy Irregular Warfare Center, ONI, Suitland, MD, the same time

"Captain Blackford, I think we're solidly onto this," Lieutenant Bruce reported.

Blackford smiled proudly at his young officer. "Okay, Lieutenant, let's hear what you got."

"Well, Captain, the deeper we dig, the more dots we seem to connect. It appears there is someone somewhere inside the intelligence community who knows about those loose nukes. I think the intel we're getting is somehow being manipulated."

"Lieutenant, you continue to amaze me. How many nukes are we talking about?"

"Sir, we have ELINT and HUMINT that alludes to at least two. But I think there could be more because what I'm seeing is inconsistent across the board with regard to total numbers."

"Anything on where they came from, their design, or yield capabilities?"

"That's what I find so interesting about this, Sir. It seems that at least one of them is a former Soviet Union missile warhead. We're seeing intercepts that suggest it might be an SS-19. That's a warhead off an inter-continental ballistic missile. It's a city buster, Sir, probably in the one-hundred megaton range, maybe larger. The other nuke is a total mystery. We haven't been able to determine what it is. All we keep seeing is that it's referred to as 'God's gift' and it will be used in the same attack. Now, more than ever, I think their reference to 'golden bird' is a direct reference to the Canary Islands. There was one obscure reference to La Palma. Perhaps La Palma is the target."

"But La Palma, Lieutenant? Why attack an island that is little more than an extinct volcano?"

Blackford rolled his chair away from his desk and rocked backward lacing his hands behind his head as if he was trying to ease the pain.

"What's the Agency have to say about this?"

"They have access to all the same intel we do and they're telling us there is one nuke and the likely target is Israel. Frankly, Sir, I don't get it."

"Yeah, it's the kind of bullshit that makes your fucking teeth itch."

"Yes, Sir, it sure does."

"Alright, I'm gonna make some phone calls to some trusted old friends and try to ferret this out. Stay on top of this, Lieutenant. You and your team are doing a shit-hot job!

"Aye-aye, Sir. Thank you, Sir."

The lieutenant left Blackford's office. Blackford picked up his secure telephone and dialed his secretary.

"Gene, please get Admiral Thornberg on a secure line for me."

Blackford and Thornberg had twice served together in the early eighties as SEAL officers in the ward rooms of SEAL Team Two and Naval Special Warfare Unit One. They knew each other well, both professionally and socially. They shared a mutual trust and had relied upon one another for the unabashed bottom line on numerous occasions - occasions that counted.

Blackford's phone buzzed.

"Captain, Admiral Thornberg is on line one."

Blackford smiled widely as he picked up the phone.

"Jim, it's Dean, thanks for taking my call. Listen, I need to run something by you that I think you may want to look into."

Chapter 14

Petra, Jordan

Sandra had tears streaming down her cheeks as she stared across the table at Boucher. Barnhart took Sandra's hand and placed it fatherly in his.

"What can you tell us?" he gently questioned.

"Think about it," she said wiping a shiny tear from her cheek. "A radio firing device on the modified nuke artillery round. Terrorists attack the Israelis and kill a bunch of women and children. You link the attack to an Iranian state supported fundamentalist terrorist group like Hamas. You know the Israelis will retaliate. You pre-position a nuke that can be command detonated in a location all intelligence indicators point to. You insure that CNN or BBC is present to record the attack. The Israelis strike what they think is the origin of the rocket attack against them in retaliation and boom! They command detonate the nuke making it look like the Israelis dropped it. The world thinks Israel resorted to nukes against a notorious terrorist enemy whom Iran supports. The terrorists think the Israelis did it. The world thinks the Israelis did it and probably, a lot of Israelis think the Israelis did it. But then intelligence reveals that the nuke wasn't dropped by the Israelis and it was really a terrorist nuke on its way to be used against Israel. It just fortunately went off before it got there. And at that point Iran is screwed any way you look at it! World opinion will unquestionably shift in favor of the Israelis right of self defense and support an attack on Iran. Once everyone figures out

138

what really happened, Israel will have attacked and neutralized Iran's nuclear weapon development complex. And it's a done deal."

"Who is 'they', Sandra?" Barnhart gently queried.

"They are Mossad. They intended to have a faction of Hamas gain control of the artillery nuke and then explode it during an Israeli strike to make it look like it detonated as a result of the attack. Iran will get the word that Hamas had control of it."

"But isn't this all a very elaborate and risky conspiracy to do what is otherwise obvious – attack Iran to stop their weapon program?"

"In my opinion it's a perfect way to both stop the peace process between Israel and the Palestinians and put Iran back in their box once and for all. The Israelis don't want a Hamas-linked Palestinian homeland on their soil and neither does the Agency. It endangers regional security. And Iran – well, how many times have you heard Iran threaten that once it has nukes it will use them to wipe Israel off the face of the planet? The U.S. Navy is currently posturing for a major offensive against Iran and the President will surely order a strike if Iran counterattacks Israel."

"I understand what you're suggesting about framing Iran, but I don't think any U.S. agency would ever knowingly allow a terrorist organization to gain control of a nuke. They may have briefed it to you like that but I don't believe for a second that Mossad or the CIA would allow a terrorist group to get custody of a working nuke just to command detonate it as part of a conspiracy to frame Iran."

Boucher interrupted, "You're right, Si. I'll bet they had the real nuke pre-positioned and they gave Hamas a decoy. So, Sandra, what's the plan for the SS-19 and where is it?"

"I wish I knew," Sandra frowned.

Boucher stared at Sandra.

"So, Sandra, why did you do it? Why did you string us along and risk our lives?"

"I had to," she replied as the tears threatened to reappear.

"You had to?"

"Yes, damn it! I had to!"

"Okay, why did you have to?"

Sandra shifted uneasily in her chair.

"Right after I joined the Agency I was assigned to the Incident Response Team. Hann headed the IRT for about two years. Well, we became very close and…"

Boucher finished her sentence. "You slept with Hann?"

"Yes," Sandra replied, her voice quivering. Boucher sat back in disgust.

"So you and Hann…?"

Sandra nodded *yes* as she sniffed and attempted to regain her composure.

"There's more," Sandra said as she raised her head to look at Barnhart. "The agent that you were working with in Tehran, well, she's my sister. Hann promised to bring her out with you. She's been there since the Gulf War and the Iranians are getting very close to her. I'm afraid she won't make it now."

"Your sister?" both Barnhart and Boucher said in astonished unison.

"I thought she was a man," Barnhart whispered. "I'm so sorry, Sandra," Barnhart said patting Sandra's hand. "Sandra, we need to find the SS-19. That is the threat we now need to concentrate on and we must prevent it from being detonated. Did it indeed arrive in Aqaba as we were told?"

Sandra nodded, "As far as I know the intel is valid."

Barnhart's concentration seemed to drift momentarily. It was obvious that he was trying to analyze the situation.

"It may be here in Petra," he mumbled. "It was the Agency that said it was on its way to Amman. We need to continue the search today. Let's get our equipment and meet in the parking lot at the tourist center in say, twenty-five minutes. We'll go in from there."

Sandra nodded agreement and left the room. Barnhart tugged on Boucher's shirt signaling him to stay behind. After Sandra had closed the door Barnhart turned to face Boucher.

"Jake, she has been used in this game the same as we have. Don't hold it against her. I happen to believe that her volunteering to tell us the truth, after she realized that she was being used to further a hidden agenda speaks very highly of her character. If I were you, I wouldn't discount that. She's a keeper. See you in twenty minutes."

Barnhart turned away from Boucher and started rummaging through his equipment, putting the necessary field equipment in his daypack. Boucher stood without comment for a moment staring at Barnhart's back before leaving the room.

Barnhart placed his Iridium satellite phone in the outer pouch of his daypack for easy access. The phone was small, concealable and if secure communications were required between him and Sandra, who also had one, it would do nicely. Barnhart returned to his van which was still parked in front of the hotel and threw his daypack on the front seat. As he started the engine, he noticed that same Arab man he had seen earlier in the elevator lobby sitting outside on a wooden bench next to the hotel's front door. The man was contentedly reading the newspaper. Barnhart still found this man to

140

be acting normally, but his suspicion was elevated slightly because the man had changed locations and was still reading the paper apparently oblivious to what was going on around him.

Barnhart drove the six blocks through town along the narrow street to the Petra Visitor's Center parking lot and immediately got out of his car, dragging his daypack across the front seat to the driver's side. He momentarily fumbled with the strap adjustments and finally pulled the pack off the seat just as Boucher and Sandra arrived. They parked several spaces away along the circular area in front of the building where the taxi cabs usually waited. They exited their car and put on small daypacks. They looked like any other tourist couple. Sandra was wearing aviator style dark sunglasses and was dressed in khaki slacks with a loose fitting, off-white cotton shirt. Boucher had wraparound sunglasses and was wearing blue jeans and a gray T-shirt. Both had cameras hanging from their necks. Barnhart watched them put on their day packs and walk toward the Petra ticket gate entrance. He casually slung his pack over his left shoulder and followed well behind.

The three didn't link up until they entered the narrow canyon leading into ancient Petra. Boucher and Sandra stopped by an enclave along the steep red rock wall and waited for Barnhart to catch up.

"Hey, Si," Boucher said, "how do you think we should do this?"

"Well for a starter, I would appreciate it if you kids would stop running and start talking to each other again."

He was breathing heavily and had begun to sweat from the exertion of walking on the loose gravel wash in the intense afternoon heat.

"Ah sorry, I guess I got carried away," Boucher replied apologetically without acknowledging Sandra.

Barnhart smiled as he again thought to himself what a good looking couple they made. If he were thirty years younger he'd be chasing a beauty like Sandra and science would not be the motive. He was really very proud of them both. Even if he could have hand picked his colleagues for this mission he couldn't have done any better. In fact, he was damn proud of them.

"Okay, I think we need to get up high so we can observe the area below. We can cover nearly the entire area that way and if we see anything suspicious we can go down and check it out."

The three journeyed about a half mile down the Petra canyon to the coliseum where a steep granite path led to the plateau above. The path, composed of well weathered stairs and steeply inclined ramps, was hand-chiseled into the side of the rock face. Over the millennium its more exposed areas had been severely eroded from exposure to the elements and fractured by several earthquakes. All in all, the path was a treacherous climb. The three of them began the arduous ascent with Barnhart in the lead. Sandra followed and Boucher brought up the rear.

Barnhart was breathing heavily. About halfway to the top, he began to speak between gulping breaths.

"Someone command-detonated that nuke in Zahie. The Israelis didn't drop it. That was not an Israeli weapon. It was just made to look like the Israelis dropped it during the air strike. Could the Israelis have intentionally sacrificed Zahie to justify their attack against Iran and at the same time generate unquestionable U.S. military support should Iran counterattack Israel? Now Amman is the target of a SS-19 warhead and it's being made to look like Iranian retaliation when in fact, someone else – a third party - may really be manipulating the whole thing. As a radical Moslem fundamentalist state, Iran will support the retaliation motive and provide additional justification to unite the Islamic states against Israel and the West. Nuking Amman has got to be a frame job against Jordan. That's why it's here. Someone wants the Government of Jordan and the stability it brings to the region eliminated. Meanwhile, the Government of Iran will distance itself politically from the method of the attack. That will drive even more world opinion against Israel and at the same time eliminate Jordan as a friend to Israel and the U.S. and as a potential threat to Iran. If Israel or any other nation retaliates it will be against Iran or maybe Syria which will very likely change the regional balance of power in Iran's favor. The whole Arab world will be behind Iran in support of the Palestinian homeland and aspirations on the Gaza Strip and Israeli-secured areas of the West Bank. Iran doesn't want Israel's real estate. They want Israel eliminated."

Neither Boucher nor Sandra commented. Barnhart hesitated as he puffed his lungs full of air.

"Sandra, I'd be interested in hearing your thoughts. I think we both know we can't go to the CIA Director of Operations with a recommended course of action based upon opinion."

Sandra paused momentarily to throw a quick non-committal glance at the acclaimed scientist who was sweating and puffing even harder now from talking during the steep climb. She marveled at his resilience and stamina.

Barnhart was so distracted by his attempt to figure out the problem that he carelessly lost his balance and fell backward. Sandra grabbed for his shirt but was unable to hold on. Gazing upward, Barnhart sprawled onto his back, bounced slightly and began rolling over the side. Short of his eyes widening, the expression on his face never changed from deep thought to surprise. Just as he began the irreversible tumble over the side a strong hand grasped his ankle, stopping him in mid-fall. Barnhart's downward momentum slammed him into the rock face as he now hung upside down by one ankle. He let out a gasp and at this point it seemed as though he finally grasped what had just happened. Above, Boucher lay face down on the rock stairs holding Barnhart's right ankle in his left hand.

"Hold on Si, I got yah! Sandra, give me a hand and we'll pull him back up."

Barnhart groaned as he peered straight down at the canyon floor sixty feet below.

"So Sandra," he asked coolly, "should we give the COS in Amman a call?"

Department of Energy Headquarters, Germantown, MD, the same time

Personnel Security Specialist Nancy McAllister's job was to screen the files for security clearance applicants. She was the first tier review and would either recommend that an applicant's file be further adjudicated or that a person be granted the Department of Energy's coveted Q-clearance. A Q-clearance means that its holder has access to nuclear weapon design and operating details. McAllister's supervisor, Tina West, stopped by to discuss a case file that McAllister had reviewed a week earlier and had "red flagged" for further action. Entering the vault-like office area where McAllister worked, West pushed the heavy steel door closed behind her, latching it with a loud metallic clank.

"Nancy, I want to discuss your review of the Cohen file."

"Sure, Tina. Have a seat while I grab the file." McAllister pulled the file in question from a five drawer safe located by her desk and opened the folder for West to see.

"Okay, give me the bottom line on Cohen and don't pull any punches."

"You got it," McAllister replied to her senior. "Ruth Cohen has been a Department of Energy contract employee for the past six years. She began her employment at Sandia National Lab where she was granted a Q-clearance. She transferred to the Department's Washington, DC headquarters four years ago on a small business contract that was won by the company she heads. Her husband is Iranian-born. They apparently met at Berkeley while he was doing his post-doctoral study and she was an undergrad. He became a Foreign Service Officer at the Department of State for a number of years and was primarily posted in the Middle East."

"Okay, I got all that. Where's the beef?"

"Ruth Cohen got her Q-clearance using her maiden name, not her husband's name."

"So what? Lot's of women keep their own name these days."

"Well, when I interviewed her last week she told me that her husband, Mark Hann, alias Mahmoud Haniyeh, is a naturalized U.S. citizen. He legally changed his name right after he got citizenship."

"Okay, what's the big deal?"

"She said he has a valid Iranian passport and that he travels to Iran several times a year to visit his family. I pulled his file and compared his clearance background data to his wife's. Get this, Tina, he renounced his citizenship to Iran the year he started his Ph.D. in Nuclear Engineering at Berkley. In fact, he became a U.S. naturalized citizen the same year. That means he absolutely should not have a valid Iranian passport. Secondly, the company that Ruth Cohen heads employs two Iranian-born naturalized citizens and Hann is listed as a part owner. Third, Hann had a record of delinquent and unpaid bills for years up to the point when his wife started her company and won the DOE contract. All of a sudden he had enough money to pay off a car loan of forty-six thousand and two credit cards totaling thirty-one thousand. They also remodeled their home without taking a second mortgage to the tune of over one-hundred thousand dollars and bought a boat for forty-six thousand. I researched his travel outside the U.S. and it seems he traveled to Paris using his U.S. passport eleven times over the last four years. And, since France is in bed with Iran he likely used his Iranian passport to fly from there to Iran."

"Damn. That's not good!"

"It gets worse. I asked Ruth Cohen for the dates when he traveled to Iran. She gave me approximate timeframes and one of them correlates closely with Hann's sudden accumulation of wealth. Tina, I think he's selling our nuclear weapon secrets to the Iranians."

"Oh shit! Do you think Mrs. Cohen knows what he's up to?"

"No, I think she's unwitting. I asked her if she had ever accompanied him to Iran and she said she hadn't. She said she doesn't even have a passport. I checked her out with Consular Affairs at the State Department and she's telling the truth. She's never had a passport in her entire life."

"What does her company do for DOE?"

"They support the NNSA Office of Defense Nuclear Nonproliferation – NA-20. Their mission is to detect, prevent, and reverse the proliferation of weapons of mass destruction, while mitigating the risks from nuclear operations."

"Damn! Where does Hann work at State?"

"He doesn't work at State anymore. He transferred over to the CIA about the same time his wife started her company and he now works for the CIA's Operations Directorate. According to the DO, his shop is involved

144

in tracking Iran's capacity to manufacture pits for nuclear weapons. He regularly visits X-division at Los Alamos National Lab and you know what X division does."

"No, actually, I only know what they do in very general terms."

"Well let's just say that X-division does the nuclear weapon design experimental physics necessary to both guarantee bomb operational surety as well as disablement of a rogue weapon. They are the center of mass for all weapon design data - both ours and everyone else's."

"So you're saying he has perfect access to how nukes are designed and function and how we keep them ready to use?"

"Exactly."

"Not good! Not good!"

"There might be more but it's just a gut feeling."

"Shoot. I need to hear everything."

"You remember a few years ago when a Los Alamos employee by the name of Debra Alderson was caught with her laptop at home and its' hard drive contained extremely sensitive weapon design data?"

"Of course I remember. The FBI investigated and as I recall they determined there was no nuclear weapon data compromise. As I remember, she was fired but not prosecuted. Didn't she have a drug and alcohol abuse problem?"

"That's right, but Hann's wife told me that he had a close friend that he always stayed with when he visited Los Alamos. I got copies of both his office telephone and e-mail records. He was calling and e-mailing Alderson regularly for over three years prior to her demise. That correspondence indicates that he was staying with her when he visited Los Alamos. She must have been the friend his wife was referring to. I think he was having an affair with her and the secrets she brought home from the lab were handed off to him."

"So you're saying he got weapon design data from her and passed it on to the Iranians?"

"Yes, that's exactly what I think he did."

"Jezzz, Nancy!"

"Yup. And his wife still has access to the technologies we employ to detect and prevent bad actors like Iran from gaining nuclear materials necessary to develop nuke weapons. What do you think their dinner conversations are like? She has two kids by him. I think he's playing her like a harp."

"Damn fine work, Nancy. It sounds like he's a fox in the henhouse. Before we set up any further interviews with Mrs. Cohen, let's get this to Counterintelligence."

Petra, Jordan

Reaching the top, the three of them sat down to catch their breath. Sandra and Boucher watched the area below as Barnhart, now breathing more normally, continued his one-sided debate.

"How do I think they'll transport it without detection? That's of course assuming that Amman or Israel is indeed the target."

Barnhart questioned as though he was debating it with Boucher and Sandra. He thought for a moment before replying to his own question.

"I'm not sure, because there are a variety of ways to mask the radiation signature. I suspect that a depleted uranium or lead-lined shipping container would work except it would be extremely large and heavy, especially with a weapon inside. That would require a large truck and a means to conceal the shipping container, which would be nearly impossible if not out of the question. It would easily be detected at a highway inspection check point."

Barnhart, now in deep thought appeared to not even hear Sandra's analysis.

"Because of the warhead's gross weight it has to be transported by truck. The truck has to be nondescript. You know - something common and indigenous. It has to possess not only radiation shielding qualities but must also have the means to conceal the nuke from inspection. A pig-type transport container is too heavy and large. What else would provide the appropriate level of shielding from radiation detection and at the same time provide concealment from border inspection?"

Boucher slowly stood and unbuttoned his top three shirt buttons.

"Back in 1996 while I was still the NEST director we supported the summer Olympics in Atlanta. The University of Georgia had an extremely large Cobalt 60 source that they used for sterilization research, among other things. They stored it at the bottom of a twenty foot deep pool of water which provided the necessary radiation shielding. The authorities were afraid that terrorists might gain access to the pool and create a radiological incident during the games, so they opted to secure the source inside a locked shipping container and left it all at the bottom of the pool."

Boucher slowly sat down and rested back against his backpack.

"I found that interesting, because the scientists I worked with said the additional shielding in the shipping container was unnecessary because the water was sufficient to adequately shield the source. I remember asking them if a weapon could be detected if it was submerged. They said that a weapon, if surrounded by several feet of water, would be virtually invisible to the state-of-the-art detection equipment and..."

Sandra interrupted him in mid-sentence. "And all you would need to do is put the RV inside a tank truck filled with water. Maybe float a couple of feet of diesel fuel on top of the water so if the hatch is opened for inspection, you'd see and smell fuel. Then, drive the truck through the checkpoint along with the hundreds of other fuel trucks that cross the border on a daily basis. And, you're home free." She slapped Boucher on the shoulder as if she was delivering the punch line of a joke.

Barnhart listened in amazement. His two colleagues appeared to have found a plausible solution to his question.

"Yes!" Barnhart announced. "Yes, it could be done! It would work! I can see no other means available. Yes, this is what we should now focus on. We should look for a tank truck coming from Petra on Highway 65. The route will probably take it west across the Dead Sea to Gnor, then north to Arad. From that point they can get it to the Golan Heights vicinity using a variety of infiltration avenues. I think we should assume that a new fire set has been successfully installed or that the original one has been modified to work. We must stop it before it can be taken across the Dead Sea to the West Bank. Jake, can you get your team moving on that now?"

Boucher inserted himself into Barnhart's one-sided conversation.

"I don't like it!"

"You don't like what?" Sandra asked.

"I don't like assuming that the target is Israel. There's just too much historical baggage in this region to make that assumption."

Sandra winced at Boucher as if challenging him to elaborate. Barnhart sat quietly, waiting to hear what Boucher had to say.

"Let's review this evolution a moment. This area is the crossroad of three continents. During the Cold War this turf was critical to the superpowers' defense. The U.S. pumped millions of dollars in aid to nearly every country in this area at one time or another - and that's what we know about. What about the 'black operations' and stuff like Ollie North was up to that we don't know about? This area just isn't as important to the U.S. or anyone else anymore because it lost its' strategic value when the Cold War ended. So the real question is who gives a shit now and why? Who is willing to risk nuclear war over this turf and what makes the risk worth it? The Iranians would risk it because they have openly said they would sacrifice their country for Islam. I can't believe that Israel or Jordan would risk it, so who's behind this, Iran, Mossad, the U.S.?"

Barnhart stirred, "Jordan and Israel have been at peace for years and Jordan has led the Arab world as a model of peaceful co-existence with Israel."

Boucher continued, "When they get wind of this, the Jordanians will shit bricks, maybe even panic and unwittingly draw world attention to the problem which will greatly complicate a successful resolution. That would likely generate immediate Israeli intervention that could expand to open conflict between Israel and Jordan."

"Maybe we need to bring in the Nuclear Emergency Support Team," Barnhart suggested.

"No, Si, NEST is out of the question because they deploy with so many people and so much equipment they require significant logistic support at their destination. In turn, this creates an unacceptable deployment signature which usually compromises the on-scene operation. Remember, NEST deploys from the U.S., so the time-distance problem involved in getting them packed up, underway and here means they won't get here in time to do much of anything. The party will be over by the time they get here."

"How about the Russians?"

"The Russians will either totally deny that the SS-19 is their warhead or invade southern Jordan until they recover it with or without the permission of the Jordanian government."

"Regardless, Israel remains the wild card to all of these courses of action," Sandra stated. "They will hammer the crap out of anyone or anything, especially after this morning's attack, if they even suspect someone is threatening them. I can't go to the Agency with any of these courses of action."

"You're right, Sandra," Boucher replied. "We need a course of action that will get the job done with a high probability of success, something that doesn't put the U.S. in the middle. We need plausible denial."

Barnhart nodded, "I suppose we have the talking done. We will just have to find that warhead and render it safe. Thank you for the good input. I think we should begin," he said pointing across the valley below, "at those large tombs over there. They're all easily accessible from the gravel road and large enough to conceal a warhead. Let's go to work."

The three walked silently in the darkness across the flat summit of Attuf Ridge and began the climb back down to the Roman Theater below. It seemed to be almost appropriate that Petra's High Place of Sacrifice, one of the most well-preserved and sacred places remaining of the ancient Nabataean creators of Petra, would be the location from which this seemingly desperate operation would stem.

The Urn Tomb was located to the left of the Royal Tombs about eight hundred meters across the gorge below. They would have to cross the main road running through Petra and then make a short climb to the tombs. Boucher was relieved that at least there was no moon visible. Moving slowly between the shadows of the rocks, the three slowly made their way towards the opposing canyon wall. The Royal Tombs looked even more imposing in the waning starlight than they did in the daytime because of the ominous shadows they cast. Sandra was in the lead about fifteen feet ahead of Barnhart, making her way around a jutting rock when she froze. Barnhart instinctively did likewise. Boucher was only trailing a few feet behind Barnhart and followed the old man's example.

They were only a few hundred yards from the multiple ground level passageways leading into the Urn Tomb. Sandra slowly pressed her body against the rock face, blending her silhouette into the shadows of the rock. Barnhart pulled Boucher over to his side and pointed ahead towards Sandra. Boucher nodded and slowly moved forward to a position behind her. Boucher noticed that she was holding a silenced automatic pistol in her right hand. Until now he hadn't realized that she was armed.

"What's up?" he whispered in her ear.

"There are two men sitting in that shadow over there by the left entrance. I need my night vision scope in the right pocket of my pack."

Boucher slowly unzipped the pocket and removed what looked like a telephoto camera lens and carefully put it in Sandra's left hand. With her index finger she turned a small ring on the rear of the scope switching it on. She then raised it to her left eye and began viewing the two men sitting in the shadows. Sandra carefully scanned the area above the men in search of others. She could find none. She turned slightly toward Boucher whispering as she handed him the scope.

"Check out the cliffs above the tombs."

Boucher took the scope and began to inspect the ledges above for human forms and signs of movement. Sandra stepped backward between Boucher and Barnhart.

"Okay, gentleman," she whispered, "we need to get inside that tomb and conduct a search."

Boucher handed the night vision scope back to Sandra. As she grasped it she caught his fingers under hers. She hesitated a moment, then squeezed Boucher's finger tips as she slid her hand onto the scope.

"We can take out those two camel jockeys and go in from the front," Boucher whispered, "or we can try to enter from above on the far right side and find our way across the tunnels to the chamber behind them."

Barnhart nodded and pointed to the right. Sandra did likewise.

"Okay, spread out and stay in the shadows."

Boucher took the point and slowly led the way across the fifty yard rock face at the base of the tomb, being careful to remain in the shadows. A few minutes later they arrived at one of the entrances on the right side. The tomb showed the damage it suffered from an earthquake in 363 AD. There was fallen rock still clogging the entrance making entry exceedingly difficult. The pillars, carved out of the solid rock, were randomly fractured and misaligned. Retrieving the night vision scope from Sandra, Boucher climbed quietly inside the small opening. He extended his hand to help Barnhart traverse the rubble as he followed. Sandra was close behind.

Inside, Boucher switched the night vision scope to active infrared so that it would generate its own light source in the almost total darkness of the tomb's interior. The three cautiously walked, climbed and crawled as they made their way to the opposite side of the tomb. Occasionally they heard the faint sound of men's voices echoing through the chambers but their words were indistinguishable. Sandra, with her pistol at the ready, stopped, facing towards the moonlit opening leading outside. The voices of the two men seemed very close. Sandra signaled Boucher to keep the night vision scope and conduct a radiation search. Her meaning was clear. She and Barnhart would remain behind and provide security while he conducted a radiation search of the rooms deep in the tomb. Boucher disappeared into the tomb's asphalt darkness. Barnhart stayed in the shadows of the entrance and Sandra settled against a crevice in the rock wall just outside.

The first room revealed no radiation abnormality. The background radiation was high because of all the naturally occurring uranium contained in the rock but not abnormal. As they moved into the second room, which appeared from its size to be a burial chamber, Boucher's detector went crazy.

"Plutonium," he whispered to himself, observing his detector's red flashing LED display. *But where?*

Using the night vision scope in conjunction with his radiation detector he systematically searched the room but he could not pinpoint a single source of radiation. He knew what that meant. It was a decoy source intended to divert the attention of a less experienced searcher. It was probably spread into the cracks on the floor of the room. They had come up short. Boucher headed back across the connecting chambers to the point of entry. At the entrance he stopped and whispered to Barnhart and Sandra.

"We need to get out of here now."

Sandra pushed past and snatched the night vision scope from Boucher's hand. She carefully surveyed the area outside, then silently exited, making her way to a concealed position by some large rocks about thirty feet away. She again scanned the surrounding area and signaled Boucher and Barnhart to join her.

The three cautiously made their way along the rock face of Royal Tombs and didn't stop until they were well inside a small nondescript tomb carved into the mountain's solid rock face several hundred yards away.

"We're in deep shit," Boucher whispered. "That was a decoy back there. Somebody wants us to think there is a weapon in that burial chamber and it's being guarded. They must know that we were on to them so they provided this ruse to slow us down or mislead us. I don't understand."

"I think I do," Sandra said abruptly. "What was the source of the tip that led us here?" Answering her own question she continued, "An intelligence tipper from whom else - the Agency; Received via official SATCOM data link."

Boucher interrupted. "Si, a few days ago you told me a story at Los Alamos about being blackballed and lied to following the Israeli bombing of the Iraqi reactor years ago. You told me of U.S. and Israeli complicity in planning and coordinating the attack. Don't you see, they're at it again! I'll bet you Israel isn't the target and I'll bet Hamas doesn't have the SS-19, if there really even is an SS-19. They're playing us for fools. Sandra, what do you know that you're not telling us?"

Boucher was clearly angry. Sandra sat down on a bench carved into the rock. Her normally controlled demeanor was shaky. She quizzically stared at Boucher, then at Barnhart before responding.

"I am afraid that we have all been played as fools. We are embroiled in a deadly game of deceit and political motive. I can add nothing to your conclusion, Jake. All I can say is that I am not one of them and I am as dedicated to resolving this incident as the both of you are. I am not a Judas and I am not the enemy. You must trust me as I have learned to trust you or we will all fail and that will undoubtedly cost thousands of lives."

Boucher could see the pain in Sandra's eyes in the dim starlight. He intuitively did trust and admire her. In fact, although he didn't want to admit it, his feelings were even stronger than that. He was falling for this smart, exceedingly capable and unpretentiously sexy, dark-haired beauty. He now felt guilty because he challenged her integrity and he felt stupid for even implying that she might be in on a conspiracy to mislead their efforts. He gently placed his hand on her arm.

"I'm sorry Sandra. I didn't mean it the way it came out. I trust you like my mother. Damn," he stammered, "I did it again! I mean like the very fine lady that you are."

Barnhart probably knew more about Boucher's feelings towards Sandra than Boucher did. He also knew that Sandra felt the same way towards Boucher. He may have been old enough to be their father but he wasn't blind.

"Okay, Sandra and Jake, I trust you both. And Jake, you may be right on track with your theory. Let's consider the alternative courses of action open to us as we get out of here. We have a one hour walk ahead of us, which should give us plenty of time to think. You know, Jake? Sometimes you really do amaze me with your thought processes. Come on, let's get out of here."

Sandra smiled, as Boucher took her hand and pulled her to her feet. She stepped outside the tomb's entrance and once again carefully checked the surrounding area with the night vision scope.

"Clear," she said as she took the lead. She was careful to remain along the shadowy, nearly vertical rock face of the narrow gorge known as the Sig. It was the Sig that provided the once secret entrance into Petra through the otherwise impenetrable mountains. Barnhart followed with Boucher close behind.

Barnhart kept reviewing the events of the past few days over and over in his mind. There were too many loose ends to put him in his comfort zone. As the three emerged from the narrow winding Sig, Barnhart stepped to the side of the dry wash by some low foliage.

"Let's take a break for a few minutes. We need to talk," he said as he sat down on a weathered rock that resembled an overstuffed chair. Sandra and Boucher joined him.

"Let's brainstorm this for a moment," he said in a muffled voice. "We know that somebody nuked Zahie in the Bakaa. No one is claiming responsibility. Hamas says the Israelis did it. The Israelis say Hamas did it. Sandra says the Mossad did it to frame Iran. The pedigree of the weapon's origin is unknown, but we do know it was a low yield weapon, probably an artillery nuke. We were sent here after a Russian SS-19 nuke which we believe might have a new fire set that we have been led to believe was developed and installed clandestinely with Iran's help. It appears the SS-19 target is undetermined but may be somewhere in Israel. It's likely the attack will occur within the next twelve to twenty-four hours. The Agency potentially located the RV here and had us focus on this location as the place to intercept and stop it. Because of the time element, location and apparent international politics involved, additional emergency response assets could not be fielded to do something as important as preventing a nuke attack against a major Israeli city."

Boucher interrupted, "We were supposed to believe that we located the weapon, which is guarded by a couple of camel jockeys, only to find that it was a decoy. We might have been observed back there or we might have, for the first time in this operation, done something unpredictable. We might now know something that we're not supposed to know. Had we continued here alone we might still be attempting to locate the SS-19."

"I'm the wild card in this, Barnhart announced. "My unannounced departure from Iran and my joining your efforts here served to put a wrench into their gears. We need to make some assumptions and work from that point."

Sandra leaned forward towards Barnhart.

"I agree. If Israel isn't the real SS-19 target, what is?"

Boucher was listening intently with his eyes fixed in a blank stare at the night sky.

"It seems to me that the Zahie nuke could not have come from a salvage effort on the Caspian. I was there and there was definitely a nuke in that hold. I saw that ship blow up and sink, remember. They just don't have what it takes to pull it off a salvage effort of that magnitude. First, it would require some very dedicated diving and salvage equipment and skilled people. Hamas neither has the equipment nor the skills to conduct such an operation. That means they would have had to either pay someone else to do it, providing that they even knew that there was a nuke onboard that ship, or there is some other party involved not associated with Hamas and Iran. That party would have to have had access to the intelligence that you and I gathered and would need the resources to conduct the salvage effort to recover the nuke from a sunken ship in the middle of the Caspian. Now who might that be?"

Sandra joined the discussion.

"What if the nuke never actually went down with the ship? What if you were fooled into believing that it did? Could someone have removed it from the hold at the last minute and somehow got it off the ship undetected? You said you saw the ship blow up and sink but the Kazahks never checked the area for survivors, did they?"

Boucher interrupted, "You might be right. Where else could the Zahie nuke have come from without the intelligence community detecting it? I'll bet the whole community wrote that nuke off when the ship sank. I must have been sent there to provide the very credibility necessary for that to happen."

Barnhart was clearly troubled. His colleagues were creating more questions than answers and he knew that what they were suggesting could be true.

"For the sake of argument let's accept that the Zahie nuke was the one from the ship. Let's also say that Hamas wasn't behind the Zahie nuking. Let's assume that Sandra's information on the CIA and Mossad's involvement wasn't accurate either. So, that leaves Iran or maybe Syria."

"It also leaves the governments of Israel and the U.S.," Boucher growled. "Let's suppose that Israel wanted to end the Palestinian problem once and for all. Let's suppose they wanted to take out the terrorist infrastructure and at the same time put both Hamas and Iran back in their boxes. Let's suppose that they framed themselves like Sandra suggests with the Zahie nuke so they could ultimately distance themselves from the SS-19 nuke attack somewhere else. Where does one of the highest Palestinian populations in the world reside? Amman. All you need to do is to take out Amman. Syria, Egypt, Saudi Arabia and Iran would almost certainly rush aid into Jordan and attempt to occupy it. Israel would meet that by the creation and occupation of a security buffer zone that would extend well into Jordan from the east bank of the Dead Sea. Israel would occupy what's left of Jordan and gain full control of the seaport of Aqaba."

Barnhart flexed his bushy eyebrows as he contemplated Boucher's analysis. Sandra picked up where Boucher let off.

"And Syria wouldn't make a move south because of U.S. pressure and support for poor little Israel along with the standing U.S. forces in Iraq. Egypt couldn't do very much about it either. Israel would be home free. The balance of power between Iraq and Iran would remain unchanged while Israel would advance its agenda, increase its security buffer zone well across the Red Sea and ultimately be the big winner of the entire event."

Barnhart interrupted. "But there is no way Israel could pull this off alone; agreed? So that leaves one last assumption to support this conspiracy theory. The U.S. must be in on it. But, I can't believe that Congress or the President would condone such an operation in the interest of Israel." He paused in thought for a moment. "While it's hard to conceive, my guess is that Israel is behind this and the real, newly elected U.S. government isn't. This must be a damn black operation. We must assume that the SS-19 is not here in Petra and that it has already made it to Amman!" Barnhart stood. "Come on," he said, "we need to head back to Amman and warn the Ambassador."

"Hold on a second," Boucher cautioned. "We're gonna need some help and my guys are ready, willing and available. I'll give them a call as soon as we get into cell phone range and put 'em on a short leash."

Barnhart and Sandra nodded their okay. The three headed up the half-mile long, dry streambed that formed the entrance into Petra and went to the tourist parking lot. Since none of them had any equipment to retrieve from the hotel they decided it was far safer to all leave directly from there in Sandra's car.

The drive north to Amman was uneventful. Boucher drove while Barnhart and Sandra dozed off. There was no conversation. All three knew the stakes were higher now than before. They knew that they would need to find the nuke before it could be detonated. Sandra was particularly troubled because she now believed that the COS at the embassy had to be in on this conspiracy and that she had been set up. She was embarrassed that she had been manipulated.

Chapter 15

Amman, Jordan, four hours later

Boucher, Barnhart and Sandra arrived in the outskirts of Amman as the still hidden sun began to brighten the early dawn. Boucher drove to the U.S. Embassy and parked outside the compound in the front parking lot facing the embassy's white concrete perimeter wall. Both Barnhart and Sandra were by now fully awake and alert.

"You know, I don't think this is a good idea," Sandra said, staring at the Jordanian guards on machine gun-equipped trucks positioned at the corners of the wall. "If we go in there and tell the Ambassador, we'll show our hand. He will surely tell the COS. Without first neutralizing the nuke threat against Amman, the cat will be out of the bag. And, that will leave someone with a loose nuke that they can still use."

Barnhart grunted acknowledgment of her point as he stared blankly at the embassy's twelve foot high, fort-like wall in front of the car.

"But if we don't provide warning and they nuke Amman, we could be responsible for the loss of thousands of innocent lives," Boucher countered.

Barnhart sat up straight in the back seat. "You're both right. We need to find that nuke and disable it. I have access to the IAEA's radiation detection and ID equipment at their office downtown. We'll need their High Purity Germanium (HPGe) portable ID unit, mobile search detectors, neutron pods and a Dewar of liquid nitrogen. Oh yeah, they also have a portable radiography unit to assist in assessment and diagnostics and they do have a limited disablement tool box. They don't have any explosive shaped charges for disablement so I guess a hand entry will have to do. Jake, can you still operate a portable ID unit and capture the spectroscopy as well as search?"

"Yes, no problem."

"Do you remember how to do an HPGe vehicle search?"

"Sure do, Si."

"Sandra, you're a trained searcher, right?"

"Yes."

Barnhart nodded back, "Alright, we know what we need to do. Let's go do it."

After retrieving the HPGe search equipment, portable radiography unit, ID unit, and disablement tools from the IAEA office they headed for the hill overlooking downtown Amman. The Marriott Hotel that Boucher and Sandra had stayed in a few days earlier was located there, predominantly perched above the city.

"I think we should begin the search on the high ground and work outward," Boucher offered. "I know we're looking for a needle in a haystack but we have to start somewhere and," he paused, "if I was going to explode a nuke at ground level in Amman I would want to get it to as high an elevation as possible to increase the blast effectiveness."

Sandra drove the car slowly up the hill toward the Marriott. Barnhart finished checking the function switches on their mobile detector ensuring that it was operating properly.

"Remember," Barnhart reminded, "because of the warhead's size and weight, we're looking for something that will most likely only be concealable in a truck or garage. Since very few houses here have garages, the street shops may be the location of choice if the nuke has been unloaded. If we get a hit on the detector we'll keep driving and come back on foot to investigate and gather the spectroscopy."

After spending about two hours systematically searching the vicinity with no success, Barnhart directed Sandra to proceed to the Citadel ruins atop a nearby hill a few miles away, in sight of their current location. The Citadel was the historic location of both Roman and Crusader ruins located on a hilltop overlooking most of Amman and King Abdulla's Royal Palace compound. Sandra drove slowly around the narrow roads that encircled the ruins and then expanded the search radius even wider by driving up and down the narrow adjoining streets. It was now late afternoon and they still had no luck. The detectors remained silent except for some occasional background anomaly that the detectors internal logic circuits would quickly filter out. Barnhart was becoming frustrated.

"How about a shwarma?" he suggested. "I'll buy."

Shwarma stands are as common to the cities of the Middle East as hotdog stands are to the cities in the U.S. It is made by slowly roasting tightly packed loaf-like chicken breasts and pork on a vertical rotisserie. The cook browns the outside against a natural gas heating element and then slices paper thin pieces from the loaf as he rotates it in front of the burner. The meat slices are then rolled in thin pita bread with some sour yogurt. The result is something about the size of an elongated egg roll that is eaten like a hotdog. Most vendors sell three shwarma and a soda for about a dollar, which provides a nutritious and inexpensive fast meal.

Sandra pulled the car over to the curb and parked in front of a small street shop. They all got out and walked over to the shwarma counter. Speaking fluent Arabic, Sandra placed the order. The cook replied to Sandra and began slicing the meat and preparing the Middle East's version of fast food. The three sat on a low wall bordering the sidewalk in the shade looking very much at home eating their shwarma and carrying on casual conversation about the weather.

Just as Barnhart was biting into his second one, a truck drove by on the street behind them and their radiation detector alarms chirped simultaneously. Barnhart was so surprised by the alarms that he spit his partially chewed mouthful on the sidewalk. Boucher jumped from Barnhart's reaction, knocking Sandra's soda can off the wall. Sandra fumbled to mute the alarm switch on her detector, dropping her uneaten shwarma onto the side walk.

"Holy mackerel!" Barnhart yelled. "That's it! That's it!"

The three ran for the car. The truck had by now disappeared on a side street leading to the main road that ran up the hill to the Citadel ruins.

"Did either of you get a look at that truck?" Barnhart asked excitedly.

"It looked like a brown colored military-style truck," Boucher yelled.

"It was a white Mercedes box truck with Arabic markings spray painted on the tailgate," Sandra replied calmly. I couldn't make out what it said but I don't believe the truck is military." Sandra started the car and pulled away from the curb. "I think I can get behind him if I go around the north side of the Citadel."

"Si, it just occurred to me that I should ask what your disablement plan is," Boucher said with a nervous laugh. "I mean, how are you going to disable it? Didn't you say the IAEA tool box is limited?"

Barnhart tapped Boucher on the shoulder, "We need to get close enough for long enough to take a spectroscopy count. Depending on the spectroscopy results, I'll have a better idea of how to deal with it. Besides," Barnhart declared, "I have my Swiss knife with me. Who needs a tool box?"

"Well, Doctor McGyver, that sure gives me a warm and fuzzy! I was beginning to think you might not know which wire to cut. Really, Si," Boucher insisted, "how do you intend to…"

Sandra interrupted Boucher. "The truck is about a hundred meters ahead of us, see it? It looks like it is turning into the entrance that the support vehicles use at the archeological dig up there. I'm going to pull off over here and park. Jake, perhaps we can play tourists and take our cameras and ID unit up there and gather a spectroscopy for Doctor Barnhart's analysis."

Boucher exited the car, grabbing the portable multi-channel ID unit concealed in a small backpack which he casually slung over his left shoulder. He then hung the camera/radiation detector around his neck. Sandra also put on a small daypack and slung her camera/radiation detector over one shoulder. Barnhart watched from the car's rear seat, being careful not to act too interested. Sandra glanced in the open car window at Barnhart, her glistening white teeth flashed inside her wide smile.

"Okay, Doc, we're off. Don't go away."

Sandra and Boucher climbed the heavily eroded stone steps leading up to the Citadel mound twenty-five meters above the street where they had parked. Barnhart watched again thinking to himself what a truly beautiful couple they made. He marveled at their courage for essentially walking up on a nuclear weapon that was probably armed and in the control of someone who intended to detonate it. It was a true weapon of mass destruction that had the potential to kill thousands, if not tens of thousands. They were risking the possibility of instantaneous vaporization when each of them could have chosen to be out of harm's way. Barnhart was very proud of his two younger colleagues. He only hoped that if he attempted disablement he wouldn't fail and become the reason for their deaths.

"I guess we'd better look like lovers," Sandra suggested as she took Boucher's hand.

Boucher smiled at her as the two strode across the grassy field toward the Citadel ruins several hundred meters away. The suspect truck was now turning onto a narrow dirt road that ran along the front of the ruins. Sandra and Boucher watched it slowly proceed toward the east side of the archeological site. On the west side of the Citadel ruins overlooking the Royal Palace grounds, about five-hundred meters opposite the archeological dig area, the Jordanian Royal Army maintained a permanent camp composed of several dozen large ragged tents for the soldiers garrisoned there and some lightly armed vehicles. The truck went completely unnoticed by the soldiers who were more interested in coping with their austere living conditions than the security of the hilltop they occupied.

Sandra now had her arm around Boucher's waist, giggling and teasing him as two lovers might routinely behave. Boucher was enjoying every moment of her attention. So much, in fact, that he almost forgot the seriousness of their mission. The pair stopped several times to pose while each took the other's picture, or so it looked to anyone observing them. All the while they were checking the radiation detectors hidden inside their cameras. Sandra snuggled close to Boucher following a picture pose and whispered in his ear. She gently kissed his check and smiled.

"I show gamma and neutron, do you?"

Boucher smiled back. "Me too," he whispered before nuzzling the side of her neck.

The truck had now parked among some plywood shanties that the archeologists used to store their equipment.

"Let's try a picture over there," Sandra said pointing to an older area of the dig which was located about fifty yards behind the truck. They approached the area walking slowly along the top of the ancient walls exposed by the dig. They saw two men leave the area of the truck and walk back down the dirt road toward the street. The men never gave Sandra and Boucher so much as a glance.

Sandra encouraged Boucher to pose for her in such a way so she could take a detector reading in the direction of the truck. She then had him take off his backpack which contained the portable spectroscopy multi-channel analyzer and position it on the stone wall behind him. She again pretended to photograph him from a series of angles and continued to playfully urge him to change his poses, finally concluding her photo session. She sauntered over to him and planted a juicy kiss on his lips.

"I have a strong gamma-neutron source coming from that truck. Hold me while the ID unit collects the spectroscopy. We'll need five minutes."

Boucher needed no further prompting. He took her in his arms and began to kiss her passionately. To his delight, she matched his ardor, caressing his neck and flattening her body up against his. He could feel every inch of her curvy form pressing hard against him, invoking reactions that he was finding difficult to control. Boucher wasn't sure if she was just a good actress or if she was really sincere, but it made little difference at the moment. The simple truth was that he was holding and kissing the woman of his dreams.

Sandra held her arms tightly around the back of Boucher's neck as she opened one eye and checked the digital watch on her left wrist.

"It's time," she whispered into Boucher's ear.

Boucher knew that meant the charade was over and the ID unit needed to be retrieved. Boucher took a few steps back, a few deep breaths to clear his head and put the pack back on switching the ID unit to the standby mode in the process. The two strode back across the ancient walls above the dig and across the field.

"Stop here," Boucher said. "I'll put the pack down so we can gather a five minute background count."

Boucher slipped the pack off, flicking the switch to the collect mode as he set it on the grass. Sandra approached him seductively, slid her arms across his shoulders and buried her fingers in his hair, once again molding her body to his.

"You know what, Jake Boucher?" she whispered.

"What?" he said, blowing in her ear.

She responded, pressing herself even closer. "I always thought you knuckle dragger types were boring. And, well, you're not such a bad guy."

Boucher chuckled without immediately answering. "You know what, Sandra Morrison?" he whispered.

"What?"

"You're the finest lady I have ever known and I," Boucher paused short of finishing the sentence, "well, I..."

Looking into his eyes Sandra gently pushed him away. "I know," she whispered. "The background is complete. Let's get the data back to Doctor Barnhart for analysis."

She slowly slid her hands from his back across his broad shoulders and down his arms, releasing his fingertips with a gentle assuring squeeze. Boucher again donned the backpack and the two strode arm in arm back across the field to the steps leading down to the street. It was nearly dark by the time they returned to the car where they found Barnhart dozing in the front seat.

"Doctor Barnhart," Sandra said, "we gathered spectrum and we saw both gamma and neutron on the detectors."

Barnhart sat up abruptly, now wide awake. "Good job! Let's take a look at it and see what we have."

Boucher handed his pack to Barnhart as he crawled into the back seat. Barnhart removed the eight pound ID unit from the pack and opened the display screen top of its palmtop computer. He switched it from the collect to the view mode and watched intently as the liquid crystal diode screen began to display the data information. This small unit had the capability to collect and store two-hundred and forty-four individual spectra, each with its own time and date stamp, then analyze and display the spectra on the small computer's LCD screen for comparative analysis.

Barnhart keyed in several commands causing the computer to run the spectra analysis calculations. In less than five minutes he was examining the spectra's counts, region of interest and conducting isotope identification. Boucher and Sandra watched him narrow down the region of interest peak counts as he grunted every time the display grew more specific.

"It's plutonium all right! Wow! Look at these lines of energy. There is plutonium and uranium here and this looks like high explosives. And, this is iron, beryllium, tritium, damn." Turning away from the computer screen to look over his shoulder at Boucher and Sandra, Barnhart summed up the analysis.

"It's about what I would expect an SS-19 warhead to look like. I believe we can say with reasonable certainty that we have a thermonuclear warhead up on that hill. The question is, what condition is it in, and is there a clock ticking?"

"How can we be sure?" Sandra asked.

Boucher answered Sandra's question. "We can't without conducting thorough diagnostics on the device and we don't have the necessary equipment to do that."

"So what do we do about it?"

Boucher thought for a second before replying.

"We must assume that the weapon is capable of its full yield and that it has a ticking clock. Waiting for the Nuclear Emergency Support Team to get here is out of the question. It would take NEST at best a day and a half providing everything went perfectly. We're going to have to attempt a disablement ourselves. I know a disablement attempt could result in full or partial yield and I recognize this is a very bad location to risk an event like that. The only thing we can do is try to move it out of Amman to reduce the risk to the human life in this city. We're going to have to steal the box truck." Boucher calmly stroked his chin. "Sandra, what do you think?"

"I think you're nuts, Jake! You're suggesting that we steal a truck with a nuclear warhead in the back that probably has a ticking clock and might go off at any second? That is not a rational course of action, Jake! It's a suicide mission!"

Barnhart eagerly responded to Sandra's charge. "You're right, Sandra. It isn't a course of action. It is an act of desperation and the only avenue we have to save many lives in this city. If we can get it far enough away from the city we will have succeeded whether we successfully disable it or not."

"Come on, I'll drive the truck," Sandra offered.

Barnhart smiled and nodded, then looked back at Boucher. "You know, Jake, I could use your help. Besides, this is going to be Pulitzer material if someone ever writes about it. The world needs to know about this for what it really is. It's about powerful nations conspiring to impose their power. It is all about deceitful, power hungry Islamic extremists who will stop at nothing to ensure their agenda continues. They'll waste their own people in the process and never lose a wink of sleep over it. They'll risk world war just to eliminate Israel and anyone else who isn't Muslim."

Barnhart looked back at Sandra who was checking her 9 mm Sig Sauer pistol to which she had attached a silencer. She pressed the slide rearward to ensure that a round was chambered and then checked that the magazine was properly installed in the gun. She replaced the gun inside her fanny pack and secured the Velcro cover flap. Boucher press checked his Novak custom built .40 caliber Browning Hi-Power pistol to ensure a round was chambered and returned it to the concealed holster inside his belt.

"One of us is going to need to remain in the car to warn our embassy once we get control of the truck," Sandra said looking at Boucher. "That means you, Jake. If we succeed in getting the truck, I want you to follow behind in the car and act as rear security. We'll head well out into the desert and attempt a disablement there. I need Dr. Barnhart to go to the truck with me. He's the only one who has a chance at disabling that nuke."

"Okay, I'll drive the car and follow you."

Sandra unfolded a city street map of Amman on the car's front seat.

"Jake, I want you to drive over to the east side entrance of the Citadel Hill. That's right here," she said placing her finger gracefully on the map. "Wait there until you see us pass you in the truck. Stay behind us far enough to keep us in sight, but not close enough to be associated with us by anyone who might try to stop us." Running her slender index finger along a road on the map she continued. "I'm going down the hill here and then I'm going out of the city on Al Jaysh Street. About a half hour out of town, I'm going to turn east on Highway 30 and go towards Al Maqat. That will put us on the highway running through the desert directly towards the Iraq border. If it goes off out there it won't hurt anyone except us and the vast majority of the fallout footprint will collapse over Iraq's western desert. If we find a place to hide the truck along the way I'm going to stop to give Doctor Barnhart a chance at disablement. Any questions?"

Boucher looked deep into her lovely brown eyes and smiled. "What do you want me to do if you're followed?"

Sandra smiled back at him. "Buy us some time. Whatever it takes."

As she got out of the car she turned back towards Boucher and kissed him

162

on the cheek. "Just don't go out of your way to be a hero. I like you just the way you are," she whispered as he and Barnhart opened the car's trunk and removed a tool bag.

Boucher closed the car's trunk and got into the driver's seat. He watched Sandra and Barnhart disappear into the black sky at the top of the steps. It was nine o'clock. There was still some light on the western horizon but otherwise, except for the lights of the surrounding city, it was dark. He took several deep breaths to relax and imagined what a thermonuclear detonation would do to the surrounding city.

Amman had a population of about one and a half million people. It was in the heart of the very area where civilization once began. It was still rich with the antiquity of where eastern and western cultures once met but it would all become a contaminated wasteland - an uninhabitable place of catastrophic ruin. It would be returned to the desert. The balance of power would surely change. Israel would finally have its West Bank border secured. The Palestinian homeland problem would be overshadowed by the destruction of one of their primary sanctuaries and they would ultimately be so weakened and eliminated they would be inconsequential as a threat to Israel. Iran would undoubtedly get blamed for supporting Hamas and U.S. retaliation would be directed against them. Iraq would likely join the rest of the world against Iran. Syria would remain quiet or suffer attack from Israel and perhaps the U.S. The Saudis would continue to get rich selling their oil to the West and take advantage of any of the spoils. All told, Jordan, as a sovereign nation, would cease to exist. Boucher shuddered at the thought. He impatiently checked his watch. It was now 2100 hours. He started the car and began the short drive along the winding road leading to the other side of the hill. He dialed his cell phone and put it on speaker.

"Pat, it's Jake."

"Hey Jake, what's up?"

"I need all you guys here in Amman."

"Of course."

"How long will it take you to round everyone up and get the G-4 in the air?"

"Well, the guys are three sheets to the wind searching for the item of concern so I suppose I can get everyone recalled and back to the airport in about an hour or two. It'll take at least another hour to load all our equipment back aboard the Gulfstream and get it pre-flighted. So I guess we could be wheels-up in about three hours, maybe a bit less. The flying time to Amman is only about an hour, so depending on where you want us to meet you we could be there in about four hours."

"Okay, gas up the Gulfstream before you leave and pack some grits. Don't kill yourselves getting here. I'll call you later and give you a rendezvous location."

"Will do. What's the mission?"

"We're going to stop a nuke attack."

"You're shitting me! Right?"

"I wish I was. Call me with your ETD when known. We'll plan our link-up then. Have your field shit and guns ready to go. You know the deal."

"Roger all. Are things okay on your end?"

"Okay for now. I'll let you know how we're doing later. If the shit hits the fan on my end, there will be a mushroom cloud above a smoking hole where I used to be standing. Out here."

Boucher smiled to himself knowing his old friend Leon Patterson would be there soon. He momentarily flashed back to the night they met. It was during the North Vietnamese 1968 Tet Offensive. Boucher and his SEAL platoon were operating in Cambodia and had set an ambush for a high level North Vietnamese officer. When the enemy patrol came along they had a black American downed pilot in tow. Boucher and his SEALs rescued Patterson. Boucher and Patterson became life-long friends. In fact, they were closer than most blood brothers. Patterson was the one man on this planet Boucher trusted above all others. He took gratification knowing his closest friend was on the way to cover his six.

Chapter 16

Amman, Jordan, Citadel Hill, thirty minutes later

The ambient light emulating from the surrounding city was too intense to render Sandra's night vision monocular of much use. Her naked eye would have to do. She and Barnhart carefully worked their way along the south side of the hill towards the parked truck remaining in the shadows of an overgrown hedge row. About one-hundred meters from the truck, they paused to momentarily observe the adjacent area for guards and any signs of movement. They saw none. They cautiously continued their progress to a concealed position behind one of the plywood tool storage shanties used by the archeological dig. Sandra stopped abruptly, poised like a cat ready to spring on its prey. Barnhart instinctively crouched down next to some scrub bushes. Looking ahead, she slowly reached down and squeezed Barnhart's arm. She then pointed to a man sitting on a chair next to a small rock pile located about ten feet in front of the truck. The man, dressed in traditional Arab garb, appeared to be unarmed.

Sandra slid her fanny pack around to her right hip and quietly opened the flap to provide instant access to her pistol. She motioned to Barnhart to remain behind. She then crept back around the plywood shelter and returned to the dark tree line that she and Barnhart had followed earlier. Sandra followed along its edge another twenty yards to the corner of the field. Stepping out of the shadows she intentionally allowed herself to be seen by the guard.

Barnhart watched as the guard stood up and walked toward Sandra. The guard stopped about five feet from Sandra where he questioned her in Arabic. She responded to the guard in Arabic but by the sound of his voice the guard seemed to challenge her answers.

Barnhart saw Sandra calmly draw her silenced pistol in a single fluid-like motion and shoot the man in the eye, killing him instantly. Without looking back at Barnhart, she returned her pistol to the fanny pack and grabbed the sprawled man by the feet. Holding one foot on either side of her waist, she dragged him into the tree line. There she carefully concealed the body behind some brush and high weeds. Sandra reappeared from the shadows moments later and walked directly to the truck, motioning Barnhart to join her.

Barnhart went to the rear of the truck and immediately lifted the canvas flap above the tailgate to check inside. There in the cargo bed's dark interior was a plywood box about the size of an office desk. Looking around at Sandra, Barnhart gave her a thumbs-up as she joined him at the rear of the truck.

"Jezzz, Sandra, what did that guy say to you?" Barnhart whispered.

"Nothing. The son of a bitch had a gun concealed under his shirt. When he went for it I capped him." Pulling the canvas back down she continued. "The civilian guards here don't carry guns. He was here to keep an eye on this truck. I'll bet the poor bastard probably didn't even know what was in it. Let's get this truck out of here."

Sandra quickly hot-wired the ignition and started the truck's engine. Barnhart swung himself onto the passenger seat next to Sandra.

"I guess it wouldn't have been his day anyway," Barnhart said half heartedly.

Sandra switched the lights on, shifted into first gear and eased the truck away from its parking spot onto the dirt road that led off the hill to the street.

"Here we go, Doctor. Hold on!" she warned, flashing a fiery smile at him.

The truck bounced through the potholes past the military camp on the opposite end of the hilltop and out onto the street. Sandra turned right, steering the truck like a pro and quickly accelerated. As they began downhill Sandra noticed a set of car headlights pull out fifty yards behind them and accelerate to match the truck's speed.

It must be Boucher, she thought.

They proceeded downhill and turned left onto Al Jaysh Street.

Sandra yelled to Barnhart over the noisy truck. "Can you see Jake back there?"

Barnhart searched hard in the rear view mirror before replying. "I think that's him back there about three-hundred yards behind us but I'm not sure."

Sandra slammed the gas pedal to the floor as the truck sluggishly sped along. It was 10 P.M. and there was little traffic headed out of Amman to slow their progress. Barnhart leaned toward Sandra so she could hear him over the noisy truck.

"I'm going to crawl in the back and see if I can get started."

Sandra nodded. Barnhart kicked out the small window that connected the truck's cab and the rear cargo area. With some difficulty he was able to hoist himself through the narrow opening into the dark cargo area. Once inside he turned on his flashlight and inspected the wooden box. Barnhart noted that the plywood box was not particularly well made. It was constructed from half inch thick plywood panels fastened over a 2x4 frame by drywall screws. By its size and design he judged that it had been built around the reentry vehicle's shipping container and the only purpose it served was to hide the RV's telltale cylindrical clamshell-like metal shipping container. Shining his light into the forklift tine slots cut into the bottom of the plywood box he could see the metal shipping container inside.

Barnhart reasoned that the box was not booby trapped with a motion sensor, because if it had, it probably would have gone off already from the truck's movement. He also figured that the box probably didn't have any photo sensor triggers either since the interior metal shipping container could be seen through the forklift slots cut into the wooden outer box. The light entering the slots alone would easily trigger a photo sensor booby trap. He began the task of removing the screws that fastened the top of the box. Barnhart held the flashlight in his mouth so he could work the screwdriver and still have a hand free to steady himself in the back of the bouncing truck. Removing the screws from the box with a screwdriver was no easy task in the back of a moving truck.

Sandra had lost sight of Boucher's headlights. There were several cars behind her, traveling at roughly the same speed she was. Turning to shout through the opening to Barnhart she could see his silhouette poised over the top of the box in the dim light of his flashlight.

"How's it coming?" she yelled over the noise of the rattling truck.

Barnhart turned his head in her direction shining the light in his mouth up and down.

"I think we lost Boucher," she yelled in his direction and then immediately returned her full attention to the road ahead.

Several minutes later she turned east onto Highway 30. Highway 30 was every bit a modern divided highway that would rival any interstate in the U.S. What was so unique about driving in Jordan on such a highway was the lack of traffic, especially at night. Private auto ownership was primarily limited to the rich. Because it had almost no oil resources of its own, Jordan was not a rich country like Saudi Arabia and Kuwait. Sandra increased her speed to seventy-five kilometers an hour which was about as fast as the old truck would go.

Sandra knew from experience the main danger in driving fast at night in Jordan was from the occasional sheep or camel that strayed away from its shepherd onto the highway. The Jordanian military had a simple countermeasure for that. They mounted the spare tire horizontally on the front bumper which acted like a cowcatcher on the front of an old train engine. It looked awkward but it worked. Sandra remained alert, ready to brake or swerve as necessary, should she encounter a stray animal.

In the back of the truck Barnhart was progressing purposefully in the disassembly of the box. Now that they were on Highway 30, the road surface had smoothed to an interstate-like quality allowing him to work more efficiently, removing the box's screws. He was finishing the removal of the second side of the box. The top and one side of the spherical gray metal clamshell container holding the RV was now clearly visible. Down on all fours, Barnhart moved around to the opposite side of the box and began removing the screws on that side. He counted the bolts holding the metal clamshell halves together. There were eight bolts on each side and they would have to be removed so that the top half of the container could be taken off to gain access to the RV inside.

Sandra sped on through the darkness, passing a large green road sign with white reflective lettering, similar to those that might be seen along any interstate in the U.S. The writing on this sign was in both Arabic and English and had a large arrow pointing straight ahead towards the Iraqi border and a left arrow towards the Syrian border. She continued straight ahead into the rocky desert wasteland. Checking her side mirrors, she could no longer see any headlights. She wondered what had happened to Boucher, but at the same time she was relieved to know there was no one following the truck. She sighed as she pressed on down the highway figuring that she could manage without Boucher. Well, sort of. She had to admit to herself that Boucher had become very special to her over the past few weeks. Taking several quick looks behind the truck, using the side mirrors, she thought, *Come on, Jake, don't leave me now.*

They had been driving for nearly an hour and Barnhart was making visible progress in the back of the truck. He completed removing the plywood from the 2x4 frame and was now disassembling the frame. As he removed a top section near the front-end he leaned down and stuck his head through the window opening into the cab.

"Sandra, where are we?" he shouted over the noisy truck.

"About a third of the way between As Safawi and Al Magat. We're well out into the desert. How are you making out back there?"

"I'm ready to remove the bolts from the shipping container. Start looking for a place to hide this truck. I'm going to need a stationary working point and your help lifting off the container's top half."

"Yes Sir!" she shouted like a soldier acknowledging a superior's order.

Twenty minutes later Sandra slowed the truck, being careful not to use the brakes. She knew the flash of a red brake light out in the desert expanse could be seen for miles and if anyone was following behind with their lights out she didn't want to cue them that she was turning off the hard road surface into the desert.

"We're going on safari. Hold on!" she shouted back to Barnhart.

She turned the truck off the hard surfaced road onto a severely rutted trail used predominantly by Bedouin nomads. She selected this trail because it led toward a gorge eroded deep into the desert floor that looked like a dark abyss about five-hundred meters ahead of them.

"Hold on!" she warned again. "I think we can hide in a gorge about a half a click ahead."

She skillfully maneuvered the truck down the narrow path that slowly took them below the desert floor. Sandra brought the truck to a stop well inside the gorge and killed the engine. She climbed up onto the truck cab roof to survey the suitability of the truck's location. Because the gorge ran perpendicular to the highway the top rear roof section of the truck was partially visible to passing traffic from the highway about five-hundred yards away. After turning in a complete circle to view the surrounding area, Sandra assessed that their location wouldn't be a problem during darkness but it would be partially visible when daylight arrived. Granted, someone traveling along the highway would have to be looking for the truck to notice it, but in the daylight its rooftop would definitely be visible from the road. She didn't like it, but it would have to do. She went around to the back of the truck and opened the rusty tailgate revealing Barnhart dripping in sweat, still hard at work.

"This is going to have to do," she said to Barnhart referring to their location with a circular sweep of her right arm. "How far along are you?"

Spitting the flashlight he was holding in his mouth onto the truck's floor he smiled calmly.

"I'm removing the last bolt on this can now. Can you help me lift the top off this thing?"

Sandra climbed up into the back of the truck without a word. The two positioned themselves at each end of the heavy container placing their hands on the lift points marked in yellow, one inch high Russian lettering.

"Sandra, let's try to lift the cover up on this side and slide it off without scraping the warhead."

"Wait! How do we know it's not booby trapped?"

"We don't and if it is, we'll never know anyway! Ready, one, two, three, lift."

Both groaned as they forced the heavy upper half of the container's metal hemispherical shell over the warhead, rolling the shell onto its side against the cargo bed's wall.

Speechless, both stood there staring at the sleek SS-19 warhead before them. The black elongated cone shaped body of the reentry vehicle appeared ominous in the faint moonlight. Barnhart wasted no time taking his hand-held spectroscopy analyzer from his backpack and began a critical analysis of the warhead contained inside the reentry cone. This was necessary to evaluate the composition of the special nuclear material contained in the weapon and determine that its physical configuration wasn't altered, which could make the weapon critically close to detonating on its own. As he ran the probe slowly along the reentry cone's smooth heat resistant body he watched the LCD screen light up.

"Its configuration is not critical. I'm going to attempt a hand entry disablement. We're going in through the bottom access port here," he said pointing to the round bottom end of the cone shaped reentry vehicle. "Sandra, look in the tool kit and see if there's a small adjustable wrench or a slip-joint pliers and a flat head screwdriver. I'll need the latex gloves as well."

Sandra passed the tools to him like a nurse would hand a surgeon his scalpel and clamps.

"Thanks. Please shine the light on my working point."

Standing slightly to Barnhart's side, Sandra focused the flashlight beam on the bottom access plate he was removing.

"Good! Good!" Barnhart commented in obvious concentration.

"How do you know what procedure to use, Doctor?"

"Actually, I'm not all that familiar with the Soviet weapon designs but I am familiar with ours. Fortunately, the law of physics applies the same no matter whose design it is. I'm not suggesting that if you've seen one you've seen 'em all. It's really a matter of what can and can't be designed into a reentry body this size because of the physical constraints involved. I know what the components of a nuclear weapon look like and how they work. It really isn't all that hard to figure it out from there. Besides, I'm not trying to design this warhead so it will properly function. I'm trying to disable it from functioning."

As he removed the rear access plate and peered inside the RV containing the nuclear warhead, he muttered.

"Damn! It looks like they replaced some of the original design components with some homemade stuff."

Sandra intuitively knew from the sound of Barnhart's voice that wasn't a good thing.

"They replaced some of the circuits here and here," Barnhart said pointing inside the cone as though Sandra could see what he was referring to. "I see one resin-potted board and," he paused, "it looks like they replaced the capacitor discharge circuit. Aaah the battery is there. They put in a different battery and wiring harness. It's very clever work, very clever indeed."

Sandra was impressed at how cool and almost academic Barnhart was as he investigated this weapon of mass destruction, capable of instantly vaporizing them and the surrounding area if it detonated.

"Sandra, I'm going to remove these bolts and try to separate the reentry cone body from the warhead. Let's see if we can use some of those 2x4s from the box to lever the back end of the cone up. Then maybe we can pull the warhead out far enough for me to get access to the fire set power source and detonators."

Sandra picked up two of the longest 2x4 pieces and wedged the ends between the reentry cone and the lower half of the shipping container from each side.

"Good," Barnhart nodded. "Now you do that side and I'll do this side. Ready. Now!"

Both she and Barnhart pushed down on the makeshift 2x4 levers with all their weight raising the rear of the RV about six inches above the shipping container.

"Okay, hold what you got while I slide this small 2x4 piece under the reentry vehicle's body."

Sandra held on with all her strength as Barnhart slid a small piece of 2x4 under the cone allowing the cone's weight to settle on the wooden brace.

"There! Good! Now, let's try the front end."

The two did the same thing again on the other end. The seven foot long reentry vehicle was now fully visible.

"Alright, I'm going to try to pry the vehicle shell forward slightly and get the weight of the warhead body on the rear 2x4. If we can slip it up just a bit I think we can get the vehicle shell off far enough to gain fire set access. Ready? Now! Push! Push! Pushhhhh! Yes!"

They had exposed the bottom one third of the warhead electronics and firing mechanism. It wasn't an ideal situation but it was adequate for Barnhart to continue his disablement attempt.

"Where is the clock timer?" Sandra asked.

Barnhart chuckled. "Its probably safe to assume that this thing has some kind of timer or radio firing device in it or it wouldn't have been left on that hill back in Amman. I haven't found anything yet. I suspect that if I do, it won't resemble the kind of clock you're expecting. I suppose you could wire some kind of conventional clock into one of these things, but the firing circuits are so sophisticated that most clock timers are too unreliable to execute the firing sequence. The timing synchronization required is down to nanoseconds. Timex and Casio don't have what it takes to make one of these puppies detonate." Barnhart glanced up at Sandra soberly. "My greater concern is that a circuit failure or circuit collapse could trigger detonation. I'm not sure what traps have been designed into this modified fire set."

Sandra grimaced. "But wouldn't they have set the timer to have gone off by now?"

"If it was up to me and I wanted to create as much death and injury as I could, I'd set it to go off at the height of Amman's rush hour. I'd detonate it when I could catch the most people outside." Pausing momentarily as he checked his watch he said, "Say, in about two and a half hours from now. And, I hope to have a disablement solution before that."

Sandra sighed, not feeling any relief from his explanation.

Old Executive Office Building, Washington DC, the same time

Newly appointed DHS Undersecretary, Denise Dunkle, or "Double Ds" as she was called behind her back, entered secure conference Room 203 and sashayed to the head of the long walnut conference table. She was a squatty, unattractive woman who had, compared to her stature, disproportionately over-sized breasts. She was not well liked by the other members of the inter-agency's counter-terrorism emergency operations community because of her know-it-all elitist mentality. Other principle deputy representatives of the inter-agency were seated around the table engaged in various conversations.

"Let's get started," Dunkle proclaimed in a loud voice while impatiently patting her hands on the table for all to see. "Hello people."

The voices around the table gradually quieted and everyone turned their attention to her.

"The purpose of this emergency meeting is to come up with a recommendation for the President on how to handle the potential threat of nuclear bombs in the hands of terrorists. As you should all already know, we were unofficially notified by our friends in Jordan that at least two nuclear weapons, either have been, or are being transported here to the United States. Jim, can you please provide an update on the situation?"

Jim Carmichael, the CIA briefer, stood and walked to the front of the room as the recessed ceiling lights were dimmed. He clicked a remote control and a brightly colored slide appeared on the digital flat screen behind him.

"Ladies and gentlemen, this briefing is classified Top Secret Special Category and must be kept within River Stone codeword channels. Two days ago we intercepted a disturbing communication posted in a high level Arabic language forum that suggested some type of terrorist operation is currently underway. It claimed the targets are the United States and Israel. According to an Israeli deep-cover intelligence operative, Islamic terrorists have been dispatched to the target locations and may now be in place, preparing to execute unspecified attacks within the next twenty-four hours."

Dunkle interrupted Carmichael in a loud voice.

"Isn't it true that neither the targets nor the types of attacks were able to be identified from the analysis of the communications?"

"Yes, the timetable of these potential attacks is unclear, although the wording pertaining to the anticipated celebration of the success of the attacks suggests that they will be carried out within the next few days."

"So, Jim," Dunkle said sarcastically, "if the intel is so sketchy what makes you think nukes are involved?"

Dunkle loved to play the "got yah" game by asking what she thought were embarrassing questions, but Carmichael was a veteran Washington briefer and had dealt with huge egos like Dunkle's numerous times.

"I never said the intelligence was sketchy, Madam Undersecretary," Carmichael curtly replied. "I said the timetable was unclear. Now, if you would allow me to continue."

Dunkle was visibly angered by Carmichael's correction of her claim. She snorted and waved him on. Carmichael nodded politely and continued the briefing.

"We were informed yesterday by the Government of Jordan that they uncovered a plot to bomb Amman using a former Soviet Union nuclear weapon acquired on the black market. We were able to confirm this through our own operatives who are taking part in locating it. While this in itself is alarming, we

173

were able to confirm, with the help of Jordan and our Embassy Amman, that there is a second plot involving at least two, perhaps three nuclear weapons. We believe these weapons are in transit to the United States.

Carmichael clicked the remote and a new slide appeared showing several exploded-view artist drawings of nuclear weapons.

"This is what we think we might be up against. The bomb on the left is a FSU artillery-fired atomic projectile, or AFAP, with a battlefield yield of about a kiloton. This is what we think may have been detonated in Lebanon two days ago. The bomb in the middle is a FSU submarine-launched torpedo with a nuclear warhead. It has an estimated yield of 5 to 8 kilotons. It was designed to kill a carrier battle group. The weapon on the right is a FSU SS-19 ICBM warhead with an estimated yield of one megaton. It's a city buster. HUMINT solidly reflects all three of these weapons are in play to one extent or another. ELINT intercepts confirm the validity of this assumption. Our challenge is to determine the source of these weapons, exactly how many there are and the intended targets. In other words, how and where did the terrorists get them, and where do they intend to explode them?"

He advanced to the next slide. This slide displayed satellite overhead imagery of the nuclear blast damage created during the Israeli air strike in Lebanon.

"The blast damage you see in this picture is what occurred in Lebanon. Based on its blast damage radius we estimated it to be about a one kiloton yield; something the size of an AFAP. We have yet to nail down who was responsible or why the bomb was detonated. The Department of Energy is doing forensic spectroscopy on the debris in an attempt to fingerprint the warhead's origin. The only fact we can confirm thus far is that the IDF jets engaged in the retaliatory bombing didn't drop it."

Carmichael advanced the next slide that simply had the word QUESTIONS on it in large blue letters. Dunkle leaned forward on her elbows to ask a question. Her breasts rested on the table making her look like she had two five pound sacks of flour tucked inside her blouse.

"Are there any tippers on the likely target cities?"

"Unfortunately, Secretary Dunkle, we don't have anything specific beyond the intelligence that leads us to believe that these weapons exist and are now, or will soon be, transported here. As such, it is the recommendation of this agency that the Threat Level be raised to Red."

"Thank you, Jim, but leave those decisions to me. That's why DHS was created, remember?"

Dunkle pointed at the Undersecretary of Energy, Ron Vallee.

"Ron, what can you tell us about detection?"

Vallee rocked back in his brown leather executive chair and frowned.

"Detection where? A building, a city, a state, or North America as a whole?"

"All of them," Dunkle tersely replied.

"Well, here in the States we have numerous radiological detection capabilities at the federal, regional, local and tribal level. We have everything from radiation detection equipped aircraft to pager-size detectors that the law enforcement types carry with them every day of the week. We have the major border check points and the major airports covered. We have NEST teams ready to deploy twenty-four seven."

"That all sounds great, Ron, but how about finding something somewhere else like overseas?"

"That's a different problem. The best thing we have going for us is intelligence. If Jim's guys can get us a solid lead, and narrow it down to a specific location within a city block or so, we're prepared to deploy anywhere and deal with it. But without specific intel, finding a shielded nuke hidden in a city is like finding the proverbial needle in a haystack. Besides, if we deploy enough of our NEST capabilities elsewhere to conduct a search and to adequately deal with the problem there, we'll not have enough capability available here to cover the home front should the continental U.S. be threatened. I guess I'm saying that we have to be damn prudent where we locate our limited capabilities so we can best protect the homeland."

"How about using your special radiation detection equipped airplanes?"

"Well that is an issue because we only have helicopters and they will have to be either shipped or flown by military transport to the area of operations. They don't have the range to fly there on their own. Secondly, my helicopters are not military helicopters. That means their rotors are not the type that easily disassemble or fold for transport. Our aircraft mechanics will have to disassemble them and prepare them to be shipped, then, reassemble them on the other end. Once reassembled, they'll need to be test flown to ensure everything works right and subsequently be recertified air worthy before we can begin to go to work and search."

"Okay, how long does all that take?" Dunkle bluntly asked.

"It will take several days on both ends not counting the actual transport time."

Vallee was interrupted by Undersecretary of Defense, Thomas Arnold.

"Hold on a second, Secretary Dunkle, this has moved from a domestic operation to an OCONUS operation. It is not a DHS mission and I would appreciate it if you would recognize that and leave the operations planning and coordination to those of us who have that mission."

"Mister Arnold, this is far bigger than arguing about whose mission space it falls in. I suggest that you, Mister Vallee and the Department of State rep come up with a plan. If it's acceptable, we'll go to the President with it."

"Ms. Dunkle, we don't even know where the nukes are so why would we deploy our NEST assets to some location outside the U.S.? A move like that would be plain stupid. I suggest you concern yourself with the security of the homeland and we'll do the heavy lifting outside the U.S."

Dunkle sat back in rage.

"Don't you dare tell me how to run my agency!" she shrilly insisted. "DHS is responsible for doing whatever it takes to protect the homeland and that is exactly what I'm going to do with or without your help!"

Arnold appeared to take some personal joy in getting Dunkle spun up. He knew full well she had many times directed her staff to gather information from their interagency counterparts so her boss, the Secretary of Homeland Security, could "scoop" the President's other Cabinet Secretaries in the President's morning briefings. The other Secretaries and Undersecretaries knew that and took full advantage of her insecurity and nebulous standing as a Cabinet-level Undersecretary whenever they could. This meeting was no different. DHS was chairing it, but from a protocol perspective, Dunkle should have asked the Departments of Defense and State to co-chair the meeting. Now she was in trouble and instead of yielding, she exposed her obvious inexperience in government and the emergency operations community – just the stuff Washington bureaucrats love to encourage and feed upon. Arnold nodded toward his longtime political friend, the Undersecretary of State, who smiled and returned the subtle nod.

Chapter 17

At the desert working point, thirty minutes later

Barnhart continued to carefully work on the warhead, systematically evaluating the components and their relationship to one another. Sandra kept checking her watch. It was now about two hours before sunrise. She was concerned for Boucher but she didn't allow it to show. The sound of an approaching helicopter could be faintly heard in the distance but both Sandra and Barnhart were too weary at this point to notice. As the sound grew louder Sandra leaned out the back of the truck straining into the darkness to see two helicopter's silhouettes in the night sky. The sound was confused and seemed to be coming from all directions as it echoed off the steep rock walls of the surrounding gorge. All at once one of the helicopters appeared overhead with a searchlight brightly illuminating the truck from above.

Sandra knew they were had. Without moving her position she raised her hands. Barnhart joined her a moment later as the two helicopters briefly circled before landing a short distance from the back of the truck. The rotor wash artificially created a storm of dust and grit that engulfed the gorge.

Four heavily armed men with submachine guns at the ready bolted from the closest helicopter's open side doors towards the truck. The helicopter's bright search light was blinding to Barnhart and Sandra. Only when the men reached the back of the truck did Sandra see that they were wearing black balaclavas to hide their faces. Two of the men forcefully pulled Barnhart and

Sandra off the back of the truck slamming them face down onto the ground at gunpoint.

The man handling Sandra ran his hands into her arm pits, across her back and down across her back side, removing the fanny pack containing her pistol. He then rolled her over and placed the muzzle of his submachine gun in her mouth. Saying nothing, he ran his free hand roughly over her breasts and down across her crotch. He rolled her back on her chest and pressed his knee into the small of her back completely immobilizing her. The pain of his weight on her spine was excruciating. He bound her hands tightly behind her back using a plastic nylon tie which cut into her wrists. Sandra was terrified and helpless but she knew better than to call out. She lay there far more concerned that the assailants would hurt the old gentleman lying next to her.

The man searching Barnhart was no less gentle. He had secured Barnhart's hands behind his back and pressed him face down in the sandy dirt with the muzzle of his sub-machinegun. Sandra realized almost immediately that they were being searched for weapons, not for identification. That meant that whoever these people were they already knew exactly who Sandra and Barnhart were. The men didn't speak as they roughly yanked Sandra and Barnhart to their feet, shoving them over to the side of the gorge where they were again forced face down on the ground.

"You okay?" she whispered.

"Yeah, just peachy."

One of the armed men remained behind to guard Barnhart and Sandra while the other three returned to the truck. A lone figure strode from the second helicopter towards the truck. Using her peripheral vision, Sandra strained to catch a glimpse of him. His silhouette looked familiar but she could not make out his face. The helicopter engines were slowly idling down, greatly reducing the noise and the dust.

Sandra risked a quick glimpse of the man when she heard his voice. His voice was familiar. It was Hann. She felt her heart sink as she began to realize the futility of the situation. She could overhear Hann talking on the radio.

"Yes sir, we have recovered control of the item. No sir, it appears that we got here in time. Yes sir, I'll handle it appropriately."

Sandra yelled above the noise at Hann. "You son-of-a-bitch, Hann! I should have known you were behind thi---!"

She never completed her sentence as the guard kicked her in the side and placed his foot on the small of her back pressing down with all his weight. As she gasped for air, Hann walked over to them.

"Well now what do we have here?" he sarcastically said.

Sandra gasped out, "You son-of-a-bitch!"

Hann laughed. "And Doctor Barnhart, you are one clever old scientist. You almost pulled it off."

"What now?" demanded Barnhart. "Are you going to shoot us or be creative and handcuff us to the weapon so we can be vaporized when it detonates?"

"Why, Doctor, you do have a sense of humor after all. Of course we're going to have to ensure that you don't talk like you did after the reactor attack. That was very embarrassing to a multitude of important people." Hann turned and casually began to walk back toward the truck.

"How did you find us?" Barnhart yelled.

"I suppose I can grant a dying man his last request," Hann offhandedly commented as he turned to face Barnhart. "We had a transponder hidden in the truck. I know it's a simple concept for us backward followers of Islam, but you must admit it's an extremely effective means to track something of value. Wouldn't you agree, Doctor?"

Barnhart didn't answer. As he looked behind Hann he could see the other three armed men backing the truck over to their helicopter and they had attached dolly wheels to the bottom of the RV shipping container.

"So what's next?" Barnhart asked. "Well, we're going to move this nuke back where it was and you and Miss Morrison are going to meet with an accident out here. I just can't imagine why you would want to come along with us and watch the incineration of Amman."

"Why Amman?"

"Oh come on, Doctor. You and I both know that the loss of Amman along with the Government of Jordan will change the balance of power in the Middle East for at least the next several hundred years, maybe longer. Israel and the U.S. will be blamed and a few days from now more nukes will arrive in the Canarys for retaliation against the U.S. The world will be thrust into war and just like the Koran prophesies predict, Islam will prevail for another thousand years. But don't worry, you and your girlfriend are going to miss all the action because you'll both be dead."

Hann turned and walked towards the truck chuckling to himself, obviously delighted with what he had just said. Barnhart turned to look back at Sandra and noticed some movement to the rear of the first helicopter coming from the direction of the road. It was a car with its lights out being wildly driven. It had to be Boucher.

The car was on a suicide path aimed directly at the closest helicopter's spinning tail rotor. Because of the helicopter's engine noise and movement from the spinning rotor blades, Boucher's approach had still not been noticed by anyone except Barnhart.

Barnhart thought, *Holy shit! He's gone nuts!*

Boucher turned the car hard to the right putting it into an intentional sideways skid and floored the gas pedal a few yards from the spinning tail rotor. Barnhart saw Boucher duck from view just prior to collision. The rear of the veering car wildly fish-tailed into the spinning tail rotor, disappearing momentarily in a cloud of dust. A loud metal-on-metal grinding sound erupted in a shower of sparks engulfing Boucher's car and the helicopter's tail section. Boucher's car leapt into the air as it careened out of control by the helicopter on a collision heading straight for the gorge's looming two story high rock face.

The helicopter lurched forward from the uplifting impact of the car under its tail. The helicopter's spinning main rotor blade was now angled down from the forward lurching impact caused by Boucher's car. One of the guards standing between the truck and helicopter, directly under the rotor blade's outer-most swath, was instantly decapitated. The helicopter pilot worked frantically to complete an emergency engine shutdown but it was too late. The bright search light on the helicopter's front underbelly flickered and went out leaving everyone temporarily blinded by the sudden onslaught of darkness.

The two guards at the rear of the truck ran in a half crouch, firing their submachine guns at Boucher's car, giving the still spinning main rotor blades a wide berth. The guard watching Barnhart and Sandra turned away from them and knelt down on one knee in a firing position facing the direction of the helicopter. He shouldered his submachine gun at the ready with his full attention toward Boucher's car.

At that instant Barnhart saw Sandra spring to her feet and rush at the back of the kneeling guard. She covered the short distance in a blur. Her attack was so overwhelming and vicious it surprised even Barnhart. Sandra, still with her hands bound by the nylon tie, side-kicked the guard just behind his right ear knocking him forward. Slamming her full weight down on the guard's back in a sitting position she brought her knees up to her chest and her bound hands forward to her heels, stepping through as if her arms were a jump rope. With her bound hands now in front of her she threw her arms over the man's head from the rear and used the nylon tie still binding her wrists as a garrote, instantaneously crushing his larynx. Using all her strength she grasped his head in both hands and snapped it sharply to the side, breaking his neck. He died without so much as a groan.

In a single fluid movement she released his head while still cradling him in front of her and grabbed the submachine gun from his limp arms. Using her left thumb to switch the selector from the auto to the semi-auto position she took aim at the two guards running toward Boucher's car. In the confusion and darkness neither of them had seen her attack their comrade. Her aim was deadly. Two surgically placed rounds hit the guard closest to Boucher's car squarely in the back of the head. The second guard reeled, barely getting off an unaimed three shot burst when Sandra's third and fourth shots hit him in the chest, knocking him to the ground. She paused for a second, aiming, before placing a final shot in the guard's left temple. She shifted her position still holding the dead guard in front of her for a clear shot at the helicopter. The pilot in the helicopter was the only one who saw Sandra kill the guards and had already opened the side door, trying hurriedly to unbuckle his seat belt and escape. Shooting through the front of the helicopter's Plexiglas canopy, she fired six shots in a moderated series, two at a time. It sounded to Barnhart like pop-pop, pop-pop, pop-pop. The pilot slumped forward, his body restrained by the shoulder harness that he had not had time to fully release.

Kennedy Irregular Warfare Center, ONI, Suitland, MD

"Captain Blackburn, I think we have something you need to hear."

"Shoot, Lieutenant."

"Well, Sir, you remember that number string we intercepted with Arabic words that meant Golden Bird?"

"Yes, you told me the number string had no correlation to the target. What about it?"

"I think we figured it out. It's the old Arabic calendar date for tomorrow. Captain, we think the attack is planned for sometime tomorrow."

"But where and how? We need those two questions answered before we can take this up the chain."

"I understand, Sir, but there is no new intel to work with. Everything we have points to the Canary Islands as a possible target and a nuke attack on our shores. Now we think we know tomorrow is *when* the attack will occur. If the Canarys are *where* and the nukes are *how*, I don't understand how that translates to an attack against the U.S. The Canarys belong to Spain."

"You and your team stay on this, Lieutenant. I need answers and I know you can figure this out."

"Aye, Sir, but the bad guys have stopped talking. Everything we've been seeing for the past few months has been like a crescendo of violence both in deeds and threats while at the same time our new President is making concessions to Arab nations in the interest of securing peaceful relationships. It's the weirdest thing. It's as if someone turned their switch off."

"Are you telling me it's the calm before the storm, Lieutenant?"

"No, Sir. It's more like violent peace."

At the desert working point

In all the confusion the second helicopter took off, creating an eye burning dust storm. Sandra released the dead guard from her arms and stood in a low crouch. The dead man slumped to the ground, his limp body in a head down sitting position then slowly toppled backward sprawling on the ground. Unfazed, with gun still at the ready, Sandra quickly surveyed the area for signs of movement before turning back to Barnhart.

"You okay, Doctor?" she asked.

"My God! I hope I never piss you off," he hoarsely replied.

She returned to the guard's body and took his knife from its sheath and threw it next to Barnhart. Barnhart cut his bindings and moved to Sandra's side doing the same for her.

"Go stop that nuke," she said.

She knelt down and took the dead guard's pistol out of the holster and handed it to Barnhart. Barnhart immediately pulled the pistol slide back slightly to ensure a round was chambered.

"How much time do you need to disable the nuke?" she asked.

Barnhart shrugged and raced towards the rear of the truck. In the process of trying to prepare the warhead for helicopter transport the guards had pulled the warhead further out of the reentry vehicle casing. This actually exposed a greater interior section of the weapon's inner working parts. Barnhart judged that they had probably checked to ensure he had not tampered with the firing circuit or accomplished a disablement. Barnhart located his flashlight and resumed work.

Sandra bounded over the two dead guards and ran to Boucher's car. As she approached she was relieved to see Boucher was not in the car. She saw the front window was broken from a dozen bullet holes and that the driver's side door was bullet riddled as well. In the moonlight she could see a splotchy blood trail across the front seat to the passenger's side door which was still partially open. The car had hit the rocky wall with considerable force, enough to demolish the entire front end. He had somehow escaped. She unconsciously sighed with relief.

Sandra made the split second decision to go after Hann. She saw him run into the gorge when Boucher's car collided with the helicopter. She left the truck and went into the narrow gorge, cautiously creeping along the furrowed wall, being careful to remain in the shadows and not silhouette herself in the moonlight. There were deep vertical creases eroded into the sides of the gorge's face that made it look like a massive open zipper under the moonlight. Ahead, the gorge turned hard to the right creating a blind turn. Sandra cautiously slowed her pace, moving across to the opposite side of the gorge to minimize her vulnerability from the opposing end of the turn. As she stepped out of the shadow into the moonlight she felt an instantaneous crushing blow to the left side of her forehead. She felt like a hammer had slammed her backward against the rock face. Her ears were ringing but she curiously felt no pain. Instead, she felt numb all over. Her legs wouldn't work. She could do little more than lie there on her side in the position she landed. Tunnel vision began to narrow her sight as consciousness slipped away. She fought to remain awake but numbly realized that it was a hopeless battle.

Hann emerged from the shadows and cautiously approached Sandra. He stood momentarily as though he was studying her body. He slowly raised his pistol and aimed it down at her head. Then he went sprawling as Boucher's smashing weight hit him from above. Both men were momentarily stunned. As they regained their composure Hann fired his pistol wildly toward Boucher. Boucher ducked behind a large rock. Hann disappeared into the darkness.

Boucher ran to Sandra's side and carefully cradled her in his arms.

"Sandra," he whispered. "Sandra, please wake up."

He examined the extent of the bullet wound to her forehead. The bullet had grazed her right temple just above the hairline, leaving one and a half inches of open flesh bleeding, but it had done nothing worse. He took her pulse. She was in shock.

"Come on babe, you're going to make it. Just hold on."

Boucher tore a piece of his shirt off and bandaged Sandra's head. Pulling her up into his lap and cradling her head on his arm, he began to talk to her.

"I wish I would have told you this before, but I will now. You are the finest lady I have ever known and I want to spend the rest of my life with you. I know you probably would never go for a guy like me, but I want you and I need you. If we get out of this, I want to marry you."

Sandra faintly groaned. Boucher cuddled her more closely, kissing her forehead lovingly. Sandra's eyes fluttered and finally opened.

Boucher smiled. "Welcome back."

Sandra managed a faint smiled and tried to speak, but Boucher touched her lips.

"Take it easy, you're okay."

As she again slipped from consciousness she whispered, "I love you too."

Boucher's lips lightly brushed Sandra's as he gently laid her on her back. He heard a helicopter land on the desert floor above the gorge and then quickly depart, its engine noise disappearing into the distance. Hann had escaped but at least Sandra had been spared.

As she regained consciousness, Boucher carefully pulled Sandra up to a standing position and put her arm over his shoulder. He wrapped his other arm around her waist and began to slowly walk her back toward the truck. She was groggy, but aware.

It was first light and the sky was slowly brightening. Boucher could see the truck about one hundred meters ahead. The helicopter was resting lifelessly about twenty meters behind the truck. He could see the car that he rammed into the helicopter wrecked against the rocky wall of the gorge. The bodies of the guards were not far from the car, resting in the contorted positions that come with sudden violent death. He walked Sandra around the back of the truck and there was Barnhart, lying beside the warhead, still working on something that looked like the inside of a stereo amplifier.

"Hey Doc!" Boucher shouted.

Barnhart nearly leapt off the truck.

"Damn it, Jake! Don't scare me like that! Can't you see I'm concentrating?" Barnhart paused a second, evaluating the appearance of Sandra and Boucher who were both covered with a mixture of dried blood, dirt and sand. "You kids sure know how to party on your first date. I thought you were both dead and if I don't get this thing disabled you will be. Could you give me a hand, Jake?"

Boucher helped Sandra to a sitting position, leaning her against the rear wheels of the truck. He squeezed her hand reassuringly before leaving her to crawl up beside Barnhart. Barnhart pointed a crooked finger at the electronic assembly in front of him.

"Okay, I'm going to remove this firing component here."

He took Boucher's hand and placed it inside the warhead firing circuitry before continuing.

"I need you to carefully pull this component down and through the gap I open in the wiring harness here. Just be careful not to break any wires or unplug the connectors. Here we go."

Barnhart carefully removed the flash drive-size component from the warhead's body and held it stationary beside the warhead's outer casing. Boucher pulled a slightly smaller sealed plastic box down through the space Barnhart had just created.

"Good. Now I'm going to separate this battery connection from the firing circuit." Barnhart carefully reached through the space and unseated a small multi-connector. "Okay, you can unplug the connectors on the firing component you're holding."

Boucher coolly completed the task.

"Good," Barnhart whispered. "Now I'm going to cut these three wires leading to the detonator circuit over here, one at a time. If you see me cut the last one we will have succeeded. If you don't, I'll see you in the light, Brother." Barnhart turned his head slightly towards Jake, "By the way, what took you so long to get here? I thought you were supposed to follow behind us in the car?."

Boucher shook his head. "Lucky for us I had a flat right after I turned onto Highway 30."

"Well, that was a pretty crazy stunt you pulled ramming your car into the helicopter's tail rotor like you did. You scared the hell out of me!"

Looking back at his working point, Barnhart cautiously snipped the wires one at a time. As he clipped the last one both men sighed in silent relief. Barnhart began to unscrew an access cover on the side of the warhead.

"We have one more thing to do to make this thing completely inoperative. We need to foul the plutonium pit. Without perfect symmetry this thing is nothing more than a conglomeration of plutonium, conventional explosives, firing circuits and sensor apparatus. Jake, the pit is highly toxic. Please hand me the gloves out of the tool bag. Dump the tools out and fill it with sand."

Barnhart put on the gloves. After carefully removing the access plate, he visually inspected the interior basketball-shaped outer shell and inner pit which resembled a centrally supported metallic tennis ball.

"Jake, break the chains off the truck's tailgate. I need to put them inside the pit cavity to foul the geometry. We'll fill it with chain and sand. Then we're going to burn it."

"Burn it?" Boucher questioned.

"Yup. Even if the explosives detonate, the geometry will be off and the thing won't yield."

Boucher broke the chains off the truck's tailgate and handed them to Barnhart. He filled the tool bag with sand and pushed it next to the old scientist.

"Good," Barnhart whispered as he pulled the bag up next to the weapon.

He carefully fed a chain section into the open inspection hole and filled the rest of the cavity with sand. He replaced the inspection plate being careful to ensure it was positioned properly.

"Alright, let's get out of here. Jake, connect the lifting slings that they were going to use to carry the container under the chopper onto the weapon's shipping container and the helicopter's skids." Leaning around the side of the truck towards Sandra he asked, "Sandra, are you okay to drive?" She nodded *yes*. "Good! I want you to drive the truck forward. The slings attached to the chopper skids will anchor the container and pull it off the back of the truck. Don't worry, it's now safe to drop. After it's on the ground I'll unhook the slings. Then I want you to turn the truck around and drive to the other side of the chopper towards the road. Wait for us there."

"Si, I'm going to drag the bodies over to the chopper."

"What about Hann's body?"

"The bastard got away," Boucher blasted.

It took no time at all to complete the tasks. It was now first light and that greatly simplified everything. Boucher dragged the guards' bodies next to the helicopter and threw their weapons into the back of the truck as Sandra drove by.

"Okay, Si," Boucher yelled, "get into the truck with Sandra. I'll be along in a second."

Barnhart hurried to the waiting truck. Looking across at Sandra in the cab he saw Boucher douse the helicopter, car and RV with fuel from one of the truck's gasoline filled gerry cans. He poured a narrow trail of gas along the ground as he walked backwards towards the truck.

"Ready." he yelled.

Sandra gave him a thumbs-up and put the truck in gear. Boucher pulled his pistol from his belt and fired the gun next to the ground in contact with the gasoline igniting the fuel. He sprinted to the cab of the truck yelling.

"Go! Go! Go!"

Sandra gunned the engine as Boucher swung himself through the open door into the cab next to Barnhart. The truck only traveled a short distance when the helicopter and car erupted in flames.

Boucher looked into the truck's side door mirror. "What happens to the special nuclear material?" he asked Barnhart. "Won't the local area be contaminated?"

"The conventional explosives the warhead contains to initiate the nuclear detonation will burn. If they get hot enough they'll explode, but there will be no nuclear yield. That's why we fouled the implosion geometry. Yes, there will be low level radiological contamination in a small footprint around the chopper but nothing of consequence. The Jordanians will have no problem cleaning it up. The SNM will remain intact but extremely dangerous to handle without toasting yourself. I suppose our embassy will offer Jordan the assistance of the Department of Energy's Consequence Management Response Team to remove the SNM. Thank God for King Abdulla."

Almost at that second the helicopter's fuel tank exploded spewing burning fuel around the disabled warhead. Sandra, Boucher and Barnhart all instinctively ducked as the blast's shock wave slammed against the truck. Searing heat immediately followed and then quickly subsided. Orange flames leapt into the sky.

Sandra turned the truck onto the asphalt, four-lane highway and shifted through the gears coaxing it up to its fastest speed. Moments later the gorge itself seemed to explode, throwing pieces of hot metal fragments from the helicopter high into the air. Black smoke billowed upward carrying sand and dust that formed an umbrella-shaped plume resembling a small mushroom cloud. The heavier fragments could be seen falling back to the desert floor making small puffs of dust as they impacted the ground. Fragments landed a few hundred yards behind the truck. Some were quite large and sounded like garbage cans hitting the street.

"Damn, Doc, I just remembered," Boucher said excitedly. "What about the locator beacon Hann said he had placed on this truck?"

"Not to worry! I removed it."

Barnhart reached into his pocket to reveal a transmitter beacon about the size of a beeper that had been obviously smashed.

"Here, a souvenir for my favorite student. Thanks for the help back there. And Sandra, thank you too. I'm glad you're okay," he mumbled. "I'm actually getting kind of fond of having you kids around."

The three of them sat there for a moment in silence before Sandra spoke.

"We need to notify the COS in Amman."

"No, he can't be trusted," Boucher countered. "I need to give Admiral Thornberg a call."

"Agreed," Barnhart said. Hann said there are nukes on their way to the Canary Islands. He said they were going to be used in an attack against the U.S. but he didn't reveal a specific target."

Boucher nodded. "We need to go to the Canarys ASAP."

Sandra chuckled. "We're in the middle of the desert, Jake. Just how do you intend to make that happen?"

"Did you forget? My guys have been working in Aqaba since we got here and they have our Gulfstream. I gave them a call while I was driving out here last night. They're on the way here to pick us up."

"Where are they going to meet us?" Sandra asked.

"Right here. Pull off the highway over there."

Sandra began to laugh. "You mean they're going to land a G-4 on this highway?"

"Yeah - No problemo," Boucher replied. "Just pull over and get well off the road surface. They'll see the smoke from the burning helo and know it's me."

Barnhart began to laugh along with Sandra. "Let me get this straight, Jake. You called your team last night and told them to find you somewhere in the desert east of Amman and look for some kind of sign?"

"Yeah, that's pretty much what I told them. Why?"

"So, I guess you expect your Gulfstream corporate jet to land here on the highway next to us any moment now?"

"Yes, I do."

It was almost fully light and the early morning sky was deep blue. A warm gentle breeze occasionally wafted over the low scrub brush spinning small clouds of tan dust a few feet above the desert floor. The residual heat emanating from the desert sand caused a shimmering chrome mirage-effect. About a half a mile behind the truck a plume of black smoke rose several hundred feet into the morning sky directly above the burning helicopter.

Boucher looked over at Sandra with a weary smile. "I thought I lost you back there."

Sandra returned his loving gaze. "I have a reason to stick around."

"I thought I lost you both," Barnhart added.

Moments later a Gulfstream touched down on the deserted highway a half a mile ahead of them. It appeared ghostly through the shimmering mirage as it taxied up next to the truck. Sandra and Barnhart couldn't stop laughing. Frank Moss and Jack Doyle were in the cockpit at the controls. Both waved to Boucher through the cockpit windows as the plane neared. Moss was wearing his signature black ball cap with DILLIGAFF embroidered above the brim in dirty white block letters. The plane came to an abrupt stop next to the truck. The side door popped open and two familiar faces appeared. Johnny Yellowhorse and Mojo Lavender bounded down the stairs. Mojo casually strode over to the truck. His white beard and mustache flowed mystically in the breeze. He studied Boucher for a few seconds before speaking.

"You look like shit, Commander. Hey, if yah-all wouldn't mind get'n onboard we really need to get back into the air before rush hour starts."

188

Book Three

Chapter 18

The Canary Islands

Rahman's navigation to the target island was flawless. His small coastal freighter had not been challenged or even paid any notice by the national authorities along his route since he left Algiers two days earlier. His transit throughout the Western Mediterranean and through the Strait of Gibraltar was so routine that he and his crew actually had time to rest. Now he was only eighteen miles east of the target island where he would plant the nukes. He could see the island on his radar scope. It was far bigger than he anticipated. He had no idea why he had been directed to drop off the nuclear weapons here or how they would be employed but it didn't matter. He was doing his part to ensure that al-Ta'ir al-Zahabi, *Golden Bird*, was a now a reality and it filled him with gratitude. *Praise be to God!*

Rahman checked his position on the navigation chart. He ran his index finger along the pencil line marking his predetermined course to the island. His freighter was nearing the western shore of the island. He stopped momentarily, pressing his finger on the island's name.

La Palma - the Canary Islands, he thought. W*hat an odd place to place bombs for detonation. Why not just take them to New York City or Washington, DC and explode them there where the infidel death toll and devastation of those cities would be ensured? No bother, this island target is God's will.*

Rahman slowed his ship to a crawl. He would soon stop his ship and loiter about half a mile from shore where he would launch two small boats that would carry the bombs to the narrow beach. Even this close to shore the water averaged about 450 feet deep. It was far too deep for the small freighter to anchor but that didn't matter. He was content that his ship could wait without its captain for a few hours while he and a chosen few would carry out their divine mission. He casually strolled out of the pilothouse onto the open bridge wing. It was now first light. The sun was just below the eastern horizon and it silhouetted the sharp terrain features of the island before him.

The island's steep volcanic face rose up from the sea to an ominous-looking 650 foot high, vertical-sided ridge that ran above the north and south shore for more than five miles in each direction. Even in the emerging early morning light the ridge looked like it was precariously poised to slide down into the sea at any moment. Rahman's attention was drawn to numerous voices as men scurried around the aft deck of his ship. Crewmen were readying the three semi-inflatable Zodiac boats.

The boats that would transport the vengeance of God ashore. The great Satan and all his followers will be annihilated just as the Prophet Mohammad predicted. Praise be to God and Islam for this day will reward the devout and punish the infidels.

Kennedy Irregular Warfare Center, ONI, Suitland, MD

"Captain Blackford, the target has to be Canarys," the young lieutenant reported. "Everything we're seeing points to the island of La Palma."

Blackford sat back in his chair.

"But why La Palma?"

"Sir, we're working it."

"I need an answer soonest."

"We're on it, Sir."

"Good."

"But, Sir, there's something else we have that might be of interest."

Blackford smiled and gave his full attention gesturing for the lieutenant to continue.

"Sir, we were looking at some recent cables from the counter-intelligence weenies and I think they might have stumbled onto something related to this."

"Let's hear it, Lieutenant."

"Apparently the DOE folks were doing some clearance reviews and they came across something that red flagged a name. Mark Hann, Iranian born, formerly Mahmoud Haniyeh, is a naturalized U.S. citizen who legally changed his name right after he got citizenship."

"And?"

"He got his Ph.D. in Nuclear Engineering at Berkley and then went to work for DOE. He was detailed to the Department of State and then later transferred to the CIA. He's a CIA operative now."

"And?"

"Well, Sir, DOE thinks he's been visiting Iran regularly for the past four years and it hasn't been authorized by the CIA. It appears the guy is a double agent."

"Okay, they caught a bad guy. How does that relate to the Canary Islands and terrorist nukes?"

"Hann is the CIA Case Officer who has been in Amman looking for the nukes and this links him to the terrorists who possess those nukes. Sir, he must be considered a terrorist himself and must be stopped before he can compromise our operations to find and stop those nukes."

"Thank you, Lieutenant. That will be all."

As the lieutenant left the office Blackford pressed his intercom.

"Gene, please get Admiral Thornberg on a secure line for me."

Blackford's phone buzzed a few moments later.

"Captain, Admiral Thornberg is on line one."

Blackford's hand hesitated above the phone a few seconds before he finally picked it up and pushed the speaker phone button connecting it to line one.

"Jim, it's Dean, I had a strange call from our old shipmate, Jake Boucher. He's inbound to La Palma in the Canary Islands. He has some of his guys with him and they're trying to chase down some loose nukes."

"Jake is where? I thought he was in Amman?"

"No, Jim, he's on his privately owned Gulfstream with some of his guys and they're still a few hours away from La Palma. Jake seems to believe that La Palma is the target for a nuke terrorist attack but he's puzzled as to the strategic importance of La Palma. I mean, why attack La Palma if the U.S. is the ultimate target?"

"My COS in Amman is on top of this Dean, and I have one of my top operatives working directly with Jake but she hasn't indicated any issues that I am aware of."

"Do you have a guy in Amman by the name of Hann?"

"Ahh, yes we do. Why?"

"We think he's gone over to the dark side. He may be a double agent."

191

"A double agent? I'll tell you what, Dean, I'll personally look into this and get back to you."

"I appreciate that, Jim. By the way, Jake asked me why La Palma might be a potential target and if so, where would the nukes likely be placed? Over the last few days we've been seeing some references to a terrorist operation that translates to 'Yellow bird' which correlates to the Canary Islands. I think Jake is onto something but I just can't figure out what the specific target is. I need your help."

"Of course, Dean, I'll get a team on it immediately."

"Thanks, Jim. I know you hold Jake in the highest esteem the same as I do. The sooner we can give him some answers the better."

"Agreed. Out here."

Blackford hit the end call button and pushed the intercom button again.

"Lieutenant Bruce?"

"Yes, Sir."

"I just got off the phone with Admiral Thornberg. The good admiral is going to personally help us but it may be too little too late. Is the any overhead imagery that might provide enough detail of La Palma to help us define a potential nuke target there?"

"Well, sir, we can check LANDSAT and some of the satellite weather imagery but what are we looking for?"

"Beats the shit out of me, Lieutenant. Look for anything out of place and look at everything in place. Figure it out."

Onboard the Gulfstream inbound to La Palma, Canary Islands

"Mossman, how much longer?" Boucher asked.

Moss pointed to the flat screen readout on the plane's dash in front of him.

"Four hours, twenty-one mikes."

Doyle who was co-piloting the sleek jet with Moss turned back towards Boucher.

"Jake, I radioed ahead to Aena Airport and have arranged a Bell 412 helicopter for us. It ain't a Blackhawk but it has good range and nearly comparable lift capability. It will be fueled and ready to go. All I need to do is sign the lease and pre-flight it. You can do an equipment trans-load while Mossman and I are taking care of the admin shit."

"Sounds good, Jackie. The faster we can get back into the air the better."

Boucher returned to his seat in the rear cabin of the plane.

"Sandra, have you had any luck raising your people?"

"Yes. They advise all indicators and warnings point to La Palma as the destination for two nukes. We're the only asset available to search for them. Jake, I don't like it."

Patterson scowled, "Yeah, me neither."

Boucher thought for a moment before responding.

"Alright everybody, listen up. We need to find those nukes before they can be moved again. We need to explore some courses of action. We need a workable concept of operations."

Her head still pounding from her previous ordeal, Sandra took a moment to order her thoughts before speaking. Her eyes met Boucher's. "Here's what we think we know. There are two nukes. They are probably large yield FSU nukes. I bet they arrived on La Palma within the last twenty-four hours. All indications point to the U.S. mainland as the eventual target. Langley thinks the fire sets have been replaced on both nukes with Iranian-built versions and they're ready to use. We don't know if they'll detonate to design yield but they will likely detonate and yield to some degree. We don't know where they've been stashed or when these nukes will be transloaded for delivery to the U.S. That said, we can assume it will happen soon."

Patterson considered Sandra's information. As the FBI's former Counter-terrorism Unit Chief he was no stranger to this kind of deductive reasoning. Turning to face Barnhart and Boucher he nodded and continued the dialog.

"We can't overlook the law enforcement aspects surrounding this case. Doctor Barnhart, you stopped a nuke from detonating in Amman. You said that nuke was an SS-19 and there was strong evidence the replacement fire set was built in Iran. Hann tried to prevent you from disabling it. Hann is a CIA-type. Apparently, he is also an Iranian-born radical Islamic extremist whose allegiance is to Iran. In my opinion he is clearly the enemy. I concur with Sandra and believe the target is the U.S. And I believe Hann is a key figure in the terrorist cell carrying out the attack."

"Yeah, I agree with all that," Mojo said, "but how are we gonna find those two nukes on an island the size of La Palma without a shit load of people on the ground to help?"

"Ya know, Mojo is right," Yellowhorse injected. "We can fly around that island all day long feel'n like we're doing good but that ain't gonna do shit if we don't know where to look."

"Okay, okay, I get it," Boucher replied. "I appreciate all the opinions but let's develop some COAs. Johnny, Billy, I'd like your input."

"Is there any available imagery that we might be able to access?" Reilly asked.

"I can tell you that the CIA doesn't watch the Canarys," Sandra offered. "Perhaps the NSA has some intercepts but I doubt they would have translated or analyzed them even if they did. I mean, the Canarys…who ties up valuable intelligence and imagery assets to watch the Canarys?"

"Exactly," Yellowhorse insisted. "Why is La Palma special? That's what I want to know – why?"

Barnhart's aged face seemed to glow. "I have an old friend at the National Geospatial-Intelligence Agency who might be able to help us. I'll give him a call and see what he thinks."

"Good, Si. I'll contact my friend at ONI and see what he can do," Boucher added.

Everyone nodded in agreement.

Boucher smiled, "Okay, we'll reconvene in thirty minutes. Hopefully we'll have some better info to go on. As soon as we land let's get the gear off this bird onto the helo. I want everyone who can to get some shuteye." Boucher readjusted his headset and mic. "Mossman and Jack, you guys will need to get the preflight on the helo done right away. I want to be fully operational as soon as possible after we land." Boucher glanced over at Sandra rubbing her temples. "Oh yeah – anyone have some aspirin? I think Sandra could use a few."

La Palma, Canary Islands, the same time

Rahman checked his watch and momentarily returned his gaze to the high ridge ashore. The sun was now cresting the horizon and there was sufficient light to see the trail that traversed the steep hillside. He knew it wouldn't be easy pulling the heavy bombs up the trail to the top but he had no doubt that the end would justify the means.

The Zodiac boats were hoisted into the sea and a bomb was subsequently hoisted into each boat and secured for transport ashore. Four crewmen manned each boat. All was now ready. Rahman strolled aft along the freighter's open weather deck occasionally peering over the side at the two boats. Every crewman on deck watched their captain climb over the ship's side into the waiting boat. Rahman nodded and the lines were cast off. Both boats sped off toward the shoreline.

The boats beached on the rocky shore where the crewman unloaded the three containers and carefully secured each of them to a field stretcher like the ones used to transport causalities. No one spoke. With Rahman in the lead, the three teams picked up their respective stretchers and began their arduous climb to the top of the 650 foot high ridge.

It took them nearly an hour of straining and sweating to reach the top but they did so without incident. Rahman, wiped the sweat from his face with his sleeve and stood at the edge of the ridge peering seaward at his ship. It seemed so small and non-threatening floating silently on a perfectly calm sea a half mile off shore. A gentle breeze coming from the water cooled his forehead.

"We have arrived," he announced to his sweating men.

He directed his men to take a short rest in the shade of some low scrub. The revving sound of engines approached from behind. Minutes later four men riding all-terrain vehicles appeared. Each was towing a trailer behind his four-wheeler. It was happening just as Rahman had been told it would. The men on the four-wheelers stopped by Rahman and his men and shut off the engines. The man on the lead four-wheeler dismounted and stood by the largest of the three bombs Rahman and his men had brought up the steep mountainside. He was a tall chiseled-looking man who exuded an ominous stance. He made a comment to the other men on the four-wheelers. Rahman didn't understand the language but it sounded like Russian. Rahman directed his men to load the bombs onto the trailers. His job was now done.

The mysterious men restarted their four-wheelers and departed for the fissure which averaged about fifteen feet deep and about ten feet wide running along most of the volcano caldron's length. Rahman knew from the target briefings that this ten mile long trench paralleled the ridge behind him. It was this trench where the deadly weapons would be planted, each separated by about two miles.

It will not be much longer, he thought, *and God will punish the infidels. There will finally be justice in the world.*

"Praise be to God," Rahman yelled.

The men immediately responded, "God is great."

He and his men were exuberant. Together, they made their way back to the beach and their inflatable boats for the return trip to his ship. Their contribution to world Islamic domination would be remembered for the next thousand years. Rahman could barely contain his joy as he climbed onboard his ship.

"It is a perfect day!" Rahman shouted to his men. "God is Great!"

His crew all cheered.

Chapter 19

The White House Situation Room, Washington, DC

Gregory Cline, the President's National Security Advisor, clicked his mic open and convened the secure video conference.

"Let's get started," he ordered in a deep raspy smoker's voice.

The other inter-agency members of the Deputies Committee that formed the counter-terrorism community's core group slowly confirmed their attendance on the secure video conference screen. This type of meeting was common-place in Washington whenever a major inter-agency decision was required to take action to counter a potential act of terrorism. The Deputies Committee was composed of the principal Deputy Secretaries of agencies in the Executive Branch who had a counter-terrorism mission. It preceded the creation of DHS by fifteen years and had served the nation well. The creation of DHS added another layer of unnecessary bureaucracy and the Deputies all knew it. Even worse, DHS's Undersecretary insisted on attending herself instead of sending her deputy. Cline began by outlining the situation to his counterparts.

"The purpose of this meeting is to provide a recommendation to the President on how to deal with the pending threat of an al Qaeda nuclear terrorist attack against the United States. We believe at least two nuclear weapons are being transported to the Canary Islands for future use against the

United States. We still don't understand the significance, if any, of their being taken to the Canarys prior to bringing them into the States. More troubling, we don't have any solid intelligence on when they may be brought into the U.S."

The DHS Undersecretary, interrupted.

"Greg, why can't our intelligence community get this information? I mean – hello-oh. How hard can it be?"

Jim Carmichael, the CIA briefer immediately responded.

"Unfortunately, Secretary Dunkle, we don't have anything specific beyond the intelligence that leads us to believe that these weapons exist and are now, or will soon be, transported to the Canarys." He pressed a button on the key pad in front of him and the wall mounted flat screen monitor switched to a picture of a map of the Canary Islands. "We don't know exactly why al Qaeda has chosen the Canary Islands as a target or if the Canarys are a target at all. There really isn't much to blow up there and the prevailing winds blow easterly so if the nukes were detonated there the fallout would most certainly be distributed over the predominantly Arab countries of North West Africa and the South Western Mediterranean. Please note the location of the Canary Islands in reference to the United States. Also note that they are almost directly in line with New York City, approximately twenty-eight hundred miles to the east and well out of range to threaten our coastal cities. We think the bombs have been cached there and will be transloaded for further transport to North America. Sources indicate these bombs will ultimately be used in an attack against the United States mainland. The target cities are unknown. In any event, we have a team of operatives on their way to the Canarys to try to locate and disable the bombs before they can be moved to our shores."

"Why wasn't I informed that the FEST had deployed?" Dunkle loudly protested.

The Foreign Emergency Support Team, or FEST, is the Nation's pointy end of the spear for resolution of acts, or potential acts, of terrorism. It is headed by a senior Department of State official from the Office of the Coordinator for Counter-terrorism and is composed of no more than sixty hand picked terrorism experts from the U.S. inter-agency counter-terrorism community. A similar team designed for U.S. domestic response is called the DEST and is headed by a senior DHS official.

"It hasn't deployed," Cline replied, "and even if it would have been deployed, DHS doesn't have a seat on the FEST. The operatives I referred to are not FEST related."

Dunkle appeared insulted. "Well, it's only courtesy to keep the complete inter-agency community informed on matters as serious as this."

"Remember, Ms. Dunkle, this entire operation is being kept within River Stone codeword channels. That means you must have a need to know and the details about our team headed to the Canarys is need to know. Now, here's what the President and the rest of us need from your agency. We need you to break out your National Response Plans. Specifically the nuclear and radiological emergency response plans to include evacuation corridors and mass casualty treatment for all our major cities. Please ensure those plans are dusted off, reviewed and are ready to implement. When intelligence identifies the target cities we'll need to have the plans briefed, distributed, and implemented as appropriate."

Dunkle tried to respond, but Cline held up his index finger cautioning her to wait as he pointed to the FBI's monitor.

"Is the FBI ready to execute its disablement mission?"

"Yes, we're ready."

"Is the DOE ready to execute its disablement mission?"

"Yes, standing by."

"Is the DOD ready to execute its disablement mission?"

"We're fully mission capable."

"To all, put your FEST deployers on a short leash. We need to get the FEST airplane loaded before close of business today." Cline checked his watch. "That's three hours from now. I want you to be ready to go wheels up within two hours from deployment notification. The Deputies Committee will issue an 'M-hour' minus two when known, so be ready."

Cline scanned the flat screen monitors and stopped on the Department of State.

"State, have you engaged the Government of Spain regarding airspace access for this potential FEST mission?"

"Negative, Greg."

"Alright, please feel them out and get back to me with any issues. If we send the FEST we won't have a lot of time to play country clearance and over-flight patty-cake. Under our MOU with the UK, I want you to let the Brits know what may be coming down. We might need their support."

Cline moved his attention to the Department of Energy's monitor.

"DOE, I want you to get your NEST team ready to deploy."

"Deploy where, Greg? CONUS or OCONUS?"

"Wherever we need them to go. Get them palletized and on a two hour deployment leash."

"Greg, I'll consolidate NEST at Sandia. We can depart from there."

"Okay, that works. DOD, by direction of the President you will provide DOE air transport for NEST. The White House will issue the directive immediately following this meeting."

Dunkle interrupted, "Greg, my deployers are ready."

"Good. I'll advise you if they're needed."

"But, I want some of my reps with the FEST."

Cline visibly winced like he was in pain. "Ms. Dunkle, I'll advise you if and when we need your help. Until that point, I need you to get those emergency response plans ready to implement. If we can figure out the target cities, we could be looking at mass evacuation and that's best case. At worst, we'll have to deal with mass casualties and mass refugee support."

"But..."

A scowling Cline interrupted Dunkle before she could continue.

"Ms. Dunkle, NO! Just do your job and get those plans ready as I asked you to do."

The Pentagon, Arlington, VA

Lester got up from his desk and ensured his office door was latched closed. He returned to his desk and hit the speaker button on his secure telephone.

"Jon, it's me. Thanks for holding. I was just told Cline put both the FEST and NEST on a two hour standby for a potential Canary Island deployment."

"That's correct. He personally chaired a Deputies Committee meeting."

"We need to encourage that FEST deployment ASAP. Can you convince Cline to authorize immediate deployment? Let's send them to Jordan. That will put them squarely in harm's way and demonstrate that our government is taking positive action."

"I don't know. Cline is trying to get his arms around this without getting into the middle of it. I think he's apprehensive now that this is all coming together."

"Apprehensive? You got to be shit'n me, Jon. He's in this as deeply as we are."

"Yeah, I know, but what if there really is a nuclear terrorist threat against the U.S.? I mean, why have the Canary Islands become the focal point all of a sudden? I thought all eyes were on Israel the way we intended?"

"We both know the real target is Amman. Come on, Jon, this is our opportunity to bomb Iran back into the Stone Age and get the rest of those radical Islamic bastards back in their box. Once we put Iran out of business, Russia and China will both have to get their oil from a different supplier and we'll be in the driver's seat instead of the back seat. It's the only way we can save our economy, eliminate Iran as an evil actor and slow the industrialization of China and Russia in one fell swoop."

"I know but I can't force him to go to the President."

"Yeah, but Cline is your boss and he's the National Security Advisor. The President will approve anything Cline puts in front of him."

"I know, I know, I know, but how am I supposed to make him do that?"

Lester sat back in his opulent brown leather executive desk chair frowning.

"Alright. I'll arrange for some non-attributable news leaks. We'll craft it to redirect public attention away from the Canarys and back to Iran and their threats to nuke Israel. And when it happens we'll have everything in place. Our heavy bombers are forward deployed. Our carriers are in position. Iran's attack on Israel will provide the catalyst we need. Israel will retaliate by nuking Tehran and we'll finish the job."

"I don't know, Ian. I'm not sure a news leak will be enough to tip the scale."

"Look, Jon, we didn't put you or Cline in there to play fiddly fuck with the President's staff. You are there to influence the President's decisions in our favor, so get it done. The sooner the FEST deploys, the better. I'll handle the rest."

Chapter 20

La Palma Airport, Canary Islands,
four and one-half hours later

Boucher gathered everyone in the main cabin of the Gulfstream.

"Listen up. Let's do a quick EEI review so we're all singing off the same sheet of music. Si, you just spoke to your geologist friend a short while ago, how about bringing us up to speed."

Barnhart rubbed his chin thoughtfully while staring out of the plane's cabin window at La Palma's mountainous horizon.

"My NGA colleague explained the geological significance of La Palma. I think I may now have some key information that answers the conundrum 'Why La Palma?' It actually seems pretty basic. Quite simply, it seems the terrorists are going to use the nukes to blast a large chunk of the Cumbre Vieja Volcano's caldron, located on the western side of La Palma, into the sea. Apparently a natural fracture already exists and the nukes will provide enough force to break a large chunk of it free. The fracture runs along the top of the caldron and is easy to see from the air."

"So you're saying a large mass like that splashing into the ocean will do what?" Patterson asked.

"It will probably create a mega-tsunami that will cross the Atlantic in about five hours and devastate the Eastern Seaboard of the U.S."

Reilly raised his hand pointing at Barnhart. "If Doc is right, we now

201

know where to look for the nukes. They'll be in that fissure you mentioned. Right, Doc?"

Moss interrupted, "So all we need to do is fly along that fissure and when we find the nukes you guys can jump out and disable them, right?"

Boucher gave Moss a puzzled glance. "Yeah, I suppose that's our best search strategy but we don't know how many there are and we only have one set of the special disablement tools. That means we can only work on one at a time. What do you think, Si?"

"We have to assume there are at least two but we need to get some folks on this to figure out how many nukes it will hypothetically take to get the job done. The fracture supposedly runs about ten miles along the caldron. I suspect it would take more than a couple of nukes to blast a mass that elongated loose. I would suppose in this case more blast is better so we should assume the bad guys have done the math and know exactly how many nukes it will take and where to place them for maximum effect."

Barnhart still had that quizzical look on his face and seemed to not hear Boucher.

"We also need to assume someone either has his finger on the detonator button or there is a clock ticking. If you recall, the bomb we disabled in the Jordanian desert had both. We got lucky. We got to it before the detonation sequence succeeded. Two nukes will present a serious disablement issue from the perspective of the time required to get the job done. Three will compound it exponentially. Jake, we may just run out of time before we can get them all disabled."

"Jezzz," Boucher gasped. "We're gonna need some help."

"So, Doc, when do you suppose this attack is planned?" Doyle asked.

"The bomb in Jordan was set to detonate mid-morning when the maximum number of people would be exposed to the blast effects," Barnhart replied.

"And it was put in place about ten hours before the morning it was set to detonate," Sandra offered.

"Alright, when would the max effects of a tsunami cause the greatest causalities along the Eastern Seaboard?" Mojo asked as he thoughtfully stroked his white beard.

"That's easy," Sandra answered, "morning rush hour, Eastern Daylight Time. Catch everyone coming to work on their way into the cities; normal traffic gridlock and nowhere to run. My God, it'll be a slaughter."

Boucher nodded. "If we factor the time it will take for the tsunami to travel across the Atlantic for an arrival along the East Coast around rush hour Eastern Daylight Time, we only have a few hours to find and disable those nukes. It's going to get dark in an hour so we need to find them while we still have daylight working for us. I gotta make a phone call. Jackie, I want you to stay here with the Gulfstream in case we need to get outta here in a hurry." Doyle nodded and gave a thumbs-up. "Mossman, we need to get our helicopter airborne now."

Moss pulled his grit-soiled DILLIGAFF hat lower on his forehead and flashed a wide smile. "Let's rock and roll."

Boucher and his crew disembarked the Gulfstream and began hurriedly off-loading their equipment from the cargo compartment. A Dassault Falcon corporate jet touched down at the same time and taxied to a nearby parking apron next to a hanger. Three men left the sleek plane with several luggage cases and headed to a hanger where they were greeted by two other men.

Kennedy Irregular Warfare Center, ONI, Suitland, MD, the same time

"Captain, take a look at this imagery product. We pulled most of it off the web along with some other open source imagery taken from the International Space Station. We merged them and digitally enhanced the detail. Note the track of that small freighter, Sir."

Blackford studied the digital flat screen presentation momentarily then put his finger on the yellow line that showed the freighter's path running through the Mediterranean Sea out into the Atlantic to La Palma. The ship was little more than a dot on the screen.

"So you're telling me this ship is a bad actor?"

"Well, Sir, there is no other explanation for it. It sailed from Tunisia four days ago and went straight to La Palma. It didn't go into port when it arrived and we can find no record of a cargo manifest on either end of the voyage. Let me advance the time a few hours and enlarge the ship a bit so you can see the deck."

Blackford watched as the lieutenant framed the area of the ship with his computer mouse and clicked the scale bar on the side of the screen.

"This is thirty minutes after the ship arrived on the west coat of La Palma. Note they are readying three rubber boats on the after deck. Now I'll advance it a few minutes at a time. Here they're lowering the boats over the side. Here they're heading to the shore. Here they're on the shore unloading what look like field stretchers. Now take a close look at this, Captain. The shore party is climbing the hillside with their stretchers. And here they're on the top."

Blackford studied the picture. "Back it out a little. I want to see the ship again."

The lieutenant moved his mouse over to the scale bar and clicked.

"That's enough," Blackford whispered. "The ship didn't depart."

"That's right, Sir. It loitered there for more than four hours. When the small boats returned they didn't have the stretchers with them. After the boats were recovered the ship departed and it's basically following the same reverse course back toward the Strait of Gibraltar. Sir, they delivered something to the top of that ridge on the west side of La Palma."

"You have any intercepts during that period?"

"No, Sir. They didn't use any radios or cell phones. They knew exactly what they were there for."

"What do you think they were there for, Lieutenant?"

"We believe they delivered at least two, maybe three, rogue nukes, Sir."

"But why that side of La Palma? The airport and the population center are on the opposite end of the island."

"We're not sure, Sir. But we think there may be a reason."

"Which is what?"

"Well, Sir, you're probably going to tell me I'm crazy but I think they're going to explode those nukes along the western top edge of that ridge."

Blackford looked puzzled as he stared at the imagery of La Palma. The Lieutenant pointed to La Palma on the screen.

"Could you track them on the imagery?"

"No, Sir, we don't have the resolution available."

"Then what makes you think they intend to blow up that ridge?"

"I don't think they're going to blow it up, Sir. They're going to blow it down."

"Explain."

"Like the other six islands in the Canary chain, La Palma was formed by a volcano. The volcano hasn't erupted in seventy years but it's still alive and rumbling. La Palma's volcano formed some very unique geology."

"Get to the point, Lieutenant. I don't give a shit about the fossil record or the frigin' continental drift."

The Lieutenant zoomed in, enlarging the west side of the island on the screen.

"You see, Sir, that particular volcano has a very unique linear caldron rather than a traditional circular caldron like most other volcanoes. This volcano's caldron stretches about ten miles along the west side of the island and rises to a height of about 450 feet above sea level. That's almost as tall as the Washington monument. This volcanic ridge is over-steep. Because it was formed volcanically, it is relatively new, geologically speaking. It hasn't had enough weather exposure to erode away its over-steep qualities so it's very prone to landslides, much like avalanches occur on mountains covered with over-steep snow. Worse yet, the caldron has fractured about one-half mile to a mile inland and slipped under its own weight about fifteen feet downward. That means there is a mass of earth about ten miles long that is anywhere from a half a mile to one mile thick hanging precariously above the sea surface to a height of 450 feet. The ocean depth is approximately 650 feet deep along the caldron. Many geologists believe that when the volcano becomes active again the tremors will cause this huge mass to break loose and slide into the sea."

Blackford scratched his head. "So you're saying that's a really bad thing, right?"

"Yes, Sir," the Lieutenant patiently answered. "That's going to be really bad and here's why. When that mountain slides into the sea and crashes to the sea floor 650 feet below, the water displaced by a mass that size will trigger a massive tsunami. This mega-tsunami will cross the Atlantic at the speed of an airliner – about 450 miles an hour. It will only take about four and one half hours for it to reach, Boston, New York City, and the coast of New Jersey. Because of the underwater topology of the Hudson River, the tsunami's energy will be focused by the deep trench that the Hudson follows as it drains east off the continental shelf. In that particular location the tsunami will build to between nine-hundred and twelve hundred feet high and completely engulf New York City."

"Holy shit!" Blackburn gasped. "What about the rest of the coastline?"

"The tsunami will devastate the entire eastern seaboard of North America from Canada to the Gulf of Mexico along with the low lying Caribbean Islands that have an unprotected northeast exposure. The waves that hit Boston will be over one-hundred and fifty feet high. The waves that hit Virginia Beach will be over two-hundred feet high. Miami and the Florida Keys will be washed over by sixty foot waves. The Eastern Seaboard will be completely devastated to a distance inland from between five to twenty miles depending on the topography. Even Washington, DC will be flooded with ten feet of water from the Chesapeake Bay surge up the Potomac River. There will be no way to hide from it and no way to stop it. The waves will keep coming with perhaps as many as eight to ten successive waves over a period of minutes to hours. It will be complete destruction of our east coast on a cataclysmic scale never seen by man. The death toll will be in the millions. The refugees will easily number three times that many. If this happens, about a third of the U.S. infrastructure will be largely devastated and may never recover. Wall Street will be washed off the face of the earth. The U.S. east coast will cease to exist as we know it today."

Blackburn sat down in astonishment. "They're going to use the nukes to break that mountain loose, aren't they?"

Lieutenant Bruce nodded. "And then gravity will take care of the rest."

"It's brilliant, simply brilliant. When are they going to conduct the attack?"

"All the intel points to tomorrow morning, Captain."

"What's so special about tomorrow?"

"It's the 19th, the Islamic holiday of Isra' Me'raj – Mohammad's Night Journey to the Heavens."

"Okay, what the hell is that all about?"

"Hell," Bruce repeated, "I guess you could say that, Sir. According to the legend, Mohammad journeyed to the Heavens and back in a single night, riding on a winged steed where he met with Allah. Allah told him that He would raise Islam up as a holy superpower and with the basic elements - earth, fire and water - defeat the Great Satan. Sir, they may have taken that as a literal prophecy to nuke a mountain into the sea to create a mega-tsunami that will eliminate the U.S. Eastern Seaboard."

"We have to get this to The White House. What's the name of that fucking volcano on La Palma?"

"The Cumbre Vieja Volcano, Sir."

A petty officer appeared, interrupting Blackford's thoughts.

"Sir, there's a Commander Jake Boucher on the phone holding for you. He says it's critical that he speaks with you."

Chapter 21

The USS Saipan

USS Saipan is the flag ship for Amphibious Squadron Eight. The five ships composing the amphibious ready group had been underway for four days heading to the Mediterranean on a great circle southerly route. They were now one-hundred and twenty miles southwest of the Azores on a northeasterly heading. Another seven-hundred miles and they would pass through the Strait of Gibraltar into the Mediterranean on their way to their patrol area off the Israeli-Lebanese coast. There they would rendezvous with and join the USS Dwight Eisenhower Battle Group which was running a full day ahead of the Amphibious Ready Group.

The Saipan's flight operations had been secured an hour earlier. The SEAL detachment riding onboard was doing an exercise run around the flight deck. Commodore Tom Laverne, who was in overall command of the Amphibious Ready Group, was smoking an after dinner cigar on the Saipan's flag bridge watching the SEALs race around the ship's expansive flight deck three stories below. The Messenger of the Watch approached Laverne startling him out of his daydream.

"Commodore, I have a flash message for you, Sir."

The messenger handed him a flat-hinged aluminum file cover marked TOP SECRET - SPECAT and saluted.

"Thank you," Laverne said returning the salute. "Standby a moment."

The messenger stepped back inside the flag bridge to give Laverne privacy. Laverne turned his back to the wind, shaking off the chill that pierced his flight jacket. He opened the metal cover and began to read the message. He knew a flash precedence message was only issued when something was of the utmost importance. This one was. After reading a few moments he looked up and turned, facing the messenger.

"Please inform my Battle Staff, the Air Boss and the SEAL Detachment Commander to meet me in the Flag Staff briefing room immediately."

"Aye, Sir."

Laverne turned back toward the Saipan's bow as if the salt-laden wind buffeting the bridge wing would cleanse his face and perhaps his thoughts. He had just been handed a bag of shit and knew it. He puffed his cigar again, then promptly plunged it into a foam cup half full of cold coffee as he stepped off the bridge wing into the warm pilot house.

Cumbre Vieja Volcano, La Palma

Moss rolled the helicopter into a shallow dive, leveling off about fifty feet above the fault line. Boucher and Patterson leaned out of the open starboard-side door. Reilly and Mojo did the same on the opposing port-side door. Moss skillfully maintained his altitude and air speed as they reconnoitered the grass and hedge-covered fault line below. Boucher marveled at Moss's piloting skills and raw nerve. He still revered Moss as both the most talented pilot he'd ever known and the damn luckiest man alive. Moss had saved his bacon a number of times during the Vietnam War as well as during last year's treasure hunt that brought him and his old SEAL platoon all back together. Boucher was forever grateful that Moss was now working as a full time partner in his security firm. Boucher's mind flashed back to their adventure a year ago that began in Cambodia in search of a 1968 airplane crash site and the gold bullion and cash they recovered worth nearly half a billion dollars. It had made them very wealthy men, even though the treasure hunt itself had almost gotten them all killed.

Below, the glint of a metallic object partially covered by foliage caught Boucher's eye, bringing him back to reality.

"You guys see that metallic object down there?" he shouted into his mic.

Moss adjusted himself so he could get a clear view from the cockpit at the fault line ditch directly below.

"Yeah, got it. Is that it?" Patterson asked.

"That sure looks like the right shape. What else could it be? Mossman, can you hover us close to it so I can check for a radioactive signature?"

Boucher sat on the deck in the open door with his legs dangling outside the hovering helicopter. He held the radiation detector as far outside the helicopter as he could to keep the fuel tanks located beneath the helicopter's cargo deck he was sitting on from mitigating the radiation signature. He carefully studied the LED window on the detector.

"I show gamma – neutron. Mossman, put us down as close as you can get us. Then move away as far as you can without losing a visual on us.

"Roger, that."

"Pat, Johnny, Mojo, you're with me. Billy, hang back with Sandra and Dr. Barnhart."

"No, Jake," Barnhart demanded, "put me down and I'll begin a disablement. You and the others find the other nukes and mark them. You can come back and help me later."

"Roger, but I want one of my guys to assist you."

"I'll do it," Sandra volunteered. "You guys need to find the other nukes."

Boucher nodded his consent.

Moss landed the Bell 412 on a relatively level spot on the ridge a few yards above the fault line. Mojo grabbed the tool bag and ran it over to the trench where the object was resting. Reilly and Sandra helped the old scientist out of the helicopter and assisted him down the steep side of the trench to the object. Both Reilly and Mojo returned to the helo and climbed inside. Mossman eased the helicopter back into the air and vanished along the trench. The jet engine noise gradually dissipated in the distance and it became eerily quiet.

The USS Saipan, the same time

Laverne sat at the head of the conference table patiently sipping his coffee. Lieutenant Morgan, the SEAL Detachment Commander was the last to enter the flag conference room located just aft of the Flag Bridge. He was still wearing his sweat soaked brown T-shirt and running shorts. No one spoke. All eyes were on Laverne.

"Thank you for assembling so quickly gentlemen. I will get to the point. A few minutes ago we received a flash precedence message with new orders. We are directed to make flank speed to within air operations proximity of La Palma in the Canary Islands. Our mission is to locate two terrorist nukes that are believed to be hidden along the Cumbre Vieja volcano's caldron and stop them from detonating. We are advised there may be additional nukes that the terrorists may be in the process of planting and arming. It is believed these nukes will be detonated sometime after midnight tonight. We are directed to do whatever it takes to locate and stop those nukes from detonating."

Laverne looked into the faces of his Chief of Staff and Operations Officer.

"Hal, turn the Group toward La Palma and make flank speed."

"Yes, Sir."

Laverne looked at his Air Boss who coordinated all aviation assets in the Group and then at Lieutenant Morgan.

"Boss, I'll need you to launch two V-22s with extended range auxiliary tanks to La Palma the moment we're in range. I'll get you the landing zone coordinates immediately following this meeting. I'll need a TOT as soon as possible."

The Air Boss nodded as he took notes.

"Lieutenant Morgan, you and your SEALs will be flown to the Cumbre Vieja Volcano on the west side of La Palma in the V-22s. Be advised that you may make contact with the terrorists who either planted these nukes or are still in the process of planting them. Therefore, you will be fully combat ready and protect yourselves as necessary."

"Aye, Sir."

"I understand that you and your team have had some 'special' technical training in dealing with WMD."

"Yes, Sir, we have and we have our tools and special explosives stowed here onboard the Saipan but we only have a single emergency destruct capability."

"Your mission will be to provide direct action search and disablement. I want you to challenge any suspicious activity. Get your men and equipment onboard the V-22s. You can brief your men on the way in."

"Aye, Sir."

"Battalion Commander, Colonel, I want a Marine security element to follow-on in helicopters the moment we are in range to launch them. If you can get them launched along with the SEALs - great! They are to protect those conducting the search and disablement operations and apprehend the terrorists if possible. Additionally, when the Group is within helicopter range I am certain we will be tasked to conduct a non-combat evacuation operation of all the civilians from the western side of La Palma so be ready. We will transport these people to our ships to get them out of immediate danger. We'll see what further action is required from there if it's deemed necessary. Colonel, the NEO mission will fall squarely in your lap. I want you to go ashore and personally command it."

"Understand, Commodore."

Laverne scanned the faces of his senior staff.

"Gentlemen, this is the real deal. There are real nukes on that island and their clocks are ticking down. The terrorists who put them there may be close by. We don't know. I don't want our ships to get any closer than twenty miles from the south east side of La Palma. That will keep us out of the blast effects radius and upwind just in case our people on the ground are unsuccessful in their disablement attempt. Based on our current position, I estimate that we will be within V-22 launch range in about fifteen minutes. I will provide the rules of engagement as soon as possible. Gentlemen, let's make ready. Any questions?"

<u>Chapter 22</u>

Cumbre Vieja Volcano, same time

Four ATVs slowly made their way up the steep trail with their headlights off. They came to a halt on the east side of the caldron just below the top of the ridge. The man on the lead ATV checked their position on his portable GPS and waved, signaling the others to follow. He then drove a short distance off the trail and stopped in a brush thicket. The others followed. All were wearing night vision goggles and dressed in nondescript black battle dress uniforms. The four heavily armed men dismounted and draped their four-wheelers with camouflage tarps. They slowly patrolled up the trail with their sub-machine guns at the ready.

In the Bell 412, same time

"How you coming along Doc?" Boucher asked over the radio.

"Not bad for a Monday," came the static-laden reply. "I'm going to attempt a hand entry."

"A hand entry? Are you nuts? Hold on a few mikes, I'm on my way!"

"No, Jake! This thing could go off any moment. I want you all out of here now! Sandra refuses to leave so she will assist me."

"Bullshit, Doc! I'm on my way!"

Moss clicked his mic open. "Jake, if you're staying, I'm staying."

"Me too!" Patterson confirmed.

"That goes for all of us, Jake," Reilly added. "We're either all coming out together or we'll end it together fighting the good fight."

"Thanks boys, I'm honored, but I need you guys to keep looking for the other nukes. Mossman touch down as close to Doctor Barnhart's working point as you can without hitting him with rotor wash. I'm gonna jump out. You guys keep looking and let me know if you find anything."

"Roger!"

Moss banked the helicopter into a hard right turn, lining up on a parallel course with La Palma's ridge and the trench fracture. "Jake, I'm gonna fly down the trench with my landing lights on. When we find Doc and Sandra, I'll touch down so you can jump out."

"Roger, keep us low so we don't miss them."

They only flew a few minutes when Moss flared the helicopter, pulling the nose up, settling in a slow descent toward the ground below. As the helo's skids momentarily found solid ground in a touch and go, Boucher jumped out and charged down into the trench to Barnhart's working point. Sandra was assisting him like a nurse in an operating room.

Barnhart was concentrating on removing the screws from the access plate at the base of the warhead.

Boucher ran his hand lightly across Sandra's back in greeting. She acknowledged him with a warm smile.

"What you got, Si?" Boucher calmly inquired.

"An SS -19 physics package with a modified fire set," Barnhart drawled without looking up.

Boucher sat down on the side of the trench and cautiously slid over next to Barnhart. "How can I help you, Si?"

"I don't think I can stop a detonation. The best I can do is try to stop it from detonating in symmetry. Hopefully, that will reduce the yield. If this thing goes off full yield it will shove about a mile of this mountainside down into the sea."

"Why can't we move it?"

"It is just too risky," Barnhart replied. "When I radiographed the firing circuit I noted a radio firing device that is not accessible through any inspection port. The amazing thing is that they designed the primary to detonate on a clock timer."

"A clock?" Boucher questioned in surprise. "I thought you said it has an RFD?"

"I did, but there's a clock ticking down as well. My guess is that the clock

213

will trigger the radio firing device so all the nukes fire simultaneously. Pretty ingenious."

"How long do we have?".

"I don't know. It's a digital timer and all I can see on the radiograph is the timer's circuitry. I can't determine how much time is left without opening this access plate and looking inside at the LCD display. There's at least one tremor switch built into this firing circuit as well. I think our only option is to do a hand entry and try to disable the fire set."

Boucher leaned forward studying the screws that held the access plate in place.

"Is there any reason why we can't cut the tremor switch out of the circuit and then put this thing on the helo and drop it into deep water?"

"Yes, a big show stopper. This is a very sophisticated firing mechanism and I'm betting it will detonate if I try to collapse parts of the energized circuit. I can't determine how many traps it has without a close diagnostic study of the fire set design and we don't have time for that. Jake, we have a clock counting down. The only way is to do a hand entry and attempt a partial disablement of some of the detonators. I don't think we can stop it from going off. All I can do is try to ensure this thing doesn't detonate in symmetry and go full yield."

"I'll radio Mossman and advise him of our plan. What do you need me to do?"

"You and Sandra carefully dig some of the dirt away from the other side so I can get better access to the inspection plate on that side. I'll continue here."

Following the radio call, Sandra and Boucher began pulling the soft volcanic earth away from the bottom side of the bomb using their hands.

Chapter 23

North end of the Cumbre Vieja Volcano caldron, the same time

Lieutenant Morgan had divided his eighteen man SEAL platoon into two elements putting one SEAL element onboard each Osprey. He did this as a force multiplier so his men could cover twice as much ground and also to reduce the odds of mission failure should one of the Ospreys crash or otherwise run into unforeseen problems requiring a mission abort. The two Ospreys carrying the SEALs had spaced themselves about a hundred yards apart and were hovering above the trench. They were using their ultra-sophisticated night vision and forward-looking infrared, or FLIR as it was called, to scan the trench below. The FLIR was also capable of seeing a heat source – a source like a lightly shielded or unshielded fissile warhead. Lieutenant Morgan's SEALs were all wearing night vision goggles and peering down from the open waist door windows and the open tail ramp. The search was slow going. Characteristic of secure voice satellite radios, Morgan's headset bleeped with two short electronic tones followed by a static-fringed voice.

"Anvil One, this is Juno Five, over."

Static ensued for a few moments. Morgan recognized the call sign as the pilot in command of the other Osprey.

"Roger, Juno Five, this is Anvil One. What you got?"

"Anvil, we intermittently hold a low flying contact at the far south end of this caldron ridge. From its flight profile I make it to be a helicopter."

"Roger Juno Five, you stay here with Anvil Two and continue search. I will take Juno Four and prosecute suspected boogie."

"Roger, Anvil. WILCO, out."

Lieutenant Morgan directed his Osprey to fly to the south end of the caldron and investigate the suspect aircraft.

South end of the Cumbre Vieja Volcano caldron, the same time

A short burst of sub-machine gun fire from above raked the side of the trench coming dangerously close to the nuclear warhead Barnhart was working on. Boucher instinctively yanked Barnhart down while yelling to Sandra to get down. Four men wearing night vision goggles and balaclavas appeared on the trail above holding their guns at a menacing ready.

"Hands up!" the leader growled. "Step away from the warhead and don't anybody try to be a hero."

Boucher helped Barnhart to his feet. The man kept his sub-machine gun pointed at Boucher.

"You three have gotten in the way for the last time. Climb up here!" he demanded waving his gun barrel along the side of the trench in his direction. "Do it now!"

Boucher took the lead pulling Barnhart by the hand. Boucher climbed a third of the way up the fifteen-foot side of the trench and turned to help Barnhart up the steep earthen wall. Sandra pushed him from behind in an effort to help him climb. At the point when Barnhart was near the top, Boucher caught a direct look from Sandra. He understood without words that she was going to make a move against their captors the moment she had an opportunity.

Barnhart clamored onto the trail above and knelt down on one knee panting. As Boucher reached for Sandra's hand she sprung forward with a veraciousness that surprised the man giving the orders and the guards standing beside him. The man, one of his guards, and Sandra tumbled down into the trench in a mass of confused grabbing, shoving and punching.

Boucher knew he only had one chance to overwhelm the other two guards standing on the trail a few feet away and he took it. He dove at the guard's mid-section, tackling him like a pro football player sacking a quarterback. The guard went down on his back under Boucher's crushing weight. Boucher snatched the sub-machine gun from the surprised guard's hands and pulled the trigger as he pressed the muzzle into the guard's neck. The guard died instantly. Boucher reeled and slammed the butt end of the submachine gun into the second guard's chest and raked it upward across his chin. The guard collapsed backward into the undergrowth. Boucher reeled around and aimed the gun down into the trench in the direction of Sandra and the others but couldn't get a clear shot.

The scene in the trench below was chaotic. Sandra had successfully stunned the leader with the surprise and ferociousness of her assault. He was dazed but the guard was twice Sandra's size which gave him a clear advantage. He was clutching Sandra's arm in one hand and had her by the throat with the other. She was fighting him for her life. Boucher couldn't get a clear shot at the guard. All he could do was try to reach Sandra and take over the fight. He leapt to the side of the trench and started to slide down when a single shot rang out from below. Everything was a blur. He saw Sandra collapse on top of the guard. The leader was getting to his feet. He had a pistol in his hand. He had shot Sandra!

Boucher came from behind and hammered him between the shoulders with his sub-machine gun. The man went down face first sprawling on the side of the trench. The guard was in the process of pushing Sandra's limp body off him when Boucher arrived. The guard attempted to regain his grip on his sub-machine gun but Boucher was now in full combat mode. He brought his gun up to his shoulder and fired two rounds into the guard's chest and two more into his right eye spewing the man's brains out the back of his head.

Boucher threw his gun aside and knelt next to Sandra pulling her into his arms. Bright red blood was frothing from a chest wound just above her left breast and from her mouth. She was breathing, but barely. He had seen wounds like this many times before. It was a sucking chest wound. He quickly pulled open her blouse, placed the palm of his hand over the wound and rolled her on her side to keep the blood from filling her lungs.

"Oh God, no!" he shouted at the heavens above.

Sandra's eyes fluttered open and she tried to speak.

"Don't talk," Boucher whispered, "I'll get help. Don't leave me now!"

Boucher yelled up at Barnhart. "Si, get on the radio to Mossman. Tell 'em I need an immediate dustoff."

Barnhart gave a thumbs-up and went back for the radio. Sandra's breathing was increasingly labored. Every breath sounded like gurgling water. Boucher took her pulse. It was weak and erratic. He was losing her and he knew it.

Barnhart appeared above. "Mossman says he's five out. We can fly her to the hospital clinic in town."

"Sandra, don't give up," Boucher pleaded. "Hold on. Please don't leave me. I love you."

Sandra's eyes fluttered open and she attempted to talk again.

"Don't talk. Help is on the way. I'll get you to a hospital."

Sandra began to cough out cupful quantities of frothing bright red blood. Boucher kept his palm on her wound but the internal damage to her lung and heart was catastrophic. She was beginning to convulse. Boucher clutched her more closely. All at once she relaxed. She opened her eyes and looked into Boucher's eyes and mouthed the words, *I love you too*. Her stare went blank and she died.

Boucher had seen death up close and personal many times before but this was too much for him to bear. He looked above and screamed, "NO!!!" at the top of his lungs and clutched her limp body tightly against his chest.

Barnhart could see the tears streaming down Boucher's cheeks. The man Jake had hit from behind slowly moved his hand toward the pistol lying in the dirt in front of him.

"Jake, he's moving!" Barnhart yelled. "Watch out, he's going for the gun!"

Boucher carefully laid Sandra's body down and stood, facing back at the man.

"You rat bastard! You dirty rat bastard! You murdering son-of-a-bitch!"

The masked man grabbed the gun and held it on Boucher as he got to his feet. He slowly climbed to the top of the trench a few yards from Barnhart.

"Get down there with your friend," he ordered.

Barnhart slid down the side of the trench and stood beside Boucher.

"Lie face down," he ordered. "Both of you – down!"

Barnhart began to get down but Boucher stood defiantly facing the man. The sound of an approaching helicopter was growing louder and louder.

"I'm gonna track you down and kill you," Boucher hissed.

The man didn't hesitate. He fired two rounds at Boucher. The first grazed Boucher in his left triceps spinning him down and to the left. The second round missed Boucher but hit the heel of Barnhart's shoe tearing it partially off. The man disappeared along the trail into the darkness.

Boucher regained his balance and grabbed the dead guard's submachine gun.

"You okay?" he shouted to Barnhart.

"Yeah, he missed me."

Boucher bounded up the side of the trench in hot pursuit. At this point the man had about a fifty yard head start on Boucher. Now, neither of the men had their NVGs. Boucher heard the engine of a four-wheeler race away a short distance ahead along the trail. He could make out the faint glow of a headlight bouncing off the low foliage. Then the approaching helicopter appeared. It was Moss. Boucher ran to a small clearing and waved blindly into the darkness. Moss was flying the helicopter completely blacked out using night vision goggles. The sky was now almost completely clouded over and a gentle rain was beginning to fall. A front had moved in and it was getting darker by the moment. As the roar of the helicopter's jet engines reached a defining crescendo and the rotor wash buffeted Boucher, he flashed back to the Jordanian desert a day earlier. There was something uncanny about the man he was now chasing that seemed familiar. *Was it his voice or the way he moved?*

"Jake, get in!" Yellowhorse's voice jolted Boucher back.

Boucher leapt into the helicopter's open side cargo door as Moss touched down and lifted off again without slowing the helicopter's forward speed. Reilly handed him a headset.

"Follow the four-wheeler on the trail ahead," Boucher shouted into the mic.

Moss banked slightly to the left aligning his heading with the four wheeler's shimmering headlight moving down the trail several hundred yards ahead.

"Stop him, Mossman, I need him alive. Be careful, he's armed."

"Roger," Moss coolly replied.

Moss passed above the four-wheeler at an altitude of about ten feet. Now in front of it, he spun the helicopter one-hundred and eighty degrees, switched on his forward landing light and blocked the path. The man on the four-wheeler was instantly blinded by the piercing bright light and veered off the trail into some low brush. The impact threw him downhill about thirty feet. The man hit the brush-covered ground hard, sprawling onto his back. Boucher leapt from the open door of the helicopter and rushed down to the stunned man. He covered the distance between the helicopter and the man in one giant step. The man rolled on his side and fumbled as he attempted to retrieve a pistol from the weed-covered ground next to him. Boucher snatched the pistol away before the man could reach it. He immediately pulled the slide back and chambered a fresh round. As the man pulled himself up to a sitting position Boucher yanked the man's balaclava off.

"Hann?" Boucher muttered in disbelief.

"What are you going to do, murder me?"

Trembling from rage, Boucher held the pistol down at his side as he peered back at Hann. He was oblivious to the noise and rotor wash as Mossman landed the helicopter a short distance away. Patterson and Mojo appeared next to Boucher. Hann began to laugh.

"It will all be over soon, my friends. When the nukes go off it will be over."

Boucher slowly raised the pistol and pointed it at Hann's chest.

"Don't do it, Jake." Patterson yelled. "You're not a murderer."

Boucher lowered his pistol slightly and stood silently contemplating the reality of the situation. He didn't feel the burning bullet wound in his left triceps that was slowly oozing blood. He seemed to be studying Hann as if he was trying to read his thoughts. After a few moments he stepped closer.

"Okay, asshole, where are the nukes?"

"Fuck you, Boucher!" Hann yelled defiantly.

Boucher kicked him in the face toppling him on his back. He put his foot on Hann's neck and pressed down with all his weight.

"Where are the nukes?"

"Fuck you, Boucher! What are you going to do, torture me in front of all these witnesses?"

"Yup, that's exactly what I'm going to do."

Boucher pointed the pistol at Hann's right knee and fired. The joint exploded exposing raw flesh and splintered bone. Hann screamed in pain as Boucher continued to hold him down by his neck.

"How many nukes?"

"You son-of-a-bitch! You and your dead bitch girlfriend are going to hell!"

Boucher kicked Hann in the ribs rolling him on his other side.

"Where are the nukes?" he calmly asked again.

"I'll have you killed! We got your wife. You thought it was a car accident. This time we'll get you."

"My wife?"

"Yeah, your wife. You're a damn fool, Boucher."

Boucher appeared stunned as he contemplated the circumstances surrounding the fatal car accident years ago that took his wife's life and nearly his son's as well. Boucher shook it off and set his jaw forward.

"Here's the deal. If you tell me what I ask you, I'll let you live. If you don't, I'm going to keep making holes in your body until you bleed out. How many nukes?"

Hann hesitated a moment. "Fuck you, asshole!"

Boucher pointed the gun at Hann's other knee and fired. Hann screamed in excruciating pain.

"Jake, don't do it," Patterson again warned his friend.

Boucher coolly smiled down at Hann, oblivious to Patterson's warning.

"Your elbows are next. How many nukes?"

"Two others," Hann whispered.

"And?"

"You bastard! You can't do this to me. This is torture. There are witnesses! I am protected under the Constitution. The Supreme Court ruled on it."

"Which elbow do you want to lose first?"

"You fucking bastard!"

Boucher calmly pointed his pistol at Hann's left elbow.

"Two nukes."

"How many?"

"Three."

"Where are they?"

"Two others here - I don't know where the third one is."

Boucher moved the pistol a few inches adjusting his aim. "Where are they?" he demanded again. Boucher removed his foot from Hann's neck and stepped on what used to be his left knee pinning him to the ground. Hann writhed in pain.

"The vent on the north end."

"You traitorous bastard! When are they going to detonate?"

Hann began to smile. Boucher aimed his pistol at Hann's left elbow.

"I just asked you a fucking question."

Hann glanced at his watch and laughed sarcastically. "Just after midnight tonight. You're too late."

Boucher turned away and walked back toward the waiting helicopter. Boucher seemed oblivious to all the ruckus and jet noise. Hann remained belligerent.

"I'll have you all killed for this! You son-of-a-bitch! I'll have your families killed and…!"

Hann pulled a hidden pistol from beneath his field jacket. A single shot rang out. Boucher's bullet struck Hann with perfect accuracy right between his eyes silencing him in mid-sentence. He lifelessly slumped backward with a dim stare.

"Jake?" Patterson questioned.

"It's not murder. It's justice!" Boucher muttered as he passed by Patterson. "Take me back to Barnhart."

Chapter 24

Cumbre Vieja Volcano, La Palma

Morgan's darkened Osprey touched down a short distance from Moss's idling helicopter and Barnhart's working point. Lieutenant Morgan along with several heavily armed SEALs rushed from the open tail ramp of the Osprey and took up defensive covering positions ready to engage. With guns at the ready, Morgan and two of his men cautiously approached Boucher who was aimlessly carrying Sandra's body. Patterson was by his side with a steadying hand on Boucher's arm.

"Don't anyone move," Morgan shouted over the noise of the Osprey's whining jet engines.

Boucher turned and faced Morgan, straining to respond. His lips were moving but no words were coming out. Morgan immediately recognized Boucher from the ship boarding operation he had run against Boucher's junk in the South China Sea a year earlier. His mind flashed back to the shootout they had with the Chinese submarine. He could picture the dead Chinese sailors sprawled on its deck and the fatal crash dive it made as smoke bellowed from the holes the SEALs had blasted through its hull. He was again looking at the man who fought so bravely by his side; a SEAL commander of legendary status. Then he recognized the black man at Boucher's side, Leon Patterson, former POW and retired FBI Supervisory Special Agent and Counter-terrorism Unit Chief; another living legend.

"Commander Boucher, Special Agent Patterson, what the hell are you doing here? We were sent in here to stop terrorists from planting nuclear weapons and destroy any they already have put in place. I damn near shot you guys." Morgan's excitement visibly waned as he focused on Sandra. "We can take the lady out to the Saipan for triage."

"She's gone," Patterson said.

"I'm sorry, Sir."

Boucher slowly laid Sandra's bloody body on a grassy spot and stepped back beside Patterson. His shoulders were slumped forward and his head was down. Patterson put a reassuring arm around his distraught friend's back.

"Jake, we have a job to finish."

Boucher stared up at the black sky as he organized his thoughts. The rain had turned into a downpour. He cocked his head left, and then to the right, letting the rain wash completely over his face. For the first time he felt a sudden chill and realized the temperature had dropped since the rain had begun and darkness had set in. Shrugging off the chill he looked over at Patterson and nodded, confirming he was okay. He then focused on Morgan.

"Lieutenant, we have a mega-ton yield SS-19 warhead over there in that ditch and there are two more nukes of unknown classification and yield somewhere along this fault line with their clocks ticking. We believe all these nukes are linked together with a radio firing device so it doesn't matter which one triggers first. They'll all still go off at the same time. You need to find the other nukes and disable them before midnight. We'll stay here and continue a hand entry on this one. We have less than two hours."

"Aye, Sir, but why not let us disable this one now? I have an emergency destruct capability with me. Don't you require assistance?"

"Do you have more than a single destruct capability with you?"

"Negative, Sir. I have only a single capability."

"When you find the other nukes, you'll need to have your disablement capability available to stop one of them. We'll take care of this one. Do you have a portable radiography unit with you?"

"No, Sir, ours is down awaiting repair."

"Then take my unit with you. Hopefully you'll find the other nukes and have time to use it. Keep your comms open with us and keep me updated."

"Roger, Commander. Be advised there is a Marine Battalion Landing Team on the way here by helicopter. They should arrive shortly after midnight. I'll advise them you're here and you're friendly."

"Good. We will be finished here by then, one way or the other."

"Commander, would you like my corpsman to bandage your shoulder wound before we go?"

Boucher realized for the first time that he had been wounded. He glanced at his shoulder and lightly wiped his hand over his blood soaked shirt.

"No, it's just a scratch. Go find those other nukes."

Boucher and Patterson returned to Barnhart in the fault line trench. Mojo and Yellowhorse were both illuminating Barnhart's working point using their night vision goggles on the active infrared mode. This additional illumination added to Barnhart's own NVG active infrared providing him ample light as he worked inside the S-19's open access port. Reilly was standing out of the way to the side of Barnhart holding the satellite telephone in one hand and the radio in the other.

"Billy, tell Mossman to shut down the helo and standby. Get me a SATCOM call through to Admiral Thornberg at the CIA. His private line is programmed in the phone's address book."

"Sure, Jake."

Reilly keyed several buttons on the phone and listened.

"Admiral Thornberg, Sir, this is Billy Reilly. I'm here with Jake Boucher who urgently needs to speak with you. I have you on speaker, Sir. I'll pass the phone over to him now."

"Very well."

Boucher grabbed the satellite phone from Reilly.

"Jim, Jake, here's the bottom line. I have an SS-19 warhead in front of me. Doctor Barnhart is attempting a hand disablement. There may be two other nukes hidden somewhere along the fault line here on La Palma. We almost had a blue on blue engagement a short while ago."

"What?"

"That's right, Jim. The SEALs off the Saipan were sent in here to stop the terrorists who planted these nukes and they were not told we were already here. My guess is someone in the mission tasking and deconfliction chain of command either made a huge mistake or they intentionally intended for me and my guys to get into a dick dragger with the SEALs. And if we had, we wouldn't have a chance at disabling these nukes before midnight. We're lucky we recognized each other."

"Jezzz, Jake. Where are the SEALs now?"

"They're looking for the other nukes toward the north end of the fault line. They said they have the capability to disable only one when they find it. If there's more, we'll be in deep shit."

"Yeah, you're right. How's your team holding up, Jake?"

"We lost Sandra Morrison."

"Morrison? How?"

"We got into a fight with some bad guys just before the SEALs showed up. She was killed in the fight. So was your man Hann and three of his henchman. They tried to stop us from disabling the SS-19."

"Hann? He's supposed to be in Amman. Are you sure?"

"Yes, Jim, Hann is the one who shot Sandra and I killed him and his accomplices."

"Did he talk?"

"Yes. He confirmed that the nukes here would detonate after midnight tonight. He said there is an additional loose nuke but he didn't tell me where it will be detonated. So according to Hann, that means there are at least three nukes here and one other we don't have a clue about that is unaccounted for."

"Damn fine work, Jake."

"Don't thank me just yet. If we're unsuccessful here there's gonna be a tsunami coming your way in the morning around rush hour."

"Yeah, I know. Hey Jake, do me a favor and keep the Hann thing to yourself. Out here."

Boucher handed the satellite phone back to Reilly and adjusted his night vision goggles.

"Si, what can I do to help?"

"Jake, get the access plate off the other side of this weapon for me," Barnhart asked. "I need to come in from that side to get to the detonators and the secondary."

Boucher and Patterson dug down to the point the inspection plate was fully exposed. Boucher quickly removed the screws holding the plate in place and removed the plate. Barnhart moved over to that side and carefully probed inside.

"Damn, I still don't have the access I need to get to the detonators. I don't think I can stop this thing from going off. All we can hope to do is disrupt the symmetry of the detonation and reduce the yield. If I can't take at least a third of them out of the circuit this thing could still go off with a significant yield. I don't know how much of a blast it's going to take to put a good portion of this hillside into the sea but we can't risk it."

"What's the next best option?" Boucher asked.

Barnhart checked his watch. "We're running out of time and options."

Reilly's radio crackled to life.

"Commander Boucher, this is Lieutenant Morgan. We've located the item of concern with our FLIR. It's down in the fault approximately one mile and a half from your position. We're investigating."

"Roger, Lieutenant, copy all. Out, here," Reilly replied.

Patterson scratched his head. "Only a mile and a half from here?" he questioned. "I thought it was supposed to be closer to the north end of the fault."

Reilly's radio crackled again. "Commander Boucher, Lieutenant Morgan. Sir, I just got a call from my guys in our other Osprey and they have just found another item of concern at the north end of the fault line. How do you want to proceed?"

Reilly checked his watch. "You know what, Jake? We're gonna run out of time."

"You're right, give me the radio. Tell Mossman to get the chopper turned up."

Reilly took off toward the helicopter. Boucher keyed the radio mic.

"Lieutenant Morgan, use my portable radiography unit. I need a quick assessment of the nuke you just found. Leave a couple of your men there to help me. You go disable the other nuke. We're on our way. ETA ten mikes."

"Roger, out."

"Billy and Johnny, I want you to stay here and assist Si." Boucher passed the radio to Reilly. "Billy, keep the channel open with me. Pat, you and Mojo are with me. Let's do it."

The White House Situation Room, the same time

"We need to hope for the best and plan for the worst," Gregory Cline declared. "The President can't just make a public announcement that there is a chance a mega tsunami might hit the entire Eastern Seaboard tomorrow morning around rush hour. That would panic most everyone into an evacuation inland and it couldn't be accomplished in the time remaining anyway. Even if we could evacuate some of the less populated areas how can we expect the police or National Guard to stay behind to be washed away and otherwise risk death. The only way is to not warn the public and hope our people on scene find all the nukes and successfully disable them."

"I disagree," Denise Dunkle flatly stated. "I say DHS notifies the public and tells everyone in the affected areas about the tsunami and we advise them to shelter in place."

Pete Barnett, the Undersecretary of the Interior, shook his head. "Shelter in place? That's a stupid unreasonable thing to ask in the face of a wall of water that will reach skyscraper proportions and hit our coastal areas at the speed of an airliner. You might as well ask the people living and working there to commit suicide."

"Yeah," Dunkle countered, "but if we officially warn the public tonight most people won't even get the word until they turn on their TVs in the morning or read the paper. The up side is that we will have gone on record as having tried to warn them and that will reduce the political backlash. The administration will be off the hook."

"Political backlash?" Barnett flatly stated. "You're worried about political backlash? Ms. Dunkle, you gotta be shitting me! You're playing politics when millions of our citizens are about to be killed by a terrorist-caused disaster of epic proportions. Why weren't you aware of the fact that something like this could happen and take preemptive steps to ensure it wouldn't? Your incompetence is astounding."

"My incompetence? How about your agency's lack of preparedness? What about the levies in New Orleans?"

"Preparedness? DHS can't even secure our borders and adequately respond with emergency aid to a hurricane, how are you going to handle the mass casualties and the catastrophic loss of infrastructure? Don't tell me, let me guess – you won't!"

Cline pounded on the tabletop. "That's enough! Do you hear me? That's enough! I didn't call this meeting for finger pointing and blame letting so let's work together and find a workable solution. As you all know, two hours ago the FEST went wheels-up on its way to La Palma. They should arrive around zero three-thirty Zulu time. They have an enhanced capability Nuclear Radiological Advisory Team with them capable of doing on-scene diagnostics and assessment. As I speak we have NEST loading their equipment on a C-17 in Albuquerque. They will launch within the hour and should arrive at La Palma around daybreak. Regretfully, they will all get there too late if those bombs go off after midnight tonight La Palma time. We have our operations centers fully manned and monitoring the situation. DHS, you are ready to implement the Federal Response Plan, correct?"

"Yes, we have activated our regional emergency operations centers and have notified all the potentially affected states along the Eastern Seaboard and Gulf of Mexico that we are conducting a no-notice emergency response exercise so they don't panic."

Cline drummed his fingers on the tabletop. "I need a sound consequence management plan to deal with the loss of life and infrastructure at the potential magnitude we anticipate along the coast. We can't stop that tsunami once it's generated so all we can do is try to deal with its consequences. I recognize it will overwhelm, if not eliminate, much of our emergency response and consequence management capabilities in the affected areas so we need to bring in outside resources. Our priority will be to save the lives of the surviving victims and prevent further loss of life, create refugee camps, move food, water and medicine to distribution points central to the refugee centers, recover the dead and dispose of the bodies before disease can grab a foothold. Finally, we will need to put our COOP and COG plans into effect along with the Federal Response Plan. The President will be ready to address the country in the morning following the event, if it happens. Let us all pray that our people on the ground in La Palma are successful."

In the Bell 412 above the Cumbre Vieja Volcano fault, the same time

Moss was flying the helicopter along the trench maintaining a twenty-five foot altitude above it. Everyone onboard was straining to detect anything in the trench below. Boucher checked his watch. It was twenty-three hundred. They had to disable all the bombs before midnight.

Patterson and Mojo excitedly grabbed Boucher's arm pointing at a flashing strobe from the trench ahead. Boucher clicked his intercom mic open.

"Mossman, we got a strobe marker ahead. Put us down close by. Stay turned up and stand by."

Moss landed the helicopter and throttled the jet engine down to conserve fuel. Two of Morgan's SEALs met Boucher at the helicopter. Boucher, Patterson, and Mojo jumped out of the helicopter and followed them down into the trench next to the weapon. It was partially covered by some scrub brush and grass and still resting on the litter used to carry it there. Boucher tested the radiation intensity using his dosimeter.

"This thing is one hot puppy. We're getting one hell of a dose. We're going to have to work fast before we get fried by the radiation. What you got?' he asked the SEALs.

"Sir, I'm Chief Springer and this is Petty Officer Branham. We did a quick single view digital radiograph. We believe this is a warhead off a submarine-launched cruise missile. It's probably a Russian design but we can't be sure. It has a crude fire set with a clock and RFD working in parallel. We didn't detect any traps. We sent the radiograph file back to the Los Alamos Home Team for further diagnostics and assessment. Recommend we stand by until they get back to us with a plan for disablement."

"You said it doesn't have any booby traps, right Chief?" Boucher yelled above the helicopter's jet engine noise nearby.

"No Sir, I said we didn't detect any traps based upon the radiograph's single side view. We didn't have time to do a front, top and rear side view.

Lieutenant Morgan had to take the radiography unit to the other working point. You're not going to risk a hand entry disablement attempt, are you?"

"No Chief, we're not. That only works for Hollywood script writers and Los Alamos nuclear weapon scientists."

"So what's the plan, Sir?"

Boucher checked his watch then studied the warhead before him.

"Chief, we're going to lift this bad boy up out of this trench and get it on the helo. We'll fly it out to deep water, drop it over the side and take our chances."

"What if it has a booby trap built into it and it goes off?"

Boucher gave the Chief a dumbfounded look, "That's called molecular dislocation! You'll never feel a thing."

"No, I mean what if it goes off and sets off the other two bombs? Then we cause the tsunami?"

Boucher felt bad for his previous reply.

"Chief, we have an SS-19 megaton-yield warhead on one end of this trench and another warhead on the other with Lieutenant Morgan. Between Lieutenant Morgan and Doctor Barnhart we only have enough disablement capability to attack two warheads with a reasonable chance of success. The clocks are ticking on all three warheads and we're running out of time but you make an excellent point. We'll wait until the last minute before we attempt moving this nuke to give the Lieutenant and Doctor Barnhart time to disable their respective nukes."

Chapter 25

Cumbre Vieja Volcano, La Palma

"Commander," Chief Springer said, "Lieutenant Morgan just radioed to advise they're ready to fire their emergency disablement charges. He's standing by for our okay."

"Okay, thanks, Chief. Stand by one." Boucher turned to Mojo. "Make sure Si and Billy know. Tell Mossman to find a shielded spot for the helo and land it. We'll hunker down here." Boucher looked back at Chief Springer. "Once Moss is on the ground go ahead and tell Morgan to shoot."

Moss landed the helicopter behind a nearby ridge and shut down the engines. Moments later the low hanging rain clouds were illuminated by a white hot flash of a high explosives detonation coming from the north end of the caldron. Its characteristic high velocity blast pressure wave passed over the hillside with a dull thud.

"My God!" Moss exclaimed over the radio. "What the hell was that? It looked like an artillery burst."

Boucher grabbed the radio and clicked his mic open, "Mossman get back over here. Land as close to us as you can, hurry!" Boucher pulled Chief Springer next to him. "Chief, get Lieutenant Morgan on the radio for me."

Moments later Boucher's headphones crackled with the familiar sound of Morgan's voice.

"Commander Boucher, this is Lieutenant Morgan, over."

"Boucher here, are you and your guys alright?"

"Ahhh, yes, Sir. We backed off and we're fine but we're not yet completely sure if we got any yield or not. So far our FLIR pictures show a relatively small smoldering crater. We'll be able to get a better estimate when we get a closer look at the crater diameter and depth. The good news is, as best as we can determine the blast didn't cause any downward movement of the mountain. We're feeling our way in closer but we're being careful to remain upwind so we don't contaminate ourselves. How's it going on your end, Sir?"

"We're almost out of time. I'll keep you info."

"Understand, Sir. Good luck. Out here."

Chief Springer grabbed Boucher's shirt. "Sir, I just received word from the Los Alamos Home Team. Their preliminary evaluation of the radiography I took of this weapon's firing circuit reveals no traps."

Boucher checked his watch and waved his men closer.

"We're out of time. There's no way the new fire set on this bomb is waterproof. If the fire set is flooded by sea water the electronic components will short out and it will malfunction. The odds of a nuclear detonation after we drop it in the water are extremely remote. This will be one less nuke we have to worry about. Give me a hand. We're gonna put this bad boy on the helo and drop it into deep water offshore."

The six men strained to lift the litter bearing the bomb. They slowly wrestled it up the steep fifteen foot side of the trench to ground level. Then they slid the bomb-laden stretcher into the open cargo side door of the waiting helicopter and climbed in behind it. Boucher put on an intercom headset and adjusted the mic close to his mouth.

"Mossman, get us well out to sea as fast as you can and stay low. We're going to throw this turd overboard once we're out over deep water."

"Roger that," Moss replied as he revved the helo's engine up to full power and pulled up on the collective. "Hey Jake, I'd be real pissed if that thing goes off before we drop it into the sea."

"You better be more concerned with the radiation dose rate you're getting right now."

"Shit, is it going to make my dick fall off or something?"

"No, it will just make it limp - forever."

Moss clicked his mic button twice in acknowledgement to Boucher as he coaxed the powerful Bell 412 helicopter into the air and turned it to a seaward heading.

"Jake, be advised we only have about twenty-five minutes of fuel left with no reserve. That's barely enough to make it back to Doctor Barnhart's working point much less make it back to the airport."

"If we don't disable all these nukes, it won't matter."

Minutes later Boucher and Patterson rolled the bomb out of the open door and watched it splash into the dark sea below.

"Bombs away," Boucher reported over his intercom. "Mossman, take us back to Barnhart."

Moss banked the helicopter hard over and headed back toward the caldron. Boucher tugged on Chief Springer's shoulder.

"Advise Lieutenant Morgan."

Springer gave Boucher a thumbs-up as he keyed his radio to Morgan.

The White House Situation Room, the same time

Gregory Cline was sitting at his desk reading the most recent situation reports when he was interrupted by a National Security Council staff member.

"Sir, we just got a report from our people on La Palma. Apparently there was a detonation when they attempted an emergency disablement."

"A nuclear detonation?"

"They don't believe so but they're investigating."

"Any movement of that caldron?"

"They don't think so."

"What's the status of the other nukes?"

"They report that they have successfully removed one nuke from the caldron's fault line and dropped it into the ocean offshore."

"And the other?"

"They're working on it."

"If that thing goes off and the mountain breaks loose we're going to have a major problem about five hours from now. Where's the FEST?"

"They're still two and half hours from La Palma but I recommend we don't land them there now because of the potential contamination risks."

"How about NEST and their consequence management response team?"

"They've been in the air for about an hour. They have about six more hours until they reach La Palma."

"Turn the FEST around and bring them home. If they end up there they'll become part of the problem instead of part of the solution. Besides, if that tsunami hits our coast we're going to need all the help we can get right here. Direct NEST to drop off its consequence management team on La Palma and return home. The Saipan Amphibious Ready Group can provide logistics support to the consequence management operations on La Palma."

232

Kennedy Irregular Warfare Center, ONI, Suitland, MD, the same time

Lieutenant Bruce gently cleared his throat, waking Captain Blackburn who was slumped awkwardly in his office desk chair with his feet resting on a low two drawer file cabinet.

"Captain, we may have stumbled on something that points to the origin of all these nukes."

"What?" Blackburn blustered groggily as he straightened up.

"Sir, we might have something that points to the origin of the nukes and the bad actors behind it all."

Blackburn took a sip of lukewarm coffee and swallowed hard.

"Let's hear it, Lieutenant."

"Well, Sir, as you know the nuke that was exploded in Lebanon last week was a command-detonated Russian artillery-fired projectile. The warhead that our people disabled in the Jordanian desert was a Russian SS-19 warhead. Now we find that there are at least three more warheads in play on La Palma in the Canaries. The SEALs destroyed what they believed was a Russian-made warhead of the type carried by a submarine launched missile. A second warhead was identified as the same design and our guys dumped it into ocean. The third is another SS-19. Sir, that's five loose nukes in eight days. You gotta ask yourself, where the hell are they all coming from and why didn't we detect their movement? I mean, why haven't we seen any indicators and warnings before last week? There's just no way all those warheads ended up in the wrong hands without anyone detecting their movement."

"You tell me, Lieutenant."

"My analysts and I think Russia is behind this, Sir. Iran is an unwitting surrogate."

"What are you suggesting?"

"Well, Sir, we think Russia either directly or indirectly provided some, if not all of those nukes to Iran so they could be used against Israel, Jordan and us."

"You gotta be shitting me, Lieutenant. There's no way Russia would do something that reckless."

"We think they have, Sir, and it is anything but reckless. Rather, it's a well planned and precisely executed strategy."

Blackburn walked over to the coffee pot and refilled his cup.

"Okay, let's say they're behind this – why?"

"It's kind of a convoluted theory to explain but it seems quite plausible."

Blackburn returned to his desk and eased back in his chair motioning for Lieutenant Bruce to sit down in the chair next to his desk.

"I have the time, Lieutenant. Go ahead and explain it to me. I'm all ears."

"As you well know, Sir, U.S. policy has succeeded in Iraq by creating the foundations for a political settlement and establishing a relatively stable government. But our simultaneous commitment in Afghanistan has been exasperated by the six years it took us to get to this point in Iraq and time has not been our friend."

"How so?"

"Because we simply didn't plan on a war of this duration and it caught us ill prepared. To be able to maintain our fronts in both Iraq and Afghanistan we have had to commit the majority of our ground fighting forces and air capabilities along with our strategic reserves. In the process we stretched our military resources dangerously thin. Worse, as we committed the majority of our available forces, our foreign policy never changed toward Russia. We remained committed to the expansion of democracy in the countries that made up the former Soviet Union. We assumed a dominant role in reshaping post-Soviet social and political institutions, as well as fostering the emergence of democratic governments and free markets."

"I was wondering when you were going to get around to Russia," Blackburn interrupted. "So get to the point, Lieutenant. I don't need any armchair quarterbacking."

Bruce smiled at his boss, taking no offense at his impatience.

"Following the collapse of the Soviet Union, the Russian Federation underwent an excruciatingly painful internal upheaval. Russia was so damaged economically, divided politically and weakened militarily, it couldn't oppose American and European involvement in its regional and internal affairs. I'm sure you remember the reports stating most Russian government officials believed that the United States was executing a well-financed CIA operation designed to exploit their weakness and provoke an anti-Russian uprising in the Ukraine aimed at destabilizing the region." Blackburn nodded affirmatively. "Well, Sir, this led to their assumption that we had a hostile intent and they began planning to counter it."

"So what's that have to do with the price of vodka in La Palma?" Blackburn impatiently demanded.

"Our policy assumed that the Russians wouldn't confront American interests in the emerging republics that once composed the former Soviet Union or anywhere else we had dominating interests like Israel, Jordan, Iraq, Iran, etc., etc. The Russians, on the other hand, realized that they had a unique opportunity to strike and that the window of opportunity would not remain open very long. They surely follow our presidential politics and saw our new president would soon be concluding the war in Iraq. They recognized this would allow us to once again consolidate our focus and return us to our pre-eminent position of being the only superpower on the planet. They knew they couldn't afford to wait for that to happen and lose their last remaining opportunity to emerge again as powerful as they once were - but they had to act quickly."

"This is all very interesting, Lieutenant, but you're killing me with all this background shit. You still haven't made the case for Russian complicity with Iran and the nukes?"

Bruce patiently smiled again and nodded.

"We have had sanctions against Iran for years and we've been playing them as fools. We threaten to attack them for being bad actors while at the same time we refuse to negotiate with them. The Russians have never participated in the sanctions against Iran. Instead, Russia became one of Iran's main oil export customers, but Russia didn't have the cash to pay for the oil. At the same time we encouraged Russia to not sell its state-of-the art nuclear and military technology to Iran. I believe the Russians recognized that their situation was untenable and they knew they had to change it before the U.S. withdraws from Iraq and Afghanistan. I think Russia carefully evaluated their situation and developed a brilliant plan designed to secure all the energy resources they need. The plan's intent was to also send a clear message to their former satellite states in the Ukraine, Baltics and Central Asia, not to mention the NATO nations that might potentially challenge their return to world power status."

"Wait a minute, Lieutenant, Russia is far weaker than we are and the world knows it."

"That's correct, Sir, but that will change if their plan succeeds. You see, Sir, by providing the tools necessary for their surrogates like Iran to do the dirty work, all Russia needs to do is step in and take advantage of the situation as the dust settles."

"So you're saying Russia knowingly provided five nukes to Iran so al Qaeda could attack their enemies and ultimately topple the U.S. from superpower status?"

"Yes, Sir, exactly and here's their plan as I believe it to be. Set off a small artillery nuke in a known terrorist training camp in Lebanon and frame the Israelis as the first to resort to nuclear weapons. A few days later, melt down Amman with a second much larger nuke and ensure Iran has its fingerprints on both attacks. Israel retaliates against Iran and the U.S. bombs Iran back into the

Stone Age to prevent Iran's counter-attack against Israel. Three more nukes detonate on the remote island of La Palma thirty-six hours later and a mega-tsunami follows five hours after that wiping the U.S. Eastern Seaboard off the map. Al Qaeda has their fingerprints all over this attack but how do we retaliate against that? Bombing the shit out of Iran again won't do squat. We can't use our ground forces even if we want to because our military is overstressed between Iraq and Afghanistan. Our homeland has been successfully attacked. The infrastructure along the U.S. Eastern Seaboard is destroyed. Wall Street has literally been washed into the sea. Millions of our citizens are dead. There are even more millions who are now refugees. We default on our national debt and the world economy goes tits up."

"I get it. Russia rushes aid to Iran and secures their oil fields. They watch the U.S. economy fail as a result of the devastation. The economies of our European NATO allies fail along with ours. Russia sends a loud and clear message to the world that they are back in the game. They provide much needed aid to the nations of the former Soviet Union as well as to those elsewhere of strategic value. Russia emerges as a major superpower that cannot be challenged economically or militarily and there's nothing we can do about it. But what about China?"

"China will not be in a position to challenge Russia or expand their sphere of influence because when the U.S. economy fails theirs will too. They own so much of our debt. If they try to step into any area Russia considers its turf, Russia will overpower them. China is no dummy. They'll read the tea leaves and stay clear."

"Lieutenant, you're a fucking genius! Now, answer me this. The nuke destined for Amman was disabled, therefore Jordan remains intact. The Israelis haven't attacked Iran and we haven't bombed them, at least not yet. Two of the three nukes we know about on La Palma have been disabled. The third may go off but probably not full yield providing our guys on the ground can prevent it, so no mega-tsunami. What's that all mean to Russia?"

"Russia will continue to strengthen its position and become increasingly more challenging toward the U.S. and NATO. They will continue to befriend South American oil producing nations like Venezuela and Nicaragua and sell them military technology for oil. They'll establish a political and military foothold on the South American continent and they know there is little we can do about it. If we take any meaningful actions against Russia, they will respond against us by bolstering Iran with advanced military technology along with their other new friends to our south. We may have foiled their plan by detecting and disabling the nuclear weapons in play but their strategy will still succeed as long as we remain in Iraq and Afghanistan and continue to encourage Russia's former satellite states to join NATO."

Cumbre Vieja Volcano, La Palma, the same time

A steady rain cut the visibility by half. Moss cautiously approached Barnhart's working point in a slow hover with his landing light on. He landed the helicopter close to where Sandra's body still lay and shut the engine down.

"Jake, Lieutenant Morgan is on the radio. I'll put it on speaker."

"Commander Boucher, this is Lieutenant Morgan. We were apparently successful in preventing a yielding detonation. I'd guess it went sub-atomic. What's your status?"

"Advise everyone to stay clear of this end. You'll know real soon if we fail."

Boucher pulled on his night vision goggles and bounded towards the ditch where Barnhart was hard at work. Barnhart had his right hand buried inside the access port on the side of the warhead. Several wires were exposed that he had cut.

"Any good news, Si?"

"I've taken three detonators off line so far but it's not enough. I want you all to leave here now and put some serious distance between this nuke and yourselves."

"Si, I'm staying with you."

"No Jake, it's too dangerous. Each detonator I cut out of the circuit will reduce the yield a few more percent – maybe eliminate it all together, but there's still gonna be a nuclear detonation and there will be a yield."

Boucher checked his watch.

"It's twenty-three forty-one. We have nineteen minutes. Can you shunt the remaining detonators?"

"That's an interesting concept. Without full radiography of the warhead and the time to assess it, my colleagues on the Los Alamos Home Team believe that the safest way to attack this weapon is to individually cut each detonator out of the firing circuit. If I shunt the detonators I'm essentially shorting the firing circuit. There is no guarantee it will work. In fact, I don't know anyone who has ever attempted it before. It's just too risky."

"Si, it's the only way."

Barnhart grunted and withdrew his hand from the access port.

"Okay, Jake. I'll give it a try. I think I can reach the trunk wires from here. I'll shunt as many of the detonators as I can reach. How much time do you need to fly us at least a mile from here and find some cover?"

"Five minutes. We'll need a few extra minutes to get from here to the helo."

"Okay, when you say it's time to leave, I'll stop what I'm doing here and we'll leave."

Boucher again checked his watch.

"We have ten minutes working time."

Barnhart nodded and returned his full attention to the circuitry inside the open access port.

Mossman had the helicopter turned up and was standing by. Boucher checked his watch.

"Si, it's time to go."

Barnhart kept working without replying.

"Si, I said it's time to go."

Barnhart was probing into the mass of wires with a needle-nose pliers in one hand and a wire cutter in the other.

"All I need is a few more minutes and I think I'll have it."

"No, Si. Now!" Boucher demanded.

"Jake, just a few more minutes and it will be better. Trust me, I'm almost there."

"Si, you used to always tell me better is the enemy of good enough."

Barnhart kept working without replying.

"Si, if you don't come with me right now voluntarily, we're going to grab you and take you."

"Alright, done," Barnhart proclaimed triumphantly. "Let's get outta here."

The men rushed to the helicopter and jumped inside. Moss throttled the engines up to full power and performed a maximum performance takeoff. He wasted no time heading the aircraft toward a high ridge. Boucher put on a headset and adjusted the mic close to his lips.

"Mossman, get us as far away as you can and find something we can hide behind before midnight. I show we have three minutes. Get me a radio link to Morgan."

Moments later Lieutenant Morgan's voice crackled through Boucher's headphones.

"Lieutenant Morgan here."

"Lieutenant, this is Boucher. Advise all your assets to take cover. We don't know how this is going to go. We may experience a major EMP."

"Roger, already done, Sir. We're clear and standing by."

Boucher held the mic button open for a moment before speaking.

"You're a good officer, Lieutenant, and you have a good platoon. I'm very proud of you and your guys."

It was then that Boucher saw Sandra's poncho-wrapped body strapped into a seat on the other side of the helicopter. Mojo and Yellowhorse were sitting on either side of the corpse holding her body in a sitting position. Boucher's face was devoid of emotion. He just stared blankly.

Chapter 26

Cumbre Vieja Volcano, La Palma

Moss flew over a nearby ridge barely clearing the top and landed in a narrow canyon. He immediately shut down the engines and turned off all electrical power. The helicopter became quiet as the rotor blades slowly wound down to a stop. The sudden quiet seemed deafening. Boucher continued to stare at Sandra's body.

"Virtus junxil, mors non separabit," Patterson respectfully annunciated, breaking the quiet.

"What did you say?" Boucher muttered.

"'Whom virtue unites, death cannot separate'."

Boucher hesitated as he contemplated his friend's words.

"Yeah," Boucher blankly replied. "Pat, I just don't get why they target those closest to me?"

"Jake, you have been at the pointy end of the spear your entire life. The bad guys pay attention to men like you because every time they come up against you they get their asses severely kicked or end up dead. They are cowards. They have no courage or honor. They kill innocent people every day without regard. Their goal is to inflict as much pain as possible on their enemies anyway they can. If it means killing a man's family members to weaken his resolve, that's exactly what they'll do. You don't negotiate with people who strap bombs on their own kids to kill other people's kids, you kill them."

Boucher looked at his long time best friend.

"You know, Pat, I've killed a lot of sons-a-bitches in my time but I never killed anyone who didn't deserve it. Trouble seems to follow me now. It seems to seek me out. I can't help but ask, why me? First my wife, my son, now Sandra, I just can't take it anymore."

A brilliant flash illuminated every droplet in the rainy night sky followed by a loud boom. The pressure wave that followed felt like getting hit in the chest by a baseball bat as it passed over them. The sky slowly grew dark again and an eerie quiet ensued. No one spoke. Then it began, first as a low almost inaudible rumble that could be felt rather than heard, then the ground beneath the helicopter began to shake. Moss had already begun the engine start procedure.

"Mossman," Boucher shouted breaking the silence, "get us the hell out of here!"

The White House Situation Room, Washington, DC, the same time

Gregory Cline, the President's National Security Advisor, hung up the phone and looked around the room at the inter-agency's senior emergency response officials.

"I just received notification that our satellites have detected an atomic detonation on La Palma. We don't know the fate of our people on the ground there. The President has been informed. DOE, where is the NEST and its consequence management team?"

"They're about two hours away from La Palma. The Brits also have a CM team on the way there from Mildenhall. They should arrive around the same time."

"Good. Is there any estimate as to the extent of fallout?"

"We can't ascertain the actual yield and the fallout lay down footprint until we get people on the ground and do the instrumentation. The good news is that the blast occurred on a small island well out in the Atlantic two hundred miles west of Morocco so the vast majority of the fallout will drift eastward and fall into the sea. The stuff that does make it ashore will mostly fall over the Sahara Desert."

"DOD, what's your status?"

"The Marines off the Saipan and her Amphibious Ready Group will support the consequence management operations as required. The ships have arrived in helicopter range and will remain upwind of the island. The helicopters will be launching shortly."

"Can anyone give me a status on casualties?"

The CIA representative spoke up. "We have a preliminary unconfirmed report of two friendly and three unknown dead."

Dunkle interrupted. "How did that happen? You never told us you had people on the ground there."

"Ms. Dunkle," Cline responded, "there are many things that happen on the planet that DHS is not briefed on and CIA operations is one of them." Dunkle began to reply but Cline held up his open hand to silence her. "You do have the National Response Plan ready to implement, don't you?".

Cumbre Vieja Volcano, La Palma

Moss had already begun the engine start procedure moments before Boucher's order. The instrument panel lights dimly illuminated Moss as he whisked through the start sequence flicking switches and monitoring gauges. The initial whine of the first jet turbine engine start was immediately followed by the second engine. The helicopter's rotors began to spin up to speed and beat the air into submission. With a guarded eye on the fast rising engine temperatures and pressures, Moss advanced both engine throttles dangerously fast, risking engine fire and turbine meltdown. In less than a minute the engines were up to maximum red line power and Moss had the helicopter poised for take-off. He flicked on the helicopter's powerful landing lights, brightly illuminating the surrounding area. The rain was now falling in torrential sheets. Even with the wipers running full speed it was almost impossible for Moss to see and clear any obstacles in his flight path. He glanced one last time at the engine temperature gauges then yelled above the jet engine noise.

"Hold the fuck on!"

He instantly pulled up on the collective initiating a maximum performance takeoff. Moss saw the torque and power gauges redline as the powerful engines strained to keep the rotor turning at constant speed. With the engines moaning and the airframe shuddering, Moss expertly piloted his aircraft as it broke contact with the ground and leapt into the air. At that precise moment the ground seemed to give way all around the helicopter in a downward slide toward the sea. Everyone was peering out of the open cargo doors and what they saw was astonishing. The entire hillside appeared to bulge outward then settle toward the ocean. The low frequency rumble it created was so intense it resonated inside everyone's entire body, blanking the helicopter's engine noise. All at once a bright red warning light began to flash on Moss's instrument panel.

"Jake," Moss yelled, "I gotta land this bad boy, we're out of gas."

"Get us on the solid ground just on other side of the slide."

"I don't have the fuel," screamed Moss.

Boucher crawled onto the communications console between the pilot and co-pilot's seat in the cockpit to get next to Moss.

"Mossman, you can do it."

"Jake, we're out of fuel. I gotta set this baby down now."

"Mossman, if you can't go up, then go down. Just get us away from this slide."

Moss banked hard to the left turning the helicopter toward the blackness of the ocean about a half mile ahead.

"Mayday, mayday, mayday, this is helicopter hotel niner three one. Seven onboard, we're going down one half mile seaward of the south vent, Cumbre Vieja Volcano, La Palma. Activating ELT." Moss calmly announced over the radio. "I say again, this is helicopter, hotel niner three one. Seven onboard. Mayday, mayday, mayday." He was no stranger to crash situations, having survived a number of them over his thirty-eight years of piloting, but this was the first time he ever ran out of gas. "Jake, all I can do is put us in the water seaward of the landslide. I'll keep us just above the water in case the engines flame out. Get ready to bail."

Boucher slapped Moss on the shoulder and returned to the cargo deck with Barnhart and his men.

"Once we're low enough over the water I want all you guys to be ready to jump on my command. Pat and Johnny, you look after Si. I'm gonna stay here. Mossman needs a swim buddy. We'll regroup once we're all in the water and make it to shore."

Patterson, grabbed Boucher's arm. His eyes were the size of saucers.

"Jake, what about the sharks?"

Boucher gave his longtime friend a quizzical look before answering.

"Pat, it's nighttime. The fucking sharks are all asleep."

Patterson forced a nervous smile and nodded, appearing to be relieved.

The White House Situation Room, the same time

Peering at the wall of video flat screens before him, Gregory Cline, the President's National Security Advisor called the secure video conference meeting to order. "We just got a real-time report from the Saipan Task

Force at La Palma. We had a small atomic yield apparently resulting from a disablement attempt. Based upon seismic monitoring, we believe the yield was somewhere in the vicinity of one to three kilotons. It seems a portion of the mountain broke loose and slid into the sea. The Saipan monitored a mayday call from one of our teams shortly after the detonation but there has been no further communication with that team. The Marines have several aircraft headed to the location to assess how much of the caldron may have collapsed into the sea. Ladies and gentlemen, we may have a tsunami on the way here."

Denise Dunkle, interrupted, "We need an accurate assessment."

"We all realize that, Ms. Dunkle, but at the moment, it's dark and raining heavily over there. Our Marines are doing everything they can, but it's slow going."

Dunkle leaned forward sprawling her huge breasts on the table. "We wouldn't be in this mess right now if you had allowed me to send my people when I told you to. But no, you let CIA and military people attempt an extremely sensitive task they were obviously incapable of adequately handling. Now we have to deal with the consequences of their incompetence."

Cline looked as though steam was going to come out of his ears.

"Ms. Dunkle, I have been more than patient with your inability to understand reality but my patience is finite. Please pay attention to what I am about to say." Dunkle's mouth dropped open. "Our people on the ground over there have valiantly risked their lives trying to beat ticking clocks in an attempt to disable three nuclear weapons and prevent a mega-tsunami from hitting our Eastern Seaboard. They succeeded by reducing the yield from as much as megatons to as little as a kiloton. If the President had approved the deployment of DHS personnel to La Palma your people would still be in the air at this very moment and those nukes would have gone off full yield. We have done the best we can with what we had and we have foiled a major attack against us."

Dunkle interrupted again. "But we still have a tsunami headed our way. Whose fault is that? It's certainly not mine."

Cline looked down and slowly shook his head in disgust as he massaged his temples.

Chapter 27

Cumbre Vieja Volcano, La Palma

Moss swooped down low over the water clearing, the landslide area. He still had the landing lights on as he headed south paralleling the rugged shoreline, staying about a hundred yards seaward. He brought the helicopter into a hover with the landing skids nearly touching the wave tops. Boucher yelled go and everyone jumped into the sea. Boucher turned and slapped Moss on the shoulder. Moss immediately jettisoned the cockpit door by his side and maneuvered the helicopter slowly forward to clear the area where the men had just entered the water when the engines flamed out. Despite Moss's attempt to cushion the crash, the helicopter hit the water hard and began to quickly settle into the sea as water flooded in through the open cargo doors.

When the spinning rotor blades hit the water, the transmission ripped from its mountings and the helo rolled upside down and began to rapidly sink. As the helo inverted amid a mass of steamy bubbles, Moss unhooked his seat harness. He hadn't anticipated being so rapidly submerged and so disoriented. He searched to find the opening where the pilot's door had been jettisoned and struggled to get free of the aircraft. Boucher was prepared for the rollover and had hyperventilated by taking deep breaths to saturate his bloodstream with oxygen just prior to ditching.

Boucher easily pulled himself free of the sinking helicopter through the wide open cargo door the others had just jumped from. He immediately began to search for Moss. The landing lights were still illuminating the surrounding sea like a tropical fish tank in a dark room. Boucher could see Moss struggling to get free of the cockpit but seemed to be losing the battle. He pulled himself forward adjacent to the cockpit area positioning himself a few feet from Moss. He reached inside and grabbed his disoriented friend by the arm pulling him away from the sinking hulk and up to the surface.

"You okay?" he yelled at Moss.

"Yeah, thanks."

"I'll be right back," Boucher yelled.

Boucher gulped a deep breath and disappeared below. Moments later he reappeared next to Moss with Sandra's body. The others swam over to Boucher.

"Head for shore," he yelled. It only took about ten minutes to reach the shore and climb a few yards up the steep mountainside well clear of the surf zone.

Minutes later two U.S. Marine Corps V-22s approached with their landing lights on. Moss signaled with his flashlight as the aircraft neared. One of the noisy V-22s slowed and transitioned to a hover, then slowly descended, landing on a small, somewhat level depression in the mountainside above while the other orbited the area of the landslide, apparently surveying its extent. Lieutenant Morgan and his SEALs jumped from the waiting aircraft's open tail ramp and made their way down to Boucher and his men.

"Everyone okay here?" Lieutenant Morgan shouted.

Boucher gave him a thumbs-up. One of Morgan's men pulled off his backpack containing a small satellite radio and handed Boucher a communications headset.

"Commander Boucher, please put this headset on. You have a secure call from Admiral Thornberg. He's standing by."

Boucher put on the headset and adjusted the mic close to his lips.

"Jim, Jake here."

Boucher pressed one of the head phones against his ear as he intently listened.

"Yeah, of course I know who Rajakovics is. I know him well. He was in command of the Kazak Special Squad when we boarded the Rakish last February in the Caspian." A look of total amazement came over Boucher's face. "I don't believe it. There's no way he is." Boucher shook his head as he listened to his old friend. "Let me get this straight, Jim. You think he is a major player in all this?" Boucher's astonishment was obvious as he sat back against the hillside. "Yeah, I'll do it for you. Out here."

Everyone was staring at Boucher. They could plainly see he was trying to make sense out of the call he had just had. Patterson leaned toward him.

"Jake, what's up?"

Boucher studied his friend for a moment before replying.

"It's the Russians."

"The Russians?" Barnhart ask dumbfounded.

"Yeah. You remember me telling you about the ship boarding operation I did for Admiral Thornberg last February in the Caspian? Well, it seems my Kazak counterpart was a Russian plant. Jim says Rajakovics is at the airport in Dakar. They identified his presence from electronic intercepts over the past hour. Apparently the Agency has been tracking him for some time. Jim says he's working out of a hanger along the flight line. He wants me to find him and bring him back to the States for interrogation."

"Well, hell, Jake," Mojo drawled, "why don't the good Admiral just have his CIA folks or the Marines grab him?"

"Because the Admiral wants to keep it quiet. Under the Long Arm

Statute, Rajakovics shows up in the States and no one asks how he got there. No fucking lawyer involvement. I have a feeling Rajakovics knows some stuff that can embarrass some very important people and Admiral Thornberg knows it."

Mojo contemplated Boucher's explanation. "You know what, Jake...I was in the Navy almost thirty years before I found out that the term, 'fucking lawyer,' was two words."

Boucher snorted and shouted over to Morgan who had been waiting a few yards away to give Boucher privacy. "Can you give us a lift back to Aena Airport, Lieutenant?"

"Let's go, Commander. I'm sure our Marines flying the V-22 would be happy to help. Besides, this rain doesn't seem to be letting up any time soon and we have a thermos of hot coffee in the plane. It might help to get the chill out for a few minutes."

Office of the Assistant Secretary of Defense for Special Operations and Low Intensity Conflict, The Pentagon, Arlington, VA, the same time

"Secretary Lester, you have a secure call from Mr. Patrick at the National Security Council," a woman's voice announced over the telephone intercom.

"Put him through to my desk, Kim."

Lester casually walked over to his office door and turned the lock, then returned to his desk. The secure telephone started ringing. Lester waited until the third ring before answering.

"Jon," he gruffly answered. "I'm putting you on speaker."

Lester clicked the speaker on and began pacing the floor in front of his desk.

"We have a problem. I just got word from our guy in the DNI's office that Admiral Thornberg is on to Rajakovics. He has tasked Boucher to bring him back here. Do you have comms with Rajakovics? We need to warn him."

"We can't raise him outside of our normal communications protocol without risk of compromise. Our next scheduled comms with him is ten hundred hours Zulu time. That's about five hours from now."

"Do you think the Israelis are on to this yet?"

"It's hard to say. They certainly know this operation is underway and it involves a bunch of moving parts. I mean – they're not stupid."

"What's the status of the tsunami?"

"No one knows. We can't determine how much of the mountain made it into the sea until daylight. It may not be enough to do the job. I guess we'll know for sure about rush hour when it comes ashore."

"Shit!" Patrick gasped. If this unravels on us, you know the consequences. Make sure everyone gets the word."

Aena Airport, La Palma

The V-22 landed and taxied to the parking apron close to where Boucher's Gulfstream was parked. Morgan stopped Boucher on the tail ramp.

"Be advised the Marine helicopters off the Saipan will be here in twenty mikes. You sure you don't want me and my guys to give you a hand?"

Boucher hesitated a moment, watching his men disembark the V-22 before turning back to Morgan.

"Thanks, Lieutenant, but no. This is something we have to do." His eyes shifted to Sandra's poncho-wrapped body which was strapped to a field stretcher located in the forward part of the cargo cabin. Morgan could read his mind.

"She'll be okay, Sir. I'll personally see to it."

Boucher patted Morgan on the shoulder and turned to leave the plane but stopped short, turning back to Morgan.

"Just out of curiosity, what did you guys ever do with those gold ingots we left you with last year when you caught up to us on that island offshore Vietnam?"

Morgan's expression betrayed his pain.

"We never told anyone we had them. When Lieutenant Murrant was killed in Afghanistan last year, we cashed them in and anonymously gave all the money to his wife. You know, they had one-year-old twin boys."

Boucher's eyes glistened with tears. He leaned forward and gently kissed Morgan on the forehead.

"Good man," he whispered.

Boucher briskly left the plane to join his men by the Gulfstream. The V-22 taxied back out onto the runway and departed into the rainy darkness.

The men assembled beneath the wing of the Gulfstream, using it as a roof from the rain. No one spoke. They just stood there silently watching Boucher. He looked into the eyes of each of his loyal old friends going slowly from one to the next silently acknowledging each with a nod.

"I'm okay," he assured them. "Admiral Thornberg asked me to apprehend a Russian double agent by the name of Rajakovics. He's working out of a hanger at the airport in Dakar. The Admiral says they monitored some phone calls he made a few hours ago. I'm gonna need some help. The Admiral wants him alive."

"What's the plan, Jake?" Doyle asked.

"Jackie, is the Gulfstream ready to go?"

"Yes, fueled and pre-flighted."

"Get'er started up. I want to be outta here before the Marines show up."

"Jake," Doyle warned, "Air Traffic Control has just closed the airport."

"Is there any reason we can't taxi and take off without clearance?"

"No problem as long as the runway isn't blocked."

"Can you do a low level out of here so they can't track us?"

"Roger, I can fly us fifty feet above the water, but that's going to significantly cut into our fuel burn rate. We'll have to get fuel at the Azores so we can make it across the pond for home on the return leg."

"No, that's exactly what they think we'll do. After we leave Dakar, plan a southerly route that takes us to Rio de Janeiro. We can puddle jump north from there after we test the tea leaves."

Chapter 28

Dakar, Senegal, two hours later

The sun had been up for an hour when they landed. The Dakar Airport was a typical dingy, foul smelling Third World airport. There was no sign of security and if it even existed, the guards were either sleeping or otherwise distracted. Doyle and Moss parked the Gulfstream near the only hanger on the field and shut down the engines. Boucher gathered everyone in the cabin area.

"Si, stay here in the Gulfstream with Jackie and Mossman. Jackie, work up a flight plan for a transatlantic. Johnny, Mojo and Billy, you're with me. Johnny, I want you to cover the back of the hanger. Mojo, you cover the front. Billy, you, Pat and I are going inside to grab Rajakovics."

Boucher pulled his Novak custom built .40 cal. Hi-Power pistol from his belt holster and did a quick press check to ensure he had a round chambered. In a single fluid motion he flipped the thumb safety up locking the hammer back at the ready and shoved the pistol firmly back into its holster.

"Any questions?" he asked his trusted old teammates.

With Boucher in the lead, the three men cautiously entered the dimly lit hanger through the open hanger doors. Surprisingly, the hanger floor was relatively uncluttered and well maintained. There was only one small plane inside undergoing engine maintenance along with a van that was parked near the front of the hanger doors. A number of doors with small frosted glass windows opening into several offices and works spaces lined the rear wall of the hanger. Two adjoining offices had lights on. Boucher noted that one of them had a flickering light – *a television*. Boucher and Reilly quietly made their way around the door. They could hear the TV blaring inside. Boucher gestured for Patterson and Reilly to follow him through the door. He held up one finger, two, three and quietly entered the office.

Rajakovics was asleep on a couch in front of the TV. A near empty bottle of vodka sat next to a glass on the table beside the couch. Boucher cautiously approached and pressed his pistol into Rajakovics' cheek.

"Get up," he ordered.

Rajakovics opened his eyes and lurched.

"Commander, what are you doing?" he asked in a heavy Russian accent.

"I'm taking you for a plane ride. Sit up and don't make any fast moves."

"Where to are you taking me?"

"To see a friend. Blindfold him Billy."

Reilly grabbed a roll of duct tape off a nearby bench and wrapped a double strip around Rajakovics' head making sure his eyes were completely covered. He and Patterson lifted Rajakovics to a standing position and Boucher searched him for weapons.

"All he's got on him is this cell phone." Boucher handed the phone to Billy. "Get all the guys on the plane. I'll be along in a few minutes. Pat and I need to have a private chat with Rajakovics. Pat, please don't let me kill this sorry ass son-of-a-bitch."

Boucher turned off the TV and turned on the ceiling light. He seated Rajakovics at the table and bound his hands behind the chair. Boucher sat down across from him placing his pistol on the table with the business end pointed at Rajakovics.

Patterson stood by the wall behind Rajakovics.

"Okay Captain, we can do this the easy way or the hard way - your call. Either way we're gonna get to the bottom of it all."

Rajakovics smiled. "You are already too far to matter my friend. The U.S. can not survive."

"How so? We stopped the nukes and the tsunami. I killed your friend Hann. You're finished."

Rajakovics smiled again. "Would you be kind to remove the tape from my eyes?"

Boucher nodded at Patterson who pulled the tape off his face.

"Thank you. It is better that I look you to explain." Rajakovics was confident and calm. "I will tell you story, Jake. You can then do what you want but you will not be able to stop it."

"I'm all ears." Boucher sprawled back in his chair keeping his hand close to his pistol.

"The U.S. is heading for collapse. The dollar is not secured by anything. The country's foreign debt has grown like an avalanche, even though in the early 1980s there was no debt. Now it is more than 11 trillion. Even now it is already collapsing. Four of the largest and oldest five banks on Wall Street have already ceased to exist, and the last is barely surviving. Their losses are the biggest in history. Now what we will see is a change in the regulatory system on a global financial scale. America will no longer be the world's financial regulator."

"You got me scared now. What's your fucking point?"

"Your lack of unified national laws and divisions among your political elite have led to these crisis conditions. It is not Russia. The U.S. will fail and break up into separate parts."

Yeah, and I guess the tsunami attack was just a joke, huh?"

"Two countries will assume your role: Russia and China."

Boucher's thoughts immediately shifted to the discovery he made of the Chinese war plans a year earlier and their plan to occupy the U.S. under the guise of emergency aid. It was a sobering memory.

"Break up into separate parts? And Russia will rule the world? I don't think so."

"Yes, and it is already too late for you. The financial problems in the U.S. will get worse. Millions of your citizens have lost their savings. Prices and unemployment are on the rise. Your auto industry and heavy manufacturing plants are on the verge of collapse, and whole cities will be left without work. Your governors are already insistently demanding money from the federal center. Dissatisfaction is growing, and at the moment it is only being held back by the hope that your new president can work miracles. But by next year, it will be clear that there are no miracles."

Boucher and Patterson's eyes met. Words were unnecessary.

"So you just thought you could speed things up by eliminating the Eastern Seaboard?"

"Sooner or later the U.S. will break up into six parts. The Atlantic coast, with its distinct and separate mentality from the rest of the U.S.; the Pacific coast, with its growing Chinese population; the South, with its Hispanics; five of the poorer central states with their large Native American populations; and the northern states, where the influence from Canada is strong and Texas, where independence movements are already on the rise. We will reclaim Alaska since it was only granted on lease, after all."

"You're out of your mind, Rajakovics!"

"I do not think so, my friend. You thought you won the Cold War but you lost your way. Join us and we will show you the way. I could have had you killed many times already but I have no interest in killing you. We are much alike, Jake, you and I. We are wolves in a world of sheep."

Boucher sat straight up. "No, Captain! You are a wolf who feeds on the sheep. I may resemble a wolf but I am a sheepdog, I protect them. Let's go."

Patterson lifted Rajakovics to his feet and turned him towards the outer door but he spun and kicked Patterson in the groin, knocking him backward onto the table and into Boucher. He freed his loosely bound hands with a snap and darted out through the door. Boucher and Patterson were close behind but he had just enough of a head start that he made it into an adjoining room, slamming the door behind. Boucher and Patterson stopped short of entering the room.

They lined up on either side of the windowless door leading to the room. They could hear a television and see light from its screen flickering through the crack beneath the door and the floor. Boucher nodded and slowly reached for the door knob but stopped short of touching it.

"I don't like it," he whispered. "I have a bad gut feeling about this."

Patterson shrugged.

"Be ready."

Boucher disappeared back into the other workroom and returned with a spool of electrical wire. He and Patterson secured it to the door knob and reeled it out to the hanger floor. Boucher slowly turned the doorknob unlatching the door.

"Run it over to that van over there. We'll use it for cover."

Patterson laid out about thirty more feet of wire being careful not to yank on the strand tied to the doorknob.

"Okay, Pat, fire in the hole."

Patterson pulled all the slack out of the wire and then gave it a hard tug. A near simultaneous explosion followed, blowing the wall out of the office they had almost entered.

"Back to the plane!" Boucher yelled.

As they exited the smoking hanger, they were met by Yellowhorse and Lavender. Mojo grabbed Boucher as he came through the door.

"What the fuck happened?"

"It was a trap. Get onboard the plane."

Moss and Doyle already had the jet engines powered up and their preflight checklist completed when Boucher secured the cabin door. He went aft into the main cabin area and sat down at a small table with Patterson, Reilly and Barnhart. The engines revved and the plane began taxiing to the runway.

"That was a close one back there," Patterson commented. "How did you know?"

"I didn't, it was a gut feeling. I just felt it."

Reilly had his laptop booted up and was reading the screen.

"Jake, I downloaded Rajakovics' call record from the SIM card in his cell phone. There are numbers here with 202, Washington, DC and 703, Northern Virginia area codes. Here's some 646, New York City numbers. And here's Hann's cell number."

"Put it into a file and e-mail it to Admiral Thornberg."

The plane's intercom crackled with Doyle's voice.

"Jake, there is a truck full of soldiers blocking the runway."

"Can you take off from the taxiway?"

"Yeah, I think it's long enough."

"Do it."

Office of the Assistant Secretary of Defense for Special Operations and Low Intensity Conflict, The Pentagon, Arlington, VA, two hours later

Lester was standing by the window in his office that overlooked Arlington National Cemetery. He observed distant movement on the cemetery's hillside. He watched as a horse drawn caisson in a military funeral procession made its way to the hilltop. The intercom on his desk crackled with a woman's voice compelling his attention back into the office.

"Secretary Lester, Mr. Patrick is holding for you on secure line two."

Lester was jarred from his daydream and hesitated before replying.

"Okay, Kim, put him through."

Lester returned to his desk and characteristically answered his phone on the third ring.

"Jon, what the fuck?"

Lester punched the speaker button and returned to the window.

"We did it! Cline has linked Boucher and his boys with the Cumbre Vieja blast and the Dakar airport bomb. Rajakovics got away and is safely on his way to Tripoli. It doesn't get any better than that."

Lester slowly paced in front of the window.

"Yeah but there's no fucking tsunami - nothing! Now what?"

"We still can't make a determination on the extent of the slide."

"Why the fuck not? It's daylight over there. Can't you just get an estimate on the volume of the displacement and do the math?"

"We did that and it's inconclusive. The only thing we're sure of is that about a cubic mile went into the sea. We don't know how fast it slid or whether it reached the bottom. Best case is that it will generate a tsunami it just won't be a big one like we intended."

"It doesn't have to be big. It just has to make it to this shore to keep our plan moving. Now where the hell is Boucher and his band of merry men?"

"Apparently they're off the radar screen. They did a deception flight out of Dakar and haven't been detected since. My people think they may be on the ground waiting us out somewhere along the African coast, or perhaps the Azores. We're just not sure."

Lester sat down in his desk chair and pulled a file from the two-drawer file safe beside his desk. He opened it and picked up the top page.

"We need to remove Admiral Thornberg. He's the only one standing in our way. He's our Achilles heel."

"Thornberg? I don't know. He's well entrenched within the new administration and the President thinks he walks on water."

"Fuck the new President. The arrogant bastard is there because we put him there. He'll do what we tell him to do or we'll remove him too."

"How about Boucher and his friends?"

"Boucher is either the craftiest bastard on the planet or he's the luckiest son of a bitch I ever saw. I'm beginning to think he can't be killed." Lester quickly reviewed the second and third pages in the file. "Okay, Jon, here's your tasker. Remove Thornberg and make it so Boucher and his men take the fall for everything. I don't care how you get it done. Just get it done. Understand?"

The White House Situation Room

Cline called the meeting to order.

"As you all know, a terrorist nuclear bomb detonated on the island of La Palma about three hours ago. The good news is it fortunately didn't detonate at full yield. The bad news is it did cause a section of the Cumbre Vieja Volcano's caldron to break free and slide into the sea. Ladies and gentlemen, there may be a tsunami on the way here. We still aren't sure. If it does arrive, we don't know how devastating it may be to our Eastern Seaboard. In what we believe is a related incident, we just got word from our embassy in Senegal that the Dakar airport was bombed about thirty minutes ago. A Gulfstream

450 corporate jet departed immediately afterward without clearance to do so. Remarkably, this same jet had arrived only moments earlier from La Palma having departed from there without clearance shortly after the nuke bombing of the Cumbre Vieja Volcano caldron. The FAA advises that this jet is registered to a privately owned Maryland-based security firm. Does the name Jake Boucher ring any bells for anyone?"

Chapter 29

Kennedy Irregular Warfare Center, ONI,
Suitland, MD, four hours later

Captain Blackburn walked from the coffee mess with an overfilled cup of coffee spilling some of it on his Navy kaki uniform crotch area, pant leg and the blue vinyl tile floor. Because of the ongoing crisis he hadn't been home in over forty hours and the lack of a good night's sleep or a complete meal was beginning to wear on him.

"Wow, that's fucking hot!" he cursed aloud just as a thirties-something female civilian intelligence analyst passed by.

"What did you just say to me?" she indignantly challenged.

Blackburn was caught off guard. He hadn't noticed her.

"Ahh, sorry. I was talking about my coffee," he replied while reaching down to brush the coffee from his now wet crotch and pant leg.

The young woman's eyes moved down to the mess he had just made and then back up to him, but she wasn't going to let it go. She knew he had a reputation as an old school officer and she saw him as crude, unsophisticated and out of touch. He was at odds with the scholarly, politically correct, elitist world she represented. She had him by the balls for sexual harassment and she knew it.

"How dare you speak to me like that!" She angrily responded. "I'm reporting this to my supervisor and filing a sexual harassment complaint. Now get out of my way!"

257

Blackburn was so taken back by her outburst he was uncharacteristically at a loss for words. All he could do was stand there and watch her storm off down the hall. After she disappeared into an office he turned back to the countertop and put two heaping spoonfuls of creamer into his coffee. Mumbling to himself he lumbered in the opposite direction down the hall into Lieutenant Bruce's office. Bruce was sitting at his computer screen with his back to the door.

"Hey Lieutenant, you'll never guess what just happened."

Bruce swiveled around and laughed.

"The Marines just killed Bin Laden?"

"Nahh, nothing that wonderfully uncomplicated. You know that blond bitch with the long hair and big tits who works in the 62 Shop at the other end of the hall?"

"Yes, Sir, I see her in the hall from time to time. She's the good looking chick with the attitude who never says thanks when I hold the door for her or even acknowledges there are other people besides her on this planet."

"Yeah, that's her. Well she just charged me with sexual harassment. You believe that shit?"

Bruce laughed. "You? A sensitive new age guy like you? No way, Sir."

"It's not funny, Lieutenant. She heard me cuss when I spilled hot coffee on my balls and she thought I was talking about her. I mean, shit, it would be different if I had told her she has a nice ass and big tits or something like that - but hot coffee? Fuck me."

Bruce laughed at his boss again. "Well, Sir, I guess we better figure this out before you're relieved from duty for cause."

Blackburn shook his head ruefully.

"Yeah, I gotta remember to quit cussing so fucking much."

Bruce turned his flat screen monitor toward Blackburn and offered him a chair.

"Here's what we've pieced together so far, Sir. According to your old friend Commander Boucher, he participated in this mission at the request of the CIA. It began in Jordan and proceeded to La Palma. He worked closely with a CIA operative by the name of Sandra Morrison, now reported to be deceased, and a Los Alamos scientist by the name of Doctor Simon Barnhart. He also had some of his old SEAL platoon members help him out along the way. I assume you know the men listed here."

Blackburn read the names on the screen.

"Yeah, I know'm all including Leon Patterson. He's the former POW who Jake rescued during the Vietnam War and who later retired from the FBI as a Supervisory Special Agent. All these guys are the ones who recovered all that gold about a year ago from a Vietnam War era crash site in Cambodia. They're all bazillionaires now."

"Exactly, Sir, so why are they involved here when they don't have to work a single second of their lives ever again?"

"What are you saying, Lieutenant?"

"Well, Sir, there is some emerging intelligence that suggests a link between them and the terrorists involved in the loose nukes and this attack."

"That's fucking preposterous!" Blackburn insisted. "I've known Jake Boucher for over thirty-eight years and there is no way he, or any of his men, is a terrorist. It's im-fucking-possible, Lieutenant!"

"Sir, it's not that I don't believe you. It's just that there is intelligence surfacing that suggests otherwise."

"Lieutenant, those men have spent their entire lives hunting down the enemies of our country and killing them. They've dedicated their lives to defending this country against a bunch of cocksuckers who hate America and want us dead. I can promise you that those men are no more affiliated with terrorists than I am."

Blackburn sat back and cautiously took a long swallow of his coffee, being careful not to spill it.

"Sir, there's one more thing you need to know. It appears that Admiral Thornberg may be complicit with the terrorists involved with the nukes."

Blackburn spit his coffee on the floor.

"No fucking way, Lieutenant! Look, I don't know where this bullshit intel is being generated but it's not credible and that's all there is to it! Pull out all the stops, investigate the sources of that intel, and get me some answers."

"Yes, Sir."

"One more thing, Lieutenant. Keep this between us."

Air Traffic Control Center, San Juan, Puerto Rico

"Mr. Alverez, we just received a call from ATC Rio reporting the arrival of our mystery plane. They advise that the plane is now parked and will remain overnight."

Alverez was the overall ATC manager at the San Juan Center. All the air traffic control shift supervisors reported to him.

"Excellent, James. Please ask Rio to notify us when the plane departs. I want you to personally stay on top of this and keep me informed the moment they file for departure. And, James, you're up for a merit raise at the end of this month and promotion by the end of this year so let's keep this between us."

"Certainly, Mr. Alverez."

El Rancho Hotel, Rio de Janeiro

The flight across the Atlantic had been uneventful for Boucher and his men. They had taken a southerly great circle route that is heavily used by commercial jets in an effort to blend in. They didn't file a high altitude instrument flight plan so they wouldn't be tracked as they crossed the Atlantic. They waited to report in to Air Traffic Control until they were about to enter Brazilian air space and then proceeded under Brazilian control to Rio. Upon arrival they immediately refueled their plane and took cabs to a nearby hotel. After checking in they assembled in Boucher's room.

"Alright everyone, listen up. I tried to raise Admiral Thornberg on the satellite phone the whole trip across the Atlantic. He's not answering any of his personal numbers and I'm concerned. I'm going to give my old friend Captain Blackburn a call and see what he knows. I need to sort this out before we depart for home. For now, get some sleep. We'll plan on a 0500 departure in the morning. Jackie and Mossman, I think we should look at Nassau for our next leg."

"No problemo, Jake."

As the men left the room Boucher focused on Barnhart who was sitting in an arm chair next to the window. The old scientist had held up remarkably well considering everything they had been through over the past several days.

"You do'n okay, Si?"

"Not bad for a Monday."

"What do you make of all this?"

"Fuller."

"Fuller?" Boucher questioned.

"That's right, Jake, Markus Fuller, remember him?"

"Sure. CIA, Area 51, but..."

"He was Hann's boss and he put Sandra in the mix with us. There never really was any expectation that we would succeed. He set us up."

"He must have also been tied into Rajakovics."

"Maybe not. What if Hann was a double agent for the Russians and Rajakovics was his handler."

Boucher looked dumbfounded.

"But why us, Si?"

"Because of who we are. When we failed it would appear that they had tried to stop this attack using the very best operators they could get. The problem we now face is that we beat the odds against us. We succeeded in stopping the attack. So, the sixty four thousand dollar question is; what are they going to do now?"

260

The old scientist rubbed his chin thoughtfully and then sucked in a long breath through his teeth awaiting Boucher's reply.

"We need to pay our friend, Markus Fuller, a visit and find out."

Kennedy Irregular Warfare Center, ONI, Suitland, MD

Blackburn's intercom buzzed.

"Yes," he said gazing into the LCD screen on the phone's face.

"Sir, you have a call from a Commander Boucher – line one."

"I'll take it here. Thanks."

Blackburn pushed the flashing button on the phone.

"Jake, it's me. What the fuck is going on?"

"Thanks for taking my call. Dean, I'm in deep shit and need your help."

"Yeah, I'll say. Deep shit is an understatement. There's intel trickling in that links you with the terrorist nukes. At least there was no tsunami. Where the hell are you, Jake?"

"Me and my guys are in Rio. Look, Dean, this is a frame job. We think the guy behind this is on your end. He's a CIA official by the name of Marcus Fuller. I don't believe for a second that's his real name. In fact, he might not really be CIA, but that's all I have to go on. He's the man who hired us to track down the loose nukes and stop them. I've been trying to reach Admiral Thornberg for the past seven hours to ask him about Fuller but he hasn't answered any of his private numbers. I'm worried about him."

"You haven't heard? It was reported that he suffered a major heart attack early this morning."

"Damn!"

"The last report I got he was in Bethesda Naval Hospital."

"Damn. He was as strong as an ox the last time I saw him. Is he going to recover?"

"I don't think anybody knows. He's been in the critical care unit since he got there, no visitors allowed."

"Dean, there's a lot at stake here. It's not about me and my guys. I need to know who Fuller is and where he is ASAP. So if you have another path you can investigate, it would sure be helpful."

"Okay, Jake. I'll get on it. Is this a good number for you?"

"Yeah, it's my satellite phone."

Chapter 30

Nassau, Bahamas, the next morning

Boucher's Gulfstream touched down beneath a cloudless sky and uneventfully taxied to the ramp parking apron where other corporate jets were parked. Moss and Doyle shut the engines down and began the post flight check list. Boucher opened the door and casually disembarked the plane with Barnhart following close behind. The moment they stepped onto the tarmac they were immediately arrested by FBI agents who were waiting in a maintenance van a short distance behind the plane's tail. They were immediately whisked off without explanation. Patterson witnessed the entire escapade from the plane's open door but couldn't react fast enough to intervene. Boucher and Barnhart were gone.

"Hey guys, get out here," Patterson shouted back inside the plane, "Jake and Si have just been carted off by FBI agents."

Mojo and Reilly ran down the stairs to the tarmac where Patterson was now standing trying to keep an eye on the van as it navigated between parked planes toward the other side of the airport.

"They're in that yellow van over there," Patterson said pointing.

"What the hell? Why did they take Jake and the Doc?" Reilly asked.

"I don't know but they obviously wanted them and not us."

Moss appeared above at the open door with binoculars.

"The van is pulling up next to a Learjet. They're boarding it. The van has moved away. They're gonna fly'm outta here."

"Back in the plane," Patterson yelled. "Mossman, get this thing fired back up. We're gonna follow'm."

Moss had already disappeared back into the cockpit and, along with Doyle, was rushing through the start-up check list."

Patterson stuck his head into the cockpit.

"Do we have enough fuel?"

Moss checked the instrument panel.

"That depends on where we're going. We can make it as far north as Baltimore and as far west as Louisville," he coolly replied.

"Can you monitor Air Traffic Control on their outbound path?"

"Yup, can do easy, Pat."

"Okay, then follow that plane."

"What about our flight clearances?" Doyle asked Patterson.

"Fuck a bunch of clearances! We'll worry about that when we get to the U.S."

Patterson rushed back to the cabin.

"Billy, can you get Captain Blackburn on the satellite phone for me?"

"Sure can. Give me a moment."

Kennedy Irregular Warfare Center, ONI, Suitland, MD

Blackburn had just arrived at work having had a good night's sleep for the first time in several days. He was sitting at his desk reading the previous night's intelligence messages when his telephone buzzed. Lieutenant Bruce was sitting across from him, notepad in hand. Blackburn casually closed the folder he had been reviewing with Bruce and reached forward, answering the phone on the third ring.

"Blackburn," he answered impassively. "Yeah, of course I remember both of you. Sure, I'll talk to Pat." Blackburn sat forward in alarm. "What? Hey Pat, can I put you on speaker? Good." Blackburn punched the speaker button. "Okay, Pat, I have one of my lieutenants here who needs to hear this. Shoot."

"We landed in Nassau about twenty minutes ago. When Jake and Doctor Barnhart disembarked our plane, FBI agents took them into custody. We saw them both put onboard a Learjet which is now taxiing toward the active runway. We're gonna follow them in our plane. We sure would like to know what the fuck is going on."

"How do you know they were FBI agents?"

"They were wearing jackets that had FBI printed on the back in big yellow lettering. Besides, I know from my FBI days that we have counter-terrorism law enforcement reciprocity with Nassau."

"Okay, Pat, I'll take it for action. By the way, you know that Marcus Fuller guy Jake asked me to locate; well after we drilled down a little and called in a few favors we learned his real name is William Mason and he heads Langley's black operations. He's a career spook. No one in my circles knows him personally. They say he's a loner."

"Where does he live?"

"I'm told he lives close to DuPont Circle in downtown DC."

"I need an address."

"I couldn't get an address on him. All I could find out is that he lives in an old church that was converted into a private dwelling. It can't be too hard to figure that out – an old church, now a home, close to DuPont Circle - how many of those could there be?"

Inside the Gulfstream above the Atlantic Ocean, twenty minutes later

The Gulfstream was climbing to a cruising altitude of thirty-nine thousand feet. They had taken off several minutes after the FBI's Learjet but had no problem catching up. Doyle and Moss had skillfully brought the Gulfstream onto the same northerly heading and were following about two miles behind the Learjet. Patterson had gathered everyone in the main cabin.

"Billy, can you arrange to have someone grab Fuller or Mason or whatever his real name is?"

"Maybe. It depends on how much time we have to pull it off."

"We need to grab him tonight and stash him in a safe house until we can question him. Is that possible?"

"I need to make some phone calls."

"Okay, do it."

Reilly grabbed the satellite phone and keyed a number into the handset.

"Haus, I need you to run a body snatch for me."

Chief Quicklinsky had been Boucher's SEAL Team platoon chief in Vietnam and had participated in the gold recovery operation Boucher and his men had run last year. He had retired from the Navy years earlier but was still regarded as a loyal, tried, tested and proven SEAL operator who was now, thanks to Boucher, independently wealthy.

"A what?" he laughed recognizing Reilly's voice. "What the hell do you have yourself into now, Billy?"

"A body snatch, Haus and I'm not alone. I have Pat, Mossman, Jackie, and Johnny here with me. We're in deep shit. We need your help."

"Where's Jake?"

"FBI agents grabbed him and a friend of his, Doctor Barnhart, on the ground in Nassau about twenty minutes ago. We're in pursuit in the Gulfstream."

"Damn, Billy, I was just settling into my condo here in Fells Point with my new girlfriend. She's the horniest woman I've ever known. Life is good these days."

"Haus, there is no one else I can go to. I need you to grab an asshole by the alias name of Fuller, Markus Fuller. His real name is William Mason. We thought he was a CIA operative but now we're not sure. The last time Jake saw him was about three weeks ago in a deep underground facility at the Nevada Test Site - Area 51."

"Oh hell, Billy," Quicklinsky replied in a chuckle, "detailed information like that ought'a make it easy to find him. Is he a space alien or some shit?"

"No, he's flesh and blood just like us. Chief, if anyone can find this ass wipe, you can. We need you to grab him and hold him until we can question him."

Quicklinsky laughed. "So you're asking me to kidnap this dickwad and hold him until you get to wherever it is I'm holding him?"

"Exactly."

"And I bet you need this done within the next twenty-four hours or less."

"Yes, ASAP."

Quicklinsky paused. "Where is he?"

"Captain Blackburn says he lives in an old church that has been converted into a residence close to DuPont Circle in downtown DC."

"I'm probably gonna need some help, Billy."

"Yeah, I know. See what you can do, Haus. Use this SATPHONE number to reach me."

"Hey, Billy."

"Yeah, Haus?"

"After I grab him I'm gonna hold him onboard the Perseverance."

"Roger that."

Office of the Assistant Secretary of Defense for Special Operations and Low Intensity Conflict, The Pentagon, Arlington, VA, two hours later

"Secretary Lester, Mr. Patrick is holding for you on secure line one."

"Put him through."

Lester uncharacteristically answered his phone on the first ring.

"Jon, what you got?"

Lester glanced to his door to ensure it was closed and then punched the speaker button.

"The FBI got Boucher and Barnhart in Nassau."

"How the fuck did that happen?"

"Cline must have been tipped and he put the Attorney General on it. It's okay. They'll be charged as terrorists. They don't know enough to implicate us or our plan."

"What does the President know?"

"Nothing. He's too busy kissing Iran's ass and trying to keep Russia pacified. Ever since he announced the troop withdrawal date from Iraq he's been trying to find a way to leverage diplomatic relations with Iran. The son of a bitch doesn't get it."

"How are the Speaker and the Majority Leader reacting?"

"They'll do what we tell'm or we'll get rid of them."

"Yeah, but how would the President react?"

"Look, the President has only been in office a short while. He's still trying to build his political coalitions and vet his administration with the world. This isn't even a speed bump on the road he's driving down. During the campaign the Vice President told the American public that the new President would be tested. So we're making sure he's being tested - big fucking deal!"

"I still don't like it. The President is a wild card. He could cause us a lot of grief if we don't keep him screwed down."

"He's one of the most narcissistic bastards on the planet. We can continue to use that to our advantage."

Inside the Gulfstream above the Atlantic Ocean

Moss clicked the intercom button, "Pat, they're landing at Manassas."

Patterson appeared in the cockpit moments later.

"Okay, let's go to Dulles. We'll clear Immigration and Customs there. I have an old FBI friend at Manassas who still flies for them. I'm gonna call him and see if I can get a track on Boucher once that Learjet lands.

Doyle turned toward Patterson. "Pat, what do you think about calling Senator Cummings? Maybe she would help us."

"Cummings? I never even thought about her. She's now the Secretary of State. She might help if there's some political gain in it for her. I'll give her a try when we land."

Chapter 31

Dirksen Senate Office Building,
Washington, DC, twelve hours later

It was déjà vu as Boucher's attention was jerked away from the events of the past few days by an amplified female voice talking to him over the loudspeaker. A year earlier he had sat before this very committee and the female voice then was that of Senator Cummings. But Cummings had been appointed the Secretary of State following the presidential election. Cummings was replaced by Senator Kelley as the committee's co-chair. Boucher had not met Kelley before but his first impression was that she was even more acidic than Cummings. *Where do they come up with these assholes?* he thought.

"So," Senator Kelley concluded, "it was at this point that you and Doctor Barnhart were arrested. Is that correct, Mr. Boucher?"

Boucher winced and replied without looking up. "We were illegally detained against our will by FBI agents in foreign sovereign territory if that's what you're referring to, Senator"

"Why does it seem that you somehow keep walking on the wrong side of the law, Mr. Boucher?" Kelley smirked at Boucher before continuing. "You and your friends just don't seem to get it, Mr. Boucher, so I will repeat what Senator Cummings told you last year when you sat before this committee. This Senate Select Committee on Intelligence is intent on preserving our nation's security. Your direct implication in this potential terrorist act casts grave doubts upon your patriotism and what you think you stand for. Are you a terrorist, Mr. Boucher?"

Boucher focused his steel-eyed glare on Kelley. "Senator, you know who and what I am and you know I am not a terrorist. You also know that Doctor

Barnhart and I have been working directly for the DNCS, so why don't you stop posturing and let's get down to business. If you want to know how we stopped a nuclear attack on Jordan and a nuclear detonation-generated tsunami from hitting our Eastern Seaboard I'm here to explain. If you want to hear about the terrorists I killed in the process and the good guys who died along the way, I'll be happy to tell you about each one in nauseating detail. Otherwise, let's stop the bullshit. Frankly, I've had enough of this committee's arrogance to last me a lifetime. I'm tired and I want to go home."

Kelley's mouth gaped open in insulted disbelief. She looked at her fellow members on the panel and then squarely at Boucher. Carefully choosing her words, she again began to speak.

"Mr. Boucher, you are no gentleman and you are not someone who this committee will believe as credible. Through your own actions you have demonstrated your contempt for the United States government and the distinguished members of this committee, and you have made it clear you are no more civilized than those terrorists who murder innocent citizens rather than respect the rule of law. Therefore, I have no further questions for you or your fellow conspirators."

A faint smile crinkled over Boucher's stone hard face. Even though he knew how the game was played he hated playing games like this. It was almost as if it was scripted. He looked over at Senator Rowland who had run against the new president and lost in the last election. Senator Rowland was from Arizona. He was unarguably a Vietnam War hero who had earned his hero status as a POW. Rowland slowly leaned forward to his microphone.

"Mr. Boucher, once again you come before us and once again I think this committee should be reminded that you are, by all definitions of the word, a hero of this country. You won the Navy Cross, this nation's second highest combat award by rescuing a POW from the hands of the enemy. You also won the Silver Star, two Bronze Stars for valor and two Purple Hearts. You were additionally awarded the Legion of Merit and Meritorious Joint Service Medal, not to mention numerous other medals awarded to you by our foreign allies like the Cross of Gallantry and the Victoria Cross. The gentleman sitting beside you, Doctor Barnhart, is a retired Los Alamos National Laboratory nuclear weapon scientist who can be directly credited with helping to win the Cold War. His career is equally distinguished. My colleague's characterization of you and Doctor Barnhart as terrorists is simply wrong and I reject even the slightest suggestion that either of you are anything less than patriots. The real issue here, and the focus of this committee, is to determine to what extent, if any, this country's national security has been compromised by your actions.

Would you be kind enough to explain for the record, exactly what you were up to and why?"

Boucher nodded at Senator Rowland acknowledging his courtesy, then paused a moment to collect his thoughts before answering.

"It began at the request of Marcus Fuller who we understood was an Agency-type. I flew to Jordon with an Agency operative by the name of Sandra Morrison. We located a Russian SS-19 nuke in Amman and Dr. Barnhart, Morrison and I took it out into the desert and disabled it."

Kelley interrupted, "And, that's where you destroyed one of our helicopters and killed five of our agents, correct?"

"No, Senator, that's not correct. We were attacked by your so called agents and we defended ourselves. The helicopter's destruction was a result of collateral damage."

"But you never seem to take prisoners, do you, Mr. Boucher? You just kill, kill, kill."

Boucher shifted in his chair and straightened up a bit.

"Yeah, that's right, Senator, I kill those who try to kill me."

Rowland interrupted. "And what happened after you disabled the nuke in Amman?"

"We realized that there were other nukes that were either on their way to La Palma in the Canary Islands or were already in place and that these nukes would ultimately be used to attack the U.S."

"How did you get to the Canarys?"

"I had my private Gulfstream pick us up in the desert and fly us there."

Kelley loudly broke in. "I want you to tell the committee exactly what you did when you reached the Canarys."

Boucher squirmed slightly. "Senator, I will only discuss that behind closed doors in the appropriate security environment which protects that information."

Kelley blistered with anger. "Mr. Boucher, you insist on behaving arrogantly and contemptuously toward this committee!"

"Wait a minute, Senator," Boucher forcefully cautioned, "you're passing judgment without the facts! Senator Kelley, do you really expect me to reveal the details about this incident in an open forum like this?"

Kelley covered her microphone and whispered to Senator Rowland. Rowland nodded in agreement. Removing her hand from the microphone Kelley took the gavel in her hand.

"Members of the committee, this session will reconvene in closed chambers in one hour."

Kelley struck her gavel and left the room. Boucher and Barnhart were led out of the room by two uniformed Capitol Policemen and taken to a small office adjacent to the hearing room. Boucher immediately recognized the room as the same one he had been taken to a year earlier when Admiral Sinclair had offered him a place in the shadow government known as the Luminous.

Chester Cove Marina, Inner Harbor, Baltimore, MD

Yellowhorse, Reilly and Mojo cast off the lines securing Boucher's seventy foot yacht to the pier and scurried aboard. Quicklinsky eased the engine throttles slowly forward and spun the boat's wheel a half a turn to the left. The throaty growl of the boat's twin 871 Detroit diesels increased proportionately as the heavy craft picked up speed heading outbound to the shipping channel beyond Fort McHenry from Baltimore's Inner Harbor. A man with his head hooded was bound to a chair in the main cabin area behind Quicklinsky. He sat quietly awaiting his fate. Dick Llina, the hospital corpsman in Boucher's former SEAL platoon, sat beside him sorting through an open field pack containing various medical and first aid materials. Even though they had all retired from the Navy years ago, Llina was still very much a part of his old SEAL platoon. Like the others, there was nothing he wouldn't do for Boucher or his former teammates. Llina assembled a hypodermic needle and filled its reservoir from a small bottle of clear fluid. After ensuring there were no air bubbles in the hypo, he injected a few milligrams of the fluid into the back of the man's arm. Within minutes the man appeared to relax.

A harbor tug passed by creating a huge wake that rolled the yacht like a wobbling top. Standing at the instrument console beside Quicklinsky, Patterson braced himself. Without saying so, both men remembered their plight in a stormy sea onboard a Chinese junk in the area of the Spratly Islands the previous year. In fact, Boucher had named this 1972 vintage Chris Craft yacht, "Perseverance," in honor of that experience and today it somehow seemed even more fitting.

Boucher homeported his yacht at the Inner Harbor and used its spacious living quarters as a floating second home. He leased office and storage spaces for his security company, International Security Strategies and Operations, in an old industrial complex close to the marina so the yacht was very convenient when he worked late hours or drank too much when bar hopping along the waterfront. But this late afternoon the Perseverance would serve as a secure location for interrogation and for whatever else it would take to make their prisoner talk. They would wait until they were well away from Baltimore in the upper Chesapeake Bay and then the gloves would come off. The man had to have realized what he was about to face.

Dirksen Senate Office Building, Washington, DC

Boucher and Barnhart sat quietly alone in the small office. Neither man spoke. Moments later there was a soft knock on the door and Secretary of State Cummings entered.

"Mr. Boucher, Dr. Barnhart I presume. I have about thirty minutes. I am here to listen."

Boucher stood and took her hand. "Madam Secretary, I never thought I'd say this, but it sure is good to see you. How did you know we were here?"

"I was told about your capture by our mutual friend, Senator Rowland."

"Ma'am, I am truly sorry that neither you nor Senator Rowland won the election. I would have been good with either one of you as president. I didn't vote for President Banner but he is now my president. Madam Secretary, you need to warn the president. Our country is in grave danger."

"How so?"

"Please sit down. This is gonna take a few minutes to explain."

Onboard Perseverance, Upper Chesapeake Bay

A police helicopter swooped low above the yacht heading south along the shore line. Quicklinsky watched it with cautious optimism hoping it was nothing more than a routine patrol and that the yacht's presence gave them no cause to return. In less than a minute the helicopter's flashing marker lights disappeared into the darkness. Quicklinsky breathed a breath of silent relief.

Patterson stood next to Llina and the bound man. Yellowhorse and Reilly positioned a video camera on a tripod directly in front of the man and then sat down on collapsible chairs they had positioned out of camera view. Quicklinsky pulled the engine throttles back to idle and nodded back to Patterson. In turn, Patterson nodded to Llina. Llina had started an IV drip on the man a few minutes earlier. He now took a hypodermic syringe and injected about fifty milligrams of fluid into the IV. He carefully checked the man's heartbeat with a stethoscope and took his pulse.

"Okay," he reported to Patterson with an approving nod.

Patterson sat down directly in front of the man. "Take his hood off and start the camera."

Yellowhorse pulled the man's hood off. The man blinked wildly as his eyes became adjusted to the light. Patterson stared back at him blankly.

"What is you name?"

"Fuller. Marcus Fuller," the man replied in a monotone.

"That's not your real name. That's your cover name. What's your real name?"

"My name?"

"What's your real name?"

"My name...Will Mason."

"Is your real name Will Mason or William Mason?"

"William Mason."

"Who do you work for, William?"

"I work for the National Clandestine Service."

"What is your job at the National Clandestine Service, William?"

"The Near East Division, I am the Director of the Near East Division."

"Did you recruit Jake Boucher and Doctor Barnhart to be your operatives?"

"Yes, they are non-official cover operatives."

"What was their mission?"

"It was hopeless. They were supposed to fail."

"William, I didn't ask you if they had been set up. I asked you what their mission was."

Mason shook his head grudgingly, "To search for a nuclear bomb."

"Where was the bomb hidden?"

Mason flinched as he hesitated, fighting his compulsion to answer. Patterson nodded at Llina who immediately increased the drip flow on the IV bag. Mason settled back in his chair.

"I'm going to ask you again, William. Where was the bomb hidden?"

"It was in Jordan."

Where did the bomb come from?"

"Kazakhstan."

"Was it a Russian weapon?"

"Yes."

"What was the target?"

"Amman."

"Why was Amman the target?"

Mason slowly wound his head in a circle as if to stretch his neck.

"William, why was Amman the target?" Patterson patiently repeated.

"To permanently change the balance of power in the Middle East."

"Were there other nukes?"

"Yes."

"How many other bombs were there, William?"

"One. It was an AFAP."

"Was that the same nuke Boucher discovered onboard the Iranian ship in the Caspian last winter?"

"Yes."

"What was the target for that nuke?"

"Lebanon."

"So that was the nuke that was detonated during the Israeli air strike against Hamas?"

"Yes," Mason shrugged, answering in a whisper.

Patterson scratched his head. "But why? What was the objective?"

"Israel will eliminate the Palestinians and Hamas, take back the Gaza and extend its security zone into Jordan."

"And I suppose Iran will be blamed. Then the U.S. will bomb Iran in support of Israel?"

"Yes and Dubai must not build nuclear power plants."

"Explain the relationship between the UAE and nuclear power plants."

"They will have Russia build twenty-three nuclear power plants all through the Middle East and they will all share the power grid throughout. They will stop using their own oil. The price per barrel will skyrocket. If the U.S. or Israel attacks their power grid they will stop selling oil to Europe and the U.S. They will only sell their oil to Russia and China. Twenty-three nuclear power plants in Arab hands is a threat beyond measure. It must be stopped now."

Patterson looked back at Reilly who was operating the video camera, "You getting this?"

"Yeah, every word. Ask him about Sandra," Reilly suggested.

"Does Sandra Morrison work for you?"

"Yes."

"Was she part of your conspiracy to nuke Amman?"

"No, she only knew about the Hamas nuke."

"How did she know?"

"She headed the recovery of that nuke from the Iranian ship, Rakish."

"Are you telling me she was onboard that ship when Boucher and the Kazak Special Squad boarded it?"

Mason relaxed and smiled as he answered, "Yes."

"Does Hann work for you?"

"Yes."

"Does Rajakovics work for you?"

"No."

"Do you know who Rajakovics is?"

"He is a Russian agent."

"Did you have anything to do with the nuke attack against the Cumbre Vieja Volcano on La Palma?"

Mason immediately became agitated and seemed confused. His breathing became rapid.

"Rajakovics, Hann…the Russians."

Llina checked Mason's pulse and heart rate. "Best to give him a rest for a few minutes."

"Okay, in a minute. Hann killed Sandra Morrison on the Cumbre Vieja Volcano and Boucher killed Hann. Rajakovics was there. Why was Hann helping Rajakovics? Was Hann a double agent?"

Mason began to hyperventilate and sweat profusely as he mumbled, "Russia… Russia will try to stop us."

"You mean Russia is behind the Cumbre Vieja Volcano attack?"

"Yes, it is Russia."

"So Russia got inside your operation and used your operation against Hamas and Iran as a cover for their attack? Iran, Hamas and al Qaeda are unwitting surrogates for Russia. I think I get it. After the tsunami wipes out the U.S. Eastern Seaboard, Russia emerges as the reigning superpower with all the energy resources they could ever want and they're in bed with the Middle East to boot." Patterson focused on Mason. "I have one more question for you, William and then you can rest. How many other U.S. government officials share in your conspiracy?"

Mason shook his head. "I am not sure. It is compartmentalized."

"Give me some names, William."

"Lester…"

"Who is Lester?"

Mason held his breath and became beet red but finally answered. "ASD SOLIC"

"You mean Assistant Secretary of Defense for Special Operations and Low Intensity Conflict Lester?"

"Yes."

"Is the president associated?"

"No, I don't think so."

"Turn off the camera, Billy. I need to pass this info along to Cummings. She gave me her private cell number in our previous call." Patterson hesitated momentarily, "He won't remember any of this...right, Dick?"

Llina smiled confidently, "I administered the drug Versed along with the sodium pentothal. That's amnesia city. He won't remember ever being here."

Dirksen Senate Office Building, Washington, DC

Cummings stopped Boucher to answer her cell phone. Listening for a moment she replied, "Yes, Mr. Patterson, this is she and I have Mr. Boucher and Dr. Barnhart here with me. I am putting you on speaker."

"Thank you, Madam Secretary. Jake, I just questioned William Mason aka Marcus Fuller. He confirmed what you thought. The Lebanon and Amman, Jordan nukes were a U.S.-supported conspiracy with Israel. The Cumbre Vieja Volcano tsunami attack was not Iranian-directed. Iran was a surrogate. It's Russia."

"Russia?" Cummings questioned in disbelief.

"Yes, Russia," Patterson insisted. "Madam Secretary, we have a very sophisticated conspiracy involving some high placed officials within our own government who have facilitated the nuke detonation in Lebanon and the attempted attack against Amman using Iran and Hamas as surrogates. That's the attack that Jake and Dr. Barnhart initially foiled a few days ago. Russia was aware of those attacks and actually facilitated them to cover their own. A Russian-backed attack against the U.S. was simultaneously underway on La Palma using the other Lebanon-Amman attack as a deception. That was an offset attack that employed a landslide-generated tsunami to wipe out the U.S. Eastern Seaboard."

"Wait a second, Mr. Patterson, to what end are these attacks intended?"

"Madam Secretary, Mason revealed that the UAE is planning to have Russia build twenty-three nuclear reactors all through the Middle East. That also means they can produce a butt load of their own plutonium. They plan on sharing the power grid throughout the Middle East so they can stop using their own oil to produce power. Russia is already in bed with Iran, so Russia will emerge the big winner. Russia will not only build the nuke power plants but they will be rewarded with a sole monopoly to the Middle East's oil production. In addition to kicking our ass they'll even trump China if they pull this off. Then Russia's gonna globally reassert itself and rule the world."

Boucher gently placed his hand on Secretary Cummings' arm.

"Madam Secretary, we'll give you Mason but you need to get me and Dr. Barnhart out of here."

Cummings sat back in her chair holding the cell phone between two fingers. "Where are you Mr. Patterson?"

"Ahh, that's not important," Patterson replied fumbling his words. "The question is where do you want me to deposit Mason? He's the key to ferreting out the conspiracy within our government."

Cummings momentarily considered Patterson's question. "Mr. Patterson, I need to know where to meet you so I can bring Dr. Barnhart and Mr. Boucher to your location. I will personally accompany them and, if you like, bring a friend – Senator Rowland."

"Mrs. Cummings, it's not that I don't trust you but that's going to draw too much attention to me and my men. At this point, that's attention we don't want or need. Please just tell me where you want me to deposit Mason. I'll provide you a video copy of his interrogation."

"You're a former FBI agent. You know the video of your coerced interrogation is inadmissible in a court of law."

"That may be true but it will give you a starting point and a record of his involvement in the conspiracy. I don't think the Attorney General is part of the conspiracy because if he was, Jake and Dr. Barnhart probably wouldn't be sitting there with you. I sure don't want to sound like I'm trying to play hardball with you but you can take it from here or I can put Mason's recorded confession on the internet and let the law of gravity take its course - your call. However, if you take the initiative, you'll go down in history as a patriot and political hero who protected the president and our democracy."

Cummings momentarily considered Patterson's offer. "Do you have a suggestion for a location to turn him over?" she replied.

"I'll call you back with a location and time. Jake, call me when you're free."

Chapter 32

Kennedy Irregular Warfare Center, ONI, Suitland, MD

"Sir, you have a call from a Mr. Patterson."

"Thank you. I'll take it here."

Blackburn waited until the petty officer departed his office and closed the door behind before pushing the speaker button.

"Pat, this is Dean. Are you guys nuts? The whole frigin' U.S. government is looking for Mason. Where the hell are you?"

"We're on Jake's yacht heading toward Baltimore. I just finished briefing Secretary Cummings over the phone. There's an old abandoned fort sitting out in the water along the channel leading in to Baltimore harbor. Its name is Fort Carol. Do you know where it is?"

"Yeah, it's on the north side of the harbor channel not too far from the Francis Scott Key Bridge. Right?"

"Yeah, that's it. We're going to drop Mason off there. Once we drop him, I'll tell Cummings and Senator Rowland he's there so they can have him taken into custody. They'll probably turn it into a media circus. I want at least an hour to get well clear and make it to the marina pier."

"Look Dean, Jake gave me a call a few minutes ago and asked me to e-mail you the file we made of the Mason interrogation. He wants you to get a copy to Admiral Thornberg soonest."

277

"Admiral Thornberg? You must not have heard."

"Heard what?"

"He died about an hour ago from unknown complications related to the heart attack he suffered yesterday."

"No way! That's too coincidental. Does Jake know?"

"I don't know. I haven't spoken with Jake."

"I'm going to meet Jake downtown. I'll tell'm the bad news then. Dean, we're going to e-mail Mason's interrogation file to you now. And, Dean..."

"Yeah, Pat?"

"Watch your six. This is a huge conspiracy with a lot of moving parts and we've only seen the tip of the iceberg."

"Will do. Out here."

Blackburn sat back in his desk chair and contemplated the situation. He was startled by a knock on the door as it flung open. He immediately recognized Lieutenant Bruce and relaxed.

"Captain, what's going on?"

"Oh, not all that much. With our help Israel tried to nuke Amman and Russia tried to annihilate our Eastern Seaboard and topple the U.S. government. We have a conspiracy that permeates our federal government to an extent yet unidentified and Russia is going to build an assload of nuclear power plants all through the Middle East and emerge as the reigning superpower. Beyond that, I'm having a great fucking day, Lieutenant."

Bruce didn't laugh. He had never seen his boss so visibly upset.

"What do you want me and my team to do, Sir?"

"There's an e-mail file on my account I want you guys to analyze."

"What's the subject line, Sir?"

"Perseverance."

U.S. Department of State, Washington, DC., two hours later

The secretary's opulent office spanned nearly half of the building's seventh floor. Cummings, Senator Rowland, Boucher and Barnhart were seated around a circular table.

"Madam Secretary, we need to apprehend Rajakovics. He has key information we need."

Cummings contemplated Boucher's suggestion. "Perhaps, but where do we look for him?"

"Madam Secretary, we got his cell phone when we tried to apprehend him in Dakar and we downloaded the SIM card. We have a record of his calls. I sent a copy of that to my old friend at the Office of Naval Intelligence to do the analysis. I am relatively certain that he can give us a solid lead. Can you keep this inside embassy channels?"

"I'm afraid not, Mr. Boucher. The Chief of Station will ultimately see any tasker I send that directs the apprehension of Rajakovics and report it back through CIA channels to their chain of command. If the CIA is as corrupted as you say it will only serve to alert everyone involved in the conspiracy. We will need another alternative."

The vault-like door swung open and Patterson entered with Captain Blackburn and Lieutenant Bruce in tow. Without greeting or introduction they took seats at the table. The door was closed by two Diplomatic Security officers who took station inside by the door. Cummings nodded to Boucher. Boucher began.

"Madam Secretary and Senator Rowland, I want to thank you for arranging this meeting and for trusting Pat and me to turn Mason over to your people. Before we begin, I want to introduce Captain Dean Blackburn and Lieutenant Bruce. Dean and I served together in the SEALs and have been friends for over thirty years. He heads the Kennedy Irregular Warfare Center at the Office of Naval Intelligence. Lieutenant Bruce is a senior intelligence analyst on Dean's staff. They have some critical information you need to hear and I thought it appropriate to break protocol and have them here to personally brief you."

Bruce passed everyone paper copies of his briefing slides and began.

"Here's the bottom line. We don't think Russia is behind this."

Cummings scratched her head and winced. "What the hell are you talking about, Lieutenant? We got a senior CIA official involved in a conspiracy who thinks Russia is pulling all the strings. We got a Russian agent at the center who thinks it's Russia. Mr. Boucher and his team think it's Russia and I think it's Russia. So what makes you think differently?"

"Well, Ma'am, we took a look at everything that's gone down and we compared that against what we know and what we think we know."

"Get to the point, Lieutenant. If it isn't Russia, then who is it?"

"Ahh, yes Ma'am. You see, Ma'am, we think there have really been three conspiracies in play here simultaneously. There was the U.S and Israeli plan to nuke Lebanon and Amman so Israel could eliminate Hamas and the Palestinians and extend its security buffer into Jordan. That would also justify the U.S. turning Iran into something that resembles the surface of the moon. And who would really care when the smoke clears? The Free World would be a better place. At the same time, Russia had an operation underway with full knowledge of the U.S.-Israeli operation and used it as a cover. The

Russian operation involved wiping out the U.S. Eastern Seaboard using a nuke-generated tsunami. That was the La Palma nuke attack that Commander Boucher and his guys stopped. Russia has plans to build twenty three nuclear power plants throughout the Middle East. They anticipated the U.S. and Israel would be successful and Iran would be shattered by the U.S. attacks and that the U.S., and for that matter, the world, would think that the nuke-generated tsunami was Islamic retaliation against the U.S. With the successful annihilation of its Eastern Seaboard, the U.S. would have to withdraw its troops in Iraq and Afghanistan as well as the Middle East in general. Russia would then be free to build its nuclear power plants and take control of the oil reserves throughout the Middle East."

Rowland sipped his coffee. "Okay, Lieutenant, where's the beef? You haven't told me who's behind the third conspiracy you believe exists."

"It's China, Sir."

"China?" Rowland said nearly spitting most of coffee he had just gulped back into his cup. "This better be good, Lieutenant."

"Yes, Sir, it's better than good," Bruce said smiling. "Last year, you may recall, Commander Boucher and his guys recovered some Chinese plans that revealed the Chinese intended to land a sizable force on our shores using specially configured container ships under the guise of emergency aid. As we know, that particular plot was foiled but the Chinese goal of world domination was not. Ever since the Cold War ended and most of the Soviet Union collapsed, China has been slowly emerging from its age old policy of isolation. It has been developing a formidable navy composed of surface combatants, submarines and as we saw last year, a massive fleet of supertankers and cargo ships - all with global resupply and war fighting support capabilities."

"My friend," Rowland appealed, "please know we love you but you need to get to the point."

Bruce smiled and nodded. "China imports over eighty percent of its oil from the Middle East. That equates to over seventeen million barrels a day that goes by tanker around the tip of India by Sri Lanka, then through the Straight of Malacca, then north through the South China Sea, past Taiwan to the East China Sea to Shanghai and up through the Yellow Sea to Tianjio and Beijing. Since 1992 China has been pedaling political influence throughout the littoral areas where they must obtain and retain sea control in order to keep the sea lanes of communication open. If you analyze China's political and military presence along their critical oil-shipping sea lanes it becomes obvious what they're up to. They have established numerous strategic naval bases and developed commercial port facilities in various countries along the route. They've built overland supply routes linking most of these locations. Sir, they even have plans to build a super canal through the Isthmus of Kra in Thailand."

"That would sure save them some time," Cummings blurted. "With that they can cut straight through from the Indian Ocean to the Gulf of Thailand and avoid the Strait of Malacca dogleg."

"Yes, Ma'am, and it gets better. We've discovered the Chinese are going to build two military bases in the South China Sea. It looks like one of them already exists in the Spratly Islands. That one will undoubtedly be upgraded and fully manned. It looks like the other will be located in Vietnam, probably Cam Ranh Bay, because of it's airhead and seabase facilities, and because it will also serve to deny India and the U.S. from using the base."

"Is the Spratly base the Chinese fort that Boucher and his guys were held prisoner in last year?" Rowland asked.

"Yes, Sir, it has to be."

"So that's why those bastards were so sensitive about Boucher's presence in the area. That's why they went nuts when he and his guys escaped the fort and sank their submarine. They might have been after him since that encounter."

"It's very likely that the people who followed Commander Boucher and Dr. Barnhart in New Mexico last month were Chinese agents. It is no secret that the Chinese currently have over three thousand Chinese military students in U.S. graduate schools throughout our country and they're all studying our strategic and military thinking. Shit, Sir, according to the FBI figures, there are more Chinese military students than there are U.S. military students. There will come a time in the not too distant future when the Chinese military will understand more about our war-fighting strategy than we do and we're allowing it happen."

Rowland leaned forward toward Bruce. "Okay, Lieutenant, what tipped you to correlate all this data and connect the dots?"

"If you recall, Sir, a few days ago Commander Boucher recovered a cell phone from a Russian agent by the name of Rajakovics when he was in Dakar. The good Commander had the SIM card downloaded and sent the file to us. We followed up with a detailed analysis of the call records and found that Rajakovics is a double agent. Actually, he was more like a free agent. He works for the Russians and he works for the Chinese. When we looked at the Chinese connection we drilled down and discovered their grand plan. The name of their plan when translated means 'String of Pearls'."

"String of Pearls?" Cummings questioned. "So if I understand it correctly, the String of Pearls is a strategically placed network of military bases, commercial and navy seaports, listening posts, even joint business ventures that can be used to guarantee the flow of oil to China?"

"Exactly," Bruce confirmed, "and it appears the seaports they've chosen are all capable of accommodating super tankers and container ships with displacements up to one hundred thousand tons. Ships that size are bigger than our largest aircraft carriers."

Cummings eased back in her chair, rubbing her temples. "I can get this to the president but before I do I think we need to identify and purge the accomplices within our own government."

"But how do we that without tipping the wrong people?" Rowland asked. "I mean, we just can't go on a witch hunt and begin arresting people."

Boucher interrupted. "When we first met and worked together last year we discovered there is a shadow government known as the Luminous that operates behind the curtain. They were behind the attack we foiled last year and they may be part of the U.S.-Israeli attempt to nuke Amman. That said, I don't see them playing ball with the Russian plot to wipe out our Eastern Seaboard or with China's plot to ultimately grab the Middle East's oil resources and attain global military superiority. I don't think they knew about those plots and they were being played for as much a fool as the U.S. government was. So, my point of view, the remaining question is simply this. If Russia has expectations of monopolizing the Middle East's energy resources and China, as we now believe, is aware of Russia's plan and was using it to cover their own, why would China let Russia succeed when there is a clear conflict between China's and Russia's ultimate goals?"

Barnhart cleared his throat. "What if China sent Rajakovics to La Palma to ensure we found those nukes so we'd report that those nukes were all Russian origin? What if after the tsunami China intended to send humanitarian aid to our devastated coast just like they wanted to do a year ago and then establish a beachhead they could expand? What if China intends to overpower and outspend Russia in the Middle East? They certainly have the cash reserves to do it if they wish and Russia couldn't even begin to compete. China has put nearly everything in place to sustain their Middle East conquest. Their only serious competitors are the U.S. and Russia. They let the U.S. and Israel take out Hamas, the Palestinians and Amman so the whole Arab world is now pissed off at the U.S. and Israel. They let Russia take out the Eastern Seaboard and make it look like Arab retaliation. They grab a foothold in the U.S. and at the same time economically attack Russia while engaging in cyber warfare and who emerges as the victor through it all? China."

"What's preventing Russia from going to war with China?" Patterson asked.

"Russia would never risk war with China," Blackburn commented. "They can't afford it and they couldn't sustain it from a logistics perspective. China has the upper hand in nearly every war fighting category - even space weapons."

Boucher lightly patted the tabletop to get everyone's attention. "We need a plan that will turn this around in our favor."

"Yes," Cummings agreed, "we need a strategy that will turn the tide in our favor."

"The String of Pearls is their Achilles heel," Blackburn flatly stated. "Draw world attention to them. Write about them. Expose China's interest in them and their significance to China. Ensure that Chinese ships have occasional eco accidents in and around them. You know oil spills, fires, unexplained explosions, maybe a collision every now and then."

Cummings interrupted, "How are we going to pull that off without compromise if our own CIA is corrupted?"

"That's what we have the Joint Special Operations Command for. Turn the SEALs and Delta Force loose on them. Just have the president do the tasking - level A-1 priority direct from the Commander in Chief. And at the same time the Secretary of State draws attention to China's interests in these strategic locations. In the name of expanding free trade you arrange for other countries to share the same business space. Create competition in these locations so China can't monopolize them. Create military and commercial bases along the same route and, where possible, compete against China for the ones they already have in their hip pocket. Begin with Thailand. We need to nip that canal China wants to build across the Isthmus of Kra in the bud and keep them using the Strait of Malacca where they're vulnerable to our submarines and aircraft."

Cummings held up her hand stopping Blackburn. "Captain, please prepare a strategic plan for my and Senator Rowland's review by the end of this week. We will work directly with you on this. By the way, when do you retire from the Navy?"

"Retire?"

"Yes. When you do, I want to hire you."

Chapter 33

Laytonsville, MD, the next morning

Boucher awoke in his own bed after a restless night's sleep. He hadn't slept in his house in over a month and it felt strange to him. It was almost too quiet. The normal creaks and groans every house has seemed oddly irritating and kept him from sleeping soundly. He couldn't get the events of the past few weeks off his mind. He kept reliving Sandra's death. He could see Hann's eyes bulge out as the back of his head splattered across the ground when he pulled the trigger. And then there was Manuel's car blowing up, the hot blinding flash of the nuclear detonation on the volcano, the blast pressure wave, Moss fighting to keep the helicopter in the air, and the crash into the sea. Boucher rolled onto his side and repositioned his pillow but he knew he wasn't going back to sleep. He finally sat up on the edge of the bed. The clock radio on the nightstand read 0600.

"Damn," he said aloud.

After shaving and dressing he walked out into the hall to the room across from his. He knocked lightly on the door.

"Pat, you awake?"

"Yeah," came a muffled reply. "What's up?"

"Let's go to breakfast before the memorial service."

"Sounds good. Give me twenty minutes for the three S's."

"Roger, meet you downstairs."

Boucher casually went to his kitchen and grabbed the keys to his truck. He threw on a jacket and walked to the barn behind his house he used as a garage for his truck. He went to pull open both barn doors but stopped short staring at the tree line about one-hundred yards behind the barn. Some chirping birds momentarily caught his attention as they playfully flitted from tree to tree. He recalled the camouflaged people he observed there a year earlier and the whack on the head he endured by unknown assailants inside his barn. His thoughts shifted to the treasure hunt he and his men undertook and the gold they recovered. Then he thought about OPLAN 5000, the Chinese garrison in the Spratly Islands where they had been held prisoner, their precarious escape and the Chinese submarine they sank.

Maybe the Senator was right, he thought. *Killing has become a way of life for me.*

"Where we goin' to eat?" a loud voice asked, catching Boucher completely off guard.

"You're gonna be goin' to the fucking memorial service tits up if you don't stop sneaking up on me," Boucher gruffly replied as he reeled to face Patterson.

Patterson realized something was wrong. Ever since Sandra was killed Boucher hadn't been acting himself and now since Admiral Thornberg's death, he had become increasingly impatient, lethargic and withdrawn.

"You okay, Jake?"

Boucher's eyes welled up and he looked away. "Am I fucked up, Pat or have I just become a magnet for bad people who desperately need someone to kill them? I used to be able to cap these assholes all day long then celebrate afterward with a few beers. Now I'm seeing ghosts. I go to bed thinking about it and I wake up thinking about it. I can't get it off my mind anymore."

"Admiral Thornberg was a good man."

"Yeah, a damn good man," Boucher replied. "Did I ever tell you about the time he saved my life, Pat?"

"It was in Granada, right?"

"Yeah, Granada. You know, the autopsy report says he died from complications resulting from his heart attack."

"Yes, you mentioned that last evening."

"I don't believe it, Pat."

"What? You think he was murdered?" Patterson asked in surprise.

"Yeah, I think he was murdered."

"Jake, what makes you believe that?"

"Because they cremated him."

285

"You lost me."

"He always wanted to be buried in Arlington with full military honors. His whole family lineage is buried there - his great grandfather, his grandfather, his dad, one of his uncles and his older brother. None of them were cremated and, like his ancestors, he never wanted cremation."

"So you think they cremated him so there could be no further analysis of his body which could, at some point, have led to the real cause of death?"

"Exactly."

"What do you think we should do about it?"

"I want to find the rat bastards who murdered him and do the same to them."

Patterson placed his hand on Boucher's shoulder. "Jake, you're gonna have to let it go. You can't continue your crusade to rid the world of its scum and you can't dwell on your conscience. It's history and there's no going back. You gotta let it go."

"Pat, you're the closest thing I'll ever have to a brother." Boucher's eyes welled up again. His voice broke hoarsely, "I miss her terribly, Pat."

"I know, Jake. Let's go have breakfast. We need to be at the church before ten hundred hours if we don't want to be late for her memorial service. Come on, I'll drive."

"Wait a minute. I'll warm up the diesel."

Boucher took his truck keys out of his pocket and pressed the remote start button. As he did a tremendous explosion erupted, blowing one of the barn doors into Patterson and Patterson into him. The entire jumble of smoking doors, barn-siding splinters, truck pieces and blast propelled bodies hit the ground about ten feet backward toward the house. Boucher momentarily blacked out but slowly regained enough consciousness to realize what had just happened. His ears were ringing and his face and side were stinging. His shirt was smoldering. He couldn't stand. His left leg wasn't working. The barn was on fire. His truck was a twisted mass of steel and completely engulfed in orange flames. He painfully raised himself to one elbow. Patterson was sprawled in a contorted position a few feet away. He had been standing between Boucher and the barn when the explosion occurred and had taken the brunt of the blast along with the impact of the barn door. Boucher dragged himself over to Patterson and took his pulse. He was alive but barely.

"No! Oh, God. No! Not you, Pat!" he pleaded. "It was supposed to be me! It was supposed to be me!"

The Burn Unit, Johns Hopkins Hospital, Baltimore, MD, five days later

Mojo and Reilly sat in the waiting area watching as Boucher checked out of the hospital. His left hand and arm were bandaged and cradled in a sling. His wore a gauze bandage over his forehead and right eye. His exposed skin was covered with a greasy cream. He limped when he walked favoring his left leg. He was lucky to be alive. The nurse scheduled his outpatient follow-up visits and cautioned him to take it easy. Boucher was unusually agreeable. All he wanted to do was leave the hospital. When he finally turned and hobbled toward his two friends he forced a smile. Mojo and Reilly stood and waited for him to cross the room.

"You look like shit, Commander," Mojo offhandedly stated.

"Yeah, I know. Where are you two assholes taking me?"

Reilly smiled at being called an asshole. "The Secretary of State is waiting to see you in her office. That's where we're taking you."

"The Department of State?"

"Yup. Secretary Cummings said she wants you there the moment you are well enough. So today you're well enough."

"Come on, Billy, I don't need that shit anymore than you do."

"She wants to talk to all of us, Dr. Barnhart included. I promised her I would deliver you to her office. The rest of the guys are gonna meet us there."

Department of State, Washington, DC, one hour later

Boucher and his men were seated at the conference table in the Secretary's private seventh floor conference room. The door suddenly opened and two plain-clothes Diplomatic Security agents entered and posted themselves at the back of the room. They were followed by three Secret Service agents who flanked the table. There was a short lull and then the door opened again. President Banner entered the room with Secretary Cummings and Senator Rowland. Boucher and all his men immediately stood. The president smiled widely.

"Please sit," he directed, taking the seat at the head of the table himself.

Boucher was clearly surprised.

Mr. Boucher, Dr. Barnhart, gentlemen, I asked Secretary Cummings to bring you here so I could personally thank you on behalf of a grateful nation. I am told that because of your heroic actions a potentially devastating tsunami was averted. I understand that the mountain did in fact slide several hundred feet into the ocean before hanging up but it didn't reach the seafloor. You risked virtually everything to save us from these attacks and uncover this conspiracy. I am aware that you lost some people very close to you in the process but that you continued on, risking your lives time and time again, to stop that tsunami. I suppose men like you must love your country above all else."

Boucher quietly glanced at his colleagues, then at Rowland and Cummings.

"Mr. President, there is a distinct difference between loving your country and being in love with your country. I voted for Senator Rowland for president and he lost to you. Rest assured, Sir, no matter who my president is I will always be in love with my country."

Boucher's men all mumbled, "Here, here."

President Banner became very serious and nodded to his security detail that left the room along with the Diplomatic Security agents. After the door was closed, Banner stood.

"Gentlemen, I don't know who I can trust anymore. I do know, however, I can trust the people in this room. We have to ferret out those enemies, both foreign and domestic, who intend to cause grave damage to our country and its government. It has become obvious to me that we cannot wait for these dangers to arrive at our shores and then try to deal with their consequences. We must be proactive, even if that means occasionally working outside the bounds of our law." Banner passed along the table. He was an impressive speaker and was even more impressive in person. "I came here today to not only thank you for your service to our country but to personally ask you for your continued help. I want you to work for me."

Boucher held up his hand stopping the president.

"Mr. President, I don't speak for those at this table and I sure don't mean to sound ungrateful, but I have worked for the government most all my life either in the military or as a federal officer in the counterterrorism community. When we went on our treasure hunt last year and grabbed the gold from that Cambodian crash site, we had no idea we would find the Operations Plans or that it would lead to the revelation of a potential Chinese attack on the U.S. This year we agreed to help the CIA stop a nuke attack in the Middle East, or at least that's what we believed we were doing, and it got a bunch of people killed. I'm done with government, Mr. President."

Banner returned to his seat. "Gentlemen, our country's economy is in dire trouble. It wouldn't take a huge catastrophe to put our nation into an unrecoverable death spiral. You know better than most, there are foreign powers poised to attack us and there may be an underlying conspiracy within this government and business community hoping to facilitate government default for their own selfish goals. As trusted, loyal Americans, I need you to help me prevent that from happening." Boucher opened his mouth to speak but Banner continued. "Please, let me be clear. You will work outside the control of any U.S. government agency or office. You will take your tasking from me through Secretary Cummings and Senator Rowland. We will answer if you call. We three and your men will be the only people who will know about this relationship. I will ensure that you and your men will be compensated for all expenses and that you will all be covered from oversight and backstopped during your operations. Are you interested now, Mr. Boucher?"

Boucher considered the president's proposition. A favorite line from Hermes flashed though his mind, *Who endeavors to reform the tiger? Indeed,* he thought, *duty is always with us – inflexible as fate.* Boucher knew that for him and his men, it was exactly that - the tiger, duty and fate.

"Mr. President, a year ago I admittedly would have never dreamed that Secretary Cummings and I would make a weird alliance and today actually trust one another. Likewise, I would not have considered you much more than a slick Chicago bureaucrat who has a way with words, but I've been wrong before." Banner smiled. "I didn't vote for you but you are nonetheless my president. If I understand correctly, you're asking us to do your dirty jobs. You want me and my guys because you know we're not a bunch of choir boys and we can operate without the oversight the government agencies all suffer. You want us because you know we'll get it done. Mr. President, we will not intentionally break U.S. law or violate our personal ethics. Does that work for you?"

"I would expect no less. Then we have an agreement?"

"One other thing, Mr. President, none of us is looking for a full time job. In fact, none of us ever need to work again if we don't want to. I guess what I'm trying to tell you is, we'll help you out from time to time but that's about it."

Banner patted the table smiling. "Gentlemen, I'll be most grateful for any help you'll give me. Thank you." Banner checked his watch, "Please excuse me but I must run back to the White House. I have a meeting with my press secretary in ten minutes." Banner paused, turning back to address everyone in the room. "Again, thank you. I won't forget what you did." He put his hand on Cummings' arm. "I'll see you and Buddy for dinner this evening, right?"

Cummings nodded affirmatively. Everyone stood and the president exited without further ado. The room almost immediately became uncomfortably silent, as if it had lost its energy.

"What now, Mr. Boucher?" Secretary Cummings asked.

Boucher turned to face her. "I'm going to sell my house and live onboard my yacht in Baltimore's Inner Harbor. I'll probably keep my hand in the game with my security company. You know how to reach me if you need me."

"Yes, I do and," she paused, "you know how to reach me."

<u>Epilogue</u>

Manuel and Indian Jack were both laid to rest without fanfare or notice by the media. There are no investigative leads and their killers have not been found. The homicide investigation has stalled but the case remains open.

The special nuclear material (SNM) that Barnhart and Boucher left behind following their disablement of the weapon in the Jordanian desert was recovered by the NEST's Consequence Management Response Team. Radiological contamination from the burned weapon was low level and easily cleaned up. The event never made the news. Bedouin nomads again graze their goats throughout the area. Jordan's King Abdulla was briefed on the circumstances of the intended attack against Amman. He continues to foster peaceful relations with Israel and strong cooperation with the U.S. in the war against terrorism. Interestingly, several weeks ago King Abdulla personally hosted a visit to Jordan for both Boucher and Barnhart. They enjoyed their stay at the King's Royal Palace grounds in Amman where he presented Boucher with a custom built Browning Hi-Power pistol which had the King's Royal Seal engraved in gold on the slide.

The events that occurred on the Canary Island of La Palma did draw media attention but were shrouded under the guise that it was a joint U.S./UK/ Spanish military training exercise. Again, NEST's Consequence Management Response Team conducted the majority of the SNM recovery and radiological contamination mitigation. The UK also assisted in this effort. Fortunately, because of the coastal nature of La Palma and the heavy rain that followed the emergency disablement attempts, much of the radiological contamination washed into the ocean. Since prior to this attempt no one had ever considered this scenario as an offset means to attack the U.S., the Department of Homeland Security now employs a think tank mix of operational planners, intelligence analysts and novelists who are dedicated to developing potential outside the box attack scenarios that border fiction. Most importantly, the part of the volcano caldron that slid into the sea remains precariously poised to break free at any time and continue to the bottom. Scientists have calculated the slide's mass and believe that it might result in a small tsunami that could hit the U.S. coastline from Maine to Virginia but that it will not cause catastrophic damage. Even so, the Canary Islands and more specifically, La Palma, are still not kept under surveillance.

DHS Undersecretary Denise Dunkle remains in her current office. She never did comprehend the severity of the threat of annihilation of the Eastern Seaboard or how the attack was actually halted. The members of the inter-agency's counterterrorism community continue to question the depth of her competence and that of her agency.

Assistant Secretary of Defense Ian Lester resigned pending charges for allegedly soliciting an undercover FBI agent in a swanky Georgetown restaurant bathroom for homosexual favors. Lester's deputy and right hand man has remained in office and is now the acting ASD/SOLIC while a suitable permanent replacement is considered.

William Mason, alias Marcus Fuller, was unexpectedly retired from the CIA for medical cause shortly after suffering what was reported by the media as a brain aneurysm and stroke. He is alive but paralyzed and completely speech impaired. His prospects for recovery are reported to be dismal. He has been moved to an assisted care facility located close to Rockville, Maryland.

Captain Dean Blackburn, was quietly relieved for cause as Commanding Officer of the Kennedy Irregular Warfare Center at the Office of Naval Intelligence last week. While he won't talk about the circumstances that led to his disfavor, everyone knows that he is under investigation on charges of sexual harassment. Apparently a young women in a different division who worked down the hall from his office has charged that he said, "Damn, you're fucking hot," as she walked by him at the coffee mess. He continues to proclaim his innocence but will likely be forced to retire from the Navy regardless of the outcome of the investigation. Lieutenant Bruce, Blackburn's trusted intelligence analyst, disgusted with how the Navy handled Blackburn and slandered his lifetime of dedicated service, submitted his letter of resignation, resigning his commission as a Naval Officer and immediate termination of service with the Navy. It is rumored that he and Blackburn have been offered new careers with the Office of the Coordinator for Counterterrorism at the U.S. Department of State and will report directly to the Ambassador at Large who heads that office.

Sandra Morrison's body was returned to the U.S. via military transport. In concert with her will she was buried in a plot overlooking the James River close to the CIA training base by Williamsburg, VA. A few former colleagues attended but there was no surviving family present. One of the attendees was a distinguished old gentleman and brilliant scientist whom no one recognized. He stood behind everyone else and spoke to no one. He remained behind at the conclusion of the funeral and waited for the cemetery workers to complete covering the grave. He left two red roses on the gravesite before leaving. A nameless star was inscribed in her honor, alongside the other nameless stars representing fallen CIA employees on the marble wall located inside the CIA's Langley, VA Headquarters' main lobby.

Dr. Barnhart has returned to his home in Los Alamos. While he has remained in close contact with Boucher, he has for all practical purposes, retired. Despite the facts and no matter what anyone argues to the opposite, he blames himself for what happened. He spends most of his days mindlessly tinkering. His latest interest involves making large bells from old compressed gas cylinders which he cuts to various lengths to vary the tone. He then installs a clapper and hangs these bells from tree branches around his yard. The bells clang in disjointed harmony as the breeze blows up into the trees from the Rio Grande River mesa below.

Leon "Pat" Patterson remains in a coma at the Johns Hopkins University Hospital Rehab Facility in Baltimore. He has had several skin graft surgeries on his face and two brain operations. While he has recovered from his burns and broken bones, Doctors aren't optimistic about his full recovery from the massive brain injury he sustained from the blast. Boucher visits him on a daily basis and reads to him. He carries on one-sided conversations as he exercises Patterson's limbs with the hope that it will stimulate his brain activity.

Boucher has fully recuperated from his injuries and now runs his security firm out of a warehouse office located a block off Patrick Street by Baltimore's Inner Harbor. He specializes in anti-piracy operations, threat assessments, and one-man jobs like unfouling ship's propellers and rudders that become entangled in things like fishing nets, or are otherwise inoperable, while far at sea. Frank "Mossman" Moss and Mojo Lavender are his only fulltime employees. They fly his plane and provide mission logistic support to him. The rest of his trusted men have all returned to their private lives. Boucher now lives onboard his yacht, "Perseverance" and has become a loner. He can occasionally be found in the Fells Point waterfront bars within walking distance of his boat. He never strays further than the waterfront or socializes with anyone but his own men. He sits quietly at the bar sipping gin martinis and usually talks to no one. The death of Sandra Morrison and Leon Patterson's neurological injuries have consumed his waking thoughts. Much like Dr. Barnhart, Boucher can't be talked out of blaming himself.

Rajakovics, the notoriously dangerous double agent for Russia and China, has still not been apprehended. The CIA has been trying to capture him but he has the uncanny ability to remain several steps ahead of those in pursuit. Some analysts tasked with tracking and targeting him joke that he's either clairvoyant, divinely advised, or damn lucky – perhaps a bit of each. Regardless, he seems impossible to capture or kill. President Banner offered Boucher and his men the opportunity to find Rajakovics and bring him back alive or dead but Boucher declined. Who knows, maybe someone will get lucky one of these days, stumble across Rajakovics and have the opportunity to kill him. The hunt continues.

The UAE is moving forward with their initiative to build twenty three commercial nuclear power plants throughout the Middle East. Reportedly, they intend to build at least twelve of these plants at coastal sites where they will collocate desalinization plants for the energy-demanding production of fresh water. There is open discussion as to which nuclear power plant design they will choose – U.S. General Electric, French Framatome or the Russian Mintyazhmash. Iran has made it clear that if the UAE builds nuclear power plants then they too should be allowed to build the same commercial plants in Iran and neither Israel nor the U.S. should have any qualms about it. Iran's argument has validity and it is supported by world opinion; Russia in particular. That notwithstanding, the UAE's power plant initiative has forced the U.S. to stand-down its deployed battle groups offshore Iran and Israel that were poised to support an Israeli attack against Iran and/or Syria. Now, in the absence of overwhelming military superiority in the form of on-scene U.S. military presence, Israel has again been required to take a defensive posture and negotiate with Hamas and the Palestinians. Jordan's King Abdulla has generously offered to broker a peace agreement between Israel, Syria and even Iran but thus far, Israel has refused his assistance. Regional tensions remain extremely high and the path to peace remains tenuous.

The End

Fact

The Cumbre Vieja Volcano on the Island of La Palma in the Canary Islands exists as described. It does have a fracture running along the length of its caldron. The hill side is over-steep and is precariously ready to slide into the sea. Many volcanologists believe it is not a matter of if but when that event will occur. When it does, a mega-tsunami will likely be generated which will cross the Atlantic Ocean at the speed of an airliner. Wave intensity models lead scientists to believe that the entire Eastern Seaboard will be devastated by waves the height of our tallest buildings resulting in millions of deaths and causalities.

There is truly only one weapon of mass destruction and that is a nuclear weapon. While classified as WMD, the effects of biological and chemical weapons pale in comparison to that of a nuclear weapon. Experts believe terrorists will obtain and use nuclear weapons during this decade. The Nuclear Emergency Support Team is our last line of defense should a terrorist nuclear weapon be discovered in the U.S. The problem is time – distance. Unfortunately, they will probably never get there in time to disable it.

The UAE does intend to build commercial nuclear power plants in the Middle East and they are in the preliminary stages of threat and vulnerability assessment for locations and plant designs. They do indeed intend to share the power grid among a number of Middle East neighbors and they plan on locating a number of their plants close to the sea to power desalinization plants. Fresh water is more valuable than oil in the Middle East but oil is the only commodity for sale on the world market. By relying on nuclear power instead of their own oil to produce power they will effectively reduce dependence on their own production, giving them oil independence and a complete monopoly on production quantities. Additionally, depending upon which reactor design they chose to build, they will have the unchecked ability to produce their own plutonium. There are several U.S.-owned companies involved in a joint venture with UAE. While they are under the watchful eye of the U.S. government, the oil rich countries with money, political independence and the political fortitude to build nuclear power plants will do as they please, with or without U.S. approval. For more on international commercial nuclear power plants visit: http://www.insc.anl.gov/plants/

A U.S. Joint Forces Command report titled, "Joint Operating Environment 2008" lists China (and Russia) as primary emerging threats in the near future. The report explains China's "String of Pearls" plan and lists their basing locations throughout the Indian and Pacific Oceans. This report is available at: www.jfcom.mil/newslink/storyarchive/2008/JOE2008.pdf

<u>Glossary of Terms</u>

AFAP –Artillery-fired atomic projectile. Developed in the 1950's for tactical battlefield use in stopping advancing Soviet forces attacking Western Europe. AFAP's are low yield nukes generally in the low single number kiloton range.

Atomic yield – Same as *nuclear yield* and *yielding detonation*. Refers to the nuclear detonation of a fissile mass that results in severe destruction, searing heat, a significant release of radiation and is usually associated with the classic mushroom cloud.

ASD/SO-LIC – Assistant Secretary of Defense for Special Operations and Low Intensity Conflict.

BDA – Battle Damage Assessment. BDA is the term applied by the military to assessing the level of damage done in an attack.

Fissile – Fissionable material in the form of highly enriched uranium and plutonium.

Ghilli suit – Uniquely fabricated camouflage suits often used by snipers. The wearer blends in with his surrounding so perfectly that he is almost impossible to spot unless he moves.

IND – Improvised Nuclear Device. An IND, when detonated results in a nuclear detonation with an atomic yield (mushroom cloud). IND's, as the name suggests, can be made from any existing nuclear weapon by modifying the fire set (or other parts necessary) to make it detonate.

Mercury Village – Consisting of barracks, a restaurant, offices and several storage buildings, Mercury is set off to one corner of the Nevada Test Site. It was built to house the scientists, technicians and maintenance people who ran and supported testing of nuclear devices at NTS.

NSC – National Security Counsel.

NTS – Nevada Test Site. Located out in the Nevada desert about 100 miles from Las Vegas NTS is larger than the State of Rohde Island. From WW-II until present, NTS has been the site of nuclear testing. Today it is in mothballs but still restricted to the public because of the residual contamination from the above and underground nuclear tests conducted there.

Non-Official Cover (NOC) – Term used for operatives working under an identity that is other than recognized official U.S. government agency cover. For example, a CIA Chief of Station working in a U.S. embassy has official cover. The host country knows he is an agent of the U.S. government. People who may occasionally operate within that country who are undeclared as U.S. government agents are NOCs.

ONI - Office of Naval Intelligence.

Physics package – That part of an atomic bomb which contains the fissile mass.

Pu-239 – Plutonium 239 is a man-made element that can only be made in a reactor. It is used as the primary fissile material in nuclear weapons.

Rigid semi-inflatable boat (RSI) – The RSI incorporates a rigid hull ringed by an inflatable tube above the waterline. They come in a variety of sizes and configurations and are perhaps one of the most seaworthy boat designs ever built. They are widely used as lifeboats and rescue craft.

RDD – Radiological Dispersal Device. Employs any radiological material and uses a conventional explosive to disperse that material causing local radiological contamination. There is no nuclear yield (mushroom cloud) involved in the detonation.

SCIF – Secure compartmented intelligence facility.

SNM – Special nuclear material. SNM is any fissile material with a level of enrichment appropriate for weapon purposes.

USAID - U.S. Agency for International Development is a semi-autonomous agency under the U.S. Department of State, concerned with fostering democracy through construction / reconstruction and development programs in emerging democracies, friends and allies.

U-235 – Uranium 235 is derived from naturally occurring uranium ore through a purification process. It is used as a fissile source in atomic weapons.

Yielding detonation - Same as *atomic yield* and *nuclear yield*. Refers to the nuclear detonation of a fissile mass that results in severe destruction, searing heat, a significant release of radiation and is usually associated with the classic mushroom cloud.

LaVergne, TN USA
08 December 2009
166395LV00002B/31/P